A Splendid Indiscretion

and

The Grand Passion

Elizabeth Mansfield

A SIGNET BOOK

SIGNET
Published by New American Library, a division of
Penguin Group (USA) Inc., 375 Hudson Street,
New York, New York 10014, USA
Penguin Group (Canada), 10 Alcorn Avenue, Toronto,
Ontario M4V 3B2, Canada (a division of Pearson Penguin Canada Inc.)
Penguin Books Ltd., 80 Strand, London WC2R 0RL, England
Penguin Ireland, 25 St. Stephen's Green, Dublin 2,
Ireland (a division of Penguin Books Ltd.)
Penguin Group (Australia), 250 Camberwell Road, Camberwell, Victoria 3124,
Australia (a division of Pearson Australia Group Pty. Ltd.)
Penguin Books India Pvt. Ltd., 11 Community Centre, Panchsheel Park,
New Delhi - 110 017, India
Penguin Group (NZ), cnr Airborne and Rosedale Roads, Albany,
Auckland 1310, New Zealand (a division of Pearson New Zealand Ltd.)
Penguin Books (South Africa) (Pty.) Ltd., 24 Sturdee Avenue,
Rosebank, Johannesburg 2196, South Africa

Penguin Books Ltd., Registered Offices:
80 Strand, London WC2R 0RL, England

Published by Signet, an imprint of New American Library, a division of Penguin Group (USA) Inc. *A Splendid Indiscretion* was previously published in a Berkley edition. *The Grand Passion* was previously published in a Jove edition.

First Signet Printing, July 2005
10   9   8   7   6   5   4   3   2   1

PUBLISHER'S NOTE
These are works of fiction. Names, characters, places, and incidents either are the product of the author's imagination or are used fictitiously, and any resemblance to actual persons, living or dead, business establishments, events, or locales is entirely coincidental.

The publisher does not have any control over and does not assume any responsibility for author or third-party Web sites or their content.

If you purchased this book without a cover you should be aware that this book is stolen property. It was reported as "unsold and destroyed" to the publisher and neither the author nor the publisher has received any payment for this "stripped book."

The scanning, uploading, and distribution of this book via the Internet or via any other means without the permission of the publisher is illegal and punishable by law. Please purchase only authorized electronic editions, and do not participate in or encourage electronic piracy of copyrighted materials. Your support of the author's rights is appreciated.

A Splendid
Indiscretion

Prologue

He'd already brushed the snow from his shoulders and was stripping off his gloves as he crossed the threshold of the inn's parlor, but he froze at the sight of the lady standing nervously before the window. "Julia! What on earth—?"

He had entered the inn in perfectly good humor, looking forward to the dinner he would be served in the private parlor (Yorkshire ham covered with the inn's famous raisin sauce, homebaked bread and a brew that attracted drinkers to the taproom from miles around) and the good night's sleep he'd have in the inn's pleasant back bedroom (the room that Goodell, the innkeeper, always managed to have available for his use), but Julia's unexpected presence caused his pleasant mood to evaporate at once.

The innkeeper at his side, who had just opened the door for him, was as startled as he was. "I beg pardon, yer lordship," he mumbled in embarrassment. "Me missus didn' tell me she'd let th' private parlor."

Ivor Griffith, Viscount Mullineaux, merely waved him away, his eyes fixed on the lady's face. "Close the door, Goodell, if you please. And don't disturb us until I call."

The innkeeper withdrew, closing the door carefully behind him. Mullineaux stared for a moment at the woman across the room. She was a creature of remarkable beauty, but Mullineaux had no need to take note of her lovely light-haired coiffure, her translucent skin, the exquisite slimness of her waist or the swell of her deliciously shaped bosom. With these attractions he was yawningly familiar. He took note only of the thick maquillage she'd applied to cover the crinkles at the corners of her large blue eyes, the blacking she'd used on her lashes, the near vulgarity of her daring decolletage, and the tension that was evident in the way she clenched her ringed fingers and bit her full nether lip. "How did you know I would stop here?" he asked coldly.

She crossed the room and threw herself against him. "Oh,

1

Griff!" she breathed into his shoulder. "I've been waiting for hours."

"I asked how you knew where to find me, ma'am."

She wound her arms tightly about his neck and looked up at him with a smile that was both mischievous and nervous. "Aubrey Tait told me you generally stop here on your way to Mullineaux Park."

Lord Mullineaux's mouth tightened. "When I next meet Aubrey I shall wring his neck," he muttered, thrusting her arms down.

"Don't blame him. I wheedled the information from him. I *had* to find you, Griff, don't you know that?"

"I don't know anything of the sort. I warned you from the start that this . . . this liaison would be short-lived."

"But Griff, I *love* you! You can't—"

"Love? You don't know what love is. You offer love as if it were a little sugary confection you can take from a silvered tin and present to whomever pleases you at the moment. Whenever the weather is gloomy, or there are no balls for which you can prepare, or poor Alcorn starts to bore you—"

"My husband *always* bores me."

Mullineaux ignored the interruption. "—that's when you look around for a diversion. And everyone knows what your favorite diversion is: finding yourself a new suitor, someone to whom you can offer one of the sweets from your little tin. Love, indeed! Love, my dear, is more than a deuced container of bon-bons."

"Griff, don't be horrid. You know that what you're saying isn't at all true."

"No? I suspect that Harrington and Lord Cloverdale and that idiot Nigel Lewis would fully agree with me."

"How can you compare those incidents with . . . with what we've had together?" the woman asked, her voice trembling. "I've never felt for *anyone* what I feel for you!"

Mullineaux raised an eyebrow icily. "Stop it, Julia. You knew from the first that this would be nothing but a light flirtation. In fact, you agreed that love would have no part in—"

"I? When did I agree to such a ridiculous arrangement?"

"Are you trying to pretend you don't remember? Then let me remind you. The scene took place in the little sitting room down the hall from the Bromwells' ballroom. You had taken me there after twisting your ankle on the dance floor during the waltz. But you hadn't twisted your ankle at all, had you, Julia? It was only one of your little ruses. However, I didn't know that, then. I was dizzy and half disguised on Bromwell's excellent madeira, and, as I recall, I had just released you from a somewhat uninhibited embrace. But instead of slapping my face and calling for Lord Alcorn to come and avenge your honor, you smiled at me tantalizingly and suggested an assignation."

Julia's eyes fell. "I do remember. You refused me. You thanked me but said that you were weary of love involvements at the moment."

"Yes, just so. Do you also remember what you answered?"

"I said, 'La, Lord Mullineaux, what's wrong with a gay little flirtation?'"

"No, not quite. What you said was, 'Love has nothing to do with this, Lord Mullineaux. I promise you *nothing more* than a gay little flirtation.'"

"But, Griff, how could I have known how I would feel? That was three months ago!"

His Lordship looked at the woman disdainfully and then walked away. He said nothing more until he'd crossed to the fireplace and kicked some life into the fire with the toe of a boot. "This discussion is neither here nor there, ma'am," he said, his eyes on the low flame. "The fact remains that your husband is beginning to suspect the worst, and I, since I have no wish to face him over pistols at dawn, realize it is time we call it quits."

"No, no!" She ran to the fireplace, pulled him round and clutched at the collar of his greatcoat. "You mustn't leave me now! You *can't!* My heart will crack in two!"

He loosed her fingers and stepped back out of her reach. "Hearts don't crack so easily, my dear." His voice was low and not unkind, but there was a finality in the tone that she couldn't miss.

She stared at him with stricken eyes. Now that she was about to lose him, he seemed more desirable than ever. Imposingly tall and well built, he had glossy chestnut hair (now falling appealingly over his forehead); eyes of ocean grey that could darken frighteningly when he was angry, like the ocean itself; a strong, thick-lipped mouth; a face slightly elongated by a square chin; broad shoulders (now emphasized by a caped greatcoat that hung open to reveal a wide, waistcoated chest and narrow hips clad in tan chamois riding breeches); and a pair of beautifully shaped legs, their muscular calves not hidden but emphasized by his high top-boots. The fact that she was now about to lose him filled her with panic. "What do you know about hearts?" she cried, wringing her hands while trying desperately to think of ways to attach him again. "Sometimes I think you don't have a heart. Please, Griff, listen to me. Though it amuses you to deny it, I know you care for me. It's Alcorn you're thinking of, isn't it? You feel guilty. But there's no need to think of him. We can run away and never see him again. We needn't see anyone we know ever again. We can go to the continent to live. The *haut monde* of the continent . . . they all understand about these situations. They will accept us with open arms. We can have new friends, new surroundings, a new life. We can have each other! We can live in Paris or Venice and be *happy*."

His eyes were fixed on her face, glinting with a forbidding anger she hadn't seen before. "Do you know what you're suggesting, ma'am?" he asked in a voice of ice. Like most of the men of the Corinthian set, who found it admirable to engage in the most competitive sports, the most excessive gambling and the most passionate amours without exhibiting a trace of emotion, he had trained his face to be impassive, but at this moment his eyes revealed much of his inner revulsion. There was no question that, whatever he might once have felt for her, he felt nothing now but disgust. "Have you no conscience? Have you given no thought to the pain and shame you'd be causing Lord Alcorn to suffer? Have you no feeling for your husband at all?"

"Why should I concern myself with—?"

Her question was cut short by a sudden pounding on the door. "Griff? Griff? Are you in there?" someone was shouting from outside the room.

"Good God!" Mullineaux threw Julia a puzzled look. "Is that *Aubrey*?"

He strode to the door and threw it open. In the corridor stood a stout, youngish fellow with red cheeks, two quivering chins and a pair of brilliant black eyes. His chest was heaving with exertion, and his breath came in gasps. "Ah, there you are!" he panted in relief. "Afraid I'd be . . . too late."

"Too late for what, you bobbing-block," Mullineaux said

curtly, stepping aside to admit the breathless fellow. "What the devil are you doing here, and why the devil did you tell Julia where to find me?"

"Never mind all that," Aubrey said, dropping into a chair and pulling out a huge handkerchief from a breast pocket. "Better run for it at once."

"Run for it? What are you talking about?"

Aubrey removed his high beaver and mopped his brow. "Rode all the way from London in the saddle," he said, explaining his breathlessness. "Made it from Knightsbridge to this Oxfordshire backwater in under three hours." He grinned up at his frowning friend proudly. "Wager even *you* couldn't have done better."

"Yes, yes, you gudgeon, it was deuced good riding. But why was it necessary to follow me . . . and in such haste?"

"Alcorn. He found some sort of note from his lady there and flew into a frenzy. Came to White's looking for you, pistol in hand. He's out for your blood, Griff. Came to warn you."

Julia gasped. Mullineaux spun about and glared at her. "Good God! What did you *say* in that note?"

"Nothing about you . . . I *swear* it! I only said that I was leaving him."

Mullineaux strode across the room and grasped her shoulders furiously. "Do you take Alcorn for a fool? A wife should know her husband better. Everyone in town is probably aware that I'm off to Wales. Did you think your husband would not notice the fact that you timed your departure to coincide with mine?"

"It never . . . I didn't think—"

He thrust her away from him in disgust. "No, of course you didn't."

Julia watched him in alarm as he turned his back on her and began to pace about the room. Aubrey was equally alarmed, for he knew there was little time for pacing. But neither Julia nor Aubrey had the courage to interrupt his lordship's cogitations. After a few moments of pacing, Mullineaux stopped at the chair that held his things and picked up his beaver.

Julia expelled a worried little breath. "Griff? What shall we d-do?" she asked helplessly.

"We?" He gave her a mirthless, sardonic snort. "*We* shall do nothing. *You*, ma'am, will remain here to face your husband, and I—"

She whitened. "Face Alcorn? But . . . why?"

"Why? Because you've made a cuckold of him once too often, and it's time to make amends."

"But I don't *want* to make amends," she said, trying to play the suffering heroine but sounding more petulant than tragic. "I want to go to Paris . . . with *you!*"

Mullineaux clapped his hat on his head, picked up his gloves and cane and came up to her. "I am not going to Paris, my dear . . . not with you or with anyone. I am going to Wales."

"That is ridiculous. What can you possibly wish to do in Wales, all alone? There is nothing to do there but look at the trees."

"I shall have a great deal to do there. My grandfather willed his library to me, hoping that when I combine it with my own, it will become one of the country's great collections. I intend to go through the catalogue to see which volumes are to be crated for shipment."

Her eyebrows rose in disbelief. "Is *that* how you intend to spend your time? It sounds a crashing bore."

"Not to me. I shall enjoy every moment."

"How nice for you. But what about me, Griff? What shall happen to me?"

"I've been trying to tell you. You say you want to go to Paris, isn't that so? Well, you may some day get there, if you play your cards well. If you use your head, you may yet prevail upon *Alcorn* to take you."

"Alcorn? Ha! How can you believe that Sir Giles Alcorn would *ever* take me abroad? You're quite off the mark." She pulled a handkerchief from her bosom and sniffed pathetically into it. "You don't know him, Griff. He'll be *livid!* He'll *never* forgive me."

"Oh, yes, he will, if you use the wiles on him that you've used so successfully on your numerous admirers. Go upstairs to the bedroom, lock the door, put on the most demure night-clothes you can find in your bag—and if you haven't anything demure, ask your abigail to lend you one of hers; I suspect that all abigails carry a supply of dowdy kerseymere night-dresses along with them—and climb into bed. Then, when Alcorn arrives and bursts in, fall into his arms and explain that you've run away—alone!—because you feared you'd lost his love. Come, come, Julia, don't look at me that way. You know just how to carry it off. All you need do is convince your husband that you truly love him, and in no time at all he'll be conveying you to the continent for a second honeymoon."

Julia looked up from her damp handkerchief, her eyes expressing clearly her lack of conviction. Facing her husband was the last thing she wanted to do. Of course, she'd known when she'd set out this morning from London that she was gambling her future on a liaison that had lost its glow, but desperation had made her reckless. Now she knew without a doubt that Lord Mullineaux was not going to run off with her. She'd lost the gamble. There was nothing left for her but to try to patch up the rift in her marriage. Perhaps Griff was right, she thought. Perhaps she could do it. But Alcorn had a quick temper and a sour nature; she would have a difficult time of it. "Second honeymoon, indeed!" she muttered bitterly. "More likely, he'll convey me to his mother's country seat, where I shall spend the rest of my life listening to her scolds and living like a *nun.*"

The thought of the flamboyant Lady Julia Alcorn living like a nun made Mullineaux and Aubrey exchange quick grins. But Aubrey, aware of the passage of time, could not permit this scene to continue much longer. "Rubbish, my dear," he said, getting up and putting a friendly arm about Julia's shoulder. "You'll have him eating out of your hand in a week, see if you don't. Meanwhile, I think you should run upstairs and ready yourself, for there isn't a moment to be lost. Alcorn's carriage was hard on my heels when I set out, you know."

Lord Mullineaux watched with knit brows as Aubrey guided her firmly to the doorway. "Can your abigail be trusted to remain silent?" he asked.

"Yes," Julia replied glumly. "The girl is completely devoted to me." She looked back over her shoulder to take a last, meaningful, tragic look at her erstwhile lover. "G-Goodbye, Griff," she murmured brokenly. "I shall n-never forget you."

When the door closed after her, Aubrey glanced at his friend dubiously. "Do you really think Alcorn will believe that she came here alone?"

"No, I don't. But there's always a chance, I suppose. When a man loves a woman, he wants to believe the best of her." He fell silent for a moment, trying to imagine how he himself would react if he were in Alcorn's shoes. Soon he shook himself from his reverie. There was no time for rumination. He glanced over at his friend, a smile of fond affection suddenly lighting his face. "Thanks for coming, Aubrey, old man. It was an act of courage to gallop so many miles in this deuced weather for my sake, and I won't forget it. But I think you'd better start back to town at once. It won't help matters if Alcorn finds you here."

"What do you mean, *I'd* better get back to town? Aren't you coming with me?"

"No. I'm on my way to Wales, remember?"

"Good. The best solution is to run for it. Not that I believed for a moment that trumpery tale about a library collection. Griff Mullineaux going off to look at books! What a hum! But Wales is as good a place as any in which to rusticate. That's just what I would do... make myself scarce for a while."

"I'm glad I have your approval," his friend muttered drily.

"But, Griff, suppose he catches up with you? Take my word, he'll force a duel. Won't be any reasoning with 'im, the state he's in. Not that I don't think you're a sure shot, old fellow, but Alcorn ain't a duffer. Bound to be some blood shed... and all sorts of trouble with the magistrates afterward. And that would be in the *best* of circumstances."

Lord Mullineaux eyed him ruefully. "If that's the best, what do you think can be the worst?"

"The worst would be a situation in which you'd take a notion to delope."

"Of course I'd delope. Do you think, after what I've done to him, that I want to *shoot* the poor fellow?"

"There, you see?" Aubrey's usually cheerful, red-cheeked face clouded in alarm. *"Knew* that's what you'd take it in your head to do—aim into the sky. There's no sense in that course, Griff. The worst might happen. He might very well *kill* you!"

"Quite so. He might at that."

"Then, good God, man, what do you intend to *do,* eh?"

Mullineaux clapped him on the shoulder and propelled him toward the door. "I shall do exactly as you advised," he said with a reassuring grin. "Run for my life."

Chapter One

Jasper Surringham, Bart., eagerly picked up *The Times* from the hall table and turned immediately to the financial page. The newspaper had been delivered only moments before and was already four days late. Delivery of the London papers was always slow to Gloucester, and since the snowfall had blocked the road to Bishop's Cleve for more than a day, delivery had been even slower. Jasper, engrossed in the long-delayed news, crossed the hall to the library while keeping his nose buried in the pages. Thus he failed to notice a thin sheet of pattern-paper that had floated to the floor from the long table where his niece was absentmindedly pinning together the parts for a new blouse. His slippered foot trod upon the pattern-paper, the paper slid forward (carrying Sir Jasper's foot with it), and he found his legs flying out from under him. With a sharp intake of breath, he landed clumsily on the polished oak floor, his tailbone and elbow painfully jarred.

The sound of his gasp and the impact of his body on the floor would ordinarily have captured the attention of anyone seated nearby, but Jasper's niece Ada was not ordinary. She was deep in thought, and when her mind was thus occupied, it took a great deal of noise to rouse her. Her uncle's fall would have gone completely unnoticed were it not for the fact that the abrupt movement of his body disturbed the air and caused the pattern-pieces on the table to fly up. Ada, distracted by the unexpected movement of the papers, looked up at them in mild surprise. "My goodness," she murmured to the pieces of tissue, attempting to catch them as they floated past her, "why are you flying away so abruptly?" She addressed the papers with a smile. "Do you think you're birds, flying off to the south for the winter?"

She succeeded in catching only two of them. The rest eluded her, some wafting serenely to the floor and others dancing up over her head and out of reach. The more she flailed about in her attempt to catch them, the more air currents she created, and the more the tissue-thin papers sailed about the room.

Jasper, wincing in pain, lifted himself up on an elbow and glared at her, furious because she was aware of neither his presence in the room nor the havoc she'd caused. "Bubble-headed female," he muttered.

She didn't look round from her task of catching the pattern-pieces. "Uncle Jasper? I didn't hear you come in."

"No, of course you didn't," he retorted sarcastically, "since I came in so *quietly*. For heaven's sake, what're you doin', jumpin' about so?"

"There must have been a sudden draught," she explained, still not looking at him. She was busy trying to capture a curved piece of paper—the pattern for the collar, she realized—that kept winging out of reach like a teasing bird.

"Yes, there was a draught," her uncle declared acerbically. "I was the one who caused it."

"Oh, I don't think so, uncle. You needn't worry about it . . . I'll catch hold of them all in the end."

"Oh, you will, will ye? Too bad ye couldn't catch *me* in the end."

"What?" The collar pattern having been captured, she now got down on her hands and knees and crept under the table to salvage the pieces that had come to rest on the floor. After collecting the last piece she turned round on all fours and crept out, coming face to face with her still-supine uncle. "Uncle Jasper, is something wrong?" she exclaimed, startled.

"Wrong? What makes you think there's something wrong?"

"You're . . . you're on the floor!" the bewildered girl exclaimed.

"Oh, you noticed that, did ye?"

Ada sat back on her heels and eyed him reprovingly. "I know I'm bubbleheaded and absentminded and not always aware of the details of my surroundings, but even *I* take notice when my uncle greets me from a position flat on the floor. May I ask what you're doing down here?"

"Ain't it obvious? I wanted to examine the condition of the ceiling from a new angle."

"Oh, *Uncle*." His niece, long familiar with Sir Jasper's sarcastic wit, his acerbic manner, and his yeoman-like speech (all of which served to mask a heart as soft as a plum pudding), shrugged and turned her attention to counting the pattern-pieces in her hands. "Here's the sleeve . . . and this is the cuff . . . but

I wonder where the yolk has gone . . ."

"You don't believe I merely wanted to examine the ceiling, eh? Then let me say that I wanted to see the world from a different viewpoint. A change o' perspective, so to speak."

". . . and the collar. Can the collar piece have gotten away from me again?"

"Are you *listenin'* to me, Ada? Here I am, stretched out on my back like a split fish laid out t' dry. Don't it occur to you to wonder *why?*"

The girl continued to count the pieces. "Did you fall?" she asked absently.

"Fall? No, no, o' course not. Why should ye conclude that I fell? I lay down here on the floor t' read my paper in comfort."

Ada gave a little giggle. But then her brows knit, and her eyes clouded over. "Oh, dear. You *did* fall. It was my fault, I suppose, or you wouldn't be so testy. You're not hurt, are you?"

"No, I ain't hurt, but it's no thanks to you that my leg ain't broken."

Ada got to her feet and looked down at her uncle in dismay. "What did I do this time?" she asked shamefacedly.

"Ye dropped one o' yer deuced pattern-papers, that's what ye did. I slipped on it. Blast it, girl, why can't ye keep yer mind on what ye do? If you weren't so scatterbrained, you could keep those papers safe where they belong."

"I'm sorry, uncle. Here, let me help you up."

"Don't touch me!" Jasper lifted himself up on his unjarred elbow and attempted to wave her off. "With yer help I shall only find myself on the floor again. Go back to yer business and let me get on wi' mine."

Ada ignored the order and helped the bony old gentleman to his feet, brushing off his trouser leg while Jasper rubbed his bruised elbow and gave his niece a final glare. Then he hobbled off with an exaggerated limp to the high-backed wing chair near the window while Ada returned to her labors.

Jasper, as soon as the pain receded, felt a nip of guilt for his earlier petulance. It wasn't Ada's fault that he'd fallen. She couldn't help it that she was so disorganized. The poor girl had always been dreamy and absentminded. Ever since her childhood he'd tried to teach her to behave in a purposeful way, but her mind seemed always to be somewhere in the clouds. He'd long since given up any hope that she would change.

Not that he didn't love the girl. The truth was—though he was not the sort to say these things aloud—he positively doted on her. She was like a daughter to him. After all, he'd raised her from the time she was five years old, after her parents (his brother and sister-in-law) had perished in the sinking of the merchant ship *Phallandre,* and he'd grown more attached to her than he would have thought possible. There was a certain charm in her dreaminess. Most of the time, this was enough to insure his love. But sometimes (he really hated to admit it) that very quality of otherworldliness could drive him to drink.

He lowered his newspaper and looked over the top of it to the table where she sat. Her hands had fallen still, and a piece of cut fabric dangled forgotten from her fingers. She was staring out the window, her mouth curved up in a little smile. Whatever was she thinking of, he wondered, when she stared out like that upon the snowy landscape she was obviously not seeing? The answer would always be a mystery to him, as well as a source of irritation. Yet he had to admit that there was something very lovely in the expression of her face in repose. There was a serenity in the smoothness of her forehead, the curve of her cheek, the silky neatness of her drawn-back brown hair, the upward curve of her lip, the unreadable pale-blue depth of her eyes. Those Italian masters who used to paint the oval-faced, sloe-eyed madonnas, they would have loved to recreate her ethereal loveliness on canvas.

The trouble was, he realized, that the world was too much for Ada. She had no interest in the minutiae of everyday life. The energies of her mind were expended on a dream world of her own, so that everything in the real world became an annoyance or a difficulty for her. Papers had a way of losing themselves out of her possession, carpets would lump up under her feet and trip her, facts would get twisted in her memory, buttons at the back of her dress would come undone—and all with irritating frequency. Jasper sighed with rueful dismay. Ada could have dealt a great deal better with life if things were simpler: if people always spoke in soft voices, if agreements were reached easily and without rancor, if houses could be run without servants, if buttons could remain permanently attached to clothing, if dress patterns could be designed with fewer than three pieces. *Oh, well,* he thought, returning his eyes to the report of the previous day's doings on the 'Change, *I've done all I can to improve the girl. What can't be cured must be endured.*

He had become completely absorbed in the financial news when the butler appeared in the doorway. Since neither Sir Jasper nor his niece bothered to look up at his entrance, Cotrell, the butler, had to clear his throat twice. "Lady Haydon t' see you, sir," he announced. "And she has Miss Cornelia with her."

Jasper groaned. Lady Dorothea Haydon, his overbearing sister, lived nearby and called often, but whenever she did, she always managed to cut up his peace. And her daughter Cornelia, in spite of being what the locals called a Diamond of the First Water, was as arrogant as her mother and made an equally irritating guest. "Why don't *you* see 'em, Ada?" he suggested, lifting up his newspaper again as if to use it as a barrier between him and his social obligations. "You don't need me. Give 'em some tea and get rid of 'em."

"What did you say, uncle?" Ada murmured absently.

"Damnation, girl, ain't you been listenin'? Don't you see Cotrell standin' in the doorway? Ain't you heard a word o' what's been exchanged between us?"

Ada's eyes focused on her uncle's face. "Oh! I'm sorry. I was thinking of the rose garden."

"The rose garden?" Jasper eyed his niece in disbelief. "The *rose garden?* It's under a foot o' snow! Why should ye be thinkin' of it *now?*"

"I was only wondering how it would look if we planted some of the new hybrid roses I've been reading about. I've always loved the rich crimson of our Chinas, of course, and they make a lovely sea of color in June, but . . ." She paused and gazed out of the window at the field of white below, the dreamy look in her eyes telling her uncle that she was seeing those blooming roses as clearly as if they were real. ". . . but wouldn't you enjoy seeing a bit of varied color in the garden for a change? Not a great deal of color—I wouldn't wish for too much excitement for the eyes, would you?—but only a touch of pink here and there. I've heard of an exciting new variety called Hume's Blush, a tea-scented China, which might be very lovely along the border, and perhaps a dozen Parson Pinks to edge the walks—"

"Ada, this is the outside of enough! Yer drivin' me to distraction, babblin' away about roses! Don't ye see Cotrell standin' there in the doorway waitin' for an answer?"

Ada blinked up at Cotrell in surprise. "Oh, I'm sorry, Cotrell. What is it you wish of me?"

The butler's lips twitched in amusement. Miss Ada's absentmindedness provided him with one of his few sources of entertainment. "Lady Dorothea and Miss Cornelia, Miss Ada. They're waiting in the sitting room."

"Oh." Ada glanced at her uncle uneasily. "And you want *me* to see them, Uncle Jasper?"

"Yes, I want you to see 'em! What have I been *sayin'* these past five minutes?"

"Very well, Uncle, if you wish me to," Ada murmured, putting down the piece of fabric that she'd absently held on to all this time, "but Aunt Dorothea will not be pleased at having no one to talk but me."

The butler cleared his throat again. "Her ladyship asked fer *you*, Sir Jasper. Fer you most partic'lar."

"Oh, she did, did she? Deuced maggoty female! Does she think I've nothin' better to do than to spend my afternoons dancin' attendance on her? Be a good girl, Ada, and see if you can fob her off."

But Ada was gazing out the window again.

"Blast it, girl, has yer mind wandered off *again?*" her uncle barked.

She looked round with a start. "What?"

"I asked you to rid us of yer aunt and yer cousin. Will ye do it or no?"

Ada's clear eyes clouded again. "I can try, of course, but you know how Aunt Dorothea . . . and Cornelia, too . . . always manage to overwhelm me."

Jasper grunted. It was quite true. Sweet-natured, dreamy Ada was no match for either her cousin or her aunt. Sooner or later, he supposed, he would have to go to the library to rescue his niece from their clutches, so he might just as well get up now. He threw his newspaper to the floor in surrender to the inevitable. "Very well, then," he said, dismissing the butler with a wave and getting up with a sigh, "let's go."

But Ada seemed to shrink in her chair. "I needn't go, need I? Since you've decided to see them after all?"

Her uncle ceased his stride to the door and turned to her,

his brows knit. "I don't understand ye, girl. Why do ye always try t' avoid company? Cornelia's yer cousin . . . a female just yer age. One would think ye'd *enjoy* havin' a bit of a gossip with her."

"We've nothing to gossip about, Uncle."

"Hummph! Most women manage to find *somethin'* t' gossip about. Why are ye always different?"

"I don't know."

He peered at the girl intently. "Why did ye say, a bit ago, that she always overwhelms ye?"

Ada's eyes fell. "I don't know why I said that. I was just being . . . fanciful."

"No, I don't think ye were." He pulled up a chair, placed it in front of hers and sat down upon it, keeping his eyes fixed on her face. "I want the truth, Ada. Is that blasted, peacocky female unkind to ye?"

"No, no. I don't want you to think— It's all in my mind, really, Uncle."

"*What's* in your mind?" He leaned forward and took her hands, his face showing nothing but loving concern. "Speak up, Ada. Dash it, girl, I *ought* to know."

Ada sighed. "I don't know if I can explain, Uncle Jasper. Cornelia and I are on good terms, I assure you. It's just that she . . . she takes such pleasure in . . . in winning over me."

He didn't understand. "Winning?"

"Yes. She's quite *accustomed* to winning, you know."

"No, I don't know. Winning what?"

"Everything."

He put a nervous hand to his forehead. "Forgive me, my love, fer bein' a dense old man, but I don't follow ye. What do ye mean by everything? Can ye be specific?"

Ada shrugged. "Playing the pianoforte. Stitching. Engaging in conversational badinage. Everything from playing shuttlecock to . . . to acquiring dance partners."

Jasper raised his brows in surprise. "But winnin' implies . . . a *competition*. Are all those things *battles* between ye?"

She dropped her eyes to her clenched hands. "It often seems so to me."

"And yer cousin *wins* these . . . these skirmishes? Always?"

Ada noted the tone of chagrin in his voice and hastened to

reassure him. "I don't mind it, uncle, really I don't. You mustn't take this seriously. I'm quite accustomed to it. I don't know why I even mentioned it."

"I'm *glad* ye mentioned it. I had no notion that ye found it so difficult to be in her company."

"I don't, usually. It's just that I'm a bit blue-deviled today. When I'm in low tide, I am not soothed by the fact that she so complacently takes for granted her superiority over me."

Her uncle frowned. "Lords it over ye, does she?"

"Yes, a bit. So please, Uncle Jasper, may I take my tea up in my room . . . just for today? Cornelia and Aunt Dorothea came to see *you*, after all . . ."

"No, I won't have it!" Jasper burst out, jumping to his feet. "I won't *have* that toplofty female lordin' it over ye! Dash it all, Ada, yer every bit as good as yer cousin. Why do ye permit her to win all the time?"

"It doesn't matter to me, Uncle, truly. Cornelia *likes* to win. It's important to her. And I don't mind it, not usually. Only today I'd sooner be . . . elsewhere."

Jasper's eyes narrowed angrily. "That's the trouble with ye, my girl. Y're *always* elsewhere. Even if y're *bodily* present, yer *mind* is elsewhere. Per'aps, if ye'd be *here* in yer mind, ye'd be able to stand up fer yerself."

Ada's eyes fell guiltily. "I'm sorry, Uncle."

"Sorry! Is that all ye can say?"

The poor girl could only bite her lip. "May I be excused?" she asked helplessly.

"No, ye may not! Ye'll go with me t' the drawin' room!" He put his hands roughly on her shoulders, turned her about and thrust her out of the room ahead of him, his anger churning inside his chest. It cut him to the heart to discover that his lovely niece thought so little of herself. He would have to do something about it. Dash it all, he thought glumly, females are a damned nuisance, even the best of them.

Ada paused at the drawing-room door and looked round at him, her eyes pleading. "Please, Uncle . . ."

"*No*, I said!" He glared at her as if, by the sheer force of his anger, he could make her strong. "If I can face them, so can you. So march! I won't permit ye t' be elsewhere today!"

Chapter Two

Lady Dorothea Haydon and her daughter had already ensconced themselves in the drawing room and, making themselves
quite at home, had rung for tea. Cornelia, elegantly tall,
deep-bosomed and fair-haired, sat lounging gracefully upon the
sofa, her left foot extended and her eyes fixed on the fashionable
galoe shoe which peeped out from beneath her skirts. Her
mother stood framed in the window, looking out upon the
snowy landscape and tapping impatiently upon the palm of her
left hand with a folded letter she held in her right.

Jasper clumped into the room, gave his sister a reluctant
peck on the cheek, nodded to Cornelia curtly and threw himself
upon an easy chair near the fire. "Well, Doro, what is it this
time?" he demanded.

"Must you always greet me with such ill grace?" Dorothea
Haydon asked in disgust. "And how many times have I asked
you not to call me Doro? Really, Jasper, no one but you has
used that name since I was a child. Even you must see how
inappropriate it is for a woman of my years."

Jasper's eyes roamed over his sister with a gleam of amusement. She was quite right. The name Doro poorly fit the woman
she'd become. She had been a lively, tomboyish child, he
remembered, but she'd turned into an overbearing dowager in
recent years. Everything about her—her tightly curled grey
hair, her ample bosom, her rigid carriage, the self-righteous
set of her mouth, even her large feet—showed her to be a
Woman of Authority. No wonder her husband had expired so
early in their marriage. Living with Dorothea must have been
a strain.

Lady Dorothea was taking no notice of her brother's rude
stare. She was looking across the room at Ada, who stood
hesitantly in the doorway. "Good heavens, girl, don't stand
there like a ninnyhammer. Come in and give your aunt a kiss.
There, that's better. Cornelia, move over and give your cousin
some room on the loveseat beside you."

Ada did as she was bid and sat down beside Cornelia, stumbling only once in her passage across the room. Her aunt watched impatiently as she settled herself. Then, with an air of carefully controlled excitement, Dorothea looked down at Jasper and waved her letter. "Shall we wait for tea," she asked, "or would you like to hear my news at once?"

"Let's hear yer news," he responded with alacrity. "The sooner ye've announced it, the sooner I can get back t' my newspaper."

Lady Dorothea, accustomed to her brother's irascibility, took no umbrage. "Very well." Her eyes, gleaming with a mysterious inner triumph, flicked from her brother to the girls on the sofa and back again. "It's a letter from the Countess Mullineaux!"

"The Countess Mullineaux?" Jasper's look of impatient irritability faded. The Countess's name was well known to him. He had never met her, of course, since he never left his Gloucester estate to go to London, but he'd heard a great deal about her from both his sister and his now-deceased sister-in-law. The Countess and Ada's mother had been great friends in their youth, and the Countess had been named godmother to Ada at the infant's christening. (Dorothea had bragged for years that she'd made a third in the friendship, but Jasper suspected that the other two women had merely tolerated her.) Jasper had been regaled for years with accounts of the famous leader of London society. Lady Mullineaux was said to have everything—charm, generosity, wit, authority, taste, education and unquestioned importance in the world of the *haut ton*. Since Ada's mother's death, they had not heard much from the famous Countess, but Ada had not had a birthday on which the Countess had not sent a lavish remembrance. "Why on earth is she writing after all this time?" he asked with upraised brows.

"Listen to the letter, and you'll soon learn," his sister said with unaccustomed eagerness. "It's the most thrilling and unexpected pass." She unfolded the missive and started to read the contents aloud. *"My dear Doro,"* she began.

"Aha!" chortled Jasper on hearing the opprobrious appellation.

His sister glared at him but went on with her letter. *"You will no doubt be surprised to hear from me after all this time, but be assured that although I haven't written I have often thought of you. The memory of your dear, lost sister is always in my heart. She, as you know, was my dearest friend, and not a day has passed since she drowned at sea that I haven't missed her. It has occurred to me lately that I have also missed the pleasure of watching her daughter grow up, and yours as well.*

"*Both girls must be of age by now. In thinking about them, I suddenly realized that neither of them has had a London season. Therefore, I wondered if one of the girls might like to spend the coming season with me. London will soon be bustling with the balls, the routs, the concerts, the plays and all the other 'divertissements' that mark a new season, and it would give me great joy to introduce a young woman to its pleasures.*

"*I wish I could invite both girls, but at my age the burden of escorting two lively young women about town might be too much for me. I leave it to you, dear Doro, and to Ada's guardian, to decide which of the girls would most benefit from the experience. Please discuss this with Sir Jasper, and let me know which of the two dear girls I can expect and the date of her arrival. I so look forward to having one of them with me. With my deepest affection, I remain yours, Celia Mullineaux.*"

Jasper's eyebrows rose in surprise. "Wants to take one of our girls to London, eh? Seems a queer start after all these years."

"Not so queer, if you know the whole," his sister responded, perching on the chair nearest to her brother and leaning forward conspiratorially. "It's that son of hers. Mabel Banning told me, when she visited last fall, that the fellow is a shocking rake. She said that his mother would love to see him tethered in respectable matrimonial harness, but he's resisted the lures of every matchmaking Mama in town, including his own, and remains in impregnable bachelorhood even though he's past thirty. Perhaps Lady Mullineaux hopes that—"

"That one of *our* girls will attract him? That's the most addled notion anyone's ever conceived, if you ask me."

Lady Haydon drew herself up in quick offense. "What's so addled about it? My Cornelia is quite capable of attracting the most *resistant* of gentlemen! Didn't she capture that guest of Lady Aldrich's at the assembly last winter? What *was* his name, my love? You know which one I mean . . . the elegant Corinthian with reddish hair whom every girl had set her cap for."

"Satterthwaite," Cornelia responded, leaning back against the pillows with a self-satisfied smile, "Sir Humphrey Satterthwaite."

Jasper frowned at mother and daughter in disgust. "I wasn't castin' any personal aspersions on anyone. Doesn't matter *who* the Countess will force on the fellow, the idea won't work."

"Why ever not?" his sister demanded.

"Because he won't favor *anyone* who's forcibly thrust under his nose. It's against human nature."

"That's ridiculous. A man would have a strange nature to reject a girl like my Cornelia merely because she is near at hand."

"Humph!" Jasper snorted scornfully. As far as he was concerned, Cornelia was a puffed-up fribble without character or substance, and he regarded any man who permitted himself to be attracted to her as beneath contempt. His sister was ridiculous to believe that a man as cosmopolitan as Mullineaux was reputed to be would cast a second glance at Cornelia, even if she *were* placed under his nose...

With a sudden gasp, he sat up in his chair, indignation dawning in his brain and spreading like a tidal wave through his chest. "Let me understand the implication of your remarks, ma'am. Are you sayin' that you mean to send *Cornelia* to London?"

"Of course that's what I'm saying. Did you think I would let such an opportunity go by? Lord Mullineaux, Celia's son, is London's most desirable eligible. Why, the income from his country estates alone must be upwards of ten thousand, and that says nothing of his worth on the 'Change."

"I don't give a rapper for Lord Mullineaux or his income. I'm concerned about your high-handed assumption that it's Cornelia who should go."

Lady Dorothea gaped at him. "But... what are you talking about? Surely you don't think that *Ada—?*"

"Of *course* I think it should be Ada!" her brother retorted furiously. "Why not?"

Dorothea drew herself up in surprised offense. "You can't be serious!"

"I'll lay *odds* he isn't serious," Cornelia remarked, smiling in languid superciliousness. "Uncle Jasper knows as well as anyone that Ada would find herself in an impossible muddle in London. Why, she's been known to get herself lost merely crossing through Bishop's Cleve."

"Just so," her mother agreed.

Sir Jasper jumped to his feet. "I'm *completely* serious!" he declared angrily. "Ada is in every way as deservin' as Cornelia to have a London season. More, if y' ask me. At least she has other things on her mind than matchmakin' and balls and fripperies. The Countess said herself that we should choose the girl who would benefit the most from the experience. Well, I say that Ada needs a bit of town-bronze more than your Cornelia does! Ain't that so, Ada?"

There was no answer. Three pair of eyes turned to the figure sitting quietly in a corner of the sofa. Ada's head was lowered, and she seemed to be studying the hands folded in her lap. "Heavens," muttered Lady Dorothea in disgust, "she hasn't been listening to a word we've said."

"*Ada!*" Jasper snapped angrily.

The girl's head came up abruptly, and her startled eyes flew from one face to another. "Is . . . s-something the matter?"

"Dash it all, girl," her uncle shouted, "we've been speakin' of matters that are of vital concern to ye. Can't you keep your mind from goin' *elsewhere* again?"

Ada's cheeks turned a deep pink. "I'm sorry, uncle. The letter from the countess set me to thoughts of . . . of my mother. It suddenly seemed that I could remember her face . . ."

Lady Dorothea snorted. "Not very likely. You were just a little bit of a creature when she was lost. But at least you were listening when I read Lady Mullineaux's proposal."

Ada's blush deepened. "No, I'm afraid I . . . I only heard the first few words . . ."

Both Dorothea and Jasper stared at her in disapproval, while Cornelia briefly (though scornfully) outlined the main points of the discussion. When she understood the thrust of the discussion she'd missed, poor Ada paled. The very *thought* of going to London to stay with a grand lady whom she'd never met and who would expect her to participate in all the doings of the social world terrified her. "But, uncle," she remonstrated, "you surely don't expect *me* to go to—?"

"Dash it, Ada, that's *exactly* what I expect!"

She fixed her pale eyes on his face in horror. "Even if I . . . I don't *wish* to?"

Jasper was nonplussed. "But *why* don't you wish it? *All* young girls want t' have come-outs and go t' balls and flirt

with dandies and collect suitors and indulge in suchlike frol-
ickin'!"

"I don't," Ada said quietly.

"Of course she doesn't," Lady Dorothea interjected. "The
very idea of muddleheaded Ada living in a fashionable household among the *haute monde* is ludicrous."

Sir Jasper drew in a furious breath. "Damnation, Doro, get
out o' my house!" he shouted, jumping to his feet. His sister
had made him livid. He bounded across the few yards which
separated them and confronted her, waving an accusing finger
under her nose. "If you're goin' to call my Ada names, you
can take yourself off right now! No, woman, don't open your
mouth, 'cause I ain't goin' t' listen to another word. Take this
flibbertigibbity daughter of yours and get out. Do you hear me,
ma'am? *Out of my house!*"

"Please, uncle," Ada said softly, rising and putting a gentle
hand on his arm, "Aunt Dorothea didn't say anything that
wasn't true. I *am* muddleheaded, and I don't have any desire
to spend the season in London, truly I don't. It wouldn't suit
me at all."

"There, you see? The girl admits it. So it's all settled.
Cornelia will go. I shall write to Celia tomor—"

"You will do *no such thing!*" Sir Jasper thundered, so fe-
rociously that his sister instinctively raised her hands in self-
protection.

"No need to shout," Cornelia said calmly, not the least
disturbed by her uncle's tantrum. "If Ada doesn't wish to go,
I don't see—"

"Never mind what Ada wishes," he barked. "Ada and I shall
talk this over when we're calmer. Then, when I can bear the
sight of you and yer mother again, we can all discuss this
matter further. In the meantime, ye'll oblige me by sayin' good
day. I've seen quite enough o' the pair of ye for the nonce."

"Really, Jasper, you can be the most *exasperating—!*" his
sister declared. "We haven't yet had our *tea!*"

"You can take your damned tea at your *own* damned house,"
her brother snarled with what he considered perfectly appropriate hospitality. He propelled his sister and her daughter firmly
to the door. "I bid ye a good afternoon." he muttered icily,
and before they could utter another word, he shut the door on
them.

Chapter Three

Ada, after the excitement and the rapidity of her pulse had faded, was not unduly discomfited by the memory of the scene in the drawing room. Such quarrels between her uncle and his overweening sister were frequent and seemed not to affect the habit of regular intercourse between the two parts of the family. Nevertheless, she couldn't help feeling a twinge of alarm at the prospect of a continuation of the discussion that had precipitated the argument. She wondered if her uncle would bring up at the dinner table the subject that made her so uncomfortable: visiting the countess in London. But, no, she told herself, he couldn't have been serious in what he'd said to his sister. He knew better than anyone that she, Ada, was too feather-brained to cope with life in London. He hadn't meant what he'd said, she was sure of that. He'd probably made that scene in the drawing room this afternoon only to vent his spleen; he'd merely been angry at his sister for paying him a visit and insisting on seeing him when he wanted to read his *Times*.

He said nothing about the matter at dinner that night, so Ada put the matter out of her mind. She told herself, in considerable relief, that he'd probably forgotten all about the subject.

But Uncle Jasper had done no such thing. He went to bed that night with the matter of the London trip so much on his mind that he could not fall asleep. The more he thought about it, the more he realized that such an experience as a stay in London with the worldly Countess Mullineaux would do his foggy-headed niece a world of good. A few months in the company of a sensible, practical, clever woman might be the making of the girl. Cornelia, much as he hated to admit it, was bound to make a successful match and live a comfortable life even if she *never* went to London for a season. She was quite beautiful, amazingly self-assured and could be very persuasive about getting what she wanted. Ada, on the other hand, seemed to be drifting through life with no focus, no goals and no

23

apparent concern for her future. If he did nothing about her, she might well end her days a lonely, eccentric, addled old maid. He made up his mind that he would present this assessment of the situation to his sister the very next day. When she understood the truth of his analysis, even *she* would agree that Ada was the logical choice to accept the Countess's invitation.

Much to his chagrin, however, the next day he learned from his valet (who was "stepping out" with Lady Dorothea's hairdresser) that her ladyship had *already* written to Countess Mullineaux accepting the invitation *in the name of her daughter!*

Nothing that his sister had done to him in the past decade so enraged him as that news. He was almost beside himself with fury. That Dorothea Haydon, his own sister, could have had so little feeling for the needs and concerns of poor Ada (who was *her* niece as well as his) made him wild. How *could* she have taken it upon herself to write that letter? Lady Mullineaux had *specifically* said that the decision was to be made *by both of them, together! How dared she make the decision alone?*

He stormed into the breakfast room where Ada was sitting on the window seat, innocently sipping her morning coffee. "Ada," he thundered, "get to yer feet at once!"

Ada gave a violent start. The coffee cup wobbled for a moment in its saucer and then tipped over, spilling the hot liquid all over the girl's skirt. "Uncle!" she cried, ignoring the spill and the precarious position of the cup in her alarm. "What's the matter?"

"Everything's the matter! Can I never say a word to ye without yer jumpin' out o' your skin? Get *up*, I say!"

Ada's hand began to tremble, sending the cup to the floor with a crash. She rose, shaking. She tried to read her uncle's face and mop her wet skirt (with a tiny, completely inadequate handkerchief) at the same time. "Have I . . . done something d-dreadful, uncle?" she asked timorously.

"Don't be a ninny! Why must ye always think ye've done somethin' dreadful? When have I ever accused ye o' doin' anythin' dreadful?"

"But you seem to be so . . . so angry . . ."

"Not at *you*, girl. At yer *aunt*."

Ada let out her frozen breath in relief. Uncle Jasper was so often angry at Aunt Dorothea that his tantrums concerning her could no longer be considered a matter of importance. "Oh, is *that* all?" she murmured under her breath and knelt to pick up the pieces of the shattered cup.

But Jasper heard her. "No, it ain't all!" he snapped. "Get up, Miss Windmill-Head. Never mind the deuced cup."

"But what—?"

"We can't waste time jabberin'. Go upstairs and pack everything y' have that's suitable for London. Y're leavin' for the Countess's town house within the hour!"

Ada was stricken speechless. She could only gape at him.

"Are ye listenin' t' me, girl? Shake yerself awake, will ye? I intend fer the carriage t' depart *within the hour*, whether ye're ready or no."

"B-But . . . Uncle *Jasper!* You can't *mean* it!"

"Can't I? I'll show ye if I mean it or not." He stalked to the door. "Cotrell!" he shouted into the corridor. "*Cotrell,* ye looby! Tell Hines t' ready the carriage! He's t' start fer London in one hour!"

Ada, still trembling in shock, followed him across the room. "But uncle, this is *ridiculous*. I told you yesterday that I didn't wish . . . I thought the matter was concluded."

"Well, it *ain't* concluded. Not as far as *I'm* concerned."

"But it *is*. I heard from the housekeeper, who had it from Aunt Dorothea's cook, that Cornelia is already packing and is intending to leave within a very few days."

"Oh, she *is*, is she? Then that's too bad fer her, ain't it? Ye'll have almost a full day's head start."

"Head st-start?" the girl echoed in dismay.

"Yes. If you arrive at the Countess's door first, ye'll be welcomed with open arms. Then, when Cornelia arrives, she'll seem like an intruder." His face brightened. "Her ladyship'll very likely send her home in disgrace." He grinned wickedly at the prospect.

Ada blinked at her uncle in rebuke. "Surely you don't mean what you're saying, Uncle. You cannot wish to use Cornelia so unkindly."

"I'll take the greatest pleasure in it, I assure you. Now go upstairs and do as I've ordered. An' tell yer abigail t' pack as well."

"S-Selena? Why?"

"She'll go with ye, o'course. Ye don't wish t' arrive at yer godmother's door like a poor little waif, do ye? Ye'll make a proper entrance, with yer own maid and yer own coachman—

I'll have Hines wear his livery—and a mountain o' baggage. Pack everythin' ye own."

"Please, Uncle," Ada begged, her heart beginning to pound in real terror, "don't ask me to do this. I've no talent for living in society. And I couldn't steal this opportunity away from my cousin, when it is something she's wanted to do all her life."

"Don't be so blasted mealy-mouthed," her uncle growled. "She has no compunction about stealin' such an opportunity from *you.*"

Ada glanced up at him tearfully. "But—"

"But me no buts, girl. Ye'll do as I say, and at once! Do you hear me?"

Ada knew her uncle well enough to realize that there was no use debating the matter. Something had made him adamant. She gave him an obedient, though a tremblingly reluctant, curtsey and started to the door.

His eyes followed her, his face set sternly. "And if ye do *anythin'* t' foil my plans—if ye get lost, or fall ill on the way, or do anythin' else t' delay yer arrival so that Cornelia makes her appearance ahead o' you—ye can be sure that my wrath will be terrible!"

Ada turned round. She was quite upset by the sudden turn her life seemed to be taking, but she was too familiar with her uncle's essential soft-heartedness to be shaken by his ranting. "Come now, uncle, that's doing it a bit too brown," she said, offering him a shaky smile in the hope that it would calm him a little. "Your wrath will be terrible, indeed. If you want to play the ogre in a fairy story, find some little child to roar at, not me."

But he would not permit himself to be softened. "I ain't playactin', Ada. I mean every word. I'm warnin' ye, girl. If ye don't make it t' London on time, I'll make ye wish you'd never been born!"

And with those fearful words, he turned her about and pushed her toward the door.

Chapter Four

It wasn't Ada's fault that the carriage wheel cracked on a rut in the road. She hadn't even *wished* for such a delay in her race to London. Once her uncle had made clear that she had no choice, she'd resigned herself to the trip. She'd had every intention of obeying her uncle's orders to the letter. What else was there for her to do?

Ada had reasoned that Uncle Jasper had her best interests at heart; thus, if he thought a trip to London would do her good, she simply assumed he was in the right. In spite of her initial repugnance toward the whole idea, she told herself to make the best of the situation. She was not a rebellious sort. She'd never enjoyed arguments or confrontation but was comfortable only in an atmosphere of peace and serenity. If the only way to achieve that serenity was to succumb to her uncle's wishes, so be it.

By the time her baggage had been loaded into the coach, and she and her abigail had climbed aboard, her equanimity had been at least partially restored. Having accepted the trip as inevitable, she'd even managed to kiss her uncle goodbye with her usual affection.

During the first hour of the journey, her misgivings about living in London with a doyenne of society continued to trouble her mind, but soon she was distracted from her thoughts by a thick-sounding cough. Selena, her abigail, was sitting opposite her, and Ada noticed at once that the woman was looking distinctly unwell. Selena, a tall, gaunt, middle-aged fussbudget who'd cared for Ada since childhood, was normally sallow in complexion, but today her cheeks were flushed as if she'd rouged them, and her eyes were decidedly watery. "Are you not feeling quite the thing, Selena?" Ada asked in concern.

"I'd *better* be feelin' the thing," Selena answered, her voice unusually hoarse. "I promised Sir Jarsper I'd get ye t' Lunnon by dark, no matter whut. He wouldn' take kin'ly t' any delay, least of all me bein' sick."

Ada sighed worriedly. "Yes, I suppose he wouldn't. Here, stretch out on the seat and let me spread the laprobe over you. At least you can doze while we ride. Perhaps a few hours of sleep will help."

While Selena slept, Ada stared out of the window, letting her mind roam where it willed. She found herself dreaming of dancing at lavish balls, staring wide-eyed at glowing theater stages, dining at luxurious tables, shopping at fashionable salons where the *modistes* were as elegant as their patrons, and indulging in all the other voluptuous indulgences that a life in town suggested to the mind. In reality, she might find herself too shy to savor these pleasures, but in dreams she found them delicious. In her dreams she could be beautiful, charming, witty and self-assured—all the things that in reality she was not.

But dreams have a kind of reality of their own in the mind of the dreamer. If the dreamer concentrates on them, she lives as much in the world of her dreams as in the real. Ada knew that if, in London, she found herself in a modiste's salon in which the dressmaker treated her with disdain and dressed her in a dowdy gown of puce broadcloth, she had only to look in the mirror of her imagination and see herself, lovely and admired, clad in a flowing creation of pale blue lustring and silver lace. If she, in reality, found herself sitting in a corner of a crowded ballroom, neglected and alone, she'd have not the slightest difficulty imagining herself whirling about the dance floor on the arm of the handsomest bachelor of the assemblage, causing havoc in the hearts of all the watchers. Therefore, although the reality of this trip to London was undoubtedly frightening, in Ada's daydreams the journey was tremendously exciting.

So of course the accident on the roadway had nothing whatever to do with her. She hadn't expected, or even wished for, a delay en route. A broken wheel was the last thing in the world she wanted. But her uncle would never believe that. He would say she'd put the rut in the road on purpose!

Hines, the coachman, studied the wrecked wheel with a frown. "We'll 'ave t' find a wheelwright, Miss Ada. An' it's comin' on t' dark. I think we'll 'ave t' put up somewheres 'til mornin'."

Selena, having been rudely awakened by the shock to the carriage when the wheel cracked, moaned miserably. "Oh, no! We *can't!*" she muttered. "Sir Jarsper'll 'ave my *head!*"

Hines searched out a wheelwright at once, but by the time the fellow appeared on the scene, it had become too dark to effect the needed repairs. He promised to make the repairs at first light, but in the meantime there was no choice for the travelers but to spend the night at the nearest inn. Fortunately, Hines knew of an inn of respectable reputation that was not more than a mile down the road. The two women plodded disconsolately toward it, Hines following with the horses. By the time they reached it, the women were chilled through.

The Black Boar was a small, modest establishment with a thatched roof. It looked quite picturesque and welcoming to Ada's weary eyes. But the interior was disappointing. The walls were grimy with the effluvia of smoky chimneys, and the stale air smelled of malt and burned grease. "Humph!" Selena sneered at her first whiff. "I 'ope the bedrooms're better kept than this. Wouldn't surprise me t' find *bedbugs*."

Ada, trying to make the best of things, ignored Selena's mutterings. She arranged for rooms for her party and ordered Selena to take to her bedroom at once. "I'll manage to eat my dinner without you," she told the abigail reassuringly. "You're looking quite ill and shouldn't remain on your feet."

The abigail was too heavy-headed to object. While Hines went off to see to the horses and to take his dinner with the inn's stablemen, Selena took herself to bed. Ada, left alone, was brought into the inn's private parlor by the innkeeper's wife, who promised to bring her a good, hot dinner as soon as she could ready it.

Ada, weary and chilled to the bone, seated herself on the hearth before the room's huge fireplace and tried to warm herself. A snuffling sound caught her attention. She looked about and found that a shaggy, unkempt collie was sharing the hearth with her, looking up at her with dark, sad eyes. "What's the matter, old fellow?" Ada murmured, bending down to pat his head. "You look as if you have the weight of the world on your shoulders."

The dog whimpered and nuzzled her arm pathetically.

"Poor fellow. I don't suppose you've been groomed in weeks." She moved closer to the animal and smoothed his coat. There were a number of welts under the fur, and as her hand passed over them, the dog shuddered in pain. "Good heavens," she said in surprise, "what on earth is wrong here?"

She peered closely under the fur. The animal was covered

with scars and cuts on which the blood had dried. The wounds had obviously never been treated. The sight sickened her. The poor dog had been beaten, often and brutally, probably with a stick! She would have liked to take a stick to the person responsible for this cruelty. Something had to be done to help the animal, that much was plain. One couldn't permit such monstrous treatment of a poor dumb beast. She smoothed the collie's ears as she wondered what action to take.

The door opened at that moment, and a gentleman—a London gentleman, if one could judge by the number of the capes of his greatcoat and the elegance of his boots—entered the room. Not noticing Ada sitting on the hearth, he shut the door, tossed his hat and cane upon the table and strode across the room to the window where he stood frowning out at the winter landscape. Ada, watching him, decided that she liked his looks. He was dressed in the first style of elegance, but there was nothing of the dandy about him. His face was strong, and his eyes, though weary, seemed kind. He seemed to be the very sort who could assist her in discovering and berating the perpetrator of the crime against the collie. "Excuse me, sir. This sweet-natured dog is in pain," she announced without preamble. "Do you think we—?"

"What?" The man wheeled about, startled. "Oh, I beg your pardon. I was not aware that anyone was in the room. I was told this is the private parlor."

"So it is. But as I was saying, this poor animal—"

The gentleman held up a hand and shook his head. "Your pardon, ma'am, if I seem confused. You haven't introduced yourself, you see, and I don't believe we've met before. Are you employed here?"

"Oh, dear," Ada murmured, abashed. "I suppose I've made a *faux pas* speaking to you as I did. I *am* sorry. But circumstances made it necessary for me to omit the niceties. This poor creature—"

The gentleman let out a small, impatient breath. "If you might forget the collie for a moment, ma'am, I would appreciate an explanation of why I find you in my private parlor. *Are* you employed here?"

"No, I am merely waiting for my dinner. But in the matter of this dog—"

"Waiting for your dinner? Then *you've* engaged this room?" He glared at the door in annoyance. "Then why didn't the

damned innkeeper—I beg your pardon, ma'am—why didn't
the idiot tell me the room had been spoken for?"

"I engaged it through his wife," Ada explained. "Perhaps
he didn't know the room had already been let."

"It seems a most inefficient way to run things," the gentleman said with a little gesture of apology, his eyes flitting over
her in what seemed to be an attempt to determine if her need
for the privacy of the parlor was greater than his. She suddenly
felt ashamed of her rumpled travelling dress and the undoubted
disorder of her hair, and her hand, without any conscious orders
from her brain, flew to the back of her head and attempted to
tuck in some trailing locks. But the gentleman had evidently
already decided that she was a gentlewoman and was making
her a bow. "Excuse me for having intruded on you," he was
saying.

"Please don't go," Ada said quickly. "I'm rather glad you
did intrude, sir, for I require your assistance. You see, I've
been trying to tell you that this poor, abused animal seems to
have been regularly beaten—"

But the gentleman was not listening. His attention had been
caught by some commotion in the innyard outside the window.
"Damnation!" he muttered under his breath. "How did he manage to trail me here?"

"I beg your pardon?" Ada asked, blinking. "I was speaking
about—"

The gentleman, however, perturbed by what he'd seen outside, was unable to pay attention to her words. His brow furrowed, and his eyes flicked quickly round the room, coming
to rest on Ada's face. He stared at her speculatively. "Excuse
me again, ma'am," he said, glancing once more out the window
and then starting across the room toward her, "but I'm about
to make you a most shocking proposal. You will undoubtedly
think me insane, but I beg you not to refuse me. I need your
help in a matter of some urgency. Bear with me, and I promise
I shall explain everything to your satisfaction afterwards."

"Yes, of course," Ada said, not understanding a word of
the gentleman's speech but determined not to be distracted from
her objective, "just as soon as we've done something about
this dear, abused creature."

The gentleman shook his head impatiently. "You don't understand, ma'am. We have no time to—"

There were voices in the corridor outside the door. "Step

aside, man," someone growled. "I know he's in there!"

"Dash it all, it's too late," the gentleman hissed, pulling Ada rudely to her feet.

Ada gaped at him openmouthed. "What—?"

They could hear the rattle of the doorknob. "Forgive me," the man muttered, brazenly taking her into his arms, "and whatever happens, for God's sake, don't give me away!" Then, before Ada could utter another sound, he pressed his lips against her mouth in a strenuous—in fact, Ada thought, very immoderate—kiss.

She was dimly aware that the door had opened, and she felt, rather than saw, that more than one person had burst into the room. But the intruders evidently stopped in their tracks, for suddenly the room was completely silent. She supposed that they were staring at her. She should, she supposed, be feeling furious and utterly humiliated. But for the moment she wasn't feeling that way at all. Here she stood, being vehemently kissed by a stranger, and she was not at all upset. The stranger was evidently skillful at the art (for his hold on her waist was so comfortably firm, and the pressure of his lips on hers was so forceful and lusty that she was convinced he'd had a great deal of practice), and, truth to tell, she was enjoying the sensation immensely. She had never been kissed by a man before (for surely one couldn't count the pecks upon the cheek that her uncle had bestowed on her over the years), but she'd dreamed of it often. This experience was not entirely *un*like her dreams, but it was different enough to be fascinating. She had anticipated the emotional upheaval a kiss of this sort might wreak, but she hadn't expected the excitement generated by its sheer physicality. The closeness of their two chests, the way her arms almost involuntarily crept up round his neck, the turmoil of her pulse, the effervescence of her blood as it raced through her veins, the heated flush that swept up through her body and into her face—all this was a revelation to her.

Before she could make mental notes of all the various sensations, she felt his hold on her relax. He lifted his head. She opened her eyes and stared up at him. He was looking down at her in some surprise. For a moment their eyes held, as if both of them were attempting to remember where they were.

A snorting, bitter laugh from the direction of the doorway broke the mood. "Well, well, my lord, what have we here?

Are you trying to pretend you've snared *another* pigeon for your coop?"

The gentleman turned toward the door with a very convincing look of surprise. "Alcorn! What are you doing here?"

A pale, narrow-shouldered, grey-haired man stood in the doorway, a large wooden box tucked under one arm. His lips were pressed together so tightly they seemed edged in white, and he was tense with suppressed rage. Behind him, the innkeeper and a number of persons from the taproom were gathered in the corridor watching the proceedings with fascination. Ada felt herself blush. The humiliation, which had thus far not had an effect, suddenly swept over her.

The man named Alcorn took a step forward, a sneer disfiguring his lined face. "You know very well what I'm doing here. I *found* my wife, my lord, and sent her home."

"Did you indeed?" The gentleman moved in front of Ada as if trying to shield her. "And what has that very interesting statement to do with me?"

Ada wished she could leave the room. This was a private conversation that had nothing to do with her. But she had another matter on her mind. She tapped the gentleman on the arm. "Please, sir, the collie must be—"

The gentleman made a slight motion with his hand to indicate to her that she shouldn't speak, but he kept his eyes fixed on the other man. "Well, Alcorn? What has that to do with me?" he repeated.

Alcorn laughed mirthlessly. "Don't take me for a fool, my lord. I know my wife was running off with you."

"So that's what this is all about, is it?" the gentleman asked with icy scorn. "You *are* a fool, Alcorn, if you believe that."

"We'll see who's the fool." Alcorn's voice shook with anger. He walked into the room and set the wooden box carefully on the table. "I've brought pistols."

There was a murmur from the onlookers. The gentleman snorted. "If you're going to talk fustian, Alcorn, at least don't do it publicly. Close the deuced door!"

Alcorn did so, slamming it loudly in the faces of the onlookers. While he was thus engaged, Ada tapped the other gentleman's shoulder again. "That poor animal is still—"

But Alcorn turned from the door and spoke up belligerently to his adversary. "Very well, we're private now. So you may as well admit, my lord, that you've been involved with my wife for some time and were going off with her to Wales."

"I admit nothing of the sort."

"Do you *deny* that you set off for Wales today in her company?"

"I set off for Wales today, yes. But if you weren't so completely blinded by your outrage, you would see that my companion is not your wife."

"Ah, yes. That lady you're so carefully shielding. Who is she, my lord? Why haven't you seen fit to introduce us?"

"I don't think it's any of your business who she is. And since she *is* a lady, I think you can understand why, under the circumstances, I would rather not reveal her name."

Alcorn walked to the side to get a better view of the young woman partially hidden by his lordship's body. "She *is* a pretty little chit. Are you trying to tell me that *she's* the one you're taking to Wales?"

"No, I'm trying *not* to tell you. Good God, man, have you no discretion? Can't you see that you're embarrassing the young lady?"

The man called Alcorn stared at his lordship suspiciously for a moment and then dropped into a chair at the table. "I don't know *what* to make of this," he muttered, passing a shaking hand over his brow. "There have been *on-dits* about you and Julia circulating about town for months. I haven't heard a word about your having a *new* connection—"

"That only proves how little one should rely upon *on-dits*," the other responded drily.

Alcorn was nonplussed. He obviously desired fervently to believe what his lordship was telling him; his eagerness to believe in his wife's innocence showed quite plainly in his face. But he didn't wish to play the gull. To counteract his gullibility, he clung to his suspicions tightly. "Dash it all," he growled, "I don't know what to believe. That embrace I observed when I burst in seemed convincingly ardent, but . . ."

"Take your buts and go home," the gentleman said in disgust. "You're decidedly in the way here, I can tell you."

"Perhaps," Alcorn said, still unsure. "Perhaps. But I wish you'd let the young lady speak for herself. You've done your best to keep her from involvement in this conversation."

"Wouldn't you, if you were in my place?"

"I suppose so. Dash it all, I realize that this entire encounter is decidedly awkward. But, my lord, I promise you that you can count on my holding my tongue about all of this . . . if your companion can convince me of the truth of your claims. So speak up, ma'am. Is it true that his lordship is . . . er . . . escorting you to Wales?"

The gentleman who'd kissed Ada so brazenly turned to her, his eyes beseeching her to support him in his lies. "Go on, my dear. Tell Lord Alcorn what he wants to know."

Ada looked from one to the other. "No," she said.

"No?" Alcorn rose slowly from his chair, his face whitening and his hand reaching for the pistol case. "Are you implying that you're *not* his . . . his . . . that is, that you're not going to Wales with his lordship?"

"I am not implying anything at all." With an air of impatience she brushed by her "protector" and strode to the door. "What I've been trying to say for the past quarter hour is that there is a poor, bruised, maltreated collie lying on the hearth whimpering in agony. And until one of you takes care of his needs and sees to it that his master is sharply reprimanded, I don't intend to say anything more to either one of you. Good evening, gentlemen."

Chapter Five

Ada paced about the slant-roofed bedroom. She was uncertain about what to do next. Could she leave her room without feeling embarrassed? What would happen if she came face-to-face with the gentleman who'd kissed her? It would be dreadful to have to endure such an encounter—she didn't think she'd be able to look into his face. She'd handled the situation very badly. She should have been more ladylike, she thought. She should have fainted in his arms when he embraced her so shamelessly; or she should have slapped his face in outrage. At the very least, she should have screamed for help. Instead she'd endured the offense with apparent equanimity, as if she were quite accustomed to having strange gentlemen snatch her up and kiss her.

So, of course, she would have to remain closeted in this tiny room. But it felt like imprisonment. She was very hungry, and she could not have her dinner without going downstairs. Furthermore, she had a deep and shameful desire to take one more peep at the gentleman's face. The episode in the downstairs parlor had been so confusing that she was left without a clear memory of his appearance. All she could bring to mind were fleeting impressions...a deep, authoritative voice...a pair of dark, unreadable eyes...broad shoulder swathed in exquisitely-cut blue superfine...thick, unruly hair. These details were not sufficient to bring his face clearly to mind. And she wished very much to be able to recreate it; that face would add a touch of excitement to her daydreams.

But she hadn't the courage to go downstairs. If she did encounter that impetuous gentleman again, she would not know how to behave. How *did* one behave after an incident such as that? Should she raise her nose and pass him by, haughty and disdainful? Should she stop, gasp and sink down in a swoon? Should she call for someone to challenge him to a duel to avenge her honor? None of these responses seemed appropriate to her nature. What, she asked herself, would Cousin Cornelia

36

do in such circumstances? Take her riding whip to him, no doubt. Well, Ada was not the sort to engage in such rodomontades. In her imagination she might concoct a dramatic encounter, but not in real life.

A knock at the door caused her to stop her pacing abruptly. She froze in her place. Who could be—?

"It's Griff," the familiar, authoritative voice said loudly. Then he added, much more softly, "Please open the door."

Feeling her blood begin to race through her veins, she unlocked the door and opened it a crack. "Y-Yes?"

The gentleman who'd kissed her stood just outside, still wearing his greatcoat and carrying his cane and beaver in his hand. "Alcorn's watching us from down below," he said in a whisper. "You've gone so far already. Do you think you can go just a bit further and let me in?"

"Let you in?" she echoed dimly. She hadn't anticipated anything like this and was utterly unprepared with a response. "I . . . I couldn't do that, sir. It would be considered . . . er . . ."

"Indiscreet?"

"Oh, yes. Indiscreet at the very least."

"But it would be a rather splendid indiscretion, my dear. It might very well save lives."

"Save lives?" She gaped at him quite stupidly. She didn't really follow what he was saying. Only two thoughts flitted across her mind: one was that she ought to slam the door in his face, and the other was that she could never bring herself to do it.

His eyes—the same kind-but-weary eyes that had made her believe, at her very first glimpse of him, that he would help her rescue the collie—gleamed with sudden, amused understanding. "You're afraid I'm going to kiss you again, is that it? Have no fear, ma'am. I promise I shall behave like a perfect gentleman. I only want Alcorn to be convinced that you and I are lovers. Once he sees that you've admitted me to your bedroom, he'll have no more doubt. He'll return to his wife, and all will be well."

As if mesmerized, Ada widened the door-opening and stepped aside. The gentleman came in and closed the door quickly behind him. After placing his hat and cane carefully upon a chest of drawers, he turned to face her. "Thank you, my dear," he said, taking her hand and lifting it to his lips. "I'm more grateful to you than I can say."

Ada trembled inwardly at her own temerity. She had admitted a strange man into her bedroom and permitted him to kiss her hand. Such behavior was undoubtedly a symptom of a hitherto unrecognized depravity of character. She should really give herself a severe scolding. She would surely do so . . . but not tonight. Tonight she would live through this exciting adventure. There was plenty of time for self-recrimination tomorrow.

She gently withdrew her hand from his grasp and glanced up at him. "I don't quite understand why you find it necessary to engage in this deception, sir, but before you explain it to me, I would like to know if you've done anything about the collie."

His eyebrows rose in amusement. "What an unusually single-minded young woman you are, ma'am, if I may be permitted to say so. You seem to have thought of nothing but that collie since we met. But you may now safely put the matter out of that tenacious mind of yours. I've taken care of it."

"Have you really? You reprimanded the innkeeper? That was good of you. I hope your reprimand was severe enough to keep the fellow from renewing his behavior after we leave this place."

"You need have no worry on that score. I removed the animal from his control."

"Did you? But how—?"

"I merely purchased the collie outright."

"*Purchased* him?" Ada's cheeks colored guiltily. "Oh, but I never meant you to go so far!"

"It was not so very far to go, ma'am. Not compared to the distance you've gone for me. I intend to present him to you as a token of my gratitude."

She stared up at him, her eyes widening. "Present him . . . to *me?*"

"Yes." His brow furrowed in confusion. "You do *like* the dog, don't you? I thought—"

"Oh, yes! He's a dear, sweet animal and has been *so* much abused. But I can't take him! I can't arrive at . . . at my destination with a large, shaggy collie in tow. It wouldn't be at all the thing to do." She looked up at her visitor worriedly. "What on earth shall I *do* with him?"

But he was not listening. He was staring down at her with the strangest expression on his face. "Has anyone ever told you that you have the most remarkable eyes?"

"What?"

"Truly, they're quite remarkable. They're so clear and pale that they seem . . . unfocused. As if you're perpetually looking beyond the present scene and seeing something else entirely."

She felt her cheeks grow hot. His expression and the tone of his voice were enigmatic; she couldn't tell if he admired what he'd described or merely found her freakish. She turned away in embarrassment. "We were talking about the collie, sir," she reminded him.

He gave a little snort of laughter. "You *are* single-minded, aren't you? But you needn't concern yourself about the dog. If you can't accept him, I'll take him with me to Wales. My caretakers have a number of dogs. They won't object to taking on another."

"Oh, sir," she said, overwhelmed, "that is truly kind of you." She turned back to him and offered him the first real smile he'd seen on her face. "Now it's *my* turn to be grateful."

"Not at all. My providing for the dog is not an act in the slightest way equal to your kindness in admitting me into your bedroom. As I said, your conduct has been quite splendid."

"My 'indiscretion,' you mean. I believe that was the word you used."

"Your indiscretion, then. But you *have* been splendid, you know. You've prevented the shedding of blood tonight."

She stared at him in disbelief. "You can't be serious."

"I'm completely serious. Alcorn had every intention of forcing a duel upon me."

"I'm quite certain that the gentleman downstairs—*Lord* Alcorn, is it?—did not really intend to use those pistols."

"Oh, but he *did*, I assure you. He came all the way from London with just that purpose in mind."

"Good heavens! He must be *demented*."

"Not at all. Any man would be inclined to reach for his pistols when he suspects he's been cuckolded."

"But surely he's demented if he believes that *you*—"

The gentleman tried to hide his amusement at her naivete. "It is good of you to assume that I'm innocent, ma'am. Would you still have agreed to help me if I were guilty?"

"Surely you aren't guilty, sir! I can't believe—"

"But I am, my dear. Quite guilty. If I were innocent, I would think myself cowardly to use a ruse like this to avoid a duel. If I were innocent, I would face Alcorn across twenty paces of open space and put a bullet in one of his arms without a qualm, just to teach him a lesson for being a fool. But since I am guilty..." He paused, sighed and walked to the window. "Since I am guilty, I cannot add to my sins by shedding his blood. I have done him enough harm by wounding his honor."

"How strange," Ada murmured, half to herself. "I took you for a proper, kindly gentleman, and now I find that you're..."

"Cowardly?" he offered dryly.

"No, no, of course not."

"Degenerate, then?"

"I was going to say a... a rake."

"But ma'am, my shocking treatment of you down in the parlor must surely have given you a clue to the depravity of my character," he said, turning from the window and cocking an eyebrow at her with a mischievous charm.

"No. I was too... surprised to make any analysis."

"Too surprised, and too preoccupied with the plight of the collie, I'd say. I think I was very fortunate that you are so single-minded. I might otherwise have found myself deep in the suds."

"Oh, I don't know," Ada said, considering the matter seriously. "Perhaps I'm the degenerate sort of female who *likes* rakes."

He shook his head. "No, I don't think so." He strode back across the room and lifted her chin in his hand. "There is nothing at all degenerate in those pale eyes of yours. And a young woman who defends abused animals with such steadfast energy can only be pure of heart."

Ada knew that he was gently teasing her and that he didn't take any of this conversation seriously. But she found the implications of these casual remarks arresting. He had touched on a question she herself had been mulling over in the back of her mind... the unexpected possibility of her own degeneracy. She had very much enjoyed his kiss... the kiss of a stranger and a rake. Didn't that mean that there was some part of her that was degenerate? "I think that character can not be so easily categorized," she said thoughtfully. "If I were so pure of heart, I would not have permitted you to enter my bedroom. And if you were as degenerate as you say, I would not feel so safe as I do, standing here unprotected while you hold my chin in your fingers like a cup."

The gentleman studied her face with fascination. "Are you saying, ma'am, that I am less degenerate than circumstances indicate and that you are more so?"

"Yes, exactly."

He laughed. "A bit of the angel in me and the devil in you, eh? Not very likely in either case, I fear. I cannot imagine even a *touch* of the devil in you, my dear, and as for me, I wasn't commended for my good behavior even as a boy." He held her chin cupped in his hand and, for a long moment, peered down at her. Her skin, which he judged was usually pale and translucent, was now charmingly rosy from her blushing discomfort at being so impudently studied. Her hair, pulled back from her face in a severe knot, looked so soft and silky that he itched to smooth back the strands that had burst from their fastenings. Her lips were deliciously full and red, and he would have thought them her most fetching feature had it not been for her large, amazingly-light eyes. Those eyes made her seem to be a creature not of this earth. Surely only angels in heaven could have eyes of such ethereal clarity! Imagine her trying to pretend she had a touch of the devil. There could not be even the *slightest* touch of evil behind those eyes. Feeling all at once a sharp twinge of guilt, he dropped his hold on her. "Well, whatever the truth, we shall not have time to debate it tonight. I've given my word to act the gentleman, and no gentleman worthy of the name would compromise a lady—especially one who's given him such unselfish assistance—by dawdling too long in her bedroom. I must leave you, ma'am."

He gave her a quick bow and went to the door. As he put his hand on the knob, however, he paused. "I wonder if Alcorn is still waiting. If only I could open the door a crack to take a look. But if I open the door and he's down there, I'll give the whole game away." He stared at the door speculatively for a moment and then shook his head. "No, no, he won't still be there. He couldn't be! Even a cawker like Alcorn wouldn't be so idiotic as to stand guard all night, would he? What do you think, ma'am?"

There was no answer. The gentleman turned about and discovered that Ada was sitting on the bed lost in thought. Puzzled, he crossed the room and knelt beside her. "Ma'am?"

She blinked and smiled at him absently. "Yes?"

"I asked what you think."

"I think it very unlikely that your behavior was reprehensible all the time. I'm sure that there were many occasions in your boyhood when you were good or kind or generous. Even now, although it is undoubtedly reprehensible to have cuckolded poor Lord Alcorn, you are doing all you can to keep from dueling with him . . . which anyone would agree is a very commendable act."

He studied her face in amazement. "But I wasn't asking you to defend my character, ma'am. We had ceased our conversation on that subject some time since. Where have you been these past few minutes?"

"Oh!" Ada's cheeks reddened at once. "I . . . I must have been . . . woolgathering."

"Woolgathering? Good God, woman, how can you be woolgathering when a strange man is in your bedroom, unable to think of a way to get out, and thus giving every indication that he will cause the ruination of your reputation?"

She twisted her fingers together in humiliation. "I'm sorry. I don't know what makes me so . . . so bubbleheaded. It's a very disturbing weakness of mine."

"Do you mean that you do this sort of thing often? Wander away mentally?"

"I'm afraid so. My uncle says my mind is *always* elsewhere."

"I suppose that shouldn't surprise me. That's what I was trying to describe in your eyes." With a shake of his head (a gesture which Ada interpreted as an indication that he was dismissing from his mind any attraction that he might earlier have felt toward her), he stood erect and looked at the door. "This is all very interesting, ma'am, but we haven't time to discuss it further. We must somehow manage to solve the *present* dilemma."

"Dilemma?"

"Yes. We have a dilemma. If I go out the door, I may come face to face with Lord Alcorn and thus give the game away. If I remain, I may ruin your reputation."

"I don't think my reputation will be ruined if you remain. You could roll up in your greatcoat on the floor near the fire and get some sleep," she suggested shyly.

"That, my dear girl," he said, touched by her innocence, "is a most generous offer. Much more generous than I deserve. If I were a true degenerate, I would certainly accept it." He smiled down at her with a warmth that stirred her pulse. "You must be closer to the truth of my character than I suspected, because I find that I *can't* accept. I will not premit the innkeeper, the servants, or anyone but Alcorn to question your reputation, as they might do if I were discovered in this room in the morning."

"Then, what—"

His brow furrowed in concentration. After a moment, he strode back to the window, threw open the casement and looked out. "My bedroom is right next door," he said. "If I can climb across on that ledge—"

She came up beside him and looked for herself. "But it's so *narrow!* You can't possibly—"

"Yes, I can. If you give me a supporting hand while I lower myself to the ledge, I'll make it."

Without waiting for a reply, he sat down on the sill and swung his legs over it. With one hand gripping her arm and the other pressing against the wall, he turned his body so that he faced the wall and slid down to the narrow ledge below the window. The ledge, barely as wide as his boot, ran along the entire width of the building. Once his feet touched it, he released his hold on her. "Thank you, my dear, for what you've done for me this night," he said as he began to edge slowly away from her.

"Never mind that," she whispered breathlessly. "Just don't fall."

He was half-way between her window and his. "Damnation," he swore suddenly. "I forgot my hat and cane!"

"Does that matter? I can give them to you in the morning."

"What if someone came into your room before you managed it? What if a housemaid or the innkeeper's wife discovered them? In such a case, this quixotic escape would have been made in vain."

"You do seem to think of all the possibilities," she murmured. "You must have had a great deal of experience in such subterfuge."

He was inching his way back toward her. "A very great deal," he responded crisply. Glancing up at her, he caught the measuring look in her eyes. "Aha. There you are. You see it now, don't you? I'm not so angelic as you thought, am I?"

"Perhaps n-not."

He looked away. "Be a good girl and get my things, will you?"

"You can't possibly hang on while holding something in your hand," she objected.

"Oh, ye of little faith. Just get them, please."

She did as she was bid. With heart beating in fear, she leaned from the window and handed him his hat. He clapped it on his head and resumed his sideward movement. When he'd almost reached his destination, he stretched out his hand toward her. "Now the cane," he instructed.

She held it by its bottom tip and reached out. He grasped the silver head, edged closer to his window and used the tip to pry open the casement above him. It took a great deal of dangerous maneuvering before the window gave way and this caused Ada a great deal of heart-stopping consternation as she watched him teetering on the ledge. When the casement finally budged, he tossed the cane inside. He then removed the hat, sent it following the cane and centered himself below the sill. Grasping the sill with both hands, he was about to heave himself up when he suddenly paused and began inching back in her direction.

"What are you doing?" she gasped. "Are you *mad,* moving back and forth along that . . . that precipice?"

"It's not as dangerous as all that. Even if I fell, the damage would not be great. We're only a story off the ground."

"But why are you doing it? What's wrong now?"

He didn't respond until he was just below her window. "You may have noticed that I haven't asked your name."

"Good God! Is *that* why you came back? To ask my *name?*"

"No, because I could more easily have asked the innkeeper in the morning. But I suddenly wondered if *you* would wonder why I hadn't."

"Why, no," she said in surprise, "I hadn't thought of that at all."

He made a rueful face. "I should have known. Your mind was probably elsewhere. But I think it only right to tell you that I don't intend to ask for your name after all."

"No? Why not?"

"Because if I knew your name, I should find myself tempted to call on you, and I don't think it would be wise to do so."

"Oh?" She was shocked at the sharp pang of disappointment which constricted her chest.

"We shouldn't suit at all, you see. Despite your kind denials, I have too much of the devil in me for such an innocent as you. And I haven't enough patience to deal with..." He hesitated while he tried to search for the right word.

"Bubbleheads?" she ventured bleakly.

"I don't believe you to be a bubblehead."

"Woolgatherers, then."

"Let us say 'dreamers.' Men of my ilk have been known to wreak havoc in the lives of innocent young dreamers, you know. So I think it better that I don't learn your name."

"You must please yourself on that score, sir," she answered quietly. "It would not be proper for me to offer my name to a stranger in any case."

"Then there's nothing left but to exchange goodnights," he said and began to inch back.

Once under his window, he grasped the sill, heaved himself up and threw himself inside, top over tail.

Ada, having seen him safe, was about to withdraw when his head and shoulders reappeared. "Goodnight, ma'am," he whispered. "I will always be grateful to you."

"Goodnight," she replied and withdrew her head. She was struck with a feeling of deep depression that the night's adventure was at an end. *What on earth is the matter with me?* she asked herself, on the verge of tears.

"Ma'am?" His hissing whisper came wafting through the night air into her still-open casement.

She took a deep breath, swallowed the tears that had lumped in her throat and leaned out again. "Yes?"

"You *do* have the most *remarkable* eyes," he said.

Chapter Six

The inn was very quiet when Ada and the still-feverish Selena sat down to breakfast. There was no sign of the gentleman who had visited her room the night before, or of Lord Alcorn either. Ada wondered if either of them were still in the hostelry. It would have brightened her mood considerably to learn that the gentleman whose face had invaded her dreams all night had not yet left, but she was too proud to ask. All through breakfast she looked up at every sound, hoping to see him standing in the doorway. She imagined him smiling at her, saying he'd changed his mind, that he'd learned her name from the inn-keeper and that he hoped she would permit him to escort her to London. "Escort me to London?" she'd ask with a flirtatious laugh. "Whatever for?"

"So that I learn where to come calling, of course," he'd respond.

But the only man who loomed up in the doorway was Hines, who announced that the wheelwright had made the repairs and that the carriage was ready to leave. Ada's dream evaporated in the bustle of departure. Selena, conscious of the hours of delay, hurried her charge into the carriage without giving the girl a moment for a backward look. By the time Ada was settled into her seat in the coach and had caught her breath, the scene of her previous night's adventure was left far behind.

"Oh, Miss Ada," the abigail wailed through the first hour of the ride, "we'll be too late. I know we'll be too late."

"Stop worrying, Selena," Ada ordered at last. "We shall not be late, I promise you."

"'Ow kin ye be sure o' that, Miss Ada? Miss Cornelia may 'ave passed us in the night!"

"I'm certain she did no such thing. You know Miss Cornelia. It will take her a week to pack her clothing."

It was this offhand remark that silenced the abigail. Anyone who was acquainted with Cornelia knew that the girl never traveled anywhere without a mountain of trunks and bandboxes.

Surely she would not have set out from Bishop's Cleve for London without her entire wardrobe, a wardrobe so extensive that it *would* require a week to pack it. Even Ada was soothed by the certainty that Cornelia was still at home, safely readying her clothing.

Selena's cough sounded worse by the time they arrived in London. She fell into a severe paroxism of gasps just as Hines was maneuvering the coach up the curved driveway of the Countess Mullineaux's town house. Ada was so concerned with soothing her stricken abigail that she failed to notice the number of carriages which lined the driveway. But when they drew up before the imposing domicile, Ada couldn't help but take note of the dignity of the building's facade. It was three stories high, its height emphasized by the tall windows which were now all brilliantly lit. Most impressive of all was the stone pediment over the wide double door. It was decorated with sculpted flags and fluting, and at the center it bore a graven coat of arms. While Ada gaped at the edifice through the coach window, the abigail sniffed pathetically into her handkerchief and spoke yearningly of her own bed in her own room in the Surringham house at Bishop's Cleve. Ada, who was convinced she'd never in her life seen a more magnificent mansion, could scarcely believe her ears. "Don't you think you'll be comfortable here in the Countess's staff quarters?" she asked her abigail.

"There ain't no place like 'ome," Selena wheezed, "'specially when yer ailin'."

"Then, Selena, why don't you go home with Hines."

"Go 'ome? T' Bishop's Cleve? Oh, Miss Ada, I *couldn't*, could I? Sir Jarsper wouldn' take it kin'ly if I deserted ye."

"You wouldn't be deserting me, my dear. Even Uncle Jasper wouldn't accuse you of that. You helped get me here safely, after all. Of course, I do believe he wanted you with me to impress the countess, but even if I had *ten* abigails in tow I wouldn't impress the countess." She sighed. "I'm just not impressive. *Cornelia* is the impressive one." In her mind's eye, Ada could imagine how Cornelia would make her arrival. She would have a coachman, an abigail and two liveried footmen. One of the footmen would lower the steps of the carriage while the other knocked at the door. Cornelia would alight with the dignity of a Royal Queen, her abigail fluttering behind her, holding aloft an umbrella to protect her charge from either sun or rain and clutching in her other hand a little case containing

Cornelia's jewelry. The Countess Mullineaux, her butler and all the household staff who would hurry to the door at the sight of Cornelia's retinue would be bound to be impressed.

Selena did not follow all of what her mistress was murmuring, but she was quite used to Ada's way of thinking. The abigail understood that Sir Jasper's primary purpose in sending her on this trip was to make certain that his niece arrived at her destination safely and on time. That she had done. As for the rest, perhaps what the girl said was right—Miss Ada was Miss Ada, and she wasn't likely to stir up much attention whether she had an abigail beside her or not. In that case, why *shouldn't* she go home? She'd be no good to anyone, sick as she was. "Are ye sure, Miss Ada?"

"Sure?"

The abigail frowned in annoyance. Miss Ada was off in the clouds again. "Are ye sure I should go 'ome? Ye'd not mind doin' without me?"

Ada shook herself into the present with an effort. "I shall miss you, of course, Selena. But I'm certain that her ladyship will be able to provide me with an abigail. So, please, go home and get yourself well again."

Hines, having unloaded the portmanteau and the two bandboxes (which held every item of clothing, every pair of shoes, every comb and brush which Ada possessed) and placed them on the doorstep, turned to Ada for further instructions. "Go along, Hines," Ada ordered. "It's time you started for home."

"We'd better wait until ye've gone inside," Hines suggested, looking at the huge oak doors dubiously.

"Why should you wait? Even if her ladyship is not at home, there are surely enough servants on hand to take care of me. Go along now. You must take poor Selena home. She needs to be put to bed as soon as possible."

Ada waved goodbye until the carriage trundled out of the curved driveway and was lost to sight. Then she took a deep breath to build up her courage and knocked at the door.

After a long wait the door was opened by a trim but elderly woman wearing a black bombazine dress with a ring of keys hanging from the belt and a frilled white mobcap. Ada was surprised. This was evidently the housekeeper. Why, she wondered, was the housekeeper answering the door? Where was the butler?

The housekeeper studied her coldly, her eyes sweeping over

Ada's form from her bonnet to her laced half-boots. "What are you doing *here?*" she asked.

The question was so rude and unexpected that Ada was at a loss. "I . . . I'm Ada Sur—"

"I know who you are, girl! You've been expected since noon. But you should have come to the back."

"The b-back?"

"Yes, you fool girl, the *back!* You shouldn't've expected to be admitted here. Especially tonight, when her ladyship's entertainin' forty for dinner. How would you feel if one of the guests, like the Duchess of York herself, should see you comin' in the front door?" She looked round over her shoulder to make sure nobody was about. "Well, you may as well come in, now you're here. You'll have to carry your things yourself; none of the footmen can be spared tonight."

Ada was so startled by this unexpected welcome that she was bereft of speech. She picked up her portmanteau and one of the bandboxes, but she had difficulty getting hold of the second bandbox. The housekeeper watched her for a moment in annoyance, but then she relented and picked it up herself. With a finger pressed cautiously against her lips, she led the way on tiptoe across the polished marble floor of the magnificent entry hall.

Ada, wearily hauling her baggage, could hear the sounds of merriment from somewhere down the hall. She followed the housekeeper to the stairway. She would not have believed that anything could surprise her after the peculiar greeting she'd just received, but when the elderly woman led her not *up* the stairs but right *past* them, she was more surprised than before. Where was this crêature leading her? she wondered. If the idea were not so preposterous, she would have believed she was being taken to the servants' quarters.

The elderly woman led her down a rear hallway to the back of the house. Surely this *was* the servants' quarters! Ada couldn't understand what was happening. If Lady Mullineaux was indeed occupied with a dinner party for forty guests, Ada didn't expect her to leave her guests and greet her with an eager embrace and tears of affection. But she certainly had a right to expect more warmth than *this!*

They came to the back stairs, where the housekeeper put down the bandbox she carried. "I suppose you haven't had supper," she said sourly. "Well, leave your things here and come down to the servants' hall. We can probably find somethin' for you without disturbin' Monsieur Albert and the staff."

"Monsieur Albert?"

"Our cook. But be sure to stay out of everyone's way. When we have a dinner party of *this* size, everyone on the kitchen staff becomes jittery."

"I . . . I'm not very h-hungry," Ada stammered. "I don't wish to be in anyone's way. If you could just show me to my room . . ."

Something in the quiver of Ada's voice caught the housekeeper's notice and softened her irritated spirits. She turned and peered into Ada's face. "Oh, dear," she muttered, suddenly friendly, "I've upset you, haven't I? I'm sorry I was so pettish. I expected you earlier, y'see. I said to Eva—she's her ladyship's dresser, y'know—I said to her when you failed to appear by four, 'She'll come in the midst of the dinner,' I said, and that's just what you did. And you can see that this is the worst possible time to show your face . . ."

"Yes," Ada managed, wondering what sort of household she'd fallen into, "I am sorry . . ."

"But you needn't look as if you'd stabbed your own mother, girl," the housekeeper said, suddenly smiling. "We'll get through the evening right enough." She put out her hand. "I'm Mrs. Mudge. You'll like me better once you get to know me. Come downstairs. We can't let you go to bed hungry, now, can we?"

The stairway led to a pleasant, square room fitted with a huge table surrounded by at least twenty chairs. "Here's where we eat," the housekeeper said. "Sit down, and I'll see what I can find for you."

She went out through a swinging door through which Ada got a glimpse of the kitchen. It was evidently a beehive of activity. Through the door came a flood of sounds—a babble of voices shouting orders both in English and French, the scuffle of feet on a wooden floor, the clatter of dishes and pans. But what interested Ada more were the smells . . . the tantalizing aroma of roasting meats and baking pastries. Ada hadn't realized how very hungry she was.

In a few minutes Mrs. Mudge returned, followed by a young maidservant with a ruddy complexion, swathed in a long apron that almost covered her clothes and a white kerchief that almost covered her hair. The maid carried a tray laden with dishes.

"This is Clara," Mrs. Mudge told Ada. "We've brought you

a bowl of soup, a bit off the end of the roast, a hot muffin, some sprouts and, of course, a pot of tea. Set the tray down here, Clara. Serve the soup, if you please, and pour me a cup of tea. They can spare you in the kitchen for a while, now that the second course's been served."

The housekeeper laid out two table settings and took a seat beside Ada, while the maid Clara set down the tray and ladled out some soup from a tureen into a bowl. She placed the bowl in front of Ada and smiled shyly at her. "It's the same soup they served upstairs," she confided in a friendly way, "so ye're bound t' like it."

"Thank you," Ada said and picked up her spoon.

Clara eyed Ada with interest as she served the tea to the housekeeper. "So yer the one who's come t' assist Mr. Finchley-Jones," she said admiringly. "I wish I had the schoolin' t' do bookwork."

Ada blinked at her. "Assist Mr. Finchley-Jones?"

"Of course," Mrs. Mudge said impatiently. "Didn't the librarian's society tell you his name when they hired you? He's a famous scholar, Mr. Finchley-Jones is. Lord Mullineaux interviewed him hisself before he engaged him."

Ada wondered briefly if she'd been daydreaming and had missed some important part of this conversation. "Lord Mullineaux?" she asked faintly.

"Her ladyship's son. He's very proud of his library, you know, and he wanted it—what did his lordship call it? Catalogued? Yes, catalogued by the best librarian in England. If his lordship engaged Mr. Finchley-Jones, you can be certain he's the best. You're a lucky girl to work for him."

Ada stared at the housekeeper as a sudden insight broke through the clouds in her mind. This entire episode, from the first moment Mrs. Mudge had opened the door, had been a *mistake*. A silly, almost farcical comedy of mistaken identity! The housekeeper had mistaken her for someone else . . . someone who was to assist this Mr. Finchley-Jones. "I think, Mrs. Mudge, that you've mistaken my identity," she began. "I'm not—"

The door to the kitchen swung open at that moment, and another aproned housemaid burst in. "Mrs. Mudge, Mrs. Mudge," she shouted breathlessly, "they're callin' fer you upstairs."

Mrs. Mudge jumped to her feet, her keys jangling. "Upstairs? Whatever for? What's gone wrong?"

"It's that protegee of 'er ladyship's. One of the footmen spilled the poivrade sauce, and a bit of it spotted 'er gown. They say she's raisin' a terrible fuss. 'Er ladyship wants ye t' take the girl upstairs and see if ye can get rid of the stain."

"There, you see?" the housekeeper flung back over her shoulder to Ada as she ran for the stairs. "I told you how it would be. Whenever there's a dinner party for so many, things are bound to be at sixes and sevens!"

Ada gazed after the housekeeper until she disappeared up the stairs. Her head was spinning with a new possibility. Upstairs, at a dinner party for forty, a "protégée" of the Countess Mullineaux was "raisin' a fuss." Could this "protégée" be—?

"Is somethin' wrong wi' the soup?" Clara was asking in friendly concern.

"N-No," Ada muttered. "Nothing."

"Then why ain't ye eatin' it? Ye ain't upset by Mrs. Mudge's scold, are ye? Ye mustn't take no notice of 'er. She's a good sort when you get to know 'er."

Ada nodded and tried to sip some of the soup. "I wonder, Clara . . . is this protégée of her ladyship called Cornelia?"

"Yes, indeed, that's 'er name. But how did ye know?"

Ada stirred her soup. "Er . . . ah . . . Mrs. Mudge must have told me."

She bent over her soup, her mind in a turmoil. It was clear that she'd arrived too late after all. Cornelia was already installed upstairs, having dinner with the Duchess of York and the other thirty-odd guests of the Countess Mullineaux. Cornelia had won again. Ada would have to make her way back to Bishop's Cleve and admit her failure. And Uncle Jasper had said that his wrath would be terrible. *I'll make ye wish ye'd never been born*—wasn't that what he'd threatened? He'd always been a kind, even soft-hearted guardian, but when he'd sent her on this journey he'd sounded angrier than ever before. For the first time in her life she was afraid to face him.

And even if she could work up the courage to face her uncle, how was she to get to Bishop's Cleve? She'd sent her carriage home without a thought for the future. She had no transportation, no pocket money, no resources of any kind. She could, she supposed, make her identity known to Countess Mullineaux and rely on her ladyship to provide the wherewithal for her return, but the prospect of such a solution was appalling. It would be mortifying to have to reveal the truth—that her uncle had forced her to engage in this humiliating race, that she'd floundered on the way, and that she needed assistance to return home. The very *thought* of telling this tale to the worldly countess made Ada feel ill.

But was else was she to do? To return home without letting the countess know of her existence would require some money. Could she possibly sell her belongings to someone in exchange for passage on the stage? But to whom could she go? Where? She was a stranger in London. She didn't even know where the stagecoach terminal was located. If only—

"Miss? *Miss?*" The maid Clara was bending over her, looking at her strangely.

Oh, dash it all, Ada thought in self-reproach, *I've done it again. I've been woolgathering!* She looked up at the maid in embarrassment. "I'm sorry, Clara. Were you asking something of me?"

"I was only askin' what ye meant when ye said a moment ago that there was some mistake concernin' yer identity. Ain't ye the one they've engaged t' assist in the liberry?"

Ada blinked at the maid, her pulse suddenly arrested. *Why not?* she asked herself. Why not stay and assist this Mr. Finchley-Jones? It would be better than admitting the truth to the Countess and being shipped home in disgrace to face Uncle Jasper's wrath. She could remain for a while safely hidden in the library and the servants' quarters, areas of the house where Cornelia was quite unlikely to appear. Why not?

It was a wonderful idea. She could stay right here, unnoticed among the household staff, until she'd saved enough money to return to Bishop's Cleve on her own. And while she stayed hidden, Uncle Jasper would believe that she had done his bidding and was having a grand time in London. He wasn't likely to discover that Cornelia had beaten her in the race, for he had made it clear that he and Lady Dorothea were no longer on speaking terms. Sooner or later, of course, he would discover the truth, but with any luck at all she should be safe for at least a fortnight. In that time she would surely be able to concoct a story to tell her uncle that would ease his wrath and make her return to her old life possible. And meanwhile, it would be very interesting to see if she could manage to live on her own resources and even earn a wage. If the experiment proved successful, she might be able to believe that she was not such a bubblehead after all.

The maid Clara had cocked her head and was frowning down at her. "Miss? Did ye hear me? 'As Mrs. Mudge made some mistake 'ere?"

She looked up at the curious maid and smiled. "No, Clara, there's no mistake. I'm Mr. Finchley-Jones's new assistant."

Chapter Seven

By the time Mrs. Mudge returned to the servants' dining hall, Ada had thought through the problem of taking on a new identity. It was all worked out in her mind. If the real assistant to Mr. Finchley-Jones had been due to arrive at noon, something serious must have prevented her from appearing. It was extremely unlikely that she would make an appearance at this late hour. Chances were good that she would not arrive at all. And since she was obviously unknown to Mrs. Mudge, she was probably unknown to Mr. Finchley-Jones as well. Therefore, Ada convinced herself, it was quite safe to continue to play the role of the librarian's assistant for the time being.

Mrs. Mudge returned to the servants' dining hall in a cheerful mood, having successfully cleaned the stains from the gown of her ladyship's new charge. "It's a most modish gown, I'd say, considerin' it ain't London made," the housekeeper revealed to Clara and Ada confidentially, seating herself beside Ada with a fresh cup of tea. "Saxe blue jaconet with satin panels. I managed to clean it with just a rub of lime soap and a wipe with a damp cloth, so the young lady didn't have to leave the party for more than a few minutes. She was very nice and proper. I don't know why Anna said she'd raised a fuss. Miss Haydon—that's her name, Miss Cornelia Haydon—was most pleasant to me . . . even offered me a vail, which of course I told her that as I am the housekeeper and not a common housemaid, I do not deign to accept."

"They should've sent fer me," muttered Clara under her breath. "I'd've taken it right enough."

"Now that's enough of that sort of talk," Mrs. Mudge admonished sharply. "You don't want to set a poor example for Miss—" She looked at Ada with a sudden blink. "What's your name, girl? I've forgotten—"

Ada had told herself she'd thought of everything, but here in the first moments of her deception she was already stumped. "My n-name?"

55

"I know I should remember. Mr. Finchley-Jones showed me the letter the society sent about you . . ."

"It's Ada. Ada S-S-Surrey."

"Surrey? That's strange." The housekeeper stared at her with knit brows. "I would swear the letter said somethin' like Latcham . . . or Letcham . . ."

"Good gracious, Mrs. Mudge," Clara interjected, "the girl knows 'er own name, don't she?"

Mrs. Mudge shrugged. "I'm gettin' old, I suppose. Don't remember things as I used to. Well, Ada, I suppose you'll be wishin' to see your room and take to your bed. Follow me. I'll show you where you'll be stayin'."

Mrs. Mudge maintained a lively monologue as she led Ada up the stairs to her room, enlarging on her impressions of Miss Haydon, her ladyship's new house guest. "A bit spoilt, I think one might say, and too mindful of her clothes and her looks, but she's a real beauty. I can see that her ladyship's pleased with the girl. This Cornelia Haydon'll suit her ladyship's purposes very well."

"Her ladyship's purposes?"

The housekeeper nodded conspiratorially. "It wouldn't do for you to bibble-babble this about, Ada, but her ladyship'd like nothin' better than to see this girl catch her son's interest. Her son is Lord Mullineaux that I've told you of. He's slipped out of more marriage traps than an eel out of nets. Never knew a gentleman so wary of gettin' hisself leg-shackled." She'd been walking ahead of Ada on the stairs, but at this point she waited for Ada to come up beside her and whispered the rest of her tale into her ear. "It's said he only interests hisself in ladies that are already wed, so that he'll be perfectly safe from matrimony. Got hisself into any number of scrapes because of his habits, I can tell you. Not that I wish you to think ill of him. Lord Mullineaux is as fine a gentleman as ever walked. Kind and generous and as devoted to his mother as anyone would wish. Once he settles down, he'll be a most ideal gentleman. It's better for a man to sow his wild oats before he's wed than after. No man makes a better husband than a reformed rake, as I've heard her ladyship say on more than one occasion. I ain't inclined to disagree with her, are you?"

"I don't know much about rakes, I'm afraid," Ada answered. But as she settled herself into the little room to which the housekeeper had brought her, she couldn't help wishing that she'd been given the opportunity to try to reform a certain rake of her own acquaintance.

It was a wish that permeated her dreams all night. In one dream she was standing at an altar in a dimly lit church beside the gentleman of the inn. It was obviously a wedding ceremony in which she was the bride, but while the groom held fast to her hand, his attention was fixed on a lady standing at his other side. "Do you know," he said to the other lady, "you have the most remarkable eyes?"

In another dream, she found herself on a strange country road. Near by, a farmer was walking down a furrow which had been newly turned. "What are you doing?" she called to him from the roadway.

"Can't you see? I'm sowing seeds."

She was startled at the familiar sound of his voice, for she was sure she'd never been in this neighborhood before and could never have seen this man. "What sort of seeds?" she asked.

"Oats," the farmer answered. "Wild oats."

"What good are wild oats?" she persisted.

"Don't you know anything, girl?" the man scoffed, crossing the field in long strides, coming up to her and cupping her chin in his hand. "If a man sows wild oats early, he's all the better for it later."

But when she looked into his strangely familiar eyes, she saw reflected in them a laughing devil, and she woke up trembling.

She resolved, as she dressed herself at daybreak for her forthcoming meeting with the awesome Mr. Finchley-Jones, that she would make every effort to put the memory of the gentleman-of-the-inn out of her mind. Thinking of him would be to no purpose, for neither of them knew the other's name and were thus unlikely ever to meet again. Remembering him in daydreams or night dreams would only distract her and make her all the more bubbleheaded. If she was to succeed in her new life with her new identity, she would need all her wits about her.

Mr. Finchley-Jones was not present in the servants' dining hall for breakfast. Clara explained to Ada that the librarian did not reside in the household but came only for the day. Mr. Finchley-Jones held a special status in the Mullineaux household. Since he was a scholar, he was considered above the servants and did not take meals with them. But he was not socially equal to her ladyship or Lord Mullineaux (though Clara revealed that his lordship had once actually sat down to lunch with his librarian while they discussed the plans for the library) and was therefore served his luncheon on a tray in the library. *Poor Mr. Finchley-Jones,* Ada thought. *Neither fish nor fowl.*

Before Mrs. Mudge bustled off to supervise the reordering of the household after the festivities of the night before, she informed Ada that the librarian always appeared in the library on the stroke of seven. "You may as well wait for him there. Since it ain't yet time, you'll have a few minutes to look round."

The library was located in a huge, high-ceilinged corner room at the back of the house. It had evidently been in disuse for some time. The windows were grimy with dust, allowing only a pale gleam of sunlight to filter through. Several beautiful leather chairs had been pushed out of the way into a corner, and a sofa against the wall had been shrouded in a Holland dustcover. That left only one piece of furniture—a long library table—in the center of the room. It was completely covered with piles of books of assorted sizes, with additional piles surrounding it on the floor. Ada had never seen so many books in her life.

Even though the atmosphere was one of disarray, one couldn't help admiring the magnificent carved oak bookshelves. They climbed up three of the walls from floor to ceiling, even over the doors and windows. Only the area over the fireplace had been kept free of shelves, probably to provide space for the huge painting which had been hung there. The painting, completely encased in a Holland cover, hovered over the room like an angular, misshapen ghost. Ada made a mental note to peep under the sheet after she'd finished her examination of the room.

The bookshelves themselves had been partially denuded of books. Those that had been removed were lying in uneven piles on the floor along the walls, while those volumes that still remained on the shelves lay this way and that in the dust, adding to the room's dismaying air of disorder and desolation. Only one place in the room stood out in unexpected, pristine neatness—a large-topped desk with a chair behind it, placed between two of the windows opposite the entrance door. Completely free of dust or chaos, the desk was as discordantly out of place as an alabaster chess piece might be if it were found in a mud puddle. The desk's wood shone, its brass fittings glowed, the leather insert on its top gleamed with polish. A serviceable but remarkably clean inkstand had been placed precisely at the center point of the rear surface, with a pen tray in front of it. Three thick notebooks lay at the exact center of the leather insert, and at their right and left were two identically high piles of notes, each one held in place by a brass paperweight in the shape of a globe.

The symmetry of the placement of the items on the desk fascinated Ada. What sort of man, she wondered, would take the time to divide his papers into two such precisely even piles? And weight them down with matching globes? But on closer examination, she was amused to discover that although both globes were indeed alike in having been engraved with maps, the map on the right-hand globe was celestial while the one on the left was terrestrial.

She was still holding the celestial globe in her hand when she heard the door open. "Don't ever," came a shrill outcry from the doorway, "*ever* touch anything on my desk!"

"Oh!" she gasped, dropping the brass ball in alarm, "I . . . I beg your pardon."

A tall, thin figure in a black coat bounded across the room and snatched up the paperweight from the floor. The man (for despite the frightened beating of her heart, Ada could now see that the black-clad apparition was indeed a man) lifted to his nose a lorgnette which hung from a black cord about his neck, clipped the nosepiece to the bridge of his nose and peered through the glasses at the little globe. Now that the first shock of his arrival had worn off, Ada saw that he looked less tall and much less ferocious than her first glimpse of him and his first shriek had led her to believe. He was a man not much above average height, but his long, thin legs and arms made him seem taller. Everything about him was thin and bony. The skin on his face stretched over high, sharp cheekbones and a sharp nose. Even his hair was thin and long, and he'd combed it to the side from a parting on the right side of his head to cover a place on his pate where he'd gone bald. He appeared to be a man in his middle years, but the intensity of his scholarly grey eyes made her realize that he was younger than he first seemed.

After examining all of the globe's surface, Mr. Finchley-

Jones breathed a sigh of relief and replaced it carefully on the desk. "There," he said more calmly, "that's better. No harm done. Although I must say, Madam, it's no thanks to you." He stared at her through the glasses. "Who are you? You can't be Miss Latcham."

"N-No, I'm . . . I'm not Miss Latcham."

"That's what I *said*. I dislike useless repetition. You didn't need to offer me such obvious information. I deduced it for myself at once."

"D-Deduced it?"

"I was given to understand that Miss Latcham had been employed by Lord Lesterbrook's librarian for twenty years. You can not have been employed by *anyone* for twenty years. I would venture to guess . . ." He pointed at her with a long, bony finger as if making an accusation. ". . . that you have not been *alive* for twenty years!"

"I am . . . p-past twenty-two."

"Then I am in the wrong, but not by much. However, since you are twenty-two and not forty-two, I am *not* in the wrong in my deduction that you are not Miss Latcham. Where, may I ask, is she?"

Ada, having decided that Mr. Finchley-Jones's bluster was not any more threatening than her uncle's, recovered her composure during this exchange and made up her mind to continue with her pretended identity to the end. "I . . . we . . . don't know where Miss Latcham has disappeared. The . . . er . . . the society sent me in her place."

"Did they indeed? And who are *you* to take her place? A little slip of a girl like you. What do you know of bibliography? I'd warrant you've never been inside a library in the entire twenty-two years of your existence."

"Then, sir, you'd be in the wrong again," Ada said bravely, putting up her chin. "I was told, Mr. Finchley-Jones, that you have an excellent reputation in scholarly circles. But jumping to conclusions seems to me not at all the mark of a scholar. One would think that a man with a scholarly mind would seek adequate information before making judgments."

"Hmmmph." Mr. Finchley-Jones peered at her through the lorgnette for a moment or two longer. Then he removed the spectacles from his nose and turned away from her. He crossed the room to a small door in the corner behind the leather chairs and disappeared inside what appeared to be a closet or retiring room. When he emerged a moment later, he was in his shirt-sleeves and waistcoat and was pulling on the second of a pair of black sleeve protectors. "You are familiar with libraries, you say?" he asked, seating himself at his desk.

"Oh, yes. We have a reasonably good one in my uncle's..." She caught herself up short. "I mean, before I was...er...orphaned..." Her voice trailed off helplessly.

"Ah, I see. It is as I suspected. You are well-born but impoverished, is that not the case?"

"Well, I..."

"So you are forced to find some way to support yourself. You must not believe that I am unsympathetic to your plight, madam, but I should have thought you more suited to a post as a governess. The art of bibliography cannot be practiced by the untrained. I warned the society of that. I had hoped to find a young scholar...a man...but Miss Latcham's experience was admirably extensive. I am sorry. You won't do. You should go to one of those agencies that find governesses for good families and ask them to find you a post as a governess."

"But I...I don't wish—"

"One shouldn't expect to be granted all one's wishes, child. If you are not suited to this work, there is nothing to be done."

"But...how do you know so quickly that I'm not suited—?"

He stopped her with a glare. "I think I have enough information to make a judgment. There was a library in your ancestral home, yes, but you are not, I hope, going to claim to have done extensive *reading*, are you? I would venture to guess that you've never *heard* of, say, Erasmus."

"I am sorry to say that you're in the wrong a third time," Ada responded, stung. She had taken on a new identity and was beginning to live the part. Poor, without resources and having nowhere to turn, the newly created Ada Surrey had to fight for her existence. "I am reasonably well-read, I think," she told him proudly. "I've read the classics, though not in Greek, a good deal of history and a bit of philosophy. I admit, however, that I am more partial to poetry and the works of Shakespeare than I am to Erasmus or Aquinas or Hume."

"Hmm." Mr. Finchley-Jones raised his eyebrows in surprise. He put on his spectacles and stared at her again. Then he shook his head in disbelief. "I must say, you don't *appear* to be the sort who reads. You seem to me to be the sort who writes romantic verses and capitalizes every noun in them. Who loves to put curlicues on her *T*'s and *Y*'s and little circles instead of dots on her *i*'s. I despise females who put circles on their *i*'s."

"I am guilty of having written romantic verse from time to time," Ada said, suppressing an urge to smile. "But I write a very neat hand. Would you like me to demonstrate?"

"Naturally I shall wish to examine your writing. It is the most important function you will be performing . . . *if* I should decide that you are suited to this post. However, we are still a long way from making such a decision, Miss . . . Miss . . ."

"Surrey. Ada Surrey."

"I admit, Miss Surrey, you seem to have more qualifications than I at first credited, but a bibliographer's assistant needs more than a good general education and a fine hand. To build a fine library, one is required to have a depth of knowledge in a wide variety of academic disciplines, a mind capable of classifying that knowledge, a sense of organization—"

"I should be surprised if you found *anyone* to fill all those requirements," Ada murmured dryly under her breath.

"I do not mean to imply that a mere assistant needs the qualifications of a fully trained bibliographer," the librarian pointed out coldly. "After all, the assistant can rely on the guidance of her employer—"

"Yes, that is what I meant," Ada assured him.

Mr. Finchley-Jones rose from his chair and came around the desk toward her. Taking off his lorgnette and using it to gesture, he proceeded to lecture the girl on the subject closest to his heart, the importance of a well-catalogued library. "It is necessary for you to understand, young woman, that there is more to setting up a fine library than listing and shelving the books. Books contain knowledge, but the knowledge in them is useless unless it can be *found*. A library has value for its books alone, but if those books are well indexed, the library becomes even more valuable. The more complete the index, the more valuable the books and the more efficiently the reader can retrieve the knowledge within them. I regret to have to admit that many collectors with whom I've come into contact still believe that a list of authors, inscribed alphabetically in a notebook, is enough of a catalogue for a private library. Why, I have even come upon some who believed that a mere *accession* list is enough! But fortunately Lord Mullineaux is not of that ilk. He has the true bibliophile's perspicacity to understand that books should be catalogued in many ways: according to subject, author, publication date, acquisition date . . ."

Ada had been nodding her agreement throughout most of this monologue, but as the bibliographer began to expound on the methods of cataloguing that he intended to pursue, she found her mind wandering. She wondered what sort of man this Lord Mullineaux was. She had not heard of many noblemen who took such interest in their books. This household into which fate had brought her was certainly a strange one.

As Mr. Finchley-Jones prosed on about the complications of bibliographical notation in a private collection, Ada's eyes wandered about the room. She began to realize that there was some sort of order in the piles of books on the floor; some of the piles had slips of paper of varying colors sticking out of them, some seemed to be grouped by similarity of size, and those on the table were distinguished by the elegance of their bindings. The librarian had evidently done a great deal of work already. She looked carefully around the room, trying to ascertain how many volumes the library contained.

Her eyes, rising from the contemplation of the piles of books on the floor to those on the shelves, fell upon the painting hanging over the fireplace. The Holland cover had slipped since she'd first looked at it, and the painting was now partially revealed. It was a portrait of a seated woman, with a gentleman standing behind her, his hand on her shoulder. There was something about the man's face that made her chest constrict.

". . . which is no small task in a library of this size," Mr. Finchley-Jones was saying. "I don't suppose you could even *guess* its size, could you, Miss Surrey?"

"Good God!" Ada murmured, her eyes fixed on the portrait.

"You find it an overwhelming question, do you?" the librarian said with a superior smile. "With the room in this condition I don't blame you. But why don't you hazard a guess?"

But the girl remained staring at the portrait with such concentration that she didn't even hear the question.

"Miss Surrey?" Mr. Finchley-Jones took a step toward her. "Miss Surrey! Haven't you been attending?"

His sharpness of tone caught her ear but could not deflect her mind. "Good God," she repeated, "who *is* that?"

Mr. Finchley-Jones frowned at her. "Who is who?"

"The man in the portrait."

"The late Lord Mullineaux, of course. With the Countess. But what has that to do with the subject of our—"

"The Countess? The *present* Countess?"

"Yes. That is she. Although I must say, Miss Surrey, I would have expected that a young woman in search of a position of employment would try to keep her mind on the subject at hand—"

"Then are you saying that the man in the portrait is the father of this Lord Mullineaux of whom you've been speaking?" Ada persisted.

"I was certainly *not* saying it, although it is quite true that you are looking at a portrait of Lord Mullineaux's parents. What I *was* saying was on the subject of the size of the library!"

Ada had torn her eyes from the portrait and turned for a moment to Mr. Finchley-Jones, but she didn't really see him. Instead, she was seeing the face of the gentleman from the inn, a face almost exactly like the one in the portrait. "Do you think, Mr. Finchley-Jones, that your Lord Mullineaux resembles this portrait of his father?" she asked, her heart pounding.

"I think, Miss Surrey, that it is none of your business. What *is* your business is to convince me that you would make a suitable assistant. I will tell you frankly that, with this tendency of yours to easy distraction, you are not succeeding in impressing me."

If she heard his reproof, she gave no sign. She was again staring fixedly at the painting. "He *does* resemble his father, doesn't he?"

"Very closely, if I'm any judge," the librarian said grudgingly. "Now may we return to the subject at hand?"

She was remembering the moment when the man with the face like the one in the portrait pounded on her bedroom door at the inn. He'd spoken a name, but she couldn't recall it. Not that it mattered. She didn't need to match the name. The man who'd kissed her at the inn was the same man who owned this library, who was the son of the Countess (her mother's best friend and her own godmother), and whom Cornelia (now lying abed upstairs in a luxurious guest bedroom) was here to snare. There wasn't any point even to *dream* of him any more. "What is his given name?" she asked anyway, unable to tear her eyes from the painting.

The librarian was glowering at her. "You are a most addlepated female. I don't see how you can pretend to believe that such conduct is suitable for a bibliographer's assistant. His lordship's given name is, I believe, Ivor."

"No," Ada murmured, shaking her head. "That wasn't it."

"Well, I *have* heard the Countess call him—"

"Don't tell me," Ada said, the sound of his lordship's voice ringing so clearly in her ears that it was more reality than memory. She turned away from the portrait with a sigh. *"Griff.* The Countess calls him Griff."

Chapter Eight

Despite his description of Ada as an addlepated female, Mr. Finchley-Jones agreed to employ her. The reasons he gave her for his decision were quite logical: first, he said, her handwriting proved to be neat and free from the feminine flourishes he so despised; second, she was indeed well-read, especially for a female of her years; and third, she seemed genuinely interested in bibliography and very willing to learn.

Deep in his heart he knew that the logical reasons he'd given the girl had nothing to do with his decision. He'd intended from the first to employ her. He'd intended to hire her even if she'd never heard of Erasmus. Or even if she always put circles on her *i*'s. She was young and very pretty, and she brought a radiance into the dingy room that had never been there before. His life's work was important to him, and his bibliographical pursuits were, he was convinced, making a real contribution to society, but he couldn't deny that his days had always been drab. Why shouldn't he permit a little brightness to enter into his life?

His outward attitude, however, showed nothing of this. He remained cold, critical and forbidding. He put her to work at once copying the publishing information from the title pages of a pile of scientific books into one of his pristine notebooks. But he helped clear a portion of the library table for her to work on and dusted off one of the leather chairs for her. And during the morning he couldn't keep himself from looking up frequently from his work and letting his eyes feast on her bent head. It was the most pleasant workday morning he'd ever spent.

When Clara brought his lunch on a tray, he excused his new assistant (so that she could take her luncheon downstairs) most reluctantly. He would have liked her to join him for luncheon, but it was not appropriate for a lowly female copyist to take her meals with a scholar-bibliographer of his importance. Clara's shrewd eyes did not miss the look on his face as he watched his assistant leave the room. "He likes ye, Ada," she giggled as the two made their way down the back stairs. "I think y' made yerself a conquest."

Ada grinned back. "Don't be silly. He thinks I'm an addlepate."

"That may be," the maid laughed, "but that never stopped a man from admirin' the addlepate's pretty mouth or tiny waist."

Ada didn't debate the point. She liked Clara and enjoyed the girl's teasing. Clara had paid her a visit in her bedroom the night before, just to get acquainted and make her feel welcome. None of the other maids had done so. It had been fun sitting on the edge of the bed with Clara, listening to the maid's description of the downstairs life, of the quirks of the various members of the staff, of the view of their employers that the servants held. Clara was a cheerful, honest, shrewd young woman who viewed her world with a lusty optimism. Ada felt that, in this life of deception she'd embarked upon, she would need a friend like Clara. The outspoken, straightforward maid would not only be a good companion but a good advisor.

The budding friendship between Ada and the housemaid turned out to be more beneficial than Ada dreamed. One night, two days after her arrival, when all the staff had retired for the night, Clara tapped at the door of Ada's tiny bedroom. When Ada opened the door, Clara refused to come in. She stood glowering in the doorway in her nightdress and worn swansdown robe. Ada could see her pursed mouth in the light of the candle the girl carried. "Clara?" she asked. "Is something amiss?"

"Sssh," Clara whispered, "someone'll 'ear." She raised the candle so that she could see Ada's face more clearly. "Who are ye, Ada?"

"What? I don't think I understand what—"

"I asked who are ye? I mean, *really*."

Ada felt her heart sinking. The past two days had been so pleasant and uneventful that she'd begun to feel safe. "Wh-Who *am* I?" she echoed, trying to hide her alarm.

Clara looked nervously up and down the narrow corridor to make certain no one else was about. "I know ye ain't Mr. Finchley-Jones's real assistant," she hissed, "so don't playact wi' me."

"What makes you say that?"

"The real one came t' the back door this noon. Miss Latcham." With another quick glance down the hall, she stepped over the threshold and closed the door quietly. "Lucky there was no one about t' answer the door but me."

"Oh, dear!" Ada dropped her eyes from her friend's face. "What did you say to her, Clara?"

"Ye don't need t' worry. I didn't give ye away. I told 'er that 'is lordship changed 'is mind about organizin' the liberry. I said that Mr. Finchley-Jones ain't no longer employed 'ere."

Ada bit her nether lip guiltily. "She . . . she must have been very upset."

"No, she wasn't. She said she'd only come t' explain t' Mr. Finchley-Jones why she 'adn't kept 'er appointment. Seems 'er sister's took ill, and she 'as to go t' Manchester t' care fer 'er, so she couldn't take the post."

"Well, that's a relief," Ada sighed. "I wouldn't have wished to deprive a worthy woman of her employment."

Clara frowned at her suspiciously. "That's very well an' good, Ada, but it don't explain 'ow you come t' be in Miss Latcham's place."

Ada shook her head unhappily and sank down upon her bed. "I can't explain it to you right now, Clara. All I can say is that I'm very grateful to you for helping me . . . and for keeping my secret."

"Ye kin *keep* yer gratitude!" Clara declared in her forthright way. "I ain't goin' t' keep yer secret unless I'm sure y' ain't up to somethin' havey-cavey. Y' ain't plannin' on robbin' 'er ladyship, are ye? Or doin' somethin' t' hurt the family?"

"No, of course not. You can't really believe that."

"I don't know what t' believe."

"Just believe that a mistake was made and I . . . I took advantage of it, that's all."

"A mistake? Ah, yes, I remember somethin' about a mistake when ye first came 'ere. You said somethin' to Mrs. Mudge about mistaken identity." She set her candle on the nighttable, sat down beside Ada and peered at her closely. "Ye never came 'ere to work in the liberry at all, did ye? Ye didn't even know anythin' about it."

Ada lowered her head. "That's right. I didn't."

"Then why *did* ye come, Ada? I suspicioned from the first y' ain't the sort fer domestic service. If ye came t' the wrong door, why didn't ye say so and leave?"

"It wasn't the wrong door."

"It wasn't?" The housemaid shook her head in confusion. "Then ye must've come t' see 'er ladyship. Well, why didn't ye do it?"

"I discovered that I was too late."

"Too late to see her ladyship? Because of the dinner party, you mean?"

"Too late to see her at all. Please don't ask me anything more, Clara. I can only tell you that my coming here was a mistake, but I didn't realize it until too late. I had neither the money nor the means to go back home, so when I realized I could find employment here, I took the chance. Some day I promise to tell you all. But meanwhile, if I swear that I mean no harm to anyone, will you remain my friend?"

"There was never no question that I'd stay yer friend," Clara said, letting go of her suspicions and permitting herself to smile. "I just wanted to know that bein' yer friend wouldn't bring me t' the gibbet." She picked up the candle and went to the door. "If we *do* end up on the gibbet, Ada," she whispered as she let herself out, "I 'ope ye'll tell me *then* what it was all about. Goodnight, m'dear."

Mr. Finchley-Jones was not entirely happy with his new assistant. She was certainly delightful to look upon and intelligent enough when she attended to his instructions. But she had an infuriating way of taking mental absences at unexpected moments. He would look up from his work and see her staring out ahead of her, her pen poised in her hand unmoving. Sometimes a simple clearing of his throat would rouse her, and she would immediately resume work, but at other times he might cough like a consumptive for five minutes without shaking her from her reverie.

Another case in point was the girl's dismaying habit of staring at the portrait. He'd made no objection to her removing the dust cover from the painting, but sometimes, when he caught her staring at it, he wished he'd not given his permission for the cover to be removed. It was done now, and he was not the sort to go back on his word—he disliked to appear indecisive—but if he'd known that she would spend long moments gazing at it, he would have ordered that the cover be kept in place. One time he'd even asked her what she found so fascinating about it. "Everything," she'd murmured. "The late Lord Mullineaux looks so assured . . . as if he understood completely what sort of man he'd made of himself and was satisfied with the result."

"Ha!" he'd responded gruffly. "That's a very fanciful interpretation. I'm told the fellow was a gambler and a notorious rake."

But Ada didn't even seem to hear him. "And her ladyship is fascinating as well. She was beautiful, wasn't she?"

"She is still beautiful. You will see that for yourself one day, for she sometimes comes to visit here to see how the work is progressing."

Ada still seemed not to hear. "But there is something about her... a self-consciousness, I think... as if she always feels the world's eyes on her. An *awareness* of her beauty that weakens her character."

"You can see all that in the painting?" he'd asked, being himself drawn into a fascinated contemplation of the portrait. But at that point she'd become aware of his presence and blushingly returned to her work.

Another problem—and this was the most serious source of his discomfiture concerning her—was her inability to keep track of the papers, lists and notes that passed through her hands. It wasn't that she lacked neatness or the ability to grasp the intricacies of the cataloguing system. No, the problem was her forgetfulness. She simply could not keep track of papers. Slips of notepaper, information cards, sheets of records somehow managed to hide themselves away from her. Long hours would then have to be spent tracking them down. One accession slip was found in a copy of *The Shepheardes Calender* (which she'd begun to read in fascination until his cough roused her) where she'd evidently placed it to use as a bookmark. An important acquisition list was found (after three hours of desperate searching) folded into a wad and wedged under the leg of her chair. "The chair was a bit wobbly," she explained sheepishly when he finally discovered it and waved it angrily under her nose.

It was when Ada was engaged in one of these humiliating searches that her ladyship, the Countess Mullineaux herself, paid her first visit to the library. In fact, Ada was on her knees at the time, searching for the second volume of a three-volume set of Grotius' *Rights of War and Peace* among the piles of books on the floor. It was Mr. Finchley-Jones, of course, who'd discovered that the volume was missing. He'd made a great outcry about it, pointing out in a tone of pained impatience that the set was very valuable and that the loss of one volume would make the other two worthless. Ada assured him that she would find it. She remembered quite clearly that she'd had it in her hand the day before when she was doing her assigned task of listing all the works in the collection on the history of jurisprudence. "I'm certain," she explained to her apoplectic employer, "that it is only temporarily mislaid." What she failed to explain was that she'd mislaid the volume when she'd come upon an ancient and very shabby book called *The Songes and Sonnettes*, poetry of Wyatt, Surrey and others, collected by a printer called Tottel. It contained so many wonderful lyric poems (many of which she'd never seen before) that she'd carried it with her to read over luncheon and then up to her bedroom to read by candlelight before retiring. Somehow, while she'd been distracted by *The Songes and Sonnettes*, the Grotius volume had disappeared.

The Countess didn't even notice the young woman kneeling on the floor in the corner. "Mr. Finchley-Jones," she clarioned from the doorway, "I have news for you from my son." She sailed into the room in a flurry of gauze ruffles (trimming a green silk morning robe that looked shockingly out of place in this room of dusty books), an open letter in her hand. "He writes from Wales that he's crated and sent you no fewer than three thousand volumes from his grandfather's collection, in addition to some interesting manuscripts and plates."

"Three thousand!" the librarian exclaimed, overwhelmed. He jumped to his feet. "Your ladyship! That is most exciting news. I had no *idea* he would be able to accomplish so much so soon."

"My son is indefatigable when he's embarked on a project that interests him. He asks me to tell you that he himself is on his way home and will give you the details of his selections in person. I think we may expect him home by tomorrow evening at the—Good God! Who is *that?*"

Ada scrambled to her feet, her heart thudding in her chest. Here was the Countess Mullineaux herself—her deceased mother's best friend, her own godmother, the mother of the gentleman she could not erase from her mind—and Ada had been discovered on her hands and knees in the dust! She brushed nervously at her skirt with one hand and pushed back her hair from her forehead with the other (leaving a wide streak of dirt across her forehead as she did so) and dropped an awkward curtsey. "Your l-ladyship," she stammered.

The Countess gaped at her. "You can't be Mr. Finchley-Jones's assistant, can you? I was under the impression she was a woman well into middle age."

"That was Miss Latcham," Mr. Finchley-Jones explained hastily. "Miss Latcham seems mysteriously to have vanished. This is Miss Ada Surrey who was sent in her place."

"Oh, I see." The Countess graciously held out her hand. "How do you do, Miss Surrey? I must say that your employer seems to be misusing you."

"But... you don't look *at all* the same," Ada murmured, staring at the Countess with a sudden, intense concentration.

"I beg your pardon?" the Countess asked, nonplussed.

"I don't think the artist's view of you was sound. You are much more lovely than—"

Her ladyship turned to the librarian in surprise. "What is this young woman babbling about, Mr. Finchley-Jones?"

"Miss Surrey, *please!*" the librarian hissed. "Forgive her, your ladyship. It's your portrait. She is quite fascinated with it."

"Oh, I *see*." She turned to Ada with a smile. "Are you saying, Miss Surrey, that the artist didn't do me justice? That is a very kind of you, considering that he painted it twenty-five years ago. Good God! A quarter of a century! I hadn't realized..." She turned to study the painting herself. "Heavens, was I ever that young? What is it you see, young woman, that you think the artist missed?"

Ada, waking up to the fact that she'd permitted herself to be distracted from reality by her first glimpse of the Countess's face, reddened in embarrassment. "The eyes, I... I think. He missed the... the sweetness in them."

Lady Mullineaux studied the young woman with interest. "I must say, Mr. Finchley-Jones, you've found yourself a most unusual assistant."

"Yes, so it seems," Mr. Finchley-Jones agreed ruefully.

"But as I was saying before we were diverted into contemplating my portrait, you seem to be using the girl ill. Do you always require that your assistants crawl about in the dirt as Miss Surrey was doing when I came in?"

The librarian winced in chagrin. "I don't ... that is, it isn't a requirement, exactly..."

"It's my fault entirely," Ada put in quickly. "I mislaid a book, and I've been searching—"

"But, my dear child, that is no excuse for him to expect you to crawl about like that. Surely, Mr. Finchley-Jones, you could have done the searching *for* her."

"Yes, but I . . . I . . ."

"What he means, my lady," Ada explained, "is that he cannot *always* be crawling about for me."

"Always?" Her ladyship's eyebrows rose curiously.

Ada twisted her fingers together behind her back and lowered her head miserably. "I'm always misplacing things, you see."

"Really?" The countess looked from the librarian to the girl and back again, her lips twitching in amusement. "That seems an odd quality for a bibliographer's assistant."

"It is an unfortunate trait, to be sure, your ladyship," Mr. Finchley-Jones said in hasty defense, "but I assure you that in every other way Miss Surrey is quite admirable. She is remarkably well-read for someone of her years, she has an excellent understanding of my goals for cataloguing Lord Mullineaux's collection, and she is a superior scribe."

The countess held up her hands. "You don't have to defend her to me, Mr. Finchley-Jones," she said, casting Ada a warm smile, "especially after she has been kind enough to describe me as having sweetness about the eyes. I certainly did not mean to imply that there was any question in my mind about the suitability of this young lady for the post. Even if there were such a question in my mind, my son would surely object to my interfering in your selection of an assistant. So, please, my dear girl . . ." She crossed the room and took Ada's hand. "What did you say your given name was?"

"Ada, your l-ladyship."

"Ada. It is a lovely name, I have a goddaughter by that name, you know. Please, Ada, you needn't look so frightened. I have no intention of sacking you, even if you *do* have a tendency to mislay things."

With that, the Countess waved her letter in a farewell gesture to Mr. Finchley-Jones and wafted to the door. "But in future, if there is any crawling about on the floor to be done, call one of the footmen to do it. Good day to you both."

Chapter Nine

The news of Lord Mullineaux's imminent return spread with amazing speed through the household, causing waves of excited activity below stairs. This unusual stir surprised Ada greatly. Since the house was already very efficiently run, she didn't know why his lordship's arrival should cause such a flurry. Clara explained that Lord Mullineaux was so popular with the household staff that they went to great lengths to welcome him on his return from a journey. Everyone from Mrs. Mudge (who saw to it that there were fresh flowers in his bedroom no matter what the season) to the cook (who prepared all his favorite delicacies for his homecoming dinner) made special efforts to please him.

Ada could only gape in wonder at the stir. Everyone seemed to know that Lord Mullineaux was a rake, yet this fact seemed not to affect the feelings of the members of the household in the least. Everyone, from the Countess to the youngest of the scullery maids, spoke of him with respect and affection. All of them were quite willing to excuse his excesses, as she had done that night at the inn.

Ada *herself* anticipated his lordship's arrival with severe inner quaking. Uppermost in her mind was the fear that he would come into the library and recognize her. What a humiliating moment that would be! It would be horrible for them both, *she* because she would have to lie about her identity and maintain her pretense of being a lowly servant in his household, and *he* because he would find someone in his own employ who knew firsthand about his rakish tendencies. It was all well and good for his lordship to accept being surrounded by a staff who knew all his secrets (and who were so devoted to him that they forgave him his trespasses), but to harbor in his own household someone who *had actually been involved with him in one of his exploits* might be beyond what one could expect of him.

And there was something else that caused Ada to quake at the prospect of Lord Mullineaux's arrival. It was the problem of Cornelia. What if Cornelia should discover her presence in the house? Ada had been dreading that possibility since her arrival, but that it might happen in front of Lord Mullineaux was an unbearable prospect. She seriously considered running away before his lordship set foot on the premises, but she was in no better position *now* to make her way back to Gloucester than she'd been on her arrival. Wages, she'd learned from Clara, were dispensed monthly. She had occupied her post for less than a fortnight. (She had never asked Mr. Finchley-Jones what her wages would be, but she'd convinced herself that the money would be sufficient for passage on the stage to Gloucester.) She had yet another fortnight to wait for her pay, and that meant that immediate flight would not be possible.

Her only consolation was the fact that she'd been able to avoid being discovered by Cornelia thus far. With any luck, she should be able to avoid a confrontation for a while longer. All she could do was hope that she could stay out of Cornelia's way for the short time that still remained.

But Cornelia's presence in the house presented still another problem for Ada. If the Countess truly intended to throw Cornelia at her son, Ada didn't wish to be a witness to the affair. It was painful enough to know that her dreams of attaching the appealing "Griff" Mullineaux to herself were quite hopeless; she certainly didn't wish to exacerbate that pain by watching Cornelia attach him. Ada had, over the years, become quite accustomed to Cornelia's taking precedence over her in all sorts of competitions both major and minor, and she'd believed that she'd trained herself to rise above petty jealousy at Cornelia's successes. But her character was not strong enough to rise above jealousy in *this* particular case. Ada had to admit to herself that she hoped with all her heart that, this time, Cornelia would fall on her face.

At the very moment that Ada was thinking these thoughts, her cousin Cornelia was discussing Lord Mullineaux's arrival with his mother. "I hope his lordship will not dislike finding a stranger in his home," she remarked as the two sat over breakfast making plans for the afternoon. Both ladies, still casually bedecked in their morning robes, were sipping their coffees while her ladyship went through the pile of invitations, bills and messages that the butler had placed at her elbow. "After all, he doesn't even know of my existence, I imagine."

"My dear child," the Countess said, glancing over at her

guest with a small frown, "I am mistress of this house. My son would be the first to assure you that, while he may be nominally the head of it, the ruling hand is mine."

Cornelia ran her fingers through her thick, still-undressed hair with languid grace. "I didn't mean to imply," she laughed, "that he would throw me out in the cold. I only meant that he might not be pleased to find it necessary to make polite conversation with a stranger after returning from a long and tiring journey."

The Countess did not answer even with a smile but merely turned her eyes back to her letters. She knew what Cornelia expected to hear in reply: *Oh, la, girl, my son will be so taken with you at first glance he'll be grateful to me forever that I arranged for you to be with us,* or words to that effect. Well, Lady Mullineaux had no intention of uttering them to feed the girl's vanity. In the fortnight that Cornelia Haydon had been with her, the Countess had had ample time to recognize the signs of vanity in her guest and to have had her fill of the girl. In fact, she was regretting that she'd ever invited her. When she'd sent the letter to Cornelia's mother in Gloucester, she had hoped that the woman would have the generosity to send Ada Surringham down. Ada was her goddaughter, after all, and had not had a mother to nurture her since she was a babe. But Dorothea had sent her own daughter, with the message that Ada herself had declined the invitation. It was too bad. Lady Mullineaux would have liked to get to know the daughter of her dear, lost friend.

Of course, she'd had a more pressing—and more selfish—purpose in mind when she'd sent the invitation. She'd hoped to find someone suitable for Griff. When she'd first glimpsed Cornelia, she'd been overjoyed. The girl seemed to embody everything the Countess had had in mind for her son. The tall, willowy, almond-eyed Cornelia was undeniably a beauty. On the three occasions since her arrival that Lady Mullineaux took her into society, the girl had been instantly surrounded by admiring men. Even Griff, she was sure, would not be immune to such spectacular looks. And the girl had other qualities to recommend her: she was of impeccable lineage, she was properly reared, she could play the pianoforte with considerable ability, and she could converse with some wit and without the simpering, giggling inanities which afflicted the conversation of so many of the females on the current Marriage Mart. But even with all these assets, Cornelia failed to win her affection. After the girl had been with her for only two days, Lady Mullineaux discovered that she'd changed her mind—she didn't wish Griff to be attracted to Cornelia after all!

It was not merely that Cornelia was vain. Lady Mullineaux could forgive that in a young beauty. She'd suffered from vanity herself in her youth. She knew how hard it was for a youthful beauty to keep from being vain; she remembered very well how it was when every man who looked at her (and it didn't matter what his age; he could be seventeen or seventy) ogled or petted her, played the poseur, flirted, flattered and behaved foolishly. How could an innocent young girl *keep* from having her head turned by such obvious admiration from the men? She remembered that she herself had been odiously conceited in her youth. It was only when she matured, after having benefited from the wise counsel of her good friend and the challenge of life with a demanding husband, that she'd realized how ephemeral and insubstantial was reliance upon a pretty face.

Yes, she could forgive Cornelia's vanity if she could see a sign that the girl's character showed promise of improvement in maturity. But the Countess could find no such sign. Instead, she discovered something else about Cornelia she could not like. It was hard to put a finger on, but there was something so . . . so complacent, so self-satisfied about the girl that at times the Countess would have liked to wring her neck. It was as if it had never occurred to the girl to doubt herself. She simply floated through life assuming that every choice she made was in the best of taste, that every remark she made was unquestionably clever, and that everything she did was right. What made these assumptions especially irritating was that Cornelia was, except for her looks, not at all above the ordinary.

But the Countess had invited her and was now trapped. She had promised to keep the girl for the season. There was no way to prevent Griff from crossing her path. What an irony! Before Cornelia had arrived, the Countess had occupied herself with plans to trap Griff into paying her heed and escorting her about town. But now that she wanted her son to ignore her guest entirely, he would undoubtedly be attracted to the girl. Why shouldn't he be? He'd been attracted to the wrong sort of female for years.

"Shall we dine at home tonight, if Lord Mullineaux arrives in time?" Cornelia asked suddenly, putting down her coffee cup.

"Yes, I expect so. I told Dolly Harrington that we were unlikely to attend her ball tonight." She looked across at Cornelia with a gleam as a hopeful idea struck her. "Why do you ask, Cornelia? Do you prefer to attend the ball tonight?" She smiled at her guest archly. "Did you perhaps plan an *assignation* at the Harringtons', my dear? If so, I have no objection to your going off to the ball without me. I'm certain that Mrs. Delafield will be willing to act as your chaperone in my place."

"Go off without you?" Cornelia dismissed the idea with a languorous wave of her hand. "I wouldn't dream of it. Besides, I wouldn't miss his lordship's homecoming for anything in the world. I think I shall wear my new green jaconet for the occasion. It is cut in the latest mode, yet it is perfectly appropriate for an intimate dinner. Didn't you say the other day that his lordship has a weakness for green?"

Lord Mullineaux arrived in plenty of time for dinner. His mother greeted him with her usual affectionate cheerfulness, hiding the fact that she felt a great deal of inner trepidation. She couldn't shake off a sense that she'd brought on a catastrophe by trying to interfere in his life. When Cornelia rustled in to the drawing room in her clinging green gown (with the décolletage cut so daringly low that the Countess felt her eyebrows climb in spite of herself), she introduced her son to her guest. Cornelia was a breathtaking sight; her green gown clung to her tall, shapely form as if it had been damped, her gold curls fell in charming disarray from a jeweled fastening at the top of her head, and her almond eyes glowed. *Good God,* the Countess thought, *my goose is cooked!*

But if Griff was taken with the girl, his mother saw no sign of it. Throughout the dinner he appeared to be preoccupied with other matters, and he gave the girl no more than the minimal attention that good manners required. Cornelia tried in vain to capture his attention by making flirtatious remarks, obvious sallies that grew more challenging and less subtle as the dinner progressed. "I've heard much about your prowess with the ladies, your lordship," she ventured with desperate coquetry at the meal's conclusion, smiling at him enticingly over her wineglass. "One common *on-dit* has it that you are able to win the most icy heart by a mere smile or an easy witticism."

"Is that what you've heard?" Griff answered indulgently. "Surely you don't credit such nonsense as that."

"I did credit it until now." She leaned back in her chair with an air of saucy disdain. "But now that I've seen your smile and heard you speak, I find that thus far you haven't been able to crack *my* icy heart."

"Then that, Miss Haydon," Griff responded with the pleasant patience one might show to a cocky child, "should be a lesson to you on the nature of *on-dits*. They are always exaggerated and should never be believed."

Her ladyship smiled to herself as they rose from the table. She should have known better than to worry about Griff. If he was to be captured, it would take more than a pretty face and a modish green gown to bait the trap.

Chapter Ten

One of Mullineaux's acquaintances had recognized his returning carriage and had immediately reported to his cronies at White's that Griff had returned from rustication. Thus it was that, early the next morning, Aubrey Tait burst into his lordship's bedroom. "Why didn't you tell me you were back?" he demanded of the sleeping figure on the bed.

Griff's valet tried valiantly to pull Aubrey from the room. "His lordship told me to wake him at eleven, Mr. Tait. *Eleven!* It is now barely ten. Wouldn't you care to wait in the breakfast room for a while? Symonds will be happy to serve you some breakfast."

"Go away, Crowley, go away. I have important matters to discuss with his lordship. Come on, Griff, wake up!"

Griff stirred, blinked up at the friend bending over him and groaned. The valet, hovering guiltily in the background, threw Griff a gesture of helplessness. Griff sat up, stretched and fixed a baleful eye on his friend. "Confound it, Aubrey, have you no feelings?"

"I *asked* Mr. Tait to wait in the breakfast room," Crowley said, throwing the intruder a look of reproach.

"It's all right, Crowley. Open the drapes, and take yourself off. We'll let the impatient Mr. Tait help me to dress in your place."

"Who," Aubrey demanded as soon as the valet had left the room, "was the magnificent creature who passed me in the outer doorway?"

"What magnificent creature?" Griff asked, yawning as he threw his legs over the side of the bed and headed for the washstand.

"Don't play games with me, Griff. You must know her. She seems to be living here." He followed his friend across the room. "I assume you know whom you have residing on your premises."

Griff lowered his face into the bowl his valet had thoughtfully filled before departing and came up sputtering. "You must mean Miss Haydon," he said, vigorously towelling. "She's a guest of my mother's. From Gloucester."

"A relation of yours?" Aubrey queried interestedly.

"No, I don't believe so. I think she's the daughter of a childhood friend of Mama's. Why are you so interested?"

"Who *wouldn't* be interested? Have you taken a good look at her? She's a regular out-and-outer!"

"Is that why you roused me, you bobbing-block? I ought to draw your cork."

Aubrey was gazing out ahead of him pensively. "I don't suppose it would do me any good to ask the Countess to introduce me. She probably invited her here in order to catch *your* eye."

"Oh, I don't think so. If an introduction means so much to you, go ahead and ask for it. Tell Mama you have my blessing."

"Thanks, old man, I will."

"Just hand me a shirt from that drawer before you go, will you?"

"I'll hand you a shirt, but I'm not going just yet. I haven't told you why I came."

Griff paused in the act of buttoning his smalls. "Was it not to worm an introduction to Miss Haydon?"

"No, for I didn't know of her existence 'til I saw her gliding out the door. She was wearing the most fetching bonnet, Griff . . . with a rose hanging over the side and brushing her cheek. I was shaken, I can tell you. Of course, she didn't even throw a glance at me. I suppose I shan't ever manage to win her attention, shall I? She stands at least a hand's breadth taller than I."

"Don't worry, old fellow. I'll have Mama whisper in her ear that you're as rich as Croesus, and you'll appear a foot taller the next time she sees you."

"Don't tease, Griff. I wouldn't mind if you *did* tell her that I'm well to pass. It's the height of vulgarity, I know, but if it would help to make her notice me . . ."

"Why don't you wait until you're introduced before you fall into despond? Who knows? Perhaps she'll adore your apple cheeks at first sight. In the meantime, see if you can find my boots, will you? If you're supposed to be taking Crowley's place, you're doing a paltry job of it."

As Griff drew on his boots, Aubrey forced his mind to return to the matter that had brought him. "I think you came back too soon," he said, sitting down beside his friend on the bed. "The Alcorn matter is still not settled, you know."

"Don't be a nodcock, Aubrey. I took care of that before I reached Wales."

"Took care of it?" Aubrey asked, confused. "What do you mean?"

"I mean that after you and I parted company in Oxfordshire, I went to a country inn called the Black Boar. It was a quiet place, quite out of the way, but Alcorn managed to find me. I thought for a while that a duel would be inevitable. But through the most fortunate circumstance, I managed to convince him that I was making off to Wales with someone else entirely."

"With someone else? You don't mean it! Are you implying that he believed there was *another* lady—?"

"Yes. Just so."

"I don't believe it! Even Alcorn wouldn't swallow such a fantastic tale!"

"But he did. And so would you, Aubrey, if I'd introduced you to the lady herself."

"You *introduced* him? To a living, breathing lady?"

Griff grinned at his friend's dumbfounded expression. "Yes, you mooncalf, she was very much alive. And, I might add, a very taking little creature in every way."

"Griff, you *Trojan!* Where did you find her? Did you dress up a tavern wench to play the role?"

"Not at all. I found a genuine lady. She had soft hands, a voice like music and the most unforgettable eyes. Alcorn was completely taken aback when he laid eyes on her."

Aubrey chortled and shook his head with admiration. "Dash it, I'd have given a monkey to see his face." But his elation quickly faded and his expression became dubious. "But, Griff," he added worriedly, "that may have been the case at the time, but the effect must have worn off afterwards. He's been heard to make threatening remarks about you at the club. I heard him do so myself, just the day before yesterday. And when the rumor spread that you were on your way home, they say he packed Julia off, kicking and screaming, to his mother in East Anglia."

"The man's a fool. If he were less severe with her, she might feel less inclined to flout him."

"Yes, but this talk don't signify where you're concerned. What will you do if Alcorn comes looking for you *again* with his pistol case under his arm?"

Griff peered into his shaving mirror and rubbed at his stubbled chin. "I can tell you what I *won't* do, Aubrey. I won't run off a second time. If the man is bound to have his duel, there can be nothing for it but to let him have his way. Shall I shave now or take you down to breakfast first?"

"Let's take breakfast. Perhaps the divine Miss Haydon will return, and you can make me known to her." He helped Griff into a dressing gown and the two headed for the door. "Are you really as indifferent to your mother's breathtaking guest as you pretend, old man?"

Griff shook his head. "It's no pretense. Something's happened to me, Aubrey, and I don't know what to make of it. I have no interest in my mother's guest, undeniably lovely as she is, or in any other female who's crossed my path lately. Except for..."

Aubrey cocked an interested eyebrow. "Except for whom?"

"The girl at the inn." He paused with his hand on the doorknob, his brows knit and his eyes puzzled. "Ever since the night at the Black Boar Inn, I haven't been able to get that young lady out of my mind."

Aubrey, just stepping over the threshold, stopped in his tracks. "What young lady?"

"The one I told you of. The one who pretended to be running off with me."

Aubrey gaped at his friend for a long moment, and then his face took on the closest approximation of a leer that his apple cheeks could manage. "Aha!" he chortled. "Don't tell me that Griff Mullineaux, who's never let a female get the best of him, has finally succumbed to a weakness of the heart!"

"I wouldn't go so far as that," Griff objected, urging his friend to the stairs. "You needn't fly into alt over this, you know. Besides," he added ruefully, "nothing can come of it."

"Come now, you don't expect me to swallow such fustian. Are you trying to make me believe that this creature from the inn—a girl who appeared out of nowhere—has spurned your advances?"

"No, that wasn't it. I didn't *make* any advances. I didn't even ask her name."

Aubrey, clumping down the stairs ahead of him, turned

round in surprise. "You clunch! Why didn't you?"

"I don't know." He lowered his head as the memories of the night in the inn assaulted his mind. "I was afraid she was a bit . . . maggoty."

"Maggoty? She was *maggoty?* Good God! I thought you disliked those muddleheaded sorts."

"I do. But she was only *slightly* maggoty. Just whimsical, you know, with her head a bit in the clouds. Very charming, all the same. I'm quite sorry, now, that I didn't get her name. If I had guessed that she would linger in my memory like this . . ."

Aubrey couldn't believe what he was hearing. He considered the matter for a while and then shook his head. "Do you know what I think? I think your journey has put you out of frame." He turned and proceeded down the stairs. "Once you've resumed your normal activities, you'll realize this is some sort of temporary aberration. A fortnight from now, or sooner, I'll remind you that you claimed to have lost your heart to a maggoty female, and you'll laugh me out of the house. Ivor Griffith, the Viscount Mullineaux, with a maggoty female! That's a tale beyond belief! If you ask me, it's a good thing you *didn't* get her name."

"Easy for you to say," Griff muttered under his breath as he followed his friend down the stairs. "You didn't see her eyes."

Chapter Eleven

Aubrey lingered on the premises until after two, but when the beautiful Miss Haydon had still not returned from her shopping trip at that late hour, he gave up the vigil and departed. Griff, taking advantage of his temporary solitude, started toward the library to see Mr. Finchley-Jones. He had intended to make the interview with the librarian his first order of business for the day, but he'd had to wait until Aubrey took his leave. Neither Aubrey nor any of his friends knew much about his bibliographical activities. He'd always been interested in books, but it was not an interest shared by his London circle. His friends were members of the Corinthian set, most of whom admired—and even envied—his reputation as a sportsman and a Lothario, but few of whom would be pleased to learn about this freakishly bookish aspect of his nature. They would think it inconsistent with his character, and they would find it as pathetic and inexplicable as his falling in love with a maggoty female.

The only person who was aware of this passionate interest in books was his mother. The Countess, although not a very great reader herself, had been educated by her husband to appreciate the value to the nation of increasing the number and quality of private libraries. When her son showed, at quite an early age, an interest in continuing the work of his father and grandfather, she encouraged him. Almost from the first it was clear to her that her son had greater intellectual gifts than his forebears and would make of the library a noteworthy achievement. It made her proud to realize that her son, who in other ways was as profligate, spoiled, self-indulgent and rakish as the other men of his class, had this one overriding interest to make his life less superficial and more purposeful than that of most of his contemporaries.

On his way down to see his bibliographer, Griff passed the sitting room where his mother sat at her desk writing letters. "Are you very busy, Mama?" he asked, pausing in the doorway.

She turned. "Only writing invitations for the ball I'm giving for Miss Haydon next week. They can wait, if you have something to speak to me about."

"A ball for Miss Haydon? I didn't know you were planning such elaborate festivities in her honor."

The Countess sighed. "I'm afraid I must. I promised her mother that I would introduce her into society. A ball is *de rigueur*."

"I see. Then I won't keep you, since you're so busy. I only wanted to ask if you'd care to come down to the library with me. I thought you might be interested to hear Finchley-Jones's report of his progress and my report on what I found in Wales."

She put down her pen at once. "Of course I'm interested, dearest. But why go down into the dust of the library? Have Mr. Finchley-Jones join us here."

While waiting for Mr. Finchley-Jones to arrive, Griff described to his mother with enthusiasm some of his discoveries in his grandfather's collection. "I didn't dream of the riches I'd find. There was a great deal of duplication, of course, but more than three thousand volumes were worthy of shipment. I'm deucedly impatient for the crates to arrive so that I can show you what I found. There's a hand-lettered Chaucer, an edition of Montaigne I didn't know existed, a tall Elzevir with the widest possible margins and several other volumes of considerable interest."

"Was there anything the equal of your Tottel's?" his mother asked, smiling at his un-Corinthian excitement.

"I doubt that I shall ever equal *that* find, Mama. A first-edition Tottel's is a jewel. A rarity of that kind is not to be found every day. Nevertheless, the Wales library held a number of gems. Grandfather may not have realized himself how many treasures he'd garnered over the years. When his books are added to mine, and all properly catalogued and indexed, you may find yourself putting up with a good many visiting scholars. How will you feel when one of your tonnish friends comes face-to-face with a shabby, bespectacled scholar in the hallway?"

"I shan't mind, my love. Not a bit. In fact, I shall make it clear to all and sundry that having scholars about the house is quite the thing. Lady Heathley has her orphanage, Tricia Farrington has her Bibles-for-the-Heathen, and I shall have my scholars."

Mr. Finchley-Jones arrived carrying several of his notebooks under his arm. As was his wont in time of stress, he chewed nervously on his underlip. Knowing full well that his lordship would not be pleased, he reported on the progress he'd made in the weeks of his lordship's absence. He was quite right. Lord Mullineaux's face fell in disappointment. "I should have thought you'd be much further along by this time," he said. "You did engage an assistant, did you not? I seem to remember your showing me a letter about a woman who had been of help to Lord Lesterbrook's librarian."

"Yes, my lord. A Miss Latcham. But she disappeared. The Bibliographical Society sent along a Miss Surrey in her place, and I engaged her. She has not the experience that Miss Latcham had, but she is quick to learn."

"Not quick enough, I daresay. Most of these entries seem to be in *your* hand. What has this Miss Surrey been *doing* for a fortnight?"

Mr. Finchley-Jones shifted uncomfortably from one foot to the other, bit his nether lip again and dropped his eyes to his shoes. "She has been . . . er . . . concentrating on jurisprudence. She has much to recommend her, my lord, but she has a tendency, sometimes, toward . . . er . . . abstraction . . ."

"Abstraction?"

"Yes, my lord. Her mind, though decidedly a good one, does sometimes . . . wander."

"Good God!" Griff muttered in disgust. "Just what we need . . . an assistant with a wandering mind. Get rid of her, Finchley-Jones, and find yourself someone capable."

"Get *rid* of her?" the librarian echoed miserably. "But I—"

"Really, Griff," his mother interjected, "aren't you being hasty? You haven't yet set eyes on Miss Surrey."

"I don't *need* to set eyes on her. You know, Mama, how I dislike these dithering females with pencils stuck in their hair and spectacles on their noses, shuffling through their stacks of tiny notes and muttering in their rusty sopranos, 'Now *where* did I put that acquisition slip? I had it *right here* in my *hand* not a *moment* ago . . .' Have I characterized your Miss Surrey rightly, Finchley-Jones?"

Mr. Finchley-Jones nodded miserably. "In some ways, I suppose . . ."

"That's quite unfair," the Countess said firmly, recollecting that the sweet child in the library had given her a charming compliment. She would not permit so lovely a girl to be summarily dismissed, not if she could help it. "Miss Surrey did not seem to me to be *at all* like that. She wasn't a *bit* dithering!"

"Oh?" Mullineaux turned to his mother with brows upraised. "You've met her, then? You found her to be efficient?"

"I'm not qualified to comment on her efficiency, although I recall that Mr. Finchley-Jones spoke highly of her abilities. I *can* say, however, that I liked her a great deal. Haven't you told me more than once that men in responsible positions, like Symonds and Finchley-Jones (and even Mrs. Mudge for that matter), should be permitted to select their own staffs?"

"Yes, of course I said that. But in this case, with the disappointing results of the last fortnight's efforts here in front of me—" He looked over at his librarian with knit brows. "I say, Finchley-Jones, do you *object* to sacking the woman?"

"Well, to be honest, your lordship, I . . . I would prefer to try her for . . . for a while longer."

"Would you indeed? It sounds to me as if you're being rather too softhearted."

"I think, Griff," her ladyship persisted, "that you should at least *see* Miss Surrey for yourself before you sack her. Perhaps when you meet her, you'll understand Mr. Finchley-Jones's reluctance to let her go."

Griff shrugged his acceptance of the suggestion and went to the bell-pull. The butler presented himself almost immediately. "Go down to the library, Symonds, and tell Miss Surrey we'd like to see her here at once."

While they waited, Griff sat down and told Finchley-Jones about some of the treasures he'd discovered in Wales. The librarian beamed in pleasure. "An early Montaigne!" he exclaimed. "I can hardly wait to see it."

Griff nodded in agreement. "I think we may find it a true rarity. Not like my Tottel, of course, but—"

"Tottel? What Tottel?"

"Good heavens, fellow, haven't you seen my Tottel? It's the star of my collection."

The librarian paled. "You have a Tottel's *Miscellany*? Not the 1557 edition, surely."

"The very one. It has *The Songes and Sonnettes* as its title. Do you mean you haven't come across it?"

"No. I probably wouldn't have believed my eyes if I had.

You should have mentioned—"

"Dash it all, how can I have overlooked mentioning it? But, man, how can you have missed seeing it for yourself? It was on the shelf with the sixteenth century poets."

"Then I know just where to find it," the librarian said in relief. "I shall seek it out as soon as I return and lock it in my desk. A volume like that should not be kept out in the open."

"Nonsense, Mr. Finchley-Jones," the Countess said. "There is no need to keep valuables under lock and key in this house. The household staff is completely trust—"

At that moment, however, the butler returned. "I'm sorry, my lord," he said, looking unusually distressed, "but Miss Surrey refuses to come."

Everyone gaped. "What's that?" his lordship barked. *"Refuses?"*

"She was very apologetic, of course, my lord. Most upset. But she is quite covered with dust, you see, the library's condition being what it is, and she insists that it would not be proper to enter your lordship's presence in all her dirt. She asks that you excuse her for today, and she hopes you will find it convenient to interview her at some other time."

"Oh, she does, does she?" Griff jumped to his feet in a fury. "I've never heard of such temerity! I'm sorry to override your wishes, Finchley-Jones, but this is the outside of enough. Like it or not, Mama, that woman is getting the sack, and *right now!*" With that, he strode angrily out the door.

"Griff, wait!" his mother begged, rising from her place and running after him.

But Lord Mullineaux paid no heed. He marched angrily down the stairs, his mother scurrying behind, trying vainly to catch up with him, and the librarian, his face a study in distress, at her heels.

His lordship burst into the library without a pause in his stride. "See here, Miss Surrey—!"

She was standing on tiptoe on the top step of a small library ladder, reaching for a book which lay neglected on a high shelf. At the sound of his voice, she wheeled precariously about on her perch gasping in alarm, the book clutched in one hand and the other flying to her mouth as if to catch the gasp before it flew into the air.

Griff froze to the spot. The girl on the ladder was dishevelled from top to toe. Strands of hair, loosened from their clasp, fell over her forehead and across her cheeks. The overskirt of her dress had been pinned up for protection against the dirt, but the underskirt and bodice were grimy, as were her hands and face. The trembling hand that covered her mouth would have served, in ordinary circumstances, as an effective mask. But the pale eyes that stared at him, horror-stricken, from her dust-streaked face could not be masked. They were instantly recognizable. "Oh, my God!" he muttered, feeling quite certain that he'd wandered into some sort of crazy dream. "It's *you!*"

His mother and Mr. Finchley-Jones burst into the room behind him. "Miss Surrey!" the librarian choked out. "What on earth—?"

Ada held the book out toward him. "It's the . . . the m-missing volume of the Grotius," she stammered. "I . . . f-found it."

Chapter Twelve

Lord Mullineaux, his eyes fixed on Ada, dismissed everyone else from the room and shut the huge library doors with a bang. "Come down from there," he ordered sharply.

Ada climbed down unsteadily. "M-May I be excused, your l-lordship?" she asked from the bottom of the ladder.

"No, you may not. There are a few questions I'd like answered first."

"I have no d-doubt there are. But I . . . I'm so v-very dusty . . ."

"Yes, so I see. Nevertheless, the dust will not keep you from telling me how you found me. Go on, my girl. Speak up!"

"*Found* you? I don't know what you mean."

He glared at her from under lowered brows. "It's the eyes, I think. Those blasted eyes. They seem so pure . . . so clear and innocent. They make it difficult for me—for *anyone*, I imagine—to suspect you of having sinister motives."

"S-Sinister motives?"

"Yes, ma'am. Sinister motives. What motives could you have other than sinister ones? Why else would you have gone to the trouble of tracking me down?"

Her light eyes widened in her streaked face. "Is that what you think? That I tracked you down?"

"Are you trying to pretend you *didn't?* That my finding the girl from the Black Boar Inn standing on a ladder in my library is sheer *coincidence?*"

"But that's . . . that's *exactly* what it is, my lord."

"Do you take me for a fool, Miss Surrey? My meeting you at the Black Boar could, I suppose, have been an accident, but all the rest? Miss Latcham's peculiar disappearance? Your timely appearance in her place? My turning out to be your employer? All of this is *coincidence?*"

She twisted her fingers together miserably. "I know it s-sounds unbelievable. I was very shocked, myself, when I saw the p-portrait."

"Portrait?"

"Yes. That one there. That's how I first learned your identity, you see. Your resemblance to your father is very marked."

"Let me make certain I understand what you're saying." He circled about her, eyeing her suspiciously as he spoke. "You applied for a post as a librarian's assistant at the establishment of a Lord Mullineaux, a gentleman quite unknown to you? And it was a complete surprise to you to find that he was, in fact, the same person you met at the Black Boar?"

"Yes. S-Something like that."

"Ha!" he snorted. "A likely story." It was too foolish a story for anyone with sense to swallow. Despite the innocence of her eyes, he couldn't swallow it. The girl was lying. Did she think she could make him accept her claim to be a household servant, even one of education like a librarian's assistant? She was quite obviously a girl of breeding. There were too many discrepancies, coincidences, unlikelihoods for her story to be accepted.

He was surprised at the powerful surge of fury smiting his chest. How dared the little minx look up at him with that expression of pained purity? He would get the truth out of her if he had to wring her neck! With a sudden turn, he grasped her waist with both his hands and lifted her up from the floor so that they were face to face. "I want the truth, girl. The *truth*. What is the motive for your establishing yourself in this house? Blackmail?"

She heard the words he spoke, but they didn't seem to have meaning. It was the anger in his voice that had significance to her. The words he said were only sounds that reverberated in her head, but the fury behind them struck her like little darts that pierced her with stabs of pain. It seemed to her that, for reasons that were completely beyond her, he hated her now. The cruel pressure of his hands grasping her waist was the physical sign of that hate. What had she done to inspire it? "Please, my lord," she managed to utter through a throat that burned, "put me d-down."

"*Tell* me! Was it a bit of blackmail you had in mind?"

"I . . . I don't even know wh-what that is."

"Don't you?" He stared at her for a moment in disbelief. She had to be lying, but he found it hard to remain unmoved by the guilelessness of her expression. She was so very innocent of face. Streaked as it was by grime, her face nevertheless seemed ethereally lovely. Her lips, trembling in agitation, were appealingly rosy and full, giving a touch of earthiness to her otherwise unworldly pallor. Her shiny brown hair, framing her face with soft tendrils of unruly curls, seemed completely in keeping with her air of artlessness. But more than anything else, her unbelievably soulful eyes, swimming in unshed tears, gazed down into his with a directness and sincerity that were almost impossible to doubt. In spite of himself, he felt his rage recede. Soon, unable to bear the look in those pained eyes, he set her down. "I thought the word was familiar to everyone," he said, turning away. "It's of Scottish origin, I believe. It refers to a letter sent by a miscreant for the purpose of extorting money from the recipient. It says, in effect, 'If you pay me the specified sum, I will not report to the world at large the heinous secret you are hiding.'"

Ada, with a sudden flash of horrified comprehension, gasped. "Are you s-suggesting, my lord, that I am here to present *you* with such a letter?"

"Are you not?"

That he could believe her capable of such a vile scheme was, to her, a final cruelty. She put a trembling hand to her mouth to keep from crying out.

He wheeled about to face her again. "Well, ma'am?"

"How can you *th-think* such a thing?" she asked, appalled. "Even if I had the sort of mind that could conceive of such a plan, what heinous secret of yours could I threaten to report?"

"Are you *joking*, ma'am? The facts you learned about my relations with Lady Alcorn would keep tongues wagging for a year!"

She looked up at him blankly. "Facts about Lady Alcorn?"

There was something so disarmingly sincere about the blankness in her eyes that he was taken aback. *But no*, he thought, *it must be a performance. A very skilled performance.* A person practicing blackmail must of necessity be adept at dissembling. He wouldn't permit himself to be disarmed. "Come now, Miss Surrey, you can't have forgotten the Alcorn business! You heard Lord Alcorn make accusations against me with your own ears."

"Oh, that." Ada sighed and brushed her still-shaking hand across her forehead in her attempt to concentrate. "Yes, of course. The Alcorn business. I'd forgotten for a moment."

"You'd *forgotten?*" He almost wanted to laugh. Such

featherheadedness was too ridiculously innocent to be feigned. She *couldn't* be pretending! Not even an actress as gifted as a Mrs. Siddons could enact sheer innocence so convincingly. He felt a surge of relief dissipating his hot anger like a sudden rain in a desert. But with the relief was an irritated impatience at her muddleheadedness. "Good God, woman," he exclaimed, shaking his head at her in wonder, "what did you think we'd been speaking of all this time?"

Her eyes welled up with tears. "I d-don't know *what* we're s-speaking of," she muttered miserably, dropping her face in her hands. "When you c-came in s-so furiously, I th-thought you were d-dissatisfied with my *l-library* work."

"I don't give a ha'penny's damn for your library work!" He pulled her hands from her face and peered down at her. Her dirty cheeks were pathetically streaked with tears. Her flooded eyes, so pale they were almost translucent, were completely unguarded and artless. Her hands trembled in his; he felt as if he'd taken hold of a pair of terrified birds. Suddenly, all he wanted to do was take her in his arms and comfort her. "Confound it, girl, when you look up at me like that I'm incapable of judgment. If you told me you were the *Queen Mother* I'd probably believe you." He lifted one hand to her cheek and absently wiped away a teardrop with his fingers. "Very well. Tell me what you want me to believe, and I shall believe it. Your name is Ada Surrey, you came here as an assistant to the librarian, and you had no idea that the man at the Black Boar would turn out to be your employer. Is that how this all came to pass?"

A look of startled guilt flashed into her eyes before she lowered them from his face. He didn't hate her, after all. He was so . . . so kind . . . so lovable . . . so forgiving. She couldn't bear to have to lie to him, even a little. But she couldn't bring herself to admit to him the whole, silly truth. "Until I saw that painting, my lord, I had no idea who you were or that you lived in this house," she said quietly.

"Hmmm." He cocked his head, studying her speculatively. "Why do I feel, all at once, that you've given me an evasive answer? Have you something else to tell me, ma'am?"

"No, my lord. Nothing."

"Are you certain? You needn't be afraid, you know. Whatever I suspected when I first saw you perched on that ladder— all my mistrust, all my fury—is quite gone. You've completely won me over. So if there is anything at all you wish to confess..."

She merely shook her lowered head.

"Dash it all," he muttered, taking an impatient turn away from her, "why should I even bother to pursue this matter? I ought simply to sack you."

"Yes, I suppose you ought."

He came back to her and lifted her chin. "But I can't, you see."

She blinked up at him. "You can't?"

"Of course not. After what you've done for me—"

"What I've done for you?" she echoed bewilderedly.

He threw up his hands. "Hang it all, woman, you *are* a bubblehead sometimes! Are you forgetting the incident of the inn *again?* Well, it may flit like a breeze through the filigree of that peculiar mind of *yours*, but *I* can't forget it quite so easily."

"Oh, the Black Boar incident again," she said with a dismissive motion of her hand. "I wish you *would* forget it. The episode reflects no credit on either one of us."

"Why so? It reflects no credit on me, certainly, but your action was positively noble."

"Perhaps. But my unc—but some might see it as positively foolhardy. Or bubbleheaded at the very least. After all, if you were a different sort of man, I might have found myself in dire straits."

But he paid no attention to her compliment to him. He was caught by her strange little stumble. "Were you going to say your uncle?" he inquired, brows knit. "Why did you stop yourself?"

She shook her head. "It was not important."

"There's a great deal you're not telling me, isn't there?" he asked with a helpless sigh, fighting the urge to shake the truth out of her. He could no longer believe her a fortune-hunter, but there was something she was holding back. He wished he could make her trust him. But continued urging was beneath him. "Never mind," he said. "I shan't press you. I shall merely take your word that this second encounter between us is merely a wild coincidence...a gigantic joke. What now, ma'am? Where shall we go from here?"

"I don't know, my lord." She recognized the sigh of acceptance in his tone. He believed her. She could sense that he had ceased his questioning and that this agonizing interview was coming to an end. She had gotten through it without inciting the wrath of the gods. The world had not trembled on its foundations nor had the walls come tumbling down about her head. She took a deep breath of relief before going on. "If you are not going to sack me, then I assume we shall go on as before."

"As before? You are amazing, do you know that, Miss Surrey? Quite amazing. Do you mean that you wish to continue to labor in the dust of the library, to continue your existence as a mere servant in this house?"

"Yes, that is what I wish."

"Even though you know and I know that this sort of labor is not what you were bred for?"

She did not take his bait. "I enjoy my work very much, my lord," was all she would say.

"What of me, ma'am? What do you expect of *me* while you continue in my employ?"

"I don't know what you mean," she said in surprise. "I don't expect anything of you."

"Don't you? You merely expect me to ignore your existence, is that it?"

"Well, I don't see what else . . ."

"No, of course you don't. You, with that cloudy brain of yours, have no recollection of the reason why, from the time of our first meeting, I didn't want to know your name. Do you recall it, ma'am? Do you remember my giving you my reason?"

Her pulse, which had calmed down considerably, began to race again. "Yes, I . . . I do recall it. You said you . . . you didn't wish to c-call on me."

"I said I didn't wish to be *tempted* to call on you. I hope you perceive ma'am, that the difference between those two statements is considerable."

There was a difference. He was implying that she'd made a mark on him. A flush of real pleasure surged up inside her, but she didn't permit herself to encourage the feeling. "I do perceive it, my lord, but since I am only a servant here, there *is* no possibility of your c-calling on me."

"Do you think I'm not aware of that? How do you suppose that makes me feel?"

She threw him a quick, enigmatic glance. "I don't know."

"Do you think it will be easy for me to ignore your existence?

Just try to imagine it, my dear." He walked to one of the windows and stared unseeing through the dusty pane. "I, who wished to avoid even knowing who you are, shall now not only know your name and where you can be found at any time of the day or night, but I shall be constantly aware that I need only to trot down to the library or pull the bell cord to indulge myself in the pleasure of gazing at those eyes of yours."

She felt herself flush again. "*Will* you indulge yourself so, my lord?" she heard herself ask.

He gave a mirthless laugh. "I shall certainly fight against the urge, my dear. It would not be considered seemly behavior for the head of the household. But as I said, it won't be easy."

There was a protracted silence in the room as she stood unmoving, watching him fixedly as the setting sun silhouetted his form in the window. *And how easy do you think it will be for me?* she asked herself in sudden bitterness. *Do you think I shall take pleasure in observing Cornelia's attempts to win your affections? Or in hearing tongues wagging about your renewed liaison with the Alcorn woman, which is what the gossips below stairs are already predicting? Or, if other prognosticators are in the right, learning that you're embarked on a new affair with another lady of easy virtue?* The prospect of living as a servant in this house, even for a fortnight, was fraught with danger for her emotions. But even if she could manage to make an escape, she wouldn't do it. This was where she had to stay . . . where she *wanted* to stay. As long as the fates permitted it, she would remain, at whatever cost, as close to this man as could be.

At last she forced herself to speak. "I don't know what you wish me to say, your lordship. If my presence here makes you uncomfortable, then I suppose you must . . . send me away."

"I've already told you I cannot." He took a deep breath before turning round to face her again. "Very well, Miss Surrey, we shall do as you suggest. We shall all go on exactly as we should have done if I'd never laid eyes on you. You will continue, in your abstracted way, to assist Mr. Finchley-Jones here in the library, and I—"

"And you will continue, in your rakish way, to have affairs and avoid duels and live as you please," she said in rejoinder, astounding herself as well as his lordship by this bitter outburst. "So you needn't sound so sorry for yourself," she added lamely.

His lordship's laugh was both surprised and rueful. "*Touché,*

Miss Surrey! A palpable hit. I didn't expect a riposte of such cutting accuracy from—"

"From a bubblehead?"

"I was going to say, from someone who not so long ago tried to point out that I must be in possession of some angelic qualities. I regret that you no longer believe those qualities exist in me."

"I *do* believe they exist, my lord. You would not have permitted me to remain in your employ if they didn't. Please forgive me for my outburst. I didn't mean to . . . I had no right to disparage your way of life."

"You had every right, having been witness to one of my life's more reprehensible displays."

"I thought we'd agreed to forget that incident," she reminded him.

"Very well, Miss Surrey. The subject is dropped. From this moment on, we go on as if our shared past had never happened. For the moment at least, you have won. But I'm well aware that there is something you haven't told me. I warn you, ma'am, that whatever it is, I shall discover it. . I intend to get to the bottom of the mystery of Ada Surrey." With that he turned back to his contemplation of the window pane. "You may go, Miss Surrey. I have kept you from your ablutions long enough."

"Thank you, my lord."

He turned round in time to see her drop a very proper curtsey and start for the door. "I hope, my dear, that you have no apprehension concerning my treatment of you," he said as she put her hand on the knob. "There is enough of the angelic in me to behave like a gentleman toward the females employed under this roof. Whatever else the gossips say about me, I'm certain they don't say that I've ever fondled an abigail or ordered a housemaid to share my bed."

"You didn't need to tell me that. You proved to me you were a gentleman that night at the inn."

"Yes, so I did. But I don't want you to think it wasn't bothersome, even then."

"*Was* it bothersome?"

"More so than I care to admit. However, I managed to act the gentleman with you then, and I shall certainly do so now."

"Yes, my lord. I was certain that you would."

When the huge double doors had closed behind her, he remained staring at them with a self-mocking smile. Yes, he would act the gentleman with her. There was no question in his mind about that. But it would be a great deal harder than it was the last time.

Chapter Thirteen

Sir Jasper had had two letters from his niece, one each week since her departure, but he had not found them satisfactory. She'd written in detail about the house, the servants, the meals and even the library, but she'd said not a word about her own state of mind. Jasper was not the sort to read between the lines; what was said outwardly was what he believed, but he was beginning to wonder if, in this case, his niece was hiding something from him. Was the girl unhappy in London?

When the butler delivered the third such missive into his hand, he hoped that this letter would tell him a bit more than the others. With a look of undisguised eagerness (for there was no one to see him, and thus there was no need to act the curmudgeon), he ensconced himself comfortably in the large easy chair in his study and broke the seal. His eyes flew over the page eagerly, but soon his eager expression changed to a frown. Ada was as uncommunicative in this letter as she'd been in the others.

He groaned aloud in irritation. If the girl was having an exciting time in the world's greatest city, there was no sign of it in these letters. The tone was cheerful enough, but the matter of the letter was the same as before: she liked Lady Mullineaux, who was kind and beautiful; the house was large by London standards and decorated in the first style of elegance; the meals were superb; the library was remarkable. Any other sort of detail—what she was doing for amusement, for example—was sadly lacking. "The library is remarkable." What sort of comment was that? He didn't force her out of the house for the purpose of examining the Mullineaux *library!* Where were the comments about balls, dances, theaters, suitors, callers, and all the other pleasantries Lady Mullineaux's letter had led him to expect?

He pulled himself out of the chair and went angrily to his desk. He would write and give her a piece of his mind. If she was enjoying herself, he wanted to know about it. And if she was not, he wanted her home at once. He prepared the nib of his pen, pulled out a sheet of paper and was about to write the salutation when the butler knocked. "Lady Dorothea is calling," Cotrell, trying not to show his surprise, announced importantly.

"Doro? You don't mean it! She ain't showed her face at this door since Ada left. Is that dashed pattern-card of a daughter with her?"

"No, Sir Jasper. She's alone. The only thing she brought is a letter."

"A letter, eh? Per'aps she's heard from Ada, too." Jasper chortled gleefully. "She must be *livid*. Wager she *still* ain't recovered from the shock o' havin' our Ada beat her Cornelia to London."

"I don't know about that, sir. She appeared to be in good spirits."

"Don't be misled, Cotrell. I know my sister. She's probably puttin' a good face on it 'cause she wants a favor from me or some such thing. But inside, she's seethin'. I know she's seethin'. Else why ain't she come callin' since that day, eh?"

"I couldn't say, Sir Jasper. Are you going to see her?"

"'Course I'm goin' t' see her. Do ye think I'd *miss* the opportunity to laugh in her face? I've been waitin' fer this chance a long, long time. Is she in the drawin' room?" He started for the door. "I say, Cotrell," he added before departing, "don't bring us tea until I ring, do ye hear? I want to have plenty o' time t' enjoy my moment o' triumph!"

Dorothea gave an uneasy start the moment she heard Jasper cross the threshold of the drawing room. Her manner confused her brother; it was nervous, yes, but there was an air of excitement underneath. Could it be that the butler was right? Had Doro recovered from her disappointment so soon? If so, he would soon overset her good spirits. He intended to make the most of this rare opportunity to gloat. "Well, well," he said jovially from the doorway, "it's been some time. How do ye go on, Doro, my dear?"

"Jasper!" she gasped, obviously relieved at the warmth of her welcome. "I'm so happy you've recovered from your... er... pet."

"Are you referrin' to the little altercation the last time ye were here? I recovered from that the very next day, as well you know."

"How would I know that?" Dorothea said, her eyebrows rising. "I haven't heard a word from or about you since our last visit."

"Oh, is *that* how ye're goin' t' play the game? All innocence and good spirits, eh? All right, ma'am. Suits me." He perched on a chair, crossed his legs jauntily, folded his arms over his chest and grinned at her. "If you can be a good loser, I can be a good winner."

"I don't know what you're babbling about, Jasper. You sound as addled as Ada. But I don't wish to precipitate another quarrel, so I'll merely tell you why I'm here. I've had a letter—"

"Have ye indeed? A letter, eh?" He had to hold himself back from rubbing his hands in glee and chortling aloud. "I don't suppose it's necessary fer me t' guess from whom."

His sister smiled. "Of course you don't need to guess. Who else's letter would concern me? Well, she writes that Lady Mullineaux is giving a ball in her honor next week and that she would be happy if I attended. I've been thinking, Jasper, that I might indulge myself this once and go. It needn't disturb anything at Mullineaux House. I would stay with my friend Mabel Banning and remain for only a month—"

"Ball?" Sir Jasper's high spirits seemed suddenly to have exploded like an overblown balloon. Why had there been nothing in *his* letter on this subject? "Did you say *ball?*"

"Yes, a ball. Not a come-out, exactly, for the girl is twenty-two, after all, but a very special ball to introduce her to society."

Jasper's face fell. "A ball in her honor?"

"Yes, of course. Didn't you think the Countess would—?"

"She's invited you to her ball? *You?* Why did she not say a word to *me* about it?"

Dorothea blinked at him. "What a very strange thing to say, Jasper. Why should you expect her to write to *you?* After the way you treated her at your last meeting—"

"How do ye know *how* I treated her at our last meeting? Our last meeting, if ye must know, was perfectly amicable—"

"Amicable? Have you gone *mad?* You ordered us out of the house! Without even a drink of tea!"

"It's *you* who's gone mad. It's *you* and *Cornelia* I ordered out of the house. Not *Ada.*"

"Who's speaking of Ada?" Dorothea peered at him worriedly. "Are you sure you're quite well?"

Jasper jumped up from his chair impatiently. "I think it's you who's sick," he accused, pointing a wagging finger at her. "You! Touched in yer upper works, if ye ask me. Who else were we speakin' of if not Ada?"

"We were speaking of *Cornelia!*" his sister shouted, waving her letter as evidence. "Who *else* would be writing from London?"

"*Ada,* that's who!" His gesturing arm with its pointing finger froze in midair. "Are you sayin' that that letter is from *Cornelia?*"

"Yes, that's what I'm saying! Come and look at it yourself, and then we'll see who's touched in his upper works!"

"Let me see that! Good God, this *is* from London. What's Cornelia doin' in London?"

"You know perfectly well what she's doing in London. What do you think our last argument was all about? Didn't we sit here in this very room and discuss the Countess Mullineaux's invitation? Really, Jasper, I'm beginning to believe you are becoming senile."

"Senile, ma'am? *Senile?* When it was I who arranged for Ada to get to London and cut your daughter out?" He laughed triumphantly at the look of shock on his sister's face. "Yes, that was all *my* doin'! So whom are you callin' senile, eh?"

Lady Dorothea rose from her chair like one in a trance. "Isn't Ada *here?*" she asked, lifting a limp hand to her breast.

"Here? How can she be here? She's in London, just as I've been sayin'. In London, with the Countess."

"With the... the Countess *Mullineaux?* At Mullineaux House?"

Jasper rolled his eyes heavenward in exasperation. "Well, I couldn't have sent her t' Buckin'ham Palace, now, could I? The invitation didn't come from there."

"But... Cornelia never wrote a *word* about it!"

"Why should she? She probably doesn't know. If she's gone to London, too, it don't follow that they've run into each other. London's a gigantic place."

"But Jasper," Lady Dorothea mumbled, utterly confused, "*Cornelia* is at Mullineaux House."

Jasper frowned at her suspiciously. "Ridiculous. Ada certainly would have mentioned—"

Dorothea sank back into her chair. "I don't know what Ada may write in her letters, jingle-brain that she is, but Cornelia would certainly have said something." She picked up the letter that had fallen from her brother's hand. "Here. Just look at this. She mentions everyone she's come in contact with. Griff Mullineaux is back from Wales, she writes. And her ladyship went with her to call on a certain Mrs. Wingate. Lady Hereford and the Princess Lieven called one morning. She met my friend Mabel Banning at the Pantheon Bazaar. She had three callers herself... she names them all: a Mr. Spencer, Sir Nigel Lewis and someone she calls Monty Moncrief. Three-and-a-half closely written pages full of names, and not once is Ada even mentioned. Here, take it and see for yourself."

Jasper shook his head bewilderedly. "I had a letter from London today myself. There's nothin' in it about Cornelia's bein' there. I don't understand what this is all about."

"Nor do I. Did you say that you sent Ada to London the day after our last conversation?"

"Yes. The very next mornin'."

"That was the very day that Cornelia departed."

Jasper walked thoughtfully back to his chair and sat down abstractedly. For a moment he said nothing. Then he looked over at his sister, his brows knit. "I dislike to say this, Doro, but I think Cornelia's lyin' to ye. If she was stayin' with Ada at Mullineaux House, Ada would certainly have mentioned it *once* in the three letters—"

"I've had *four* from Cornelia," his sister retorted. "Perhaps it's *Ada* who's lying."

"Ada don't lie. You know that. Besides, I have proof! Ada's abigail—and ye know that Selena's a reliable woman if ever there was one—went to London with her. She then took ill and came home. But not before havin' delivered the girl right to the Countess's door. Told me so herself, with the coachman backin' the story in every detail."

Lady Dorothea shrugged helplessly. "I don't know what to make of this, Jasper. But Cornelia doesn't lie either. And I, too, have proof. Look at this, that Cornelia tucked into her letter."

"What is it?"

"It's a gilt-edged invitation to the ball. It's written in the Countess's own hand, and it has a few informal words of regards to me from the Countess herself, scrawled across the bottom. What do you make of that, eh? You cannot imagine it to be a forgery, can you? Even *you* cannot believe that

Cornelia would go as far as forgery!"

Jasper examined the card, nonplussed. Then he sagged against the back of his chair, his spirit gone. "Then what do ye make o' this, Doro? What's goin' on there at Mullineaux House that makes each one o' the girls invisible t' the other?"

"I don't have the slightest idea. But this, of course, makes me quite decided. I shall leave for London in two days' time and shall get to the bottom of this at once. You have my word, Jasper. I shall solve this riddle and get word to you in the first post."

He fixed a lugubrious eye on his sister and shook his head. "I ain't goin' to wait fer word from you, Doro. I'm goin' myself."

"Very well. Perhaps that *would* be best. We can go in my carriage. I'll stop for you at first light, the day after tomorrow. That would bring us to London by evening of—"

"Do you think I'd be able t' bear waitin' till the day after tomorrow? I wouldn't get a wink o' sleep or a minute o' peace in my mind!" He rose from his chair abruptly and strode toward the door. "I'm goin' right now . . . or at least as soon as Cotrell can call fer the carriage. Yer welcome t' come along, Doro, but I ain't goin' to stop along the way fer any trumpery reason whatsoever."

"But I can't come now! I haven't packed. And neither have you, Jasper. I know this whole situation is worrisome, but you can't run off to London without so much as a hairbrush or a change of clothes."

"Yes, I can. Cotrell can throw a few necessaries into a bag for me—and for you, too, if ye had a mind—and I can purchase whatever I need once I get there. But there's no need fer you t' hurry yerself. Take yer time an' pack yer fineries. When ye finally arrive, Doro, you can find me at Fenton's Hotel. Cotrell! *Cotrell,* ye sluggard! Where are ye?" Without another glance in her direction, he hurried from the room.

She stared after him in a daze, a hand pressed upon her heaving bosom. Then, with a sudden shake of her body, like a dog shedding raindrops from its coat, she jumped to her feet. "I'm coming with you," she shouted excitedly. "Do you hear me, Jasper? Wait for me!"

Chapter Fourteen

"I don't know how I'll be able to face his lordship," Mr. Finchley-Jones muttered miserably as he climbed down from the library stepladder after his desperate examination of the last book on the last shelf in the room. "Such a loss will be impossible for him to bear."

"But it's only a book," Ada said, attempting to be soothing.

"Only a book! Only a *book!* I'll have you know, Miss Surrey, that the *Miscellany* is one of the most prized of rare books. Tottel printed only seven small editions of it between 1557 and 1574, each extant copy of which is precious, but the 1557 edition is the most prized of all. Most collectors only *dream* of finding it. But to have owned it and then *lost* it—" He shuddered at the horror of it. "It doesn't bear thinking of."

"Don't lose hope, Mr. Finchley-Jones," Ada said, turning back to the work at her table. "Books don't just disappear. The missing treasure will turn up, probably in the most unlikely place. I myself once left a book under the sprinkling can in the rose garden. I didn't find it again for months, for it was the last time I sprinkled the flowers that fall."

"Yes, I quite believe it of you," the librarian said reprovingly.

"So it will be this time," she said cheerfully, ignoring his little slur.

The librarian sighed hopelessly. "That's what I shall say to his lordship, of course. 'It's bound to turn up,' I'll say. But I don't really believe it. The Tottel's been stolen. A magnificent, 1557 Tottel—stolen! I can think of no other explanation."

"There *must* be another explanation," Ada insisted. "I know almost everyone on staff by this time, and no one of them seems to me to be dishonest. And furthermore, none of them seems remotely interested in books or the doings in this library. Whenever I speak of library matters at the table, they are all very quick to change the subject. There are not many people

106

in the world, it seems, who have your fascination with books."

"But, my dear girl, it requires only *one* of them to be a thief. You admit you do not know them all. And even if you did, you cannot be certain that you've correctly judged all their characters. It is the nature of a thief to hide his true character. He could easily have fooled you as to his real nature. You, if I may say so, are not the sort to see the evil that lurks in people's hearts, being so very good yourself."

"Thank you, Mr. Finchley-Jones, for your kind opinion, but I am neither so good nor so gullible as you think me."

She returned to her task of listing, by author, the books on jurisprudence which had become her special responsibility, but she found it difficult to keep her mind on the work. She wondered if Finchley-Jones had been right about her judgment of people. She tried to bring, one by one, the faces of the household servants to her mind, to see if she could determine any signs of dishonesty or wickedness in any of them. But on examination each one she conjured up seemed to be open, honest and free of guile. Yet the book was gone. Could she swear that none of them was capable of stealing it? How could one really tell what was in the secret heart of another?

Mr. Finchley-Jones, meanwhile, was gazing at her bent head adoringly. The girl was quite the prettiest creature ever to have come his way. He never got his fill of staring at her. More than once he'd considered the prospect of asking for her hand. But as often as the thought had come to him, he'd as often thrust it aside. He was almost forty years old and had long ago decided that marriage was not for him. He was very precise in his habits and style of living and did not relish the prospect of making adjustments to suit a female. Women were, in general, a messy breed. They were given to emotional outbursts of tears, to leaving their pots of facial preparations uncovered on their dressing tables, to licking chicken grease from their fingers, to dusting only the tops of things, to manhandling a man's possessions, to all sorts of other, repulsive tricks of behavior. Not that he'd seen Ada indulge in many of these quirks, but he had seen her cry, and she was very forgetful and addled. He knew enough about women to surmise that even if some of them were charming in their youth, they invariably developed these repulsive traits in later years.

Still, Ada Surrey had something about her that was unique. She seemed very much a lady. Though merely a servant in this household, she had an air of gentility that was unmistakable. For her he might forgive an open jar on the dressing table. To have her with him always, to be able to gaze at those wonderful eyes and shiny hair at any time of day or night, might be joy enough to make her absentmindedness and other feminine weaknesses bearable. Perhaps he should reconsider his stand on the subject of wedlock. For a girl like Ada, a change of heart might be in order.

"Have you ever thought, Miss Surrey, that taking care of a husband, a home and children might be more suited to you than library work?" he asked suddenly.

Ada was conjuring up the face of Symonds, the butler, in her mind. Could Symonds, she was asking herself, be capable of deceit? "Yes, Mr. Finchley-Jones," she murmured absently.

"I am glad to hear you say that," he said, taking a deep breath and beginning to pace about the room. "I believe that I can offer you the sort of life you would wish for, and, undoubtedly, better than a young woman in your circumstances could have expected. I am not without resources. An uncle of mine left me a legacy which is sizeable enough to have permitted me to follow my chosen profession without undue concern with remuneration. Fortunately, however, my employers thus far have been quite generous, and I've been able to live within my means, without touching my inheritance. With (if I do say so myself) shrewd investment of that inheritance, my income is now more than seven hundred per annum. For the past few years I've made my home in rented rooms, but with my present income I could certainly afford a pleasant house in one of the recently settled sections north of the New Road. What do you think of that, Miss Surrey?"

"What, sir?" she asked, blinking up at him.

"Don't you think a house north of the New Road would suit a newly wedded couple?"

"Oh, yes, I expect so," she agreed, deciding in her mind that Symonds the butler was too loyal to the family to even *contemplate* doing them an injury.

"Good. I would have no objection to your employing a housemaid and cook, provided they were exceptionally neat and tidy in their personal habits. I'm sure that you will have surmised by this time—even though our acquaintance has not been long—that I am a man of precise habits. I cannot endure slovenliness of any sort, so any servant I decide to employ must be impeccable in conduct and appearance."

"Yes, of course," Ada said, thinking about the two footmen who assisted Symonds. They were the youngest of the six footmen on staff (being not much above nineteen years in age) and were given to making ribald remarks. But Ada could not imagine them being deceitful. She rather liked their lusty sense of fun. Ribald remarks were a sign of high spirits, nothing more. She doubted very much that they, singly or together, would choose to engage in anything dishonest.

"As I said, we have not known each other for very long—a little more than a fortnight only—but we've worked together for many hours each day. When one thinks about it, one might court a lady for a year, calling on her weekly, without spending as much time in her company as I have in yours. So I don't believe it to be hasty to come to a decision at this time. After all, it is already clear that we have similar likes. We both enjoy quiet contemplation, we both refrain from easy intercourse with strangers, we both prefer reading to other pastimes . . . isn't that so?"

"I beg your pardon?" She was now reviewing the upstairs maids in her mind. Clara was, of course, beyond reproach, and the talkative Sally, who was close to sixty years old and had been with the Mullineaux family for forty-five of those years, was not likely to turn dishonest at this stage of her life.

"Reading *is* your favorite pastime, is it not?" he repeated.

"Reading and gardening, I suppose," she answered, wondering briefly why he was asking so personal a question. But her mind returned at once to the problem at hand—the honesty of the staff. There was Mrs. Mudge, of course. Mrs. Mudge had a mercurial temper. Could she, in a moment of anger, bring herself to steal something from her beloved Lord Mullineaux? It was not at all likely.

"There is every reason to believe we would have a happy life," the librarian went on thoughtfully. "I may be called, from time to time, to travel to parts of Britain some distance from home, but I would not accept a commission that would keep me from home for great lengths of time. In any case, most of this nation's serious library work is taking place right here in London. You can expect me to return to hearth and home almost every evening at sunset. It is a pleasant prospect, is it not?—

you greeting me at the door, both of us sitting down to sup in our little dining room (which should face south, I think, for the best evening light), then settling down together in our own library (for I have not stinted in acquiring a considerable collection of my own) where we would spend the evening reading, sometimes even aloud, I on my easy chair and you on a hassock with your head resting on my knee? In fact, the prospect is more than pleasant. It is quite delightful, is it not?"

"Oh, yes," she muttered abstractedly. "Delightful." But her cogitations were becoming less than delightful. Whereas she couldn't choose a particular person on whom she might pin a suspicion, there were a number of members of the staff about whom it would be difficult to swear *with absolute certainty* that they would never do a dishonest act. The French cook, for example, kept to himself; everyone considered him a man of mystery. And Mrs. Mudge *was* temperamental. The young footmen *were* bawdy and high-spirited. And then there was Grisha, the stable man, who'd come from Russia; some of the staff whispered that he'd run away from his home in Murmansk because he'd murdered someone there. None of them had aroused her suspicions before, but perhaps that was because she was gullible. She still believed that none of them would steal anything in this house. But she couldn't be certain. She had to admit that perhaps Finchley-Jones was right after all.

"Then you agree with me, my dear?" he was asking.

She gave a reluctant shrug and smiled up at him ruefully. "Yes, I think, after all, that I do."

His face reddened in pleased surprise. "You *do?* Oh, my dear *girl—!*"

"Yes, I do. I've been thinking it over carefully these past few minutes, and I've come to the conclusion that there is much in what you say."

"Ada, my dear!" He crossed the room to her chair, his eyes misty. "I hope I may call you Ada from now on. You have made me the ... the happiest of men!" He lifted her hand to his lips. "I'm quite overcome. Please ... forgive me." And he ran off to the tiny closet room in which he always changed his clothes and shut the door.

She stared after him in astonishment. Had there been tears in his eyes? But why? What could account for so peculiar a reaction to her simple statement that she agreed with his judgment that a theft of the *Miscellany* was a possibility? Her agreement seemed to have touched his emotions with unwarranted force. Good heavens, was it possible that even *Finchley-Jones* had deeper aspects to his nature than she'd supposed?

Chapter Fifteen

Clara was sitting on Ada's little bed, munching an apple, while Ada sat on the room's only chair, stitching a newly-washed-and-ironed white tucker on the blue bombazine dress that she would wear the next day. Clara had recently finished relating to Ada the day's gossip, mostly concerning Mrs. Mudge's speculation about the romantic prospects of her ladyship's houseguest. The housekeeper and the staff were impressed with the number of suitors who had called on Miss Haydon that day. "Three this afternoon alone," Clara reported, "an' she ain't yet 'ad 'er ball." She leaned back against the pillow and lifted her weary legs up on the coverlet with a sigh. "Once 'er ladyship shows 'er protegee to all the *ton,* there'll be no end t' the knockin' at the——" Her eye fell on a shadowy object in the corner. "What's that book doin' there on the floor?"

"What book?" Ada asked, not looking up from her sewing.

"That one there. In the corner."

Ada looked round. "Oh, yes. *The Songes and Sonnettes.* I'd forgotten all about it. I really must remember to return it to the library one of these days. I've been using it to prop up the mirror, which stands too low for me to see the top of my hair. I'm sure that Mr. Finchley-Jones would not approve of my using one of his books for that purpose."

"Ye could ask one o' the footmen to 'ang the mirror proper," Clara suggested. "That cheeky Lawrence'd do it if ye asked 'im." She grinned wickedly at her friend. "'E'd do anythin' ye asked . . . gladly."

"Come now, Clara, are you implying that Lawrence is taken with me? He's a mere child!"

"Ye can't say 'child' about a chap that's almost nineteen. An' nineteen is about time fer a chap t' turn top over tail over a girl. Lawrence is top over tail about you, my girl, or I don't know my name is Clara."

"Your name is Clara, but that doesn't make you right. If you're to be believed, every man on staff is enamored of me."

"No, I didn't never say that. Howsomever, there's a *few* of 'em in that condition. 'Ave ye noticed that Mr. Finchley-Jones 'as been smellin' of April and May the past few days? I ain't never seen him like that afore. All smiles 'e is!"

"Smiles? That proves how little you know of him. The poor man's worried sick! He hasn't yet got up enough courage to tell his lordship that his library's greatest treasure has disappeared."

Clara shrugged. "It's true I don't know anything about that, but I do know that the man glows like a candle when 'e looks at ye." She took a final nibble of what was left of her apple, got to her feet and tossed the core into the grate of the tiny fireplace. "If ye've a mind, Ada," she teased, throwing her friend a leering look, "ye could worm an offer from that there gentleman."

"An *offer?*" Ada shook her head in amusement. "You can't mean it."

"Easy as pie. As my pa used to say, 'e's a pigeon ripe for the pluckin'. A girl could do worse, Ada." She threw herself back upon the bed and raised her legs again. "Mr. Finchley-Jones is a proper gen'leman."

"Yes, he is," Ada agreed, a mischievous twinkle lighting her eyes. "And so handsome, too."

Clara giggled. "Just so. If ye find scarecrows 'andsome."

"I think he's more like a crow than a scarecrow. But that is quite beside the point. I'm not good enough for Mr. Finchley-Jones. What ordinary woman is?" Ada held an imaginary lorgnette to her nose and looked at her friend with pursed lips. "Don't you realize, madam, that a wife for Mr. Finchley-Jones cannot be an ordinary female?" she asked in a good imitation of the librarian's nasal manner of speech. "She must be precise, meticulous, exact. In a word, faultless."

"Oh, quite right," Clara agreed with a snort. "She can't never touch 'is papers nor move 'is possessions even an inch from where 'e's placed 'em . . ."

Ada grinned. "Nor misplace so much as a comma when she copies his notes . . ."

"Nor leave out the thing connectin' 'is names. What do ye call it, Ada?"

"The hyphen." She burst into a laugh. "Can you imagine the poor girl who marries him, Clara? She'll have to go through life being Mrs. Finchley Hyphen Jones!"

Clara guffawed. "There must be *some* female we know who'd be good enough fer 'im," she said, putting her hands behind her head and grinning up at the ceiling speculatively. "Somewheres in this world there's someone who's the perfect match—" She suddenly gave a wicked little cackle as a ludicrous idea burst into her mind. "I know just the female who'd suit! *Miss Haydon!*"

Ada gaped at her for a moment and then choked. "Good heavens! *Cornelia?*" The thought was so funny that her needlework slipped from her lap unnoticed.

Clara hugged herself with delight at her puckish notion. "Wouldn' that be—what is it Mrs. Mudge is always sayin'?— deevine retribution? Instead of snatchin' up *'is lordship* fer 'erself, it'd be *deevine retribution* fer Miss Haydon to be paired with Finchley-Jones."

"Why, Clara," Ada said reprovingly, trying not to laugh, "one would think you didn't wish Miss Haydon well. Don't you *like* her ladyship's beautiful houseguest?"

"Not much," Clara said frankly. "Thinks she comes out o' the top drawer, she does. Always talks t' me like I was an insect wi' a bad smell. Wrinkles 'er nose up, like this, when she speaks t' me." Clara gave a regretful sigh. "Acourse, she'd never look twice at Mr. Finchley-Jones. Not she. She'll 'ave more suitors than she'll know what t' do with when the ball is over."

"Yes, I'm sure she will," Ada murmured, picking up her sewing.

"Ye should see 'er ballgown, Ada! Green *peau de soie*, wi' seed pearls an' sparklers sewed all over the bosom. Fair took my breath away when I saw Mrs. Prentiss—the Countess's seamstress, y' know—fittin' it on 'er." Clara made a moue. "She'll 'ave the gentlemen buzzin' round 'er like bees."

"I suppose so." Ada poked her needle into the fabric viciously. "Lord Mullineaux, too, I'd wager."

"Wouldn't be a bit surprised," Clara agreed. "That's why I think it would be deevine retribution fer 'er to be paired wi' Finchley-Jones." She grinned again as the appealing vision reshaped itself in her mind. "Can't ye just *see* it, Ada? Just think o' their bedroom, fer instance, (if ye could imagine they're the sort t' share a bedroom). Can you picture it? 'Er gowns an' frills an' furbelows strewn all about *'er* side o' their bedroom, lookin' like a mingle-mangle; while on 'is side everything neat as a pin."

Ada, unable to help herself, gurgled at the vision. "There she'd be, all dressed for a ball, while he'd insist that they stay home and *read* together!"

"Exac'ly! Wouldn't that be just like 'im? Wishin' t' stay at 'ome an' read?" Clara chuckled heartily. "And no novels, neither. Only very serious stuff."

"Of course. Frivolity is not to be permitted." A giggle, made up of pure delirium, bubbled out of Ada. "Can you envision my cousin Cornelia being forced to sit and listen to Finchley-Jones reading Grotius aloud? All three volumes of *The Rights of War and Peace?*"

Ada dissolved in laughter, but Clara stiffened. Ada had made a slip, and Clara did not miss it. She sat up straight and stared at her friend with knit brows. "I don't know who this Grotius is, acourse," she said carefully, "but I take it yer *cousin* wouldn't find 'im t' be entertainin'."

"Entertaining?" Ada wiped the tears of laughter from her cheeks. "She'd find him dull as dishwater after three pages, much less three vol—" Her smile suddenly faded. *"What* did you say?"

"I said, yer cousin Cornelia wouldn't much care fer this Grotius."

"Oh, dear," Ada winced, putting a hand to her mouth. "I seem to have spilt some beans."

"It's true, then?" Clara asked tightly. "Cornelia Haydon, 'er ladyship's guest, is yer *cousin?*"

"Yes, it's true."

"Might you be a well-born lady then?"

Ada glanced at her worriedly. "Would it trouble you if I were?"

Clara looked her up and down, her face wary. "I should 'ave knowed." She got up and edged toward the door, rubbing her hands on her apron nervously. "What's a fine lady like you doin' in the servants' quarters anyway? 'Tain't right nor fair."

"Clara! Wait a moment, please. Good heavens, you're behaving as if I'm here to spy on you."

"What *are* ye doin' 'ere, then?"

"Certainly not spying. I only . . . I needed to earn some money."

Clara snorted. "Ye should 'ave asked yer cousin t' give ye some. They're sayin' downstairs that 'er ballgown alone cost more'n three 'undred pounds. Surely she could 'ave spared you somethin', even if it meant she'd 'ave t' choose a gown fer the ball not quite so posh."

"I couldn't ask—"

"Y'know, Ada, or whatever yer name really is, it ain't easy fer me t' believe that it's *money* what brought ye here. Yer wages fer laborin' away in the liberry won't amount t' much. Not fer a lady's needs, anyway. Ye wouldn't earn three 'undred pounds if ye worked 'ere fer *six years!*"

"I know. But I couldn't ask Cornelia. It would be another defeat for me. Besides, she doesn't know I'm here, and I don't want to tell her. I was . . . it was I who was supposed to be Countess Mullineaux's guest, you see."

"What's that? *You?* I don't understand. If it was supposed to be you, why ain't ye—?"

"Please, Clara, sit down again. I'll try to explain it all to you. You promised to remain my friend, remember? Even to the gibbet, you said. Don't desert me now."

Clara, eyeing her suspiciously, allowed herself to be led back to the bed. "I'll stay fer a bit . . . but only if ye agree t' tell me the true tale. Though I don't know as I'll ever believe that a fine lady truly needs t' work below stairs."

The night was well advanced before Clara was satisfied that she'd heard the whole story, but by the time they embraced and bade each other goodnight they were fast friends again. The stiffness that Clara had felt when first realizing that Ada was far above her in station was soon eased by the sincerity of Ada's warm affection for her. But affection and a renewed friendship did not keep Clara from telling Ada that she was a fool. "Ye should've asked her ladyship fer help right away," she insisted. "She would've taken you in, and it would be *you* havin' a green *peau de soie* gown and bein' the center of eyes at a ball."

"No, Clara. I would be playing second fiddle to Cornelia again, and I have quite enough of that at home. Once I'd heard that Cornelia had arrived here before me, I knew I'd lost the game."

Clara frowned. "That's nonsense. Ye can't lose a game ye didn't even play!"

Ada blinked at her friend in surprise. Was Clara right? Had

she been cowardly in not entering the lists in the battle to conquer London? She considered the matter for a moment and then shook her head. "What sense was there in playing the game? With Cornelia so beautiful and clever, what chance had *I* to make a mark? It would have been difficult enough for me to make a satisfactory impression on the *ton* if I'd been here alone, but in competition with Cornelia it would have been impossible. I would only have made the Countess ashamed of me, bubblehead that I am."

Clara remained unconvinced, but she agreed that matters were now too far advanced to change. Familiar with Cornelia's character as she was, Clara could understand Ada's reluctance to ask Cornelia for any help. Cornelia would certainly laugh at her and hold her up to riducule before the family. It was bad enough that Ada was forced to endure Cornelia's annoying condescension at home in Bishop's Cleve; here in London the girl had a right to be free of it.

It was also clear to Clara that Ada did not wish to disappoint the Countess, who had been her mother's best friend and was her own godmother. If she'd been courageous enough to introduce herself to her ladyship from the first, matters might have turned out better than the timid girl expected, but Clara had to admit that it was too late to do so now.

With all the problems made plain, Clara finally understood why Ada needed her wages. She wanted to make her way home without seeking help from either the Countess or Cornelia. "Don't you see?" Ada explained. "The person called Ada Surrey, as soon as she's earned enough money to travel, will disappear. Ada Surringham will reappear in Bishop's Cleve as if she'd never left. No one but Uncle Jasper will ever have to know anything about the whole foolish escapade."

Clara, despite her reservations, promised with a full heart to do all she could to keep the knowledge of Ada's presence from her cousin and her true identity from everyone else. "I'll help you buy yer passage on the stage. But I'll tell ye frankly, Ada, that I'll miss Ada Surrey when she disappears. I ain't 'ad a friend like you ever afore."

They embraced tearfully. "Nor I you, Clara. Not ever."

Later, waiting for sleep to come, Ada went over her conversation with Clara in her mind. She was glad she'd finally revealed herself. It would be good to have someone to confide in. The only thing she'd held back from Clara was the story of her relationship with Lord Mullineaux. The feelings generated by her two encounters with his lordship were still too new and fragile to be spoken of aloud.

She twisted about under the coverlet in discomfort. Her emotions, when she thought about Griff Mullineaux, were so chaotic that they frightened her. She knew what those emotions signified, of course. She had read so much about the emotions of love that she'd recognized her symptoms at once. Even at the inn she'd known the name of the illness that had struck her. What she didn't know was the cure.

Love was something she'd dreamed of often. She'd always wanted to fall in love. She'd imagined the sort of man he would be: gentle, soft-spoken, wise, patient. She had seen him in her mind quite clearly. He'd be fair-haired and clear of eye, with a smooth, high forehead, a serene expression and a ready laugh. She supposed he'd be a vicar or a country squire with a small estate, someone whose social obligations were modest and whose friends were not fashionable, so that he wouldn't be embarrassed by a wife who was absentminded and a bit of a bubblehead. Even in her wildest dreams, Ada hadn't imagined falling in love with a dark-eyed, devilishly attractive rake of low morals and high income, who would kiss her before he even learned her name and who would decide, before they'd been acquainted for an hour, that she was a completely unsuitable consort for a man of wealth and fashion.

So love had struck, as she'd heard it so often did, with blind inaccuracy. Now she would have to face the dire consequences. One of those consequences might be being forced to watch (from this unfortunate position below stairs) cousin Cornelia, in her green *peau de soie* gown, catch Griff in her net. That would be a painful experience indeed. Her only hope was to arrange to leave this house *before* a romance between her cousin and Griff Mullineaux had time to develop. It was true that she'd decided, only a short time ago, that she wanted to remain here as long as possible, to be close to this man who had somehow, without warning, taken possession of her thoughts. But after tonight (after experiencing the feeling of being discovered, and realizing that things would have been much worse for her if the discovery had been made, not by Clara, but by Cornelia or her ladyship) she knew she had to get away. And soon.

Feeling stifled, she threw off the covers and crept out of

bed. She climbed up on a chair to reach the tiny round window which was the room's only source of fresh air. She pushed it open and peered out into the black, starless night. Yes, she thought sadly, she would leave soon. She would have to endure the night of the ball, of course—that was to occur in only two days' time—but with the receipt of her month's wages and with Clara's help, she might very well manage her escape a few days later. Once she was home again, far from Griff Mullineaux's dynamic presence and the scene of what would undoubtedly become Cornelia's triumph, she might begin to find a cure for this terrible disease that had so unexpectedly overwhelmed her.

Chapter Sixteen

Aubrey was hanging about again. He had tried on three separate occasions to arrange for an introduction to the magnificent Miss Haydon, but his timing was always off. The first time she was out shopping; the next time she was taking tea with Sir Nigel Lewis, and Aubrey was reluctant to interrupt; and the third time she was occupied with her ladyship's seamstress who was fitting her ballgown. "Where is she today?" he demanded of his friend as they sat at the breakfast-room table lingering over their coffees. "I'm determined to accomplish this mission today."

"I don't know where she is," Griff said irritably. "I can't be expected to keep track of her comings and goings."

Aubrey glared at him. "You're not trying to keep her for yourself, are you? That wouldn't be playing fair."

"Don't be a clunch. I've already told you that the girl doesn't interest me."

"Yes, so you did, but I think it's all a hum. Trying to pretend that you're smitten with another girl! The day that Griff Mullineaux is so smitten with a female that he's blind to the charms of someone like Miss Haydon will be the day I give up my tailor."

Griff gave a reluctant laugh. He was in a vile mood, and he didn't feel up to exchanging pleasantries with Aubrey this morning. He hated having to admit to himself that his mood had anything to do with his confused emotions about the young lady working in his library. It was less bothersome to attribute this depressed state to the news Finchley-Jones brought to him this morning. But Aubrey had accidentally put his finger on a strange truth—if this Miss Haydon was really such a diamond, how was it that he, the notorious libertine, had never noticed? Something was decidedly wrong with him. "I know how much Weston's tailoring means to a man of your girth, old fellow, but if you're going to make rash statements of that sort, perhaps you'd better start looking for someone else to cut your coats," he muttered glumly.

"What? Are you still pretending to be infatuated? With the same female you told me of? The maggoty one?"

Griff threw his friend a look of disgust. "I don't want to talk about it. Do you think I have nothing on my mind but females and tailors and suchlike fripperies? After what I learned this morning, your problem concerning Miss Haydon is the last thing on my mind."

"What did you learn this morning?" his friend inquired curiously.

"You wouldn't be interested. It's about my library."

"Your library? This pucker you're in is caused by your *library*? I don't believe it."

"You may believe what you like, Aubrey. Only go away and let me brood in peace."

Aubrey ignored the order and simply reached for another biscuit. "Very well, I'll believe you. What's so troublesome about your library?"

"I've just been told that my Tottel is missing."

"You don't mean it!" Aubrey cried in mock horror. "Lost your *Tottel?* That's dreadful! Tragic! Cataclysmic!" Then, calmly buttering his biscuit, he asked, "What on earth is a Tottel?"

"Not what, you gudgeon. Who. Tottel was a publisher in the sixteenth century. He published a collection of verse known as the *Miscellany*. Have you never heard of Tottel's *Miscellany?*"

"No, can't say I have." He paused in the act of bringing the biscuit to his mouth and peered at his friend in sudden, quite sincere alarm. "I say, Griff, you're not going to tell me you're turning bookish!"

"I've always been 'bookish.' I hope you won't be too badly shocked to learn that I've managed, in the past few years, to gather together a very commendable library. The Tottel was the gem of my collection."

"Good God," his friend said, aghast. "I wouldn't have believed it of you. Griff Mullineaux, bookish!" He took a quick bite to steady his nerves. "I *am* badly shocked, I must say. This is quite upsetting news to learn about someone you thought you knew well . . . someone you considered your very best friend in the world. I don't mind your confiding this piece of information to *me*, old chap, because I'd remain fond of you no matter what aberration appeared in your character, but I wouldn't say anything to anyone else about this if I were you. Wouldn't do to have it bruited about that you were bookish."

"Damnation, Aubrey, don't talk fustian," Griff muttered, dismissing Aubrey's raving with a mere toss of his head. "You don't realize what this loss means to me. A Tottel is a rarity. Collectors may search a lifetime without finding one. Try to imagine the blow it is, after having tasted the joy of acquiring it, to have it disappear!"

"Books don't disappear," Aubrey responded with bland indifference, looking under the covered platters to discover if any more of the smoked fish lurked beneath. "The thing is bound to turn up somewhere."

"I hope so. I've sent for Symonds and Mrs. Mudge to see what can be done about locating it. You're welcome to stay, old man, but I don't think you'll find the interview entertaining."

"Oh, yes, I shall. This view of Griff Mullineaux as a man of books is *vastly* entertaining. I wouldn't miss it for the world."

"Perhaps you'll be rewarded with the arrival of Miss Haydon at the end, eh?"

Aubrey shrugged. "After putting up with all this talk of literature, I *deserve* that reward."

Symonds and Mrs. Mudge both presented themselves to his lordship when his breakfast was finished. He explained what had happened very carefully. "I don't wish you to give the staff the impression that they are under the slightest suspicion of theft," he explained. "Theft of such an object, when there are many other articles about the house of equal or greater value, like her ladyship's jewelry, is quite unlikely."

"That's right," Aubrey put in. "It's only a book, after all."

Griff threw him a silencing glare. "It is my conviction," he went on to the heads of the staff, "that the book has somehow been misplaced. It is lying somewhere, in some out-of-the-way corner, unnoticed and forgotten. I know that I'm giving you both an enormous task—there are so many rooms, closets, niches and cubbyholes in the house in which a book may lodge. But, dash it all, it must be found!"

"Yes, my lord," Symonds said. "We shall make a thorough search. But I hope, my lord, that you'll be patient with us.

There *is* the ball tomorrow, you know."

"The ball?" Griff winced in annoyance. "Oh, damnation, I'd forgotten for a moment about the deuced ball." He rubbed his forehead disconsolately. "I suppose you must do what is necessary to make ready for it. Naturally, that must come first."

"Not first, your lordship," the butler said sympathetically, "but at least simultaneously. We shall manage to search while making the party preparations."

"Thank you, Symonds."

"Beg pardon, your lordship," Mrs. Mudge asked timidly, "but p'rhaps you can describe the book, so's we know what we're searchin' for."

"Yes, of course I can. It has a reddish-brown cover of tooled leather, somewhat worn at the corners. The pages are hand-cut, which means that the edges are rough and a great deal yellowed. On the spine are the words *The Songes and Sonnettes*, in gilt letters, spelled the old-fashioned way, with the *e* on Song and the *double-t* and *e* on Sonnet. That's about all I can think of."

"That's quite enough, I should say," Aubrey observed with amusement. "If ever *I'm* misplaced, I hope you can describe me half so well."

Aubrey lingered for another hour, but his "reward" did not appear. He took his leave, vowing to return as soon as possible for another chance. "I must have an introduction to her before the ball, or I shan't be able to find the opportunity to inscribe my name on her dance card!" he said worriedly before departing.

Griff saw him to the door and then set off down the hall toward his study. Aubrey's remark about the ball had set him thinking. His friend was looking forward to the ball but he was not. The house was already at sixes and sevens, with servants dashing about making ready, with deliveries of chairs and china and champagne and potted greenery, and with his mother preoccupied with preparations. And it would be worse tomorrow. His mother had already told him that the Corinthian manner of making a brief appearance, dancing one dance, sampling one pastry and one glass of champagne and then making off for a gaming hell would not do. He was expected, this time, to remain for the entire evening, to dance every dance, and to escort the guest of honor to the buffet. He would obey his mother's request, of course, but he could anticipate nothing enjoyable about the experience.

However, there was one way the ball might be made as interesting for him as it evidently was for Aubrey. If he, like Aubrey, could sign the dance card of a young lady who'd captured his eye, the evening might be saved. The ball might turn out to be an exciting event if Miss Ada Surrey were present. Why not? he asked himself. His mother would not object, would she, to giving a card to the librarian's assistant? What would be so wrong with that?

At that moment, as if she'd materialized from his thoughts, Miss Surrey appeared down the hall. She had evidently taken her luncheon in the servants' hall and was returning to the library by the back stairs. He hurried his step. "Miss Surrey?" he called.

She turned round with a start, peered uneasily into the gloom of the hallway and then recognized him. "Good afternoon, your lordship," she said with a little bob of a curtsey.

"I was just thinking of you," he admitted, catching up with her.

"Were you?"

"Yes." He grinned down at her. "I was wishing you would permit me to sign your dance card."

"My what?"

"Your dance card. For tomorrow's ball."

"Is this some sort of joke, my lord? Or is it the fashion among the *haut ton* of London for the nobility to dance with the servants at their balls?"

"No, unfortunately it's not the fashion, though I can think of many fashions that have much less to be said for them. However, you, my girl, will receive a card for the ball this afternoon. Tomorrow night you will attend the festivities as a guest, not a servant. I hope that answers your question. Now that we have that matter cleared, I wish an answer to *my* question. May I have the first dance with you?"

Her eyes flew to his face. Even in the shadows of the rear hallway, she could see the eager gleam in his eyes. Her heart bounced up in her chest. How lovely it would be, she thought, to appear at the ball and walk onto the dance floor on Griff Mullineaux's arm for the very first dance. The blood sparkled in her veins at the mere thought of it. "It is most kind of you to ask me, my lord, but you're being impetuous, are you not? Won't you be escorting the *guest of honor* for the first dance?"

His face clouded. "Damnation, I didn't think of that. I suppose I shall have to." He frowned down at her in sudden suspicion. "For a librarian's assistant, you're very well informed on the rites and customs of the *haut monde* galas, are you not?"

She hoped that, in the hall's dimness, he wouldn't see her flush. "Well, I . . . I read a great deal," she explained lamely.

"That answer, ma'am, is a weak attempt to flummery me, I think. But it did me no good to quiz you before, and I expect I would get no better results now. So let us return to the subject I introduced earlier. Your dance card."

"I thought the matter was closed."

"No, not at all. Only the matter of the first dance. We shall now discuss the *second* dance. There can be no objection to my dancing *that* one with you, can there?"

"There certainly can, but we needn't go into that, for I won't be there."

"But I just explained to you that you *will* be there."

She shook her head. "I'm afraid, my lord, that it's quite impossible. It is not my place—"

"Hang it, girl, must you be so rigidly conventional? You were not so at our first meeting. Listen to me, my dear, and try to believe me. Once you've received an invitation, then it's as much your 'place' to attend the festivities as any other guest's."

"I do thank you for asking, my lord—"

"Griff. Call me Griff. I can not enjoy waltzing with anyone who calls me my lord."

She held up her hand as if to ward off an attack, but her expression was adamant. "I do thank you for asking, *my lord,* but if I have the right to be invited, I must also be given the right to refuse."

He caught her raised hand in his and brought it to his lips. "Don't refuse me, girl," he begged urgently. "The evening will be unbearable without you."

"Don't!" she whispered, a catch in her throat. "You shouldn't . . . you promised you wouldn't . . ."

"Wouldn't what?"

"Wouldn't flirt with me."

"I never made such a ridiculous promise."

"Yes, you did," she insisted, struggling to free her hand. "You said you . . . never fondle the housemaids."

"You're no housemaid. And this isn't fondling. I'm merely holding your hand. Even this . . ." He pulled her to him and encircled her waist with his arm. "Even *this* cannot be called fondling." Putting his cheek against hers, he hummed a strain into her ear and led her in a waltzing turn down the corridor.

She felt positively light-headed, floating down the length of the rear hallway in his arms. She had danced the waltz twice before, once at a Bishop's Cleve assembly and once at a private party. Each time she'd tripped over her partner's feet. This time she felt as if she were dancing on air. Every step was right. He whirled her about as easily as if she were a phantom, insubstantial, graceful and completely weightless. For a moment she lost her sense of time and place. They weren't master and servant or even Ada Surringham and the Viscount Mullineaux. They were Cinderella and the Prince, Juliet and Romeo, Eve and Adam. She didn't want the moment to end.

He didn't stop until they'd come to the dark end of the hall. And when he ceased dancing, he didn't release his hold on her. Breathless, they seemed to cling together. "Come to the ball," he whispered in her ear. "Please."

"Oh, Griff," she breathed against his chest, unable to return to reality.

"Does that mean yes?"

She forced herself back into the present. She would not behave like a bubblehead with him, if she could help it. "No, of course not. You know I mustn't—"

"I know nothing of the sort. Why not?"

"I have no gown, for one thing—"

"Mama will find one for you."

"I couldn't ask her to . . . besides, she would never . . . and Mrs. Mudge would have apoplexy . . . and the whole staff would take offen—" But he kissed her before she could finish.

He hadn't intended to do it. He hadn't intended to do any of the foolish things he'd done in the past few minutes. She was a dithering, maggoty, bubbleheaded female who was, on the one hand, too innocent to be taken advantage of but who, on the other hand, was too impossibly unsuitable to consider courting seriously. He'd known from the first that he should have nothing to do with her.

But every time he looked at her, something happened to his

common sense. It collapsed, dissolved, completely deserted him. One look in those eyes of hers and he lost his resolve. He realized now that for days he'd yearned to hold her in his arms and kiss her like this. She was soft, light and completely pliant in his hold. It was the most damnable pass! Never had he met a girl with whom he was so ill-matched, yet never before had a girl felt so right in his embrace. If he let himself go, as he was doing at this moment, he might forget himself enough to make the girl an offer! This strange, mysterious, absentminded, unbefitting creature might reel him in as no girl had managed to do before.

He'd better get hold of himself before there was real harm done. This girl was not for him. Slowly, with painful effort, he eased his hold on her. "Now, *that*," he said as he let her go, trying to hide his breathlessness and appear casual, "might be called fondling."

She sensed, at once, the change in him. She'd been carried away, blissful and dizzy, into a place that was completely new to her. She'd never felt so happy. She wondered if perhaps she were dreaming all this, although the excitement of her feelings was stronger than ever she'd experienced in a dream. But if this were real, she wouldn't have the courage to permit herself to waltz like a wraith in Griff's arms and to surrender—and respond like an eager little tart—to his kiss. Why, from the way he was embracing her, she could almost believe he cared for her. So this *couldn't* be reality. She simply couldn't believe this was really happening to her. Reality never turned out this way—not for her. Therefore, this was merely one of her dreams, though an especially thrilling and vivid one, and she might as well relax and enjoy it.

But it had turned out to be reality, after all. She knew it as soon as she felt him stiffen. He had kissed her, true, but all too soon he'd thought better of it. "Yes," she said, turning away so that he couldn't see the extent of her disappointment, "I think you might . . . call it f-fondling."

"I am sorry," he said in a subdued voice. "I *did* promise not to—"

Far away, down the length of the hall, someone opened the front door. The sound jarred them both. Griff was quick to notice how Ada wheeled about in terror. Footsteps appeared to be approaching. Griff looked over his shoulder. "It's only Mama's guest, Miss Haydon," he said soothingly. "You've no need to be embarrassed; we haven't been seen. Besides, even if we *had* been seen, the embarrassment would all be on my side, not on yours."

"Nevertheless, I must go," Ada whispered uneasily.

"There, you see? She hasn't even noticed us. She's going to the front stairs."

Ada felt so agonizingly deflated that she almost didn't care if Cornelia spotted her or not, but she had to get away from Griff's painful proximity. "Good day, your lordship."

"Wait!" He caught her hand again. "What about tomorrow?"

Cornelia, at the foot of the stairs, heard a sound from the shadows. "Griff? Is that you back there?" she asked, peering into the darkness.

"Damnation," he cursed softly under his breath, tightening his hold on Ada. "Well?"

"No, not tomorrow." Ada pulled her hand free and flew to the back stairs. "Please," she whispered tearfully as she disappeared from his sight, "don't ask me again."

Chapter Seventeen

The day of the ball dawned darkly, the sun obscured by a heavy covering of black clouds and the air heavy with an icy wetness. By six a drizzle began to fall with a cold persistence that seemed to promise a long stay. But not only the weather was forboding; human circumstances, too, were not propitious. The day began badly for almost everyone at Mullineaux House.

The first of the residents to receive bad news was Ada. The news was signaled by an urgent knocking at her door just as she'd arisen, a little past dawn, and begun her ablutions. It was Clara. "Ada, open up," she whispered nervously. "I 'ave somethin' t' tell ye."

Ada, shivering in the cold of her room, padded barefoot to the door. One look at Clara's face told her there was something very wrong. "What on earth's the matter?" she asked, stepping aside to let the housemaid enter.

"The book," Clara whispered dramatically as she shut the door. "That one in the corner, that ye said ye'd been usin' t' prop up yer mirror... I think it's the missin' treasure."

Ada stared at her uncomprehendingly. "Are you speaking of the book that Mr. Finchley-Jones has been searching for?"

"*Everyone's* searchin' fer it now. Even Mrs. Mudge. She tole the entire staff first thing this mornin' that 'is lordship ordered the place combed from top t' bottom. Mrs. Mudge explained what the book looked like an' said how we was all t' keep our eyes open fer it—"

"But, Clara, that book on the floor isn't the one. It *couldn't* be. The missing book is Tottel's *Miscellany*. Whatever made you think—?"

"That ain't the name Mrs. Mudge tole us. It was like the name you said the other night. Songs an'... an', ye know... those poems."

"Sonnets?" Ada asked in dawning horror.

"That's it. Sonnets with a double-*t* an' a *e*."

"Good God!" Ada dashed across the room and fell to her

knees, groping under her little table with trembling hands. She picked up the book, sat down on the floor and opened it to the title page. "Oh, Clara, it *is* the one! Here's the name Tottel large as life at the bottom of the page! I never even *noticed*. How could I be so featherbrained?"

"The question is, girl, what t' do now?" Clara said worriedly. "Mrs. Mudge is bound t' think ye filched it."

"*Filched* it? Oh, heavens! Will she believe I'm a *thief?*"

"I don't know, Ada. Prob'ly will. I think she's more likely t' believe ye a thief than a featherbrain."

"I'm not at all sure I wouldn't rather she *did* think that," Ada mumbled ruefully. "Oh, dear, I don't know what to do! Shall I just take this down to the library and confess to Mr. Finchley-Jones? He'll surely sack me when he realizes I've had this treasure all this time."

"'E might at that, even if it breaks 'is 'eart t' do it. Arfter all, it'll go 'ard with 'im t' face Lord Mullineaux an' tell 'im that 'is assistant 'as been usin' that precious book t'—"

"To prop up her mirror!" Ada finished, shuddering. "Oh, my God! How could I have done it?" She ran her hands over the book's leather cover to ascertain how much damage her carelessness had done to the binding.

"I think ye should keep yer clapper tight behind yer stumps fer a while," Clara said thoughtfully. "Today ain't the best time fer confession."

"You mean say nothing?" Ada asked, wide-eyed.

"Fer the time bein'. Now, while things is so skimble-skamble on account o' the ball, they might be real short with ye, t' get the matter over with and out o' the way, ye know. But if ye wait 'til the ball's done with, things'll be calmer an' tempers won't be as likely t' boil over."

"You're probably right, Clara, but I don't think I can bear waiting. How can I keep my mouth shut about so serious an offense? I'll *really* feel like a thief if I say nothing."

"It's only fer a day. Take my advice, Ada. Keepin' still is the smartest thing t' do fer now."

So Ada nodded her agreement, Clara went off about her business, and Ada finished with her dressing. But when she reported to the library to begin her day's work, she could hardly look Mr. Finchley-Jones in the eye, so uncomfortable was she in her hidden guilt.

Her ladyship also started her day with bad news. No sooner

had she opened her eyes than her abigail informed her that a dreadful scene was taking place in the kitchen. The lobster for the patties (which were to be the highlight of the buffet) had failed to arrive, and Monsieur Albert, the French chef, was having a tantrum in the kitchen over it. He'd spent the past half hour, the abigail reported, screeching to the undercooks and the gaggle of scullery maids who were gaping at him in frozen alarm that *"il est trop tard pour changer le menu,"* and that if her ladyship could not do something *"immédiatement,"* he was going to his room *"pour faire mes valises."*

Her ladyship sighed in resignation as she pulled herself from her bed. It was going to be one of those days, she told herself glumly, that made one wish one could escape to the Indies.

Cornelia's bad news came somewhat later that morning. It was during a mid-morning breakfast that the realization broke upon her that, in spite of all her efforts, she was not making an impression on Lord Mullineaux. She had come to breakfast early in order to encounter his lordship there, and she'd worn her most magnificent morning robe for the occasion. It was a rose-colored masterpiece in lacy *point de tulle* worked in a most intricate pattern, through the holes of which a white satin underdress could be detected. She'd tied the overdress tightly under the breast and let the neck edge fall low on her shoulders. She knew it made the most of her dewy morning skin. In addition, it rustled when she walked and emphasized her tall, willowy grace.

But she'd done even more to her appearance before descending to the breakfast room. She'd let her hair fall loosely to her shoulders, and she'd brushed a smidgeon of blacking on her lashes. Every little touch was calculated to suggest a sleepy informality that was bound to be enticing to any man of normal appetite. Both her mirror and her abigail had told her that she looked delectable.

She found his lordship at the table, as she'd expected. He was alone. She stood posed in the doorway for more than a minute before he looked up, but he was apparently engrossed in perusing a sheaf of papers which seemed to be nothing more than neatly copied lists. When he *did* look up, he rose politely, held a chair for her, murmured something about its being a shame it was raining on the day of the ball, and returned to his lists. She tried three times to engage him in conversation, but she received mere monosyllables in response. "I've wasted my most fetching robe on you," she muttered irritably at last.

"What's that?" he responded, looking up. "Did you say something about a fetching robe?" Then, realizing what she meant, he threw her a somewhat abashed grin. "I'm sorry, Cornelia. It *is* fetching. I should have said something."

"If you truly think it fetching, why don't you pay some attention to me? Why is it so difficult for me to hold your eye?" she demanded, pouting.

"Because, my dear, my library work demands my attention, too." Without a touch of guilt, he returned that attention to his papers. He was quite familiar with the tricks of accomplished flirts, and he was not in the least susceptible to them. Suddenly, he looked across the table at her with a glimmer of amusement in his eyes. "However, Cornelia, if you linger over your coffee just a bit longer," he suggested, "my friend Aubrey will be dropping in. Aubrey has been most eager to make your acquaintance. There is no one in the world who would appreciate the charm of your most becoming *dishabille* more than Aubrey."

Cornelia rose from her chair like an angry hawk rising with a flapping of its wings from the limb of a tree that had been shaken by a sudden squall. She felt as if she'd been doused with cold water. Never before in her life had a gentleman tried to palm her off on someone else! That his lordship wanted to do so was quite the last straw. Without another word she'd stalked from the room in a sulk. The incident threatened to ruin her joy in the entire day.

His lordship watched her departure with a touch of mischievous merriment in his eyes. The girl was self-centered and spoiled, and he'd found the temptation to give her a set-down quite irresistible. He didn't think he'd been too unkind. If he'd wrenched her from her complacency and disturbed her mood, the upset would only last a little while. When tonight's festivities were over, and she'd become the belle of the *ton*, she would completely forget his little slight.

Of course, he was well aware that he'd spoiled her morning. What he didn't know was that his own morning—and afternoon and evening as well—were to be filled with disturbances a great deal more wrenching than the one he'd dealt his mother's guest.

The first of those disturbances occurred a short time later, with the arrival of Aubrey. The fellow was in a belligerent mood, declaring that he would not vacate the premises until he was given an introduction to the young woman of his dreams. Griff felt a flush of sympathy for poor Aubrey, knowing how often the fellow had made the attempt to meet Cornelia, and he was perfectly willing to oblige, but he feared that he did not stand in Cornelia's good graces because of what had happened in the breakfast room only a short while earlier. Thus he decided that the best way to arrange the introduction would be through the good offices of his mother.

He searched for his mother high and low, finally tracking her down in the kitchen. He tried valiantly to convince her to come upstairs and oblige his friend, but Lady Mullineaux was too preoccupied to take the time. "I'm sorry, dearest, but I haven't yet discovered what has happened to the lobsters, so I must remain available to keep Monsieur Albert calm. And when the lobsters *do* arrive, I shall have to solve several other problems—an insufficiency of champagne glasses, for one. Clark and Debenham's delivered only half the number I ordered. We cannot serve champagne in wine goblets, you know; we'd be the laughing stock of London. Furthermore, Symonds tells me that the Regent has sent a message that he will honor us with his presence after all; that means I must completely rearrange the seating for supper. I am quite at my wit's end, dearest, so please go away and deal with Aubrey's problem yourself."

Griff tried his very best, sending Symonds to plead with Cornelia to come downstairs for only a brief quarter hour, but the girl adamantly refused. After the incident that morning, Griff was not surprised. But Aubrey, who knew nothing of the little contretemps at the breakfast table, could not understand why the girl had refused to make an appearance. "Can she have taken me in dislike without even knowing me?" he asked uneasily. "Has she heard something disgraceful about me, do you suppose?"

"I say, Aubrey Tait, what disgraceful thing have you done?" Griff teased. But reading the frustration on his friend's face, he changed his tone. "I think she's just too busy preparing for this evening," he added, trying to be comforting.

"Preparing for this evening? But it's not even noon!"

"Oh, well, you know how women are. They can fuss over their gowns or their coiffures all day."

Aubrey dropped into a chair in the drawing room and sullenly refused to leave. "I shall wait," he declared stubbornly. "I shall wait if it takes *hours!* After all, she ain't likely to remain upstairs closeted in her room all day. Sooner or later she's bound to make an appearance. And when she does, I'll be here."

Griff shrugged. "Suit yourself, old fellow. Make yourself at home for as long as you like. But I hope you won't mind if I go about my own business."

His first order of business was an interview with his librarian. While Aubrey settled deeply into his chair, put his feet up on a hassock and indulged in a desultory perusal of the *Times,* Griff and Mr. Finchley-Jones put their heads together over the shapely Sheraton table that was the jewel of the drawing room and went over the now completed list of books on English history. Mr. Finchley-Jones made suggestions for needed additions (which he read to his employer from still another list) and wrote notations beside those works whose purchase his lordship approved. When their business was completed, and Mr. Finchley-Jones rose to leave, Lord Mullineaux held up a hand to detain him. "I was wondering, Mr. Finchley-Jones, if you would like to attend tonight's festivities."

Both Finchley-Jones and Aubrey looked up, startled. *"I,* my lord?" the librarian asked, his lorgnette slipping from his nose in his surprise.

"My mother and I would be pleased if you came... and Miss Surrey, too, of course."

Finchley-Jones flushed with pleasure. "Why, your lordship, I... I'm overwhelmed! Such an invitation is quite unprecedented. I do thank you, and Lady Mullineaux, too, most sincerely. I... We shall be honored to attend."

Griff was aware that Aubrey was watching the scene with curiosity, but he went on anyway. "I know you cannot speak for her, but do you think Miss Surrey could be persuaded to join you? I have the impression that she might be too diffident to—"

"I'm quite *sure* that I can persuade her," Mr. Finchley-Jones said with what Griff felt was a rather obnoxious self-assurance.

"Are you indeed?" he asked, his tone suddenly growing chilly.

Finchley-Jones looked down at the spectacles swinging on his chest like a pendant and smiled complacently. "You see, your lordship, I am fortunate to be able to announce to you that Miss Surrey has recently consented to become my wife, so I—"

"What?" Griff felt as if someone had landed a hard blow to his midsection. "What did you say?" he asked again, frozen-faced.

"I don't blame you for being surprised," the librarian said, keeping his eyes lowered modestly. "You are thinking, I suppose, that I am somewhat advanced in years for this sort of change in my way of life—"

"I am thinking, fellow," Griff interrupted curtly, trying to keep his voice level and his temper even, "that I can't have heard you properly! Did you say that you asked Ada Surrey to marry you?"

The tone of voice in which the question was asked, though not loud, had such a timbre of angry shock that it disturbed not only Mr. Finchley-Jones but Aubrey. Both heads came up abruptly. "Yes, I did," Mr. Finchley-Jones said, his smile dying. "Doesn't your lordship approve of—?"

"Of course I don't approve!" his lordship barked, jumping to his feet. "Are you trying to pretend the girl accepted you?"

Mr. Finchley-Jones, although as impressed as anyone in his station with the awesomeness of rank and wealth, was not a milksop. He drew himself up to his full height and raised his lorgnette to his eyes. "There is no need for me to pretend, my lord," he said proudly. "She did accept me."

"I don't believe it! Why wouldn't she have told me—?"

"Told you, my lord? Why should she have—?"

Aubrey leaned forward in his chair. "I say, Griff," he asked in amazement, "this chit you're speaking of . . . she ain't the one, is she?"

"The one?" the librarian echoed, looking round at Aubrey in confusion.

"You know," Aubrey persisted, ignoring the librarian and keeping his shrewd eyes fixed on his friend's face, "the maggoty one you told me of."

"Shut up, Aubrey," Griff snapped. "Stay out of this."

"I don't understand, your lordship," Mr. Finchley-Jones said uneasily. "Other than meeting her in the library, are you acquainted with my betrothed?"

"I'm more than 'acquainted' with her! I know her well enough to know that what you say is ridiculous." He leaned on the table with one hand and pointed a threatening finger at his librarian with the other. "So don't refer to her as your 'betrothed' ever again!"

Mr. Finchley-Jones stuck out his chin stubbornly. "Miss Surrey *is* my betrothed, and I shall refer to her as such so long as it remains true," he declared bravely. "And when it is no longer true, my lord, I shall refer to her as *my wife!*"

Griff glared at the fellow, fighting an urge to throttle him. Then he threw up his hands in frustration. "I think, Finchley-Jones, that you've *lost your wits!*"

"I hope you'll pardon me for saying this, my lord, but perhaps *you* have lost *yours!*"

"Well, let's find out, shall we?" His lordship strode to the bellrope, but before he could pull it, the butler appeared in the doorway. "I'm sorry to disturb you, my lord, but—"

"Not at all," Griff said. "You're just the man I wanted. Find Miss Surrey and tell her she's wanted in the library. *At once,* mind!"

"Yes, my lord," the butler said, looking uncomfortable, "but first I must tell you that there's a . . . a certain someone at the door."

"A certain someone?" He glared at the butler in irritation. "What kind of announcement is that?"

"A certain . . . lady." That Symonds disapproved of the "certain lady" was obvious.

"Has everyone gone mad today?" Griff growled. "The lady has a name, I presu—"

Before he could finish, the sound of rushing slippers and the rustle of a cloak drew all their eyes to the doorway. Julia Alcorn came running in, her rain-spattered cloak billowing behind her and its hood slipping down to reveal a head of disheveled hair. "I couldn't wait, Griff," she cried tearfully, dashing up to him in complete disregard of the others in the room. "He's coming! With his *pistols!*"

"Oh, good God!" muttered Aubrey. "Here we go again!"

Chapter Eighteen

Griff groaned in impatience. "Julia, what have you done now?" he asked disgustedly.

"Don't be angry with me," she said with a hoarse catch in her voice. She looked quickly around the room like an actress surveying the audience, and, as impervious to the presence of Aubrey and Finchley-Jones as an actress would be to a full balcony, continued with her scene. "I had to tell him, dearest. I *had* to."

"Tell him what?"

"He threatened to send me back to his mother if I didn't! Oh, Griff, you don't know how that threat cuts into my soul! Life with his mother is...*unspeakable*. So...so I admitted it."

"Yes, my dear, so you've told me. But *what* is it that you admitted?"

"That I ran off with you when you went to Wales."

"But that's not true! He knows it isn't true. Confound it, Julia, you went back home with him, didn't you? He saw me at the Black Boar with..." Griff hesitated, not willing to go further in this ill-assorted company.

"You're referring to the girl in the inn, aren't you?" Julia asked.

His brows snapped together. "How did you know about her?"

She gave a careless shrug. "Giles Alcorn doesn't keep secrets from his wife. He told me all about the incident at the Black Boar."

Griff's eyes burned with fury. "He did, did he?"

"I told him that that was all a pretense, that the girl was probably some lightskirt you'd hired for the performance. You must have played your part magnificently, Griff, for I had a great deal of difficulty convincing him that I spoke the truth."

"It's why you *wanted* him to believe it was a performance that I don't understand," Griff muttered, wondering what had

137

ever possessed him to become involved with this troublesome woman in the first place.

"Because she'd rather throw *you* to the wolves than face her mother-in-law, that's why," Aubrey said, as disgusted as his friend by this latest turn of events.

Griff put a hand to his forehead. "Very well, ma'am, you've warned me. I am obliged to you for coming, but I think it would be best for all concerned if you would now return to your home."

"But Griff, you're not going to remain here and *wait* for him, are you? We may still have time to—"

"To do what, my love?" came a voice from the doorway. Everyone looked up to see Alcorn standing there, face white and pistol case under his arm. "To make off together to Wales again? Did you really think I wouldn't follow you to Wales?"

"Good afternoon, Alcorn," Griff said drily. "It wanted only your presence to make this party complete. Come in, come in."

"I think, my lord," said Alcorn, "that I am not in the mood for a party. Can you rid us of all these onlookers?"

"That's a bit high-handed of you, isn't it?" Aubrey demanded, rising from his chair and stepping forward. "This ain't your house."

"True, Tait, too true," Alcorn said with a pained smile, "but I nevertheless have an aversion to having my private affairs discussed before strangers."

"I shall be glad to withdraw, my lord," Finchley-Jones offered stiffly. "Do you wish me to return at a later hour?"

"No, I don't wish you to withdraw at all," Griff said shortly. "We have an important matter to conclude. Alcorn, if you don't wish to discuss private matters before strangers, you can take your wife and go. You may come back to continue the discussion at another time, if you find you still wish to do so."

"Oh, no, Mullineaux, you won't be rid of me as easily as that. I've come here to settle matters with you once and for all."

"And how do you intend to that, eh? Have a duel right here in the drawing room?"

"Griff, no!" Julia cried, throwing her arms about his neck in the manner befitting a true Cheltenham tragedy. "I won't let you shed blood over me!"

"How touching," Alcorn said bitterly, sneering at his wife.

"Very cleverly phrased, too, my dear. With those words one can't be sure if you're protecting your husband or your lover. If only you'd thrown your arms about *my* neck when you said them, I might almost have believed it was *my* blood you wanted to protect."

"*Your* blood ain't going to be shed, Alcorn, and you know it," Aubrey said furiously.

"No? I'm flattered, Tait, that you think so highly of my prowess with the pistol."

"I *don't* think highly of your prowess, you gudgeon. I happen to know that Griff won't shoot you. He intends to delope."

"That's enough, Aubrey," Griff said curtly. "Sit back down in your chair again and don't upset yourself. There isn't going to be any duel."

"I should hope not, indeed!" This was said by a new voice. All eyes turned to see Lady Mullineaux entering the room briskly. Julia backed away from Griff and self-consciously adjusted her cloak to cover her décolletage. Aubrey jumped up from his chair again, and Finchley-Jones made a stiff bow. Only Lord Alcorn failed to alter his position to acknowledge her ladyship's arrival.

"Welcome to this *ménage*, Mama," Griff said, throwing her a rueful grin. "Perhaps your presence will restore some semblance of sanity."

Her ladyship surveyed them all with thinly disguised disdain. "How can you—*all* of you—be so thoughtless as to stand about like this, babbling on about *holding duels in my drawing room*, when I'm expecting guests to begin to arrive before three more hours have passed? Really, Julia, my dear, have you no sense of time? I sent you and Alcorn a card, did I not? Why aren't you home dressing?"

"I believe, Mama," Mullineaux said, looking at Alcorn pointedly, "that they were about to leave to do just that."

"Ha! Do you think I have dancing on my mind at a time like this?" Alcorn ranted. "I've come to demand *satisfaction*, and satisfaction is what I shall have!"

"Very well, Alcorn," Mullineaux said with a helpless shrug, "if you insist on acting the fool, you may have your duel."

"Oh, how delightful," Lady Mullineaux said with ironic disgust. "Is that the sort of sanity you were referring to a moment ago?"

"Don't worry, Mama. The duel will not take place here."

"So you say," Alcorn muttered threateningly.

"So I say, Alcorn. Not here and not now. If there is to be a duel at all, it must be done properly. Aubrey will call on your second (if you can find someone idiotic enough to second you in this foolishness) tomorrow to make the arrangements."

Julia gave a terrified shriek. "No, Griff! You mustn't!"

"Be still, Julia," Lady Mullineaux said curtly. "If you had only learned to exercise some discretion and a touch of self-control, matters might not have come to this."

"They would have come to this in any case," Lord Alcorn said, his manner becoming a little more calm. "A man can not be made a cuckold without taking measures."

"Yes, but he needn't carry on like a looby so that the whole world knows it," Aubrey put in.

"That's *enough*, Aubrey," Griff ordered.

"Very well, Mullineaux, my second will call on Tait before nightfall tomorrow," Alcorn agreed, and then turned to the Countess with a stiff bow. "Your ladyship, I hope you will forgive us this untimely intrusion. Come, Julia. We shall take our leave."

He held out his arm to his wife, but the lady recoiled. "I'm not going with you!" she cried. "Never!"

"Oh, Julia, *really!*" Lady Mullineaux said in disgust. "Must you make a scene in my drawing room? And today, of all days? Do, please, behave like a sensible woman and go home."

"You don't *understand*, your ladyship," Julia quivered. "If I go home with him, he'll send me to his *moth—*"

"I beg your pardon," came a voice from the doorway. "Excuse me for this intrusion, your lordship, but be assured I wouldn't interrupt if this were not a matter of the utmost importance." In came Cornelia, still clad in her "fetching" morning robe and leading a red-faced, angry Clara by the ear.

"Damnation!" Griff muttered under his breath. "*Now* what?"

"*Griff,*" Aubrey whispered to his friend excitedly, his eager eyes drinking in the ravishing vision, "it's *she!* She's come down! At last I'll have my chance!"

"Gracious!" the Countess exclaimed, striding across the room and releasing Cornelia's hold on her housemaid. "What is happening here?"

"I believe," Cornelia announced importantly, speaking directly to Griff, "that *this* is the thief who stole your missing treasure."

The librarian, who had been observing these proceedings with the fascination natural to someone who spends most of his life in the somnolence of bookrooms, gave a start, his lorgnette dropping from his nose again. "Are you referring to the *Miscellany?*" he asked eagerly.

Griff's eyebrows rose. "My *Tottel?* This girl stole it?"

The entire company, whose attention had been captured by Cornelia's extravagant beauty, now turned their eyes to the flushed, unhappy housemaid. "How unpleasant," Julia murmured, "not to be able to trust one's servants."

"But what Miss 'Aydon says . . . it ain't *true,* m' lord," Clara declared, glaring at Cornelia belligerently.

"Of course it isn't," Lady Mullineaux said soothingly. "Whatever made you think, Cornelia, that Clara—who's been with us for *years*—could be the culprit?"

"It's as plain as day, your ladyship," Cornelia said confidently. "She was assisting my abigail in readying my costume for tonight, when I noticed a leather-bound volume in the corner of a shelf in the wardrobe in my room. You know the wardrobe, my lady. The painted oak, with double doors—"

"Yes, I know the one. Do go on."

Cornelia nodded and turned back to face his lordship. "Of course, I thought immediately that it must be your missing book. 'Climb up, girl,' I said to this creature here, 'and get that volume down. I think it may be Lord Mullineaux's treasure.' And do you know what she said?"

"No, of course we don't," Griff said impatiently. "That's what we're waiting to hear."

"She said, 'No need to bother. That isn't the one.' She turned out to be right, of course. It was only a circulating library copy of Matthew Lewis's *Bravo of Venice,* which some forgetful guest must have left behind and which some careless housemaid—like *this* one, I have no doubt—had pushed aside. Now, I ask you, Griff, if this chit's remark isn't an incriminating one. How can she have known it wasn't the missing volume if she didn't have information to the contrary? I've been questioning her for the past half-hour, but I've not been able to get a further word out of her."

"*Do* you know something about the missing book, Clara?" Lady Mullineaux asked gently.

Clara looked at her mistress miserably for a moment, and then her glance dropped to the floor. "Can't say, m' lady."

"*Won't* say, you mean," Cornelia snapped.

"See here, girl," Griff said, crossing the room and peering at the housemaid closely, "if you know something about my Tottel, it will go better with you to confess openly. If you took it without realizing what it was, or if you found it somewhere and became frightened . . ."

"'Tain't nothin' like that, m'lord," Clara said nervously. "'Tain't my tale t' tell."

"Then whose tale is it?"

But Clara refused to answer.

"*I* might be able to answer that," Cornelia offered. "My abigail says that this creature and your librarian's assistant are thick as thieves. An apt expression in this case, I believe. It seems quite plain that the two of them plotted the theft together."

"*My* assistant?" Finchley-Jones took a nervous step forward. "Miss *Surrey?*"

Cornelia looked at the librarian coldly. "I assume, by that question, that *you* are the librarian. Well, you can't expect *me* to know the name of your assistant, now, can you?"

"Dash it all," Griff muttered furiously, "why does Miss Surrey's name crop up in every household crisis?"

"My lord, you can not believe *my betrothed* had anything to do with stealing the Tottel!" the librarian said, appalled.

Finchley-Jones's repeated use of the appellation "betrothed," added to the other nuisances that had beset Griff this afternoon, caused his temper to explode. "Confound it, Finchley-Jones," he thundered, "*stop calling her your betrothed!*"

Lady Mullineaux stared at her son in amazement. "Griff! What on earth's the matter with you? How *can* you speak to Mr. Finchley-Jones in that manner?"

"There's nothing wrong with my manner, Mama. The fellow insists on making the ridiculous claim that he's betrothed to my . . . to Miss Surrey."

"I don't understand," she said, puzzled. "What has that to do with *you?*"

"That is exactly what I was wondering, your ladyship," Finchley-Jones put in.

"Asked him the very same thing myself," Aubrey said, his eyes gleaming mischievously with the certainty that *he* knew the real reason for Griff's extraordinary behavior.

Griff felt a flush creep up from his neck to his ears. "I have my reasons," he said awkwardly. "It seems to me that—"

"My lord?" It was the long-awaited Symonds who stood in the doorway this time.

"Ah, Symonds," Griff said with relief, "there you are. I was beginning to wonder if you were neglecting your duties."

"You know better than that, my lord," the butler replied complacently.

"But, dash it, I don't see Miss Surrey with you. Where is she?"

"I can't seem to find her, my lord. But—"

"Did you look in the library?" Finchley-Jones spoke up nervously.

"Of course. First thing. She's not there, nor is she in her room. But, my lord, there's something else . . ."

"I hope, Symonds, you've not brought us *another* crisis," the Countess remarked. "I don't think I could bear it."

The butler looked at her with as much sympathy as he could appropriately show. "I'm not certain, my lady. It's a pair of callers."

"Callers?" Griff groaned in disgust. "Send them away, man. We can't deal with callers now. Just send them away and go to find Miss Surrey."

"But they insist on seeing her ladyship," the butler said. "They are quite adamant."

"Who are they, for heaven's sake?" her ladyship inquired. "Do we know them?"

"They said that their names will be well known to you. The gentleman is a Sir Jasper Surringham and the lady said you would know her by the name of . . ." He hesitated for a moment, his mouth giving just a hint of his distaste at having to say the word. ". . . Doro."

"Good heavens!" Cornelia exclaimed. "It's *Mama!*"

"Your mother and Sir Jasper!" The Countess clasped her hands together in delight. "Oh, how lovely! They must have come for your ball. Hurry, Symonds, you must fetch them here to us at once. Don't keep them waiting!"

"Yes, my lady," Symonds said, bowing.

But before the butler could leave, Griff's irritated voice stopped him. "And then, Symonds, continue to search for Miss Surrey. I don't want to see you again until you've found her and brought her here! Is that clear?"

The butler bowed again and departed. For the first time

since the Alcorns' arrival, a silence fell upon the party. It was an appropriate time for the Alcorns' and Finchley-Jones to take their leaves, but somehow they made no move to do so. Clara, however, edged nervously toward the door. She understood that matters were about to reach a dramatic climax for her friend, and she anxiously watched for an opportunity to slip out of the room so that she might dash up to the servants' quarters and warn her.

Aubrey, meanwhile, realized that this might finally be his opportunity. "I say, Griff," he muttered *sotto voce,* "do you think that, while we're waiting for the new arrivals, you might introduce me to—?"

"And where," the object of his adoration said nastily to the housemaid at just that moment, "do you think you're going?"

"I beg pardon, ma'am," Clara responded nervously, "I didn't think ye wanted me round no more. Might I be . . . excused?"

"Not yet, young woman," Griff said abstractedly. "Just stay where you are." Unwilling to let anyone guess the turmoil churning within him, Griff remained leaning on the Sheraton table, a picture of outward calm. But he felt like a lion who was chained to his place in a cage and unable to pace about. His reaction to Finchley-Jones's claim to be betrothed to *his* Ada was more violent than he was willing to admit. His mother and his friend had asked what business it was of his, but he was reluctant to answer. The truth was that he couldn't bear the thought of her marrying Finchley-Jones (or anyone else, for that matter), but what right had he to object, unless he intended to marry the girl himself? Marrying her, however, was out of the question. She was impossible. Everything that was happening this afternoon seemed tied up in some way to her maggoty behavior. How could he marry so muddled a female?

The protracted silence roused Alcorn to the realization that he'd long overstayed his intention to depart. "Perhaps it is time, Mullineaux, for *us* to take our leave," he said. "It's quite plain, Julia, that this is not the time for you to air our problems. Let us go."

"No!" Julia said stubbornly. "I've already told you that I won't—"

But at that moment Lady Dorothea appeared in the doorway, raindrops still glistening on her bonnet. *"Cornelia,* my dearest!" she cried in relief, throwing her arms about her daughter's neck in an emotional embrace.

"Doro!" Lady Mullineaux held out a hand in greeting as soon as Cornelia had broken from her mother's arms. "How lovely to see you!"

"Celia!" Lady Dorothea cried, taking the Countess into a second embrace.

"Mama, for heaven's sake," Cornelia scolded after the usual expressions of delight in each other's appearances had been exchanged, "why didn't you *tell* us you were coming?"

But Lady Dorothea could only beam at her daughter and dab at her tearful eyes. "Oh, Cornelia," she murmured thankfully, "you *are* here!"

"What a strange thing to say," Lady Mullineaux remarked. "Of course she's here."

Sir Jasper, who'd followed his sister in and had stood waiting in the background during the exchange of greetings, could contain himself no longer. "You, ma'am, are the Countess Mullineaux, I take it," he said bluntly, making a quick leg before her and putting out his hand. "I'm Jasper Surringham. I don't like roundaboutation, so I'll ask ye straight out. What have ye done with my niece?"

The Countess smiled at him warmly and took the proffered hand. "Nothing dreadful, Sir Jasper, as you can see. She looks blooming, wouldn't you say?"

"Not *that* one!" he growled irritably. "My *Ada!*"

"Who?" Lady Mullineaux asked, not comprehending what he'd asked.

"Ada?" Griff asked, arrested.

"Ada?" Finchley-Jones echoed weakly.

"My Ada!" Jasper repeated impatiently. "Ada, your goddaughter and my niece."

"I don't know what you mean, Sir Jasper," her ladyship said. "I haven't seen your Ada since her birth."

Jasper's face paled. "Are ye sayin', my lady, that she *ain't here?* I sent her to ye more'n three weeks ago!"

"You sent her here? To me? But *Cornelia* is the one who came!"

"You see, Jasper?" Dorothea said triumphantly, embracing her daughter again in delight, "I *told* you it would be so. Cornelia doesn't lie."

Jasper's knees began to tremble. "But the letters..." he muttered, shaken. "She's sent me three letters, all from London. Can she have gone to the wrong house?"

Cornelia, following the conversation with growing amusement, gave a scornful laugh. "Don't tell me that my featherheaded cousin has lost herself again!"

"Isn't that just like Ada?" Dorothea murmured with the selfsatisfied pity that comes from feeling superior to the one being pitied. "She's probably living somewhere not far from here and thinking that she's safe among the Mullineauxs!"

"Come now, Doro. You don't really believe the girl can have found a home among strangers without knowing who they are!" Lady Mullineaux objected. "Do you wish me to believe the girl is witless?"

"I'll have ye know, Celia Mullineaux, that my Ada has more brains—and more character, too—than any young woman I've ever known." Jasper glared directly at Cornelia and Dorothea as he spoke. "An' *present* company *ain't* excepted!"

Griff, his brows knit, looked over at his mother. "There *is* an Ada in this house, you know."

"Good heavens!" Lady Mullineaux's eyes widened. "You don't mean *the girl in the library!*"

A murmur rose in the room. Aubrey sank down in his chair agape. Clara groaned aloud. Mr. Finchley-Jones squealed. "Are you accusing my betrothed *again?*" he demanded in an injured falsetto.

"Damnation, man," Griff snarled, "if you call her your betrothed *once more*, I give you my word I shall land you a facer you won't forget."

"I think I'm becoming quite confused," her ladyship confessed. "Are you saying, Mr. Finchley-Jones, that, being betrothed to Miss Surrey, you believe her to be who she says she is?"

"Yes, your ladyship, I am."

"While on the other hand, you, Griff, believe her to be Sir Jasper's niece?"

"I think it more than likely." Throwing a dagger look at his librarian, he added, "And much more likely than the possibility that she's betrothed to this... this mooncalf!"

Finchley-Jones had had more than his nerves could bear. "You'll eat those words, my lord!" he yowled, waving a knobby, shaking finger under his employer's nose. "You wait and see!

You'll *eat* them! She'll tell you herself, as soon as she comes in—"

"If ever she *does* come in," Griff muttered, throwing an impatient look at the door. "Where on earth can she be hiding?"

"Let me find 'er, m'lord," Clara offered eagerly. "I think I might know where—"

"Not on your life," Cornelia said. "Don't let her go, Griff. She'll only take this opportunity to warn this Ada away."

Jasper had been following these exchanges with intent concentration. "Do I understand ye all t' be sayin' that my Ada *is* in this house?"

"Nonsense," Cornelia declared, feeling quite convinced that her innocuous little cousin and the librarian's assistant could not be one and the same. Ada Surringham could never have managed to create so much interest in her doings as this chit from the library seemed to have done. "If she were here, wouldn't I have seen her?"

"Not necessarily," Lady Mullineaux suggested. "You haven't visited our library since you arrived, have you? Since the girl works there—"

"My Ada? Works in yer *library?*" Jasper asked, horrified.

Celia Mullineaux looked at the elderly man guiltily. "I really don't know, Sir Jasper. If she does, it was without my knowledge or consent, I assure you."

"An' I suppose it was also without yer knowledge or consent that she's gotten herself betrothed t' that scarecrow there?"

"She's *not* betrothed to him!" Griff said through clenched teeth.

"She *is!*" Finchley-Jones insisted, close to hysteria.

"Oh, what a dreadful coil this all is," the Countess murmured.

"Please, m' lord, send me t' find 'er," Clara begged, edging toward the door again.

"I think it would be better—" his lordship began, but a movement at the door stayed his tongue.

It was Symonds in the doorway. "Miss Ada Surrey, my lord," he announced. "She would like a moment of your time, to confess something to you."

"Well, well," Griff said with a perverse satisfaction, "it's about time. Let her in, Symonds, by all means."

Symonds moved aside and Ada, a shabby leather-bound book clutched to her breast, stepped over the threshold. With her eyes lowered in fright she launched immediately into her confession. "I have something I must tell you, my lor—" Her eyes lifted. Gasping in shock, she whitened at the sight of the ten pair of eyes staring at her.

"Come in, Miss Surrey," Griff said with a spider-to-the-fly leer. "We've been waiting for you."

Chapter Nineteen

Her first thought was that a group of constables had gathered to arrest her for thievery. But then she saw her uncle. "Oh, my *God!*" she breathed, wincing.

"Ada!" Jasper gasped, half in relief and half in anger, while everyone in the room began to speak at once.

"Heavens, it *is* she!" Lady Mullineaux muttered to herself. "How could I have failed to recognize the likeness in her eyes? Her mother's eyes *exactly!*"

"Good Lord!" exclaimed Alcorn at the same time, coming to life in excited surprise. "It's the *girl from the Black Boar!* I say, Mullineaux, it's the outside of enough, even for one of your set, to keep your mistress in your own house!"

"Mistress?" Jasper said, his voice choking as he wheeled about. "Did that fellow say *mistress?*"

"No, of course not," Lady Mullineaux assured him quickly while throwing Alcorn a look of angry disapproval. "This is all some sort of mistake—"

"Dash it all, Alcorn," Aubrey said in an outraged undervoice, "hold your blasted tongue."

"*Ada Surringham!*" Cornelia said amid all the babble, striding across the room in a fury, "have you been hiding in the library *all this time?*" Her ire was caused by sheer jealousy at the overwhelming attention being paid to her dowdy, absent-minded, innocuous little cousin (although she had no conscious awareness of this jealousy, being incapable of achieving the objectivity necessary to analyze the weaknesses of one's own character).

Meanwhile, Finchley-Jones dropped down on the nearest chair, his bravado completely deflated. "Then . . . she *isn't* really Ada Surrey, is she?" he mumbled to nobody in particular.

"Never mind all this," Griff said, silencing the uproar with tight-lipped authority and focusing his attention on the girl in the doorway. "It doesn't matter if you're Ada Surrey or Ada Surringham or the daughter of Mama's French cook. Just tell

149

this jobbernowl here that you're *not* betrothed to him!"

Julia, who'd been staring in openmouthed astonishment not at Ada or at Griff but at her husband, spoke up at that moment. "What did you mean, his *mistress?*" she demanded of Alcorn. "I thought the girl at the Black Boar was only a *pretense!*"

Alcorn gave an evil chuckle. "Well, my dear, your lover evidently pulled the wool over your eyes as well as mine. Not only was it no pretense, but she's *still with him!* It is just as I told you when I brought you home from Oxfordshire; Mullineaux has replaced you with someone else."

Julia swung round to Griff, her eyes blazing. It was one thing to be given up in the name of honor; it was quite something else to be replaced, especially by a mere slip of a girl at least five years younger than she. "Is this *true*, Griff?"

"Julia," Griff responded wearily, "go home."

"Answer the question!" Jasper demanded in an agony of confusion. *"Have you compromised my Ada?"*

It was Alcorn who took it upon himself to answer the question. "I don't know who you are, sir, or why this should concern you, even if you *are* the girl's uncle," he said fatuously, quite enjoying the situation now that his wife was getting this much-deserved set-down, "but I can tell you with absolute certainty that Mullineaux spent the night in your niece's bedroom at the Black Boar. I saw him go in with my own eyes."

"You are a *mawworm*, Alcorn," Aubrey said with loathing. "If Griff doesn't fire at you in the duel, I might very well shoot you myself!"

"Oh, my Lord!" Jasper groaned, tottering toward the nearest chair. "Give me a hand, someone. I must . . . sit down."

"You needn't concern yourself any more about the duel, Tait," Alcorn said, cheerfully ignoring the blow he'd dealt the shaken old man. "I think, now that Lord Mullineaux's interests have turned in another direction, I'm quite ready to forgive and forget."

"Magnanimous of you," Griff muttered drily, trying to help Sir Jasper into a chair while keeping his eyes fixed on the wide-eyed girl still standing frozen in the doorway.

"Take yer damned hands off me, ye lecher," Jasper barked, pushing Griff away.

"Take me h-home!" Julia wailed, throwing herself into her husband's arms. "I want to g-go home!"

"Before anyone leaves," Lady Mullineaux suggested, giving

what she hoped was an encouraging smile to the sweet child standing so stiffly in the doorway, "shouldn't we let the poor girl speak for herself?" This was her goddaughter, and a pure innocent (if the expression in those remarkable eyes was to be believed). It was not possible that all the accusations being thrown at her head could be true. "I'm sure there are a few simple explanations she can make to clear everything up, aren't there, my dear?"

Ada's eyes flew from face to face in sheer terror before fixing themselves on Lady Mullineaux's countenance. "Wh-What is it you wish me t-to explain, ma'am?"

The frightened little question stirred a reaction in almost everyone present. "What do we wish ye t' *explain?*" her uncle roared, his voice booming over everyone else's. "*Everything*, that's what!"

There was such a babble of shouts and demands and questions that Ada recoiled. Griff alone said nothing. He knew more of the answers than any of the others in the room, but he was filled with so strong a sense of irritation that it choked him like rage. The girl was infuriating! How had she managed to get herself into such a coil? He told himself that he was positively *enjoying* watching her being tortured by these questions and accusations. She *deserved* to suffer, blast her!

After a moment, however, he held up a hand for silence. "One at a time, please," he ordered. "I'm sure Miss Surringham—it is Miss Surringham, is it not, ma'am?—will be glad to respond to everyone in due course."

"*I*, for one, have no need for questions," Cornelia said in a voice heavy with scorn, "except to ask my 'beloved' cousin if the reason she hid from me in the library all this time was simply because of her dithering, childish cowardice!"

"There are several questions *I* would like to ask, of course," Mr. Finchley-Jones said, forcing himself to speak calmly, although his voice quivered in a register much higher than his normal, nasal tones, "but the most troublesome of them must be answered first. *Did* you, my dear, have anything to do with the theft of the Tottel?"

"*What?*" Aubrey asked, amazed. "Is *that* what's most important to you, you cod's-head? Ain't you going to ask if she's *betrothed* to you?"

"I have no need to ask that," Finchley-Jones responded with pompous certitude. "I already know she is."

"B-Betrothed?" Ada managed, blinking at him.

The librarian paled. "Don't you remember? I know you are sometimes a little woolly-headed, but surely on a matter such as this . . . ! I asked if you didn't agree that we should suit, and you said you'd given it some thought and that you *did* agree. Please say you remember!"

Ada did nothing but gape at him.

"Please say *something*, girl," Aubrey muttered. "*Are* you betrothed to this book-fellow or *ain't you?*"

"Oh, who cares a fig about that!" Julia declared. "What I want to know is if Griff really did go to your bedroom at the Black Boar Inn!"

Sir Jasper nodded in agreement. "Ada, my love, tell us the truth," he begged, quite stricken. "He didn't do such a thing, did he?"

"Of course he didn't," Lady Mullineaux said, patting Jasper's arm soothingly. "My son may be something of a libertine, but I don't believe him capable of seducing innocent young girls."

"Nevertheless, Countess," Alcorn insisted, "I did see them embracing at the inn, and I saw him enter her room. It *was* you at the inn, wasn't it, Miss Surringham? I couldn't be mistaken about that, could I?"

"The question I find much more interesting, Ada, is why you didn't tell me the truth about who you really were," the Countess said thoughtfully. "Am I so forbidding that you had to lie to me?"

If there were any more questions, no one asked them. Every eye was fixed on the girl in the doorway. Ada, however, seemed incapable of speech. She merely stood transfixed in the doorway, her eyes darting from one to the other like a trapped animal watching its trappers, her book still clutched to her breast in terror.

"Well, ma'am, we're waiting," Griff said, fighting back an almost irresistible urge to lift her in his arms and take her away from this inquisition. *She deserves all this*, he told himself, hardening his heart. "You've heard all the questions. What have you to say for yourself?"

Ada stared at them all for a long moment, her eyes filling with tears. Then she took a deep breath and opened her lips to speak, causing everyone in the room to lean forward in rapt attention. "Yes," she said softly. "Yes."

"*Yes?*" echoed someone in disgust. "Is that an answer?"

A veritable torrent of disgruntled remarks followed. "Egad, is something *wrong* with the girl?" Alcorn muttered.

"What on earth does she mean?"

"What sort of response is *that,* I'd like to know?"

It was another uproar. Griff held up a hand to silence them again. "Surely, girl," he said, scowling, "you can do better than that."

"But th-that *is* my answer," Ada said, her lips trembling and tears running down her cheeks. "Yes, I am Miss Surringham, and yes, I did lie to everyone about that. Yes, my cousin is quite right about my cowardice . . . I *was* too cowardly to admit to her and to my uncle that I'd arrived here too late. And about the b-betrothal to Mr. Finchley-Jones, I must say yes to that, too. I don't remember his asking m-me, but I do remember saying that I agree with him . . . about something. I must have been woolgathering, but if he says that it was an *offer* which I agreed to, then I . . . I suppose it must be so. And if I agreed to his offer, then I must indeed c-consider myself his betrothed. As for the situation at the Black Boar, you know the answer as well as I, my lord. It is also yes. Yes, you *d-did* come to my bedroom at the Black Boar, as you v-very well know, and yes, it was I whom Lord Alcorn saw being embraced by you in the dining room of the inn. I . . . I'm sorry, Uncle Jasper, to have brought such sh-shame on you, but my answer is yes to . . . to everything having to do with the Black Boar Inn. And I must give a yes even to you, your ladyship. I *did* find you f-forbidding and was ashamed to admit to you that I had come all this way in Cornelia's wake. I should n-never have come. I should have known that I'd be in her wake th-this time, too. And . . . and the final yes, your lordship . . . I *did* take your book. Here . . . I've b-brought it back to you. The truth is that I thought the m-missing book was c-called the *Miscellany,* so I had no idea that this, being c-called the *Songes and Sonnettes,* was the Tottel. I know it was featherheaded of me n-not to have noticed, but if you th-think I f-filched it on purpose, I don't m-mind. I'd rather be thought a thief than a b-bubblehead, although with all th-these yeses, I know you m-must really judge me to be b-both!"

She dashed the tears from her cheeks with the back of one hand and thrust the Tottel into Griff's arms with the other. Everyone in the room was staring at her, stricken speechless.

She looked round at them one last time and then ran to the door. "Ada—!" Griff said, his voice hoarse. He took a step toward her.

She paused in the doorway and shook her head, keeping her face turned away. "Please let me g-go, your lordship," she said with a little, negative gesture of her hand. "I h-haven't anything else to s-say, except that if you are going to c-call the magistrates to take m-me to prison, they can find me w-waiting in my room." With that, and one last little sob, she was gone.

Chapter Twenty

After Ada's disappearance, no one moved. Each seemed to be experiencing a feeling of dismay, not at Ada's behavior but at his own. Although the girl's little speech had been filled with admissions of guilt, the aura she'd left behind was one of innocence. Everyone in the room, even Cornelia, wondered how much his or her conduct had contributed to Ada's obvious misery. Only Clara was not smitten with guilt, and thus it was she who recovered first. "Ain't ye all ashamed o' yersels?" she muttered, stalking to the door. "Drivin' the poor thing t' tears with yer questions! An' if yer sittin' there thinkin' that she's done anything out o' the way, yer touched in yer upper works. I don't care that she said yes t'all yer accusations. I wouldn't care if she confessed t' murderin' 'er grandmama. Anyone who knows 'er at all would know she couldn't do nothing bad. The worst thing ye can say she done was t' use that there book as a prop fer 'er mirror!"

Having spoken her mind, she flew quickly out of the room. She had no doubt that "deevine retribution" for her insolence would be delivered upon her head at any moment, but at least it would not be in the drawing room in front of all those strangers.

"That saucy chit should be sacked at once," Cornelia muttered as soon as she'd recovered her usual aplomb.

"That saucy chit," Griff said, leaning against the table, an abstracted expression in his eyes, "is quite right. Ada hasn't done anything wrong, and it was despicable of us all to set on her like that."

"Are you saying, old fellow, that the girl is *not* your mistress?" Alcorn asked nastily, trying (despite an inner instinct that told him he was wrong) to cling to his comfortable conclusions.

"Really, Lord Alcorn," the Countess said, "isn't it plain as the nose on your face that she couldn't be? A child like that wouldn't even know how to go about it!"

"You're right, my lady," Jasper said, rising from his chair, the ruddy color returning to his cheeks as his spirit recovered its normal resiliency. "I don't know what made me even *think* it could be true. I know my girl; she may be a bit absentminded at times, but she hasn't the nature fer subterfuge or indecency. I owe her an apology fer thinkin' otherwise."

"Then why did she admit to all that business at the Black Boar?" Julia demanded.

"To protect me, I think," Griff admitted. "She agreed to the *pretense* of an affair to help me prevent a duel, and when she saw Alcorn here today, she didn't want to undo what we'd done. I assure you, Sir Jasper, that that's all it was—a pretense. If I'd known her better, I would never have asked her even to *pretend* to such behavior. Forgive me for it. But she was not in the least compromised by the pretense. My valet can vouch for that. He saw me climb into the window of my own room only a short while after I entered hers."

"So *that's* how it was done! In at her door and out at her window, eh?" Lord Alcorn muttered. "I ought to put a bullet into you for that trick alone!"

"I've heard enough about bullets and duels," the Countess said coldly. "Take your wife home, Lord Alcorn. After listening to your blustering this afternoon without much comment, I think I've earned the right to offer some advice. Spend a little more of your energies in attending to your wife—in listening to her wishes and trying to please her—and a little less on trying to arrange duels. If you do, perhaps you'd find your life more satisfying."

"Yes, Alcorn, take me home," Julia agreed with a sigh. "I'm feeling worn to the bone. I think I'm becoming to old for these theatrics. Perhaps I shall go to your mother's after all. I shall sit near the fire with her all day, rocking and embroidering, trying to grow old with grace and serenity."

"You, old?" her husband said, tenderly placing the hood of her cloak on her head. "Never, my dear, never." As he led her to the door, he glanced back at the Countess with a questioning glance. The Countess nodded her approval. Pleased with himself, Alcorn leaned down and whispered in his wife's ear, "And I shan't send you to my mother, so you needn't worry about that. I don't intend to let you out of my sight again."

Julia looked up at him in surprise. Then, with a quick glance over her shoulder at Griff, she sighed in meek acceptance of her fate. However, even in this significant moment (which she was wise enough to realize was the start of a new life of obedient, compliant, wifely boredom), Julia was conscious of the audience's eyes on her and made the most of her exit. Resting her head prettily upon her husband's shoulder, she let him lead her from the room.

The Countess expelled a relieved breath at their departure. "And now, Doro, let me take you upstairs and show you to your room. You, too, Sir Jasper. We all must begin to ready ourselves, you know. I hope you haven't forgotten tonight's festivities."

"Oh, yes, Mama," Cornelia agreed, her face clearing for the first time that afternoon, "do come upstairs. You must see the gown I've chosen for the ball."

The ladies and Sir Jasper left the room. Mr. Finchley-Jones and Aubrey were the only guests remaining in Griff's company. Mr. Finchley-Jones took out a handkerchief, removed his spectacles and began to rub them briskly. "I think that perhaps I owe you an apology, your lordship."

"Whatever for?" Griff asked.

"It seems that I am not betrothed after all."

Griff shrugged. "On the contrary, the lady admitted that you are."

"The lady admitted to a great many things that apparently are not quite true."

"I'm glad you see it that way, Finchley-Jones," Aubrey put in. "It seems to me that it wouldn't be fair to expect the girl to live up to a bargain she wasn't aware of agreeing to."

"No, it wouldn't," the librarian agreed. He put his lorgnette back on his nose with renewed firmness and faced his employer once again. "But I must tell you, my lord, that I intend to renew my suit as soon as an opportunity presents itself."

"You must do as you think best," Griff said quietly.

"But you really don't approve, do you?" the librarian accused. "Why is that, your lordship? Do you think that the lady is too far above me in birth and station?"

"I have no right either to approve or disapprove," Griff told him. "And as for her station, I have known of cases where the disparity is far greater and yet the matches led to sound marriages."

"I say, Griff, you ain't *encouraging* the fellow, are you?"

"Are you, your lordship?" Finchley-Jones inquired, studying his employer dubiously.

Griff looked up at his librarian with what seemed to be an effort. His mind seemed to be preoccupied, and it was with great difficulty that he focused on Finchley-Jones's question. "I'm neither encouraging nor discouraging. I'm merely pointing out that you have every right to do as you wish in this matter."

The librarian frowned. "I see. Well, then, there's not much more to be said. I intend to pursue my suit at the first opportunity. I owe it to the lady . . . and to myself."

"Yes, I think you do," Griff agreed. "But you will understand if I refrain from wishing you good luck in that endeavor."

"Oh, yes. Quite well. I am not familiar with the ways of the polite world, your lordship, but I am not such a fool that I did not recognize the . . . er . . . feelings that exist between you and Miss Surrey . . . Surringham—"

"Clever of you, old boy," Aubrey muttered drily under his breath.

"I suppose," Finchley-Jones went on, "that I am unlikely to succeed in my suit. However, if I fail, I shall not repine. It became clear to me this afternoon that Miss Surringham is not quite what I thought she was."

Aubrey glared at the fellow belligerently. "I hope you ain't suggesting, you greenhead, that there's something *wrong* with Miss Surringham?"

"Never mind, Aubrey," Griff said in restraint. "I don't think it appropriate to discuss Miss Surringham's character at the moment."

"I quite agree," the librarian said. "I have my opinion, and discussion is unlikely to change it." He lowered his head and cleared his throat. "I trust, my lord, that this . . . er . . . rivalry . . . will not interfere with our association in the library work."

"Of course it won't," his lordship assured him. "In fact, I wish you will take this damned Tottel and put it somewhere safe. I've had enough difficulty over it to last me a lifetime."

"Yes, my lord. At once." The librarian took hold of the book and glanced down at it with awe before taking his departure. One glance at the worn volume and all the afternoon's tension seemed to vanish from his face. With the Tottel in his hands, he was himself again. His touch and the way he looked at the book were more loving and tender than they would ever be toward a woman.

As soon as Finchley-Jones had left, Aubrey leaned back in his chair. "Whew!" he said, putting his feet up on the hassock. "What an afternoon! For a while, I thought we'd have shooting right here in the drawing room. That Alcorn is a damned nail!"

Griff, still abstracted, brushed his hair from his forehead with the back of a hand. "I must say, Aubrey, you were a brick throughout all that nonsense. Don't think I wasn't aware of your loyalty."

"Hummph!" Aubrey grunted in acknowledgment.

Something in the sound caught Griff's attention. "Is something wrong, Aubrey? You sounded gruff. I think this afternoon has been difficult for both of us. Would you care to join me in a madeira?"

"No, I wouldn't," Aubrey said frankly. "Not in the mood to drink with you today."

Griff's right eyebrow climbed up. "No? Why not?"

"Something on my mind. I'm going to say it flat out before taking myself off." He took a deep breath before going on. "I have a good mind to call you out myself, Griff."

"Call me out? Is this some sort of joke? Whatever for?"

"For calling that sweet chit a maggoty female!"

Griff turned to his friend, now fully attentive. "By the term 'sweet chit,' do you mean Ada?"

"Of course I mean Ada! Who else?"

"You liked her, eh?"

"Who wouldn't? You certainly weren't very kind to her. And how could you describe her as maggoty?"

Griff threw his friend a rueful glance. "Because she *is* maggoty. Using my Tottel to shore up her mirror! I should have wrung her neck."

"If I hear any more about that deuced book, I'll wring *your* neck! Maggoty indeed! If you ask me, you're damned lucky to have won the affections of a girl like that."

"Do you think I've won her affections?"

"Without a doubt. It's midsummer moon with her as far as you're concerned."

Griff frowned and turned away. "An expert in these matters, are you?"

'Not in the least. But anyone with half an eye could have seen it when she looked at you today. Even that clunch

Finchley-Jones saw it. Are you going to offer for her, Griff?"

"Offer for her? Are you mad?" Griff strode across the room, pushed aside the fireplace screen and gave the grate a vicious kick, sending a shower of sparks flying up into the room. "Dash it, I'm as confused as a schoolboy. I had all I could do to keep from taking her into my arms this afternoon when she made that brave little speech. But she *is* such a deuced bubblehead, you know. How can one wed a girl like that?" He stared into the flickering flames glumly. "Can you imagine what life would be like with her? I'd be spending my days listening to her answering questions I'd asked an hour before, watching her lose her spectacles for the tenth time in a day, or searching for my *Times* that she's somehow mislaid. I think, in those circumstances, I'd be bound to turn nasty. You know how little patience I have for maggoty females."

"Don't use that word in connection with her again, Griff, I warn you. If you do, I shall plant you a facer! I suppose she *is*, as your librarian said, a little woolly-headed, and I ain't saying that a woolly-headed female would suit Griff Mullineaux as a wife, but to call the girl maggoty is going too far."

Griff turned his head to throw his friend a contrite grin. "Very well, that word will never again cross my lips. Shall we send for the madeira and drink on it?"

"No, not for me." With a real effort of will, he pulled himself from the chair. "I'd better get home and change."

Griff had turned back to his melancholy contemplation of the fire. "I'll see you out, then," he said without turning.

"No need for that. I can see myself to the door." Aubrey crossed to a pier table near the door where he'd left his hat and cane so many hours earlier. Picking them up, he remarked, "It's been a most interesting afternoon. Can't remember when I've been so vastly entertained."

"Oh, yes. Vastly entertaining," Griff muttered bitterly. "Lives falling apart everywhere, but vastly entertaining."

"Nevertheless, it was as good as a play."

Griff again noticed something in his friend's voice. Turning, he peered at him in sudden suspicion. "You don't look as if you've been entertained," he said. "You look a bit down in the mouth."

"Do I?" Aubrey shrugged. "If I do, it's only because I'm not looking forward to tonight's affair with the eagerness I felt earlier."

"Confound it," Griff swore in annoyance with himself, "it's because of Cornelia, isn't it? I never managed the introduction! I'm a selfish clod. But cheer up, old fellow, I'll make it up to you at once. I'll get the girl down here if I have to drag her by the hair! Just wait right here—"

"No, Griff, don't bother," his friend said glumly.

Griff stopped in the doorway. "Why not?"

"I don't know." Aubrey put on his hat, adjusted the angle and strolled out into the hallway. "It's funny, but . . . after hearing her talk to her little cousin the way she did today . . . I seem to have changed."

"Changed? In what way changed?"

"It's hard to explain. She doesn't look the same to me."

"Are you saying, old man, that you no longer want to capture Cornelia's attention? I find that hard to believe. Less than an hour ago you were whispering to me that she was ravishing."

Aubrey shook his head, nonplussed. "Can't account for it at all, Griff," he said as he sauntered down the hall, "but the ravishing Cornelia don't seem quite so beautiful after all."

Chapter Twenty-One

Ada sat huddled in a corner of her bed, her knees up under her chin and her arms embracing her legs, staring out ahead of her with unseeing eyes, daydreaming. She'd made a complete fool of herself before everyone who mattered in her life, but she felt to drained to weep. When the bottom falls out of one's world, tears seem inadequate. Ada had only one way of coping with disaster, and that was to escape from the reality of it. She was very good at that sort of escape. In daydreams she always found comfort.

At this moment, she was imagining herself the heroine in a slightly altered world. In her dream, she was a self-assured, capable, sensible noblewoman—very much like the Countess, but younger. She was married to a handsome, dashing Viscount who happened to be named Griff, and she presided over his home with amazing competence. Her parties were always the talk of the *ton;* perfect down to the smallest detail, they were universally admired. A card for one of her galas was the most sought-after of all social invitations. Everyone from the influential Princess Lieven to the Regent himself found it remarkable that Ada Mullineaux's parties never suffered from the slightest disaster; her famous lobster patties were never overcooked, the champagne was never warm, the guests were never incompatible, the rooms were never too hot, and no one ever had to walk from his coach in the rain. In her dream, the Regent arrived at her door, kissed her hand and said, "How is it, Lady Ada, that the rain never falls on the evenings of your galas?"

Her husband, who stood beside her greeting the guests, looked down at her with unmistakable affection and took it upon himself to respond. "Didn't you know, Prinny, that my Ada is especially favored by the Almighty?"

"Yes, I know. You are a lucky dog, Griff Mullineaux. Everyone says that she—"

A knock on the door caused her dream to evaporate instantly. She knew that it *couldn't* be the magistrates—Lady Mullineaux would certainly not permit her son to send for them to arrest her very own goddaughter—but her heart hammered nervously in her chest anyway. "Wh-who's there?"

"It's I, my love, Celia Mullineaux. I've come to fetch you to your new room."

"New room?" Ada opened the door warily. "What new—?"

"You surely didn't think I would permit my very own god-daughter to remain in the servants' quarters, did you?" The Countess stood before the door, smiling at her fondly. Looming behind her was Clara, her ruddy face beaming brightly enough to light up the dark hallway. "Clara will help you move your things. You'll like having her as your own abigail, won't you?"

Ada could do nothing but gape. Clara, as she passed her coming into the room, hissed in her ear, "Say 'yes,' you noddy, afore she changes 'er mind!"

"Oh . . . y-yes, yes, of course, but . . ."

"I want to hear no buts," her ladyship ordered. "I'm quite put out with you already for hiding your identity. Now, don't look so stricken. I'm more put out with *myself* for not recognizing you immediately when I met you in the library. If only I had known who you were, I would have been able to present *you* tonight along with Cornelia. It would have made me so happy to be able to do so. But I won't permit you, you foolish child, to deny me any further opportunities to fuss over you. Come along, like a good girl, and don't argue. We have a great deal to do before the guests begin to arrive. I have a gown and a seamstress waiting in the lavender bedroom, where you shall stay as long as this visit lasts."

Her ladyship did not wait for a reply but merely turned and started down the corridor with a purposeful stride. Ada had no choice but to scamper after her. Clara tottered along in the rear, carrying as many of Ada's belongings as she could bear in her arms. "But your ladyship," Ada said breathlessly, trying to keep up with the energetic woman, "I can't—"

"You must call me Cecy, as your mother did," her ladyship threw over her shoulder."

"Oh, I couldn't *possibly*—"

"Of course you can," her ladyship assured her. "You must learn, my dearest girl, to overcome this distressing tendency of yours to belittle yourself."

"'Ear, 'ear!" Clara chortled from the rear.

Before she knew how it had happened, Ada found herself standing before a tall mirror in the prettiest bedroom she'd ever seen, being fitted into a ball gown of shiny, light blue lustring trimmed with corded satin. The seamstress was nipping in some seams to tighten the high waistline, but the gown otherwise was a perfect fit. Clara assisted the seamstress by pulling out pins when directed to do so, but when not thus occupied, she passed the time by grinning in happy admiration at her friend in the mirror.

"I knew it would suit you," her ladyship said, also looking happily at Ada's reflection in the mirror. Lady Mullineaux was overjoyed that the girl she'd liked so much in the library had turned out to be her goddaughter. And she was very pleased with herself for having found, in so short a time, the perfect gown for her goddaughter to wear to tonight's ball. She could do nothing about the fact that Cornelia would be the star of the evening, but at least Ada would not be overlooked. Not with the blue-and-silver creation which she'd managed to find among her stored clothes. "I used to wear it when I was young," she said, admiring the way the full skirt fell away from a knot of gathers at the rear, low-cut neckline, "but it doesn't suit a woman my age, so it's been on the shelf for many years. I assure you, no one will guess it's a hand-me-down."

"It is beautiful, my la...Cecy, but I can't take it. I don't...wish to attend the ball in any case."

"But you *must* attend," her ladyship insisted. "My dear, you must do it for me! Don't you know how long I've yearned to have you here with me, to fuss over you and dress you and show you off to my friends?"

"*Me,* your ladyship? But you have *Cornelia.*"

"Cornelia is...well, let us not say what Cornelia is. She is very beautiful, of course, and I've enjoyed having her with me, but she is not as special to me as you are. Besides, she has a very devoted mother of her own, while you have none. And I have no daughter of my own. Won't you let me have the pleasure of playing your mother?"

"But...you have a son—"

Lady Mullineaux laughed. "Yes, so I do." She studied the girl's face in the mirror with a sudden intent interest. "What do you think of my libertinish son, Ada?"

"He is not really libertinish, I believe," Ada said, coloring.

"It seems to me that he is . . . very kind and . . . m-manly . . ."

"Yes, I quite agree," her ladyship said, her curiosity satisfied. "But a son is not the same as a daughter, you know. Besides, it is many years since Griff Mullineaux needed mothering. So you see, my love, I *need* you. Will you say you'll come to the ball and make your godmother happy?"

"If you put it like that, my la . . . Cecy, how can I say no?"

Her ladyship tried to embrace her goddaughter and received a puncture with a pin for her pains. "Oh, well," she laughed, "first things first. There will be a time for embracing later." She remained in the room until the seamstress finished the alteration and draped Ada with the silver gauze overdress that gave the gown its finishing touch. "There!" her ladyship said, studying Ada with her head cocked. "You look lovely. And now I must rush off and ready myself. Clara, I shall leave it to you to dress my girl's hair. Take down that knot and let a curl fall over her shoulder. She's too young to wear her hair in so severe a style."

"Yes, m'lady," the beaming Clara promised. "I'll 'ave 'er brushed an' ready in a trice."

"And when you've finished, come to me in my bedroom. I have a string of pearls for Ada to wear tonight, so as soon as you're free, Clara, please come and fetch them. Now, now, Ada my love, don't open your mouth to object. They are a very special gift that I've been saving for you since you were born."

This time they *did* embrace. "Oh, Lady Cecy," Ada said, quite overcome, "you are being t-too k-kind to me. I d-don't deserve it."

"You see? You *do* need a mother," Lady Mullineaux said, her voice also choked with emotion. "You need a mother to tell you how very deserving you are."

After she took her leave, Clara let out a whoop of joy. "Ain't this the most wonderful pass?" she chortled, hugging her friend, gathering her up in a tight hold and whirling her about the room in a hilarious polka. "Did ye ever *dream* that things'd turn out s' fine?"

"I dreamed it, Clara," Ada said when she'd fallen down upon the bed to catch her breath. "In fact I'm not certain that I'm not dreaming now."

"I'll pinch ye, ye goosecap, an' then ye'll be certain." Clara, grinning, took her hand and pulled her up. "Come on, get up an' let me dress yer 'air. Oh, Ada, isn't that gown a wonder? Ye'll be the most beautiful girl at the ball, see if ye ain't!"

• The thought of attending the ball caused Ada's glow to fade. She didn't want to go to the ball and face Lord Mullineaux again. The look on his face when she'd come in with his book was engraved on her soul like a brand. She could still hear the scornful irony of his voice when he'd said, *Come in, Miss Surringham. It is Miss Surringham, isn't it?* "Must I go, Clara?" she asked plaintively as she sat down at the charming ebony and brass dressing table topped with marble. "I shall only make a fool of myself again."

"Look at yerself, girl," Clara said firmly. "Look at the girl in the mirror. Are ye tryin' t' pretend she ain't goin' to be the belle o' the evenin'?"

Ada looked. The dress seemed to emphasize the color of her eyes, and the gauzy overdress made her seem wrapped in a cloud. Clara was brushing her hair into one long coil, and by the time she placed it over her shoulder (shockingly bare because of the low décolletage of the gown), Ada hardly recognized the girl looking back at her. That was not a country mouse in the glass but a very presentable young woman. Ada blushed at the unaccustomed feeling of looking pretty. "I hardly know it's I," she whispered.

Clara knelt down beside her. "Ye know, Ada," she said conspiratorially, "I think we were wrong about 'er ladyship wishin' fer Miss 'Aydon t' wed 'is lordship. I think she 'as 'er eye on *you!*"

Ada felt her heart constrict. "Don't even *think* such a thing, Clara! His lordship doesn't approve of me."

"Because of that *book?*" Clara stood up, laughing scornfully. "When 'e sees ye tonight, 'e'll forget all about the blasted book. Y'know, it's my view ye'd make 'is lordship a *perfect* wife." She burst into a guffaw. "Better even than ye'd make fer Mr. Finchley-Jones! When ye wed 'is lordship, Ada, an' set up yer own establishment, will ye take me as yer abigail?"

"You can be with me forever, Clara, if you want to. But don't go on about my marrying his lordship. I don't think I shall ever marry anyone."

"That's rot. But I won't speak of it if ye don't wish it. Now, ye just sit tight an' wait fer me. I'm goin' t' fetch the pearls."

* * *

When the family and the houseguests gathered in the drawing room before the guests were due to arrive, Ada's entrance caused a pleasant stir. She had paused in the doorway, hesitating in nervous fear of facing the same people who had, only two hours earlier, been witnesses to the most humiliating scene of her life. The first person to notice her was her godmother. "Ah, Ada," the Countess said in delighted greeting, coming to the door and taking her in. She kissed Ada's cheek and nodded with approval at her appearance. Then she turned and announced to the assemblage, "See, everyone, what a lovely goddaughter I have!"

Her uncle beamed proudly at the picture Ada made, and he came over and whispered into her ear an apology for his earlier behavior. "We won't say anythin' more about yer hidin' in the library all these weeks, either. If ye'll forgive me, I'll forgive you."

Symonds, passing among the company with a tray of glasses of champagne, so far forgot himself as to gape at her transformation, and Lawrence, the underfootman (who Clara had said was enamored of her and who was stationed at the drawing-room doorway to open and close the doors), gasped aloud when he recognized her.

"Good heavens, Ada," Lady Dorothea exclaimed in grudging admiration, "you haven't a *thing* out of place. I'd almost not have known you."

But Ada hardly heard her. She was heart-stoppingly conscious of the fact that Lord Mullineaux himself was approaching. His lordship gazed down at her with an unmistakable glow in his eyes. "You take my breath away," he murmured and kissed her hand.

"Thank you, my lord," she said in a tiny voice, unable to meet his eyes.

"We *do* have an understanding about the second dance, do we not?" he asked with a grin.

But Cornelia chose that moment to make *her* entrance, and beside *that* everything else paled. The girl was truly magnificent in her green silk gown that whispered as she walked. Her eyes were shining, her manner was animated, and it was plain to everyone that the evening would be hers.

And so it proved to be. From the moment the ball officially began, when his lordship walked onto the dance floor with Cornelia on his arm to the first flourish of the music, Cornelia held every eye. She was surrounded as soon as the dance ended, and for the rest of the evening she was never without a circle of eager admirers.

Ada was asked to dance the first dance by a callow youth who looked to be not a day over twenty. He was not particularly adept at the movement of the dance, and Ada was not adept at avoiding his errors. As a result, her toes were mangled by the dance's end, there was a dark smudge on one of her stockings, and the fellow had managed to step upon the hem of her gown and tear a piece completely off.

She wanted to run off and hide, but she *was* promised to Griff, she supposed, for the second dance. She refused two other invitations while she waited for him, but he was nowhere to be seen. When the dancers had all taken their places in the sets and the music began, she felt sick with humiliation. Tears formed in the corners of her eyes. If they actually slid down her cheeks and were seen by anyone in the crowd, she knew she would die of embarrassment. To avoid that fate, she went quickly out of the ballroom amd down the hall.

She found herself in the back part of the hallway, just opposite the library. That room, she knew, was not open to the partygoers. If there was anywhere in the house to hide, that was the place. She opened the door and slipped into the darkened room. She knew her way about quite well and was able, without mishap, to find the lamp on her worktable and light it with the tinderbox she knew was kept on the mantel. But before she could sit down and take a deep breath, the door opened. "I thought I'd find you here," Mr. Finchley-Jones said.

He came in without being asked and shut the door behind him. Ada was surprised to see how elegantly he was garbed. The points of his shirt were as high as those of the greatest dandy, his neckerchief was beautifully tied, his coat was well cut, his ecru waistcoat was in the best of taste, and his dancing shoes bore a pair of dashing rosettes. "You look very fine, Mr. Finchley-Jones," she said. "Are you enjoying the ball?"

"Not very much," he said, taking a stance midway between the door and her table. "I've spent the past half-hour searching through the crowd for you."

"For me?" she asked, suddenly feeling uncomfortable.

"Yes, Miss Surringham, for you. There is something I feel must be . . . er . . . clarified between us."

Only then did she remember. "You're referring to the

. . . betrothal that was mentioned this afternoon, I suppose."

"Yes. I am sorry that we did not understand each other during our last conversation on the subject."

"It is I who should be sorry, Mr. Finchley-Jones. It's inexcusable for a woman to be woolgathering when a gentleman is . . . is making an offer."

"I, however, will be happy to excuse you, ma'am. I know your tendency to be absentminded. I knew it when I offered. Of course, I did *not* know that you are a Surringham and a protégée of my employers. If I had known, I don't think I would have presumed . . ."

Ada did not wish to hurt him. Having no experience in dealing with unwelcome suitors, she wondered what she was expected to say. "I do not consider it a presumption, sir," she told him, sinking down on her familiar chair. "Your having made me an offer is very flattering, I assure you. However, under the circumstances, I shan't hold you to it."

"Nor I hold *you* to it." He advanced a step closer to her. "I've thought it over very carefully since this afternoon, and I've decided that the only gentlemanly thing to do is to make the offer again, ascertaining quite particularly *this time* that you are attending me with full consciousness."

"I am attending you, sir, but—"

"But you do not wish to accept?"

She looked over at him in the room's dim light, feeling an unaccountable urge to laugh. "I have the distinct feeling, Mr. Finchley-Jones, that you are hoping I won't. Have the events of the afternoon affected your original intentions?"

She felt rather than saw him wince. "I did find the details of your . . . er . . . escapades . . . rather shocking," he admitted.

"And you would be relieved, I think, to hear me refuse you. Well, sir, you may be happy. You have been as gentlemanly as humanly possible, and I absolve you of all obligations to me."

There was a moment of awkward silence. Then Mr. Finchley-Jones gave her a low, formal bow and turned to go. At the door, he paused. "Tell me, Miss Surringham, if you had been attending the first time I offered for you, would you have accepted me then?"

She shook her head. "No, I'm sorry, Mr. Finchley-Jones, but I would not."

He sighed a sad, deep sigh. "I see. It is too bad. For a

while, I was so . . . joyful." Then he took himself in hand. He had been made a fool of, made to suffer and had been rejected. He would not retreat without a parting shot of his own. "You have someone else in your heart, I know. I feel quite sorry for you, Miss Surringham. The one you dream of is not for you."

Ada stiffened. "What can you possibly know of my dreams, sir?" she asked coldly.

"I am bookish, Miss Surringham, but not blind. But his lordship will not make the mistake I made, the mistake of offering for you. He thinks you a maggoty female. That was his very word for you. Maggoty. I myself heard him say it."

With that cruel shot, he turned about on his rosetted shoes and left her alone.

Chapter Twenty-Two

The rain had not abated all day, so not one of Lady Mullineaux's guests was able to come to the party on foot. By the time the Regent arrived, the crush of carriages outside Mullineaux House was dreadful. No lady wished to make her entrance with rain spattered on her best cloak or soaked into her carefully curled coiffure, so every driver was ordered to maneuver his carriage as close to the front door as possible. Thus it was that the Prince Regent's own carriage collided with that of Lord and Lady Somerset, causing irritation and ill feelings on both sides. Griff, called upon to untangle the coil and soothe ruffled feelings, was therefore not in the ballroom during the second dance. He and Prinny were on intimate terms, however, and after Griff had accompanied his highness up the stairs and across the ballroom (the entire party having divided itself into two rows and formed an aisle down the center of the room along which the Regent, his retinue, Lady Mullineaux and her son paraded, Prinny stopping to shake hands and exchange quips with the many guests with whom he was on easy terms) and finally ensconced him at one of the card tables in the card room off the ballroom, he was able to excuse himself without giving offense. He immediately went to look for Ada to make his apologies.

But he couldn't find her. He searched the dance floor, the dowager's corner, and along the sides of the room where the chairs and sofas were lined up. He looked behind every potted palm. She was not there. He even sent a footman up to her old room in the servants' quarters and her new room in the west wing, but she was not to be found.

It was Finchley-Jones who led him to her. The librarian had come up to him to say goodnight. "Thank you, your lordship, for inviting me," he said stiffly, "but it is time for me to retire."

"Nonsense, Finchley-Jones," Griff said firmly, "you must stay for supper. My mother has arranged a veritable feast which I'm certain you will find worth the wait. By the way, you haven't seen Miss Surringham anywhere, have you? I've been looking for her."

Finchley-Jones looked at him strangely. "I saw her a short while ago. I think you'll find her in the library."

"The library? Why on earth is she hiding there?" But he didn't wait for an answer.

He crossed the hallway almost at a run and threw open the door. In the faint light of the lamp he saw that her head was resting on her arms folded on the table. Was the girl *asleep?* "Ada?" he asked, his voice tentative.

She started, her head coming up abruptly, and he could see that she'd been weeping. "Your *l-lordship!*" she said in obvious alarm.

"I didn't mean to startle you." He came in and closed the door. "I only came to claim my dance."

She shifted round on her chair so that he couldn't see her face. "You m-missed your dance," she said, brushing away the wetness from her cheeks with one unsteady hand.

"Yes, I know. I do apologize for that. My duties as host prevented my appearing. Prinny arrived at just the wrong moment, you see, and—"

"There's no need to explain," she said in a distant, formal way that was completely unlike her. "I did very well without you."

"Did you indeed? Who was the bounder who took my place?" he asked, trying to lighten her mood. "I shall challenge him to a duel—swords, of course—and run him through."

She didn't laugh. "I didn't dance. I was here, receiving an offer of marriage."

"Oh?" He came forward curiously. "Has Finchley-Jones been at it again?"

"Yes, but he was . . . quite relieved when I refused him." She lowered her head, still keeping her face averted. "It seems that, when a gentleman becomes familiar with . . . with the quirks in my character, he realizes how fortunate he is not to have any connection with me."

He walked round her chair and stood for a moment looking down at her. Then he lifted her chin. In the dim light the tears on her cheeks sparkled like diamonds, and her eyes looked almost ghostly. "Finchley-Jones is an ass," he muttered, feeling a decided constriction in his chest at the sight of her.

"Mr. Finchley-Jones is a gentleman of rare good sense,"

she said. Her manner was strangely cold. "He knows better than to ally himself with a . . . a . . . m-maggoty female."

Griff drew in a breath and dropped his hold on her. "Maggoty?" He could feel his hands tighten into fists. "Did he call you that?"

"No, but I . . . Never mind. I don't wish to talk about it any more."

"But I'm afraid you must. You see, I intend to make an offer for you myself."

Her remarkable eyes widened in shock. "You?"

"Yes, I. Shall I get down on one knee and do it now?"

She put out her hands as if in terror. "No! If this is some sort of joke, my lord, I must tell you that I am not amused by it."

He stared at her in confusion. "You behave as if an offer from me would revolt you. You must know by this time that I love you, Ada. What makes you think I'm joking?"

"You must be joking! You've told me several times that you don't care for bubbleheaded females. And after today you're surely aware of how bubbleheaded I really am."

"I was beastly to you today. I admit it. It was because I realized how much I loved you . . . and I hated myself for it. I didn't want to love you, you see. Despite my reputation as a libertine, I've never really loved a woman before."

"No!" She held her hands up to her ears. "I don't want to listen to this. I don't want to be told that you l-love me in spite of yourself!" She jumped to her feet. "You told Mr. Finchley-Jones that I'm a maggoty female, did you not? Then surely you will thank me, when you've had time to think this over, for not permitting you make me an offer. Let it never be said that the notorious libertine, Ivor Griffith Viscount Mullineaux, attached himself to someone maggoty!"

She turned and made a dash for the door, but he caught up with her in two long strides and pulled her into his arms. "Maggoty you may be," he muttered, tightening his hold, "but you do make the most irresistibly trenchant speeches." He held her imprisoned against him with one arm and lifted her face tenderly with his free hand. "I love you, idiot girl," he said softly, "and I think you love me. Don't you realize that nothing else matters?"

He kissed her then, and for a long time nothing else did matter. She could only marvel at the singing in her blood, the dizzying magic of his nearness, the inexpressible superiority of his actual, physical closeness to her imagined dreams. The experience was too exciting to permit her to think of anything else.

But the moment he released her, the pain returned. She *was* a maggoty female, and as soon as he'd recovered from this temporary madness he would wonder how he'd forgotten that fact. It was her place to help him remember it. "Please," she said breathlessly, holding him off, "don't kiss me again. There is a great deal else that matters. You don't know what I'm really like. If you did, you'd never wish to—"

"Ada, *listen* to me! I don't care about—"

"You *must* care. We are speaking of wedlock, not a night in a country inn. If we were wed, I should drive you to distraction in a week. Do you know that I sometimes don't remember what day of the week it is? And I—"

"Is this going to be another of your trenchant speeches, my dear? If so, why don't we sit down, with you comfortably settled on my lap, and—"

"No. I don't want you anywhere near me. Stand over there, please, and listen. I am *worse* than maggoty. I am completely *impossible!* Ask Uncle Jasper. I start upstairs to get something from my bedroom, and before I've reached the first landing I've forgotten where I'm going and why. I trip over carpets that haven't got a lump. I knock over the sugar bowl when reaching for the scones because I'm thinking of something else and not looking. My uncle has been searching for *three years* for a map of his property that I misplaced! I mix up the pattern pieces for the simplest kind of clothing. I once put *sleeves* into a *skirt*. Speaking of skirts, the entire village of Bishop's Cleve is familiar with the tale of my dinner with the vicar. The vicar's wife had given me a brooch for my birthday, you see, and later, when we were invited there for dinner, Uncle Jasper reminded me that it would be unforgivable not to wear it. Well, the brooch had a broken catch, and I had to fuss with it endlessly to make it stick—with Uncle Jasper shouting from downstairs for me to hurry. I finally managed to close the clasp, I threw my cloak over me and ran out. When we arrived at the vicar's— with half the town present and watching—the maid took my cloak and there I stood wearing nothing on my lower limbs but my undergarments. I'd forgotten to put on my skirt!"

Griff choked. "Ada," he managed, trying not to guffaw, "there's no need for—"

"There *is* a need. There is! You can't love someone like me . . . not for long. Think about it! Think of the sort of life it would be. You'd miss one of your favorite books and find it, after months of searching, in my flower shed, stuck behind the compost pile. I'd jot down a message from your friend about a place to meet, and when you got there you'd find that you'd arrived at precisely the right location and hour but the wrong day. I'd stitch a wonderful new waistcoat as a gift for you, and you'd discover that I'd set in the watch pocket upside down. I'd give you a half-dozen healthy children, but I'd never remember their names. I'd pay the bills, some of them twice. I'd send invitations to our parties to all the wrong people. I'd misdirect your letters. I'd put salt in the sugar bowl or lemon in your coffee. I'd leave my embroidery stand in just the place for you to trip over in the dark. I'd come to breakfast wearing my lovely new robe inside out. I'd spend hours looking for my spectacles and find them either in the flour bin, the linen closet or sitting right on my nose. You'd be leaving on a journey, and at the door I'd hand *you* the list of household chores for the day and kiss the *butler* goodbye. Who can marry such a one as I?"

Griff laughed and pulled her to him again. "I'll endure it all . . . except the butler. I will *not* have my wife kissing the butler."

But she pushed him away. "I know it sounds amusing, but it's *not!* I'm really *like* that. You don't want to marry a maggoty female. You said so! *Admit* it!"

Griff shrugged and turned away. What she said was quite true. He wanted her with every breath he took, but he didn't know if he could really bear living the sort of life she described. It was the same stumbling block that had barred their path since the first day they'd met. "I love you, Ada," he said, "but I can't pretend that I'd enjoy the constant turmoil that you describe."

There was a moment of silence. When he looked round, she was standing at the door. "Thank you for your offer, Griff," she said, subdued and saddened. "I shall always remember that you l-loved me for a while."

He took a step toward her. "Don't refuse me, girl. We may

be able to adjust to one another." He gave her a quick, hopeful grin. "Besides, my mother thinks you're perfect for me, and her judgment has always been impeccable."

Ada shook her head. "She wanted Cornelia for you at first. Everyone below stairs said so."

"No, she didn't. She doesn't like Cornelia much. Neither do I, for that matter. It's you we want, both of us."

Ada's eyes filled as she shook her head. "Nevertheless, you should wed Cornelia, Griff. I know she's arrogant and a bit spoiled," she said in a choked voice as she went out the door, "but at l-least she has some *sense!*"

Chapter Twenty-Three

The day following the ball was, of course, a beautiful day.
The sun shone in a clear, sparkling sky and there was the smell
of spring in the air. But everyone at Mullineaux House slept
late. Even the early spring weather failed to rouse the household. The ball had not ended until dawn, and everyone from
her ladyship to the lowliest scullery maid was exhausted.

The servants, of course, were not privileged to stay abed
until noon as the Countess and her guests were, and by nine
they were busily at work tidying up the wreckage that two
hundred partygoers had left behind. Thus it was that Mrs.
Mudge discovered that Clara was gone. That led to a second
discovery and then a third, and then Lady Mullineaux's dresser
scampered down the hall to her mistress's bedroom and woke
her up. Her ladyship yawned, frowned, looked at her clock
and glared. "It is not yet ten, girl. Have you gone mad?"

The abigail merely held out a folded note. Her ladyship took
it with knit brows, opened it, read it, put a hand to her head,
read it again and leaped out of bed. Throwing on a flimsy
dressing gown, she ran down the hall in her bare feet and threw
open the door to Ada's room. It was true. The bed had not
been slept in, the drawers and chests had been emptied, and
nothing remained of her goddaughter but a blue and silver ball
gown laid out on the bed, a string of pearls resting on a velvet
cushion on the dressing table and one shabby little half-boot
lying forgotten under a chair.

A quarter-of-an-hour later, now fully dressed and unaccom-
panied, her ladyship marched down the hall in another direction. She carried the ballgown over her shoulder, the pearls
and the shoe in one hand and the note in the other. She came
to the door of her son's bedroom and, without knocking, strode
into the room. In unmotherly fury, she shook the sleeping
fellow's shoulder roughly. "Get up, you gamecock, and tell
me what you had to do with this!" she ordered.

Griff, roused from a deep sleep, rolled over, opened one

eye, winced and pulled himself up reluctantly to a sitting position. "Mama?" he asked thickly. "Is somethin' amiss?"

"Read this!"

Griff rubbed his eyes, ran a hand through a tangle of unruly hair and took the note his mother was waving under his nose. *Dearest Lady Cecy,* he read, *I hope you will find it in your heart to forgive me for leaving in this unorthodox way, but it seems to me the best thing to do. Coming here was my first mistake and remaining was my second. I do not want to make a third one. I belong at home in Bishop's Cleve. I don't seem quite so foolish there as I do everywhere else. Or at least there everyone expects me to make muddles, so the consequences don't seem quite so horrifying. It was so kind of you to try to salvage something from the disaster I had made, but you must remember that you originally wrote that escorting two young women through a London season would be too much for you. I cannot in good conscience force that burden on you.*

I have other reasons, too, which make it urgent that I leave, so please do not feel that it is in any way your fault that I've gone. You were so sincere in what you said about wishing to play my mother that, if other matters were not so pressing, I would have stayed merely on your urging. But please believe that it was impossible for me to stay, under any circumstances.

Uncle Jasper is, of course, happy to take me home. He always feels, when he is away from home, like a fish out of water. I must also tell you that Clara goes with us. She is very sorry to leave your employ without having given sufficient notice, but she hopes that, in the circumstances, you will forgive her. She and I have become such good friends that we do not wish to be parted.

It was wonderful to be your daughter, even for one night, and I shall never forget anything that happened during last evening. Thank you for the use of the gown and the pearls. But thank you most of all for the many kind words you said to me. I shall always remember you with the greatest affection. Your loving goddaughter, Ada.

Griff stared at the letter a long while after his eyes had ceased to read it. His lips were white-edged, and his mother thought there was something in his expression that indicated that a troublesome turmoil was going on within him. "So she's gone home," he said at last, his voice shaking with a tightly controlled fury. "What has it to do with me?"

"Do you take your mother for a fool, fellow? Assignations at country inns, quarrels over nothing taking on deep significance, meaningful glances exchanged in crowded rooms, blushes and palings at the mention of certain names . . . what do you think those things are symptoms of?"

"Are you speaking of *me*, Mama? Have I been showing such symptoms?"

"You and she both. What have you done to her to make her run away?"

"Nothing," he said, flipping angrily over on his side, burying his face in his pillow and pulling the cover over his head in dismissal. "Nothing at all."

She pulled the cover back. "Tell me!" she demanded.

"Very well, if you must know," he said, sitting up again, "I committed an unspeakable crime against her. I asked her to marry me."

Lady Mullineaux's eyes widened. "Really, Griff?" Her face lit up in delight. "Is this *true?*"

"Yes, but you needn't get out the champagne," he said gruffly. "She won't have me."

"That's ridiculous. The girl adores you."

"So it seems. All the girls who adore me run for the hills when I offer for them."

"Don't be a clunch. She must have had a reason . . ."

"Oh, yes. She had a very good reason. She knew I have little liking for bubbleheads."

"Good God, Griff," his mother gasped, appalled, "you didn't call her that, did you?"

"Many times."

"You *are* a clunch. *Why?*"

"That is an idiotic question. I called her one because she *is* one. One of the worst. Ask her. She'll tell you so herself. At length!"

Lady Mullineaux sank down on the bed, confused. "But if you found her so, why did you offer for her?"

Griff gave an exaggerated shrug of self-disgust. "Thus love doth make bubbleheads of us all," he muttered.

"And she refused you?" his mother asked in disbelief.

"She did indeed. In that, at least, she had better sense than I."

She looked at her son askance. "Are you trying to pretend you're *glad* she refused you?"

"I feel like the devil, if you want the truth. But I'll get over it. And when I do, I will get down on my knees and thank God for sparing me from making the worst mistake of my life."

."Will you indeed? I think you'll *regret* this the rest of your life."

"What are you saying, Mama? I hope you're not suggesting that I go after her."

"That's exactly what I'm suggesting."

"Then I'm sorry to disappoint you, but that's the last thing I intend to do. The girl's a damned bubblehead, and this damned note is but another bit of damned evidence—as if I needed *more* evidence than I already have—that she'll never change."

"Watch your tongue, you insolent make-bait," his mother chided, slapping his wrist. "If I were a girl to whom you'd made an offer, I'd refuse you, too."

"Thank you, Mama. It's always comforting for a man to know that his mother is so completely devoted to him." He threw himself back down upon the pillows and burrowed into them again. "Now go away and let me sulk in peace."

She stared at the lump under the coverlet that was her son, sighed, gathered up her things and started out. "She didn't even keep the pearls I gave her," she said sadly.

"Mmmmph," said the lump under the coverlet.

"And she left this shoe behind."

"Shoe?" He threw off the covers and sat up again. "What shoe?"

"This one," Lady Mullineaux said, tossing it over to him.

He turned the worn, shapely little half-boot over in his hand, staring at it as if it were a talisman. "It wanted only this," he said at last, disgust and unhappiness warring within him. "My final, romantic vision of my lady love: I can see her now, misty-eyed and ethereal, limping toward her carriage wearing the mate of this on one foot and only a stocking on the other. Who but my Ada could leave behind *one shoe?* Honestly, Mama, I think that girl will drive me mad."

Chapter Twenty-Four

A fortnight passed and then a month, but Griff did not "get over it." In fact "it" became worse daily. He felt like the devil all the time. Aubrey began to complain that he always seemed abstracted. "You haven't won at cards in weeks, because you don't have your mind on the game. And you let Sefton's nag beat yours last week, which you'd never have done in your right mind. At least a dozen of us are out of pocket because of you, Griff." He gave his friend a look of lugubrious sympathy. "It's that bubbleheaded girl you're thinking of, isn't it? I hate to say this, old man, but this thing's made you as bubbleheaded as she!"

There was something in what Aubrey said. Griff *felt* bubbleheaded. His days passed in a kind of grey fog, in which he heard people's voices as if from a distance or saw their faces indistinctly. His life had lost its savor, its sharpness, its clean edges.

Meanwhile, Cornelia, realizing that she would not win Griff's attention, gave up and became betrothed to Sir Nigel Lewis. The Countess found the news amusing. "Two dignified, self-absorbed, good-looking fribbles," she said to her son, laughing. "I think they will suit very well."

The signs of spring in the air were then becoming more pronounced. There was a smell of lilac on the breeze, and the wind, whipping around the corners of the streets, had lost its sting. The days were like wine, but to Griff every beautiful sign of new life was painful; he had no one with whom to walk or to share the sights and smells. When he could bear the days no longer, he capitulated. "I'm going to Gloucester, Mama," he announced one morning at breakfast.

His mother's face lit up in excitement, relief and anticipation. "For Ada?"

"If she'll have me."

"But I thought," Lady Mullineaux remarked, watching her

181

son's face with fascination, "that you couldn't abide bubble-heads."

"I thought so too. But since I've become so bubbleheaded myself, the prospect of wedding one seems not only bearable but almost desirable."

He threw a clean shirt and some linens into a bag and set out that very day, driving a curricle and pair. He drove all through the day and night and presented himself at the door of the Surringham house in Bishop's Cleve the very next morning. He was bursting with an eagerness he knew was appropriate only to very young boys, but his youthful excitement was doomed to be short-lived. Cotrell, the butler, struck him to the bone with the news that Miss Surringham was not home and was not expected in the near future.

Griff felt so cruelly disappointed that the shock made him positively weak in the knees. "Not expected?" he gasped, almost bereft of breath. "Where *is* she?"

"I'm afraid I couldn't say, my lord."

"Then who *can* say?" Griff barked in irritation. "Is Sir Jasper at home?"

It took an endless five minutes before he was led into Jasper's sitting room, and the greeting he received after the wait was scarcely what a civilized man might expect. Jasper gave him no welcome at all. Instead he greeted him with a scowl and a pointing finger. "This nonsense is all *your* fault, Mullineaux," he bellowed as soon as Griff appeared in the doorway. "If it weren't fer you, she'd never have done it."

"Done what? I don't know what you're shouting about, Surringham. What nonsense are you speaking of?"

"Ada's disappearance."

Griff paled. "Disappearance?" he echoed faintly, sinking into the nearest chair.

"Left me a note, sayin' she's goin' away fer a month. T' prove t' herself an' t' the world, she said, that she's as levelheaded and competent as anyone. Didn't take a penny with her, nor leave me an address where she can be found. Damned silly female. We were perfectly content as things were before. Then you came along t' turn her head, an' now look at the muddle. I'm so worried I can hardly sleep o' nights!"

Griff questioned the man for a long while, but it became increasingly apparent that he would learn no more. The old fellow had told all he knew. Griff finally said his adieux and went to the door in utter depression. He had not a clue as to where Ada might have gone. Where could he *begin* to look for her? If Sir Jasper couldn't 'sleep o' nights,' what was *his* fate to be? Was it really his fault that she'd run off like this? Had he, with his critical superiority, driven her to this?

He went down the steps of the house and walked to his waiting horses so absorbed in self-abasement that he didn't at first hear his name being called.

"Yer lordship? Lord Mullineaux?" someone was calling in a hissing whisper.

He looked round at last. Beckoning him from a corner of the house was a ruddy-faced young woman in an apron and mobcap. "Is it . . . Clara?" he asked, his brows knit. Then his forehead cleared. *Clara!* The very person who might help!

She dropped a curtsey. "Yes, m'lord, it's me. Y're lookin' fer Ada, I expect. I tho't ye might be comin' t' find 'er."

"Did Ada think so, too?"

Clara shook her head. "She wouldn't let 'erself believe it. And now she's gone to be a governess, y' see. She'll never speak t' me fer tellin' ye, but I can't bear t' see ye go without seein' 'er."

"A *governess?* She's working as a governess? But why on earth—?"

"Tis on'y fer a while, see? To show she can do it without makin' a muddle. She said she wants t' show ye she ain't maggoty."

Griff winced. "This *is* my fault, dash it! I don't suppose she told you where she went?"

"She did. Do ye think she'd ever fergive me if I tol' ye?"

"I don't know, Clara, but *I'll* never forgive you if you don't."

Clara studied his face in a dither of indecision. "Tell me, yer lordship," she asked uneasily, "what do ye want t' find 'er *for?*"

"I'll answer *that* question, girl, when you've answered mine. Is it a bargain?"

Clara nodded. "She's at Willow Haven, 'bout six miles down the road. The lady who she works fer is Mrs. Upshaw. There, I've tole ye. Now, then, m'lord—"

"I want to find her to *marry* her, of course," he said, starting off at a run for his carriage. "That is, after I wring her neck!"

*   *   *

Willow Haven was a rambling cottage with a thatched roof, but its size, its appointments and its well-kept trimmings gave evidence that its owners were prosperous. Thus Griff was surprised to hear screams, shouts and the sounds of general confusion when he approached the polished oak door. Nevertheless, he knocked briskly. His knock was answered by a maid wearing a neat apron but a worried expression. From somewhere behind her a baby cried, a child whined, another shouted and a woman screamed. The voice of the screaming woman was not Ada's. "Yes, sir?" the maid inquired.

"Is Miss Ada Surringham within?"

The maid looked at him in surprise, bit her lip and shook her head. "No, sir, she ain't."

"Dash it," Griff cursed under his breath. "Can you tell me when she'll be back?" he asked the maid with ill-concealed impatience.

"She ain't comin' back. Do ye wish t' see the Missus?"

Griff shrugged. "I suppose I must."

The maid led him into a sunny sitting room and disappeared. In another moment a youngish, rather pretty but overweight woman came in. She looked distressed and harried, and she carried the crying baby in her arms. Clinging to her skirt was a sullen-looking little boy of five or six. "Were you asking about Miss Surringham, sir?"

"I was, and I am. I was told she was in your employ."

The woman's eyes filled with tears. "She was, sir, until a little while ago. I had to dismiss her."

"*Bad* Mama," the little boy pouted. "I want Miss Ada *back!*"

"Be still, Timmy," his mother begged. "The gentleman and I are talking. You mustn't interrupt." She looked up at her caller unhappily. "He behaved so much better when Miss Ada was here."

"Then, ma'am, why on earth did you dismiss her?"

"I hated to do it, really I did. She is the loveliest young woman. But when Rachel ran into the drawing room *stark naked*, just when I was serving tea to Miss Faversham and her mother—"

Griff eyed the woman with fascinated concentration. "Rachel?"

"My little girl. She's four. It's she you can hear whining in her cradle."

"Ah, I see. She ran out of her cradle naked, you say?"

"Out of the tub. Miss Ada was supposed to be bathing her, but Timmy came to her with a book, asking questions as he always does, and Miss Ada became so absorbed in telling him the story that Rachel climbed out all by herself and ran out to the drawing room. You can imagine how hideously embarrassed I was."

"I *like* Miss Ada's stories," Timmy declared. "I want Miss Ada *back*."

"Well, you can't *have* her back!" Mrs. Upshaw snapped. "Really, I'm at my wit's end. I don't know what I shall do without her, until I find someone else, of course . . ."

"So it was merely this one little incident which caused you to sack her?" Griff inquired.

"If you'd seen Miss Faversham's face, you would not say a 'little incident.' And her mother almost *swooned*. It was quite the last straw."

"The last straw?"

"I mean, after all, there'd been the business with the paste, too!"

"The paste?"

"I know it *looks* like porridge, but *really!* How can anyone have confused the porridge with the paste? The porridge was in a *bowl* and the paste in a *jar!*"

"She confused them, did she?"

"More than once. After all, one can't have one's children eating paste, can one, even if it's only flour paste? And that wasn't all, you know."

"It wasn't?"

"No. There was the time she filled the tub without putting the stopper into the drain. She kept filling it with kettle after kettle full of water without even *noticing* that it was running out the bottom and puddling up on the floor!"

The little boy laughed. "Puddling on th' floor!" he chortled, and clapped his hands. "Happy, happy, happy!"

Griff glanced down at the child, puzzled. "What does he mean, happy, happy, happy?"

"I don't know, exactly. He does that when he's pleased about something." The woman's tears spilled over and down her cheeks. "But I must say that's how things were with Miss Ada . . . happy, happy, happy. There was something about her, you know, that made you feel cheerful just to look at her."

She shifted the bawling baby to her other shoulder, pulled out a handkerchief with her free hand and sniffed mournfully into it. "I hated to let her go, really I did. But I knew, the day she walked the empty hand-carriage, that she wasn't fit for this sort of work."

"Empty hand-carriage?" Griff asked, unable to help himself.

"Yes. It's a little wagonlike thing with four wheels, for taking the baby for an airing. She took it out for a stroll one day and forgot to put the *baby* in!"

"I see," Griff managed, choking.

Mrs. Upshaw mopped her eyes and, having relieved herself of some of her feelings of guilt by relating all these episodes to her visitor, became more calm. "Have you come to see her home?" she asked, really taking note of her visitor for the first time. "I asked her if someone was going to call for her, but she said she would walk. Perhaps she forgot about you. She tends to be a bit absentminded, you know."

The little boy emerged from behind his mother's skirts and ran to Griff. *"Bad* man!" he shouted, punching furiously at Griff's legs. *"Don't* take Miss Ada home! I want her *back!"*

It took several minutes more for Griff to extricate himself from Mrs. Upshaw and her noisy brood, but he was shortly tooling down the road, his heart again pounding in boyish eagerness. He didn't know how he'd missed passing Ada earlier, for he'd just come up this same road. Perhaps she'd sat down to rest behind a hedge, and he hadn't seen her. This time he would keep his eyes open.

Only a very few minutes passed before he did see her. She was struggling wearily along, her bonnet askew, the hem of her dress sweeping the dust of the road, and the large portmanteau she was pulling behind her scraping and bumping on the ground. From the rear she looked pathetic and silly and helpless and utterly beautiful.

He drew up alongside her. "May I offer you a ride, ma'am?" he asked.

"No, thank—" She glanced up, blinked, and dropped her portmanteau with a thud. *"Griff!"*

He leaped down and enveloped her in his arms before she could utter another word. They kissed hungrily for a long moment. "I think that perhaps you're glad to see me," he murmured breathlessly when he lifted his head.

The joyful look in her eyes faded. "No, I'm not," she said, turning her head away. "You don't kn-know! I'm an utter *f-failure!*"

"Are you? That sounds serious. You must tell me all about it." He picked up her portmanteau and tossed it into the curricle. "But first let me help you up."

"I shan't ride with you," she declared, pulling her arm from his grasp. "You've come to persuade me to change my mind, and I won't! I can't! You don't *know*—!"

He pulled her into his arms again. "I know one thing, Ada. When I look at you, I feel happy, happy, happy."

She gaped at him in amazement. "You saw *Timmy!* How—?"

"Never mind how. But if you're going to make one of your trenchant speeches about how you failed as a governess, you may save your breath. If I'd wanted to wed a governess, I would have advertised for one in *The Times.*"

"Nevertheless, I'm as muddleheaded as I ever was. So nothing's really changed."

"*I've* changed. I've decided I'm just like Timmy. I don't care how muddleheaded you are, for when I'm with you I'm happy, happy, happy. I find I can't be without you, Ada. I become muddleheaded myself when you're not near."

She looked up at him as if she couldn't quite believe what he was saying, but, seeing something unmistakably fond and warm gleaming in his eyes, she reddened, sighed, and hid her face in his coat. "You can't really wish to marry such a maggoty creature as I am!" she murmured.

"Yes, I can, as soon as it can be contrived. I intend to wed you with as much pomp and ceremony as befits the future Viscountess Mullineaux."

"Oh, G-Griff!" She gave a tremulous little laugh. "I shall probably trip over my bridal train, fall on my face, and embarrass you before all of London society."

He put his cheek against her hair. "No doubt you will. But I'm so besotted that I shall probably find your pratfalls utterly charming."

Eventually they were seated side by side in the curricle watching the horses amble slowly along toward home. Ada, filled with a joyousness so overwhelming that she knew she could not be dreaming, snuggled against his shoulder. "Imagine your coming all this way," she murmured blissfully, "just to offer for me again!"

"I didn't come for that purpose at all," he said blandly. "The offer was merely an afterthought."

She sat up in mock hauteur. "An afterthought, indeed! Then why *did* you come?"

"I came, my love, to even up the score. Once you made a noble sacrifice for my sake, remember?"

"I remember. You called it a splendid indiscretion."

"So it was. I shall always be indebted to you for it. So I decided to make a noble sacrifice for you."

"You don't say! What sort of sacrifice?"

"A sacrifice of time and effort on your behalf. I came all this way—at great personal cost, mind you—to deliver something you had left behind."

"Something I'd left behind?"

"Yes." He put his hand into the largest of his coat pockets and pulled something out. "Something you must have missed dreadfully."

"There was nothing I missed dreadfully . . . except you, of course."

"Thank you, my love, but this is something more practical and necessary to your daily well-being than even I am. I couldn't bear to think of you limping about without it. So here it is, with my compliments."

And, with a broad grin, he dropped the little half-boot into her lap.

THE GRAND
PASSION

❧ *Prologue* ❧

Matthew John Lotherwood, the Marquis of Bradbourne, had no interest in having his fortune told. From his place near the doorway of his aunt's enormous ballroom, he eyed with amused disdain the long line of guests who stood waiting like gullible sheep to hear the gypsy woman (hired by his aunt, Lady Wetherfield, for the occasion) read their fortunes in their palms, on cards, or in her crystal ball. Throughout the many hours of the ball's duration, a steady stream of the most *haute* of London's *ton* had been waiting in that line. "Mooncalves and cods-heads the lot of them," Lotherwood said to a crony standing nearby, and they both, laughing, turned and made their way through the crowd to the buffet.

Lady Wetherfield's annual ball was always a squeeze. Even the most jaded of partygoers was eager to accept an invitation to one of her galas, for she could always be counted on to provide something more than dancing and a supper of lobster cakes and champagne. She invariably added a distinctive touch—a group of Turkish dancers in native dress, perhaps, or a troupe of acrobatic jugglers. The *ton* agreed that no one was better than Letitia Wetherfield at surprising her guests with some sort of original, enjoyable entertainment. This year was no exception. In fact, it was beginning to look as if her special surprise this evening—the fortune-telling gypsy woman —might turn out to be one of her greatest successes.

Lady Wetherfield had installed her gypsy (a certain

1

Madame Zyto) on the balcony overlooking the ballroom, under a colorful tent-top of green and gold striped duck cloth, expecting to attract some mild interest from the older females who did not dance. She didn't dream, however, that almost every one of her one hundred and fifty guests would wish for a reading. Getting a glimpse into one's future was proving to be a most popular diversion.

Lotherwood, finding the crowd around the buffet too dense, gave up the struggle and turned away from the food. He leaned against one of the ballroom's fluted pillars and amused himself by studying the faces of the guests waiting to see the gypsy. The women were eager and impatient, but the men consistently pretended to indifference. It was farcical to him to note that, while they were undeterred by a wait of almost an hour, the men scoffed loudly and disparagingly as they stood in line, not one of them admitting to feeling even the least bit of credulity in the efficacy of fortune-telling in general or this gypsy in particular. But he couldn't fail to notice that, when they sat down at the gypsy's table, despite their previous pretense of scorn for this whole activity, they all paid fascinated attention to every look on the gypsy's face and every word she uttered. And when they left her company and climbed down the stairs again, they were either vociferously elated or noticeably dejected by what they'd heard.

"Ain't you going to hear what she has to say, Matt?" came a voice at his elbow. He turned to find his friend, Lord Kelsey, at his side. Randolph Kelsey, overdressed as usual in a striped satin waistcoat and sporting the highest shirtpoints in the room, was observing the gypsy through his quizzing glass. "You ought to go up there before too long, you know. The queue'll only get longer once supper's over."

"Not I," Lotherwood answered with a shrug. "I've nothing much to learn about my future, now that I'm leg-shackled."

Lord Kelsey laughed. "You're right. As a betrothed man, your future is too disgustingly clear."

Lotherwood sighed in rueful agreement. It *was* too disgustingly clear. He'd held back from wedlock for as long as he could, but finally, at thirty-two, he could postpone it no longer. For all these years he'd been contentedly living the life of the Compleat Corinthian—young, strong, and wealthy, he'd concentrated his energies on nothing more than sports and amusements. Like others of his set, he'd not permitted himself to become involved in anything serious. Every subject—war, politics, the national economy, even marital love—was to be taken lightly and made the object only of witticisms. Sport was the primary interest of the true Corinthian, but even in this he did not become emotionally involved. Whether he won or lost the game, the Corinthian greeted the result with equal imperturbability. The playing was all.

Lotherwood was one of the fortunate ones who excelled at everything he tried, but his reputation as a sportsman was particularly enviable in horsemanship. When it came to horses, whatever the sport (riding, handling the ribbons, riding to the hounds), there was hardly an honor he hadn't won. But lately he'd begun to find the excitement of the chase wearing thin. He was in his thirties now; he had begun to realize that it was time to put aside these boyish pursuits and turn his attention to more mature concerns.

He'd already taken the first step toward his future by becoming betrothed. His betrothal was completely in keeping with Corinthian tradition: the girl he'd chosen was as pretty, well-bred, lighthearted, and accomplished as anyone on the Marriage Mart, and, most important, one did not have to lose one's head over her. No true Sporting Gentleman would allow himself to be shattered by love. In love, as in sport, one kept one's head.

His friend Dolph Kelsey was certainly in the right of it, Lotherwood realized as he stood watching the fortune-teller do her work. His future *was* disgustingly clear. No gypsy would have trouble guessing it, for it promised to be a completely predictable existence: quiet years on his Essex estates dealing with the business of the lands, raising a brood of children, and settling down each evening at his hearth with an unexceptional wife. What could a gypsy tell him about his future that he didn't already know?

The two gentleman continued to observe the gypsy at her work. The woman was undoubtedly talented, Lotherwood thought as he watched. She was a withered old crone, but her long, gnarled fingers showed a youthful agility as they flipped through her cards or lingered lovingly on her crystal ball. Madame Zyto sat behind a round, draped table like a queen holding a series of private audiences, dispensing futures, dark or bright, with a dignified, awesome disinterest. There was an exotic witchery in the almost skeletal shape of her cheeks and the blackness of her eyes. "Why don't you go up there, Dolph?" Lotherwood suggested suddenly. "You'll probably be vastly entertained."

"I already have. She told me I'm soon to be wed, to a girl of much sweetness. Did you ever hear the like? There ain't a girl in all of our acquaintance whom I could describe as one of 'much sweetness.' Can you?"

Lotherwood shook his head. "Not one, with the exception of the lovely young chit who's hurrying toward us right now."

Dolph turned and peered at the approaching figure through his glass. "Oh, your Viola! Well, I can't count *her*, now that you've staked your claim."

And indeed the young lady approaching did have an aspect of charming sweetness. Viola Lovell was slightly under average height, with a figure that was both slim and softly rounded. She wore a rose-colored gown that shed a glow upon a complexion unmarred by the slightest imperfection, although at the moment the additional glow was not needed. The girl was pink with excitement, and her bronze-gold curls bounced as she hurried toward them. "Oh, Matt," she cried as she drew near, "it was simply amazing! The gypsy woman knew *everything about me!* It was quite uncanny. She must be *bewitched!*"

"Really, Vi?" Dolph asked curiously. "What did she tell you?"

"She knew my age to the month, and that I had a married sister who is with child. And she said that I excelled at the pianoforte and that I would be wed this summer! Is that not remarkable?"

Lotherwood tucked her arm in his and patted her hand soothingly. "Don't excite yourself, my dear. I see nothing very remarkable in that. Every young woman of education excels at the pianoforte, does she not? And as for your being wed in summer, since our banns were announced this very week in *The Times*, it is hardly surprising that the gypsy foretold the wedding."

"But she could not have known who I was, could she? There are at least one hundred and fifty people here."

Lord Kelsey smiled down at her indulgently and took her other arm. "But Miss Bubblehead, don't you know that almost every one of the hundred and fifty are babbling about your betrothal? The gypsy's bound to have heard something of it."

The gentlemen, as if in accordance with a prearranged plan, turned to lead her toward the buffet tables. But Viola hung back. "Oh, pooh! I don't believe she can have known me," she insisted. "There's something otherworldly about the woman, really there is. Matt, please, you *must* go up to hear what she says to you! I shall *die* of curiosity if you don't."

Lotherwood, having been frustrated earlier in his attempt to get to the buffet, was by this time much more interested in his aunt's famous lobster cakes than in bothering about a wizened old fortune-teller. "Anyone in the room can tell you my fortune, if you're so curious," he told his betrothed. "Ask Dolph, here. Tell her, Dolph. Make a prediction that I shall settle down in Essex with a charming wife and become a docile and respectable husband—"

"*Please,* Matt!" Viola implored. "Perhaps she'll foresee that we shall travel abroad! Would *that* convince you that she has mystical powers?"

"Since there's hardly a couple of our acquaintance who does *not* travel abroad on their wedding trip, I would be more impressed with her powers if she'd foresee *no* sea voyage in my future," Lotherwood teased. But Viola's eyes were looking up into his with such beseeching charm that he had to surrender.

He left his betrothed in Kelsey's care and joined the queue waiting for the gypsy with the good sportsmanship of a Corinthian who'd lost a contest. But the line moved very slowly, and by the time Lotherwood was seated at the table on the balcony, his usually easygoing nature had been pushed to its limits. Moreover, the way Madame Zyto cocked her head and fixed a glittering eye on him did nothing to assuage his irritation. "Get on with it, woman," he muttered. "I've already waited over an hour. I want to get to the buffet before the lobster's gone."

"Ye're an 'andsome vun, ain't ye, ye gamecock?" the crone chortled in brazen rudeness, studying his face carefully. Her accent was made of a strange combination of cockney and Romany, yet the words were clear and distinct and the voice free of the hoarseness of old age. "The ladies mus' tumble ower each-other for a smile from ye. Dark 'air, thick lips, poverful chin. Just the sort o' looks ve females itch for."

Lotherwood raised his brows, both disgusted and amused. "I thought you were to tell the *future,* ma'am," he reminded her pointedly.

"Oh, I see yer future right enough." She passed her hands lightly over her crystal ball but barely looked at it. "Ye're t' be married . . . right soon."

"Yes, so you said to my betrothed. You told her summer."

"Did I? Per'aps so." She shuffled her worn but still colorful cards. "*Your* vedding vill be sooner."

"Oh?" Lotherwood gave a snorting laugh. "How can I possibly be wed before my bride?"

The gypsy woman smiled back, revealing two horrid black teeth. "Because, m' lord, yer betrothed ain't going t' *be* yer bride."

"Indeed?"

"Ah, yes, indeed, indeed. Yer bride'll be somevun else entire."

"You don't say!" He leaned forward and placed his elbows on her table. "Can you see in this crystal ball of yours just who that bride will be?"

The gypsy woman nodded. With a jangle of her bracelets she passed her hands over her ball again and peered within. "I can see 'er plain as a pack-saddle. Tall, she is, vith short, dark 'air." She looked up and cackled loudly. "You can see 'er, too, if ye've a mind."

"I? How can I see her? I thought no one could see into your crystal ball but yourself."

"Not in the ball. Down there, below."

"What?" Lotherwood found himself enthralled despite himself. "Do you mean she's *here?*"

The gypsy woman, smiling an enigmatic smile, lifted her hand. With a long, misshapen, beringed finger she led his eye over the railing and down below to where a group of ladies sat on divans beside the dance floor. Lotherwood rose from his chair and leaned over the banister. Among the seated dowagers was a young woman with thick, dark, cropped curls. At that moment she turned her head and looked up, meeting his eyes. Lotherwood felt a peculiar shock; it seemed as if an inner clock that always beat within his chest suddenly stopped working. The feeling was only momentary, but he couldn't imagine what had brought it on. Was it the eyes looking up at him? He was loathe to admit to himself that those eyes had a mesmerizing effect on him, but they were certainly remarkable—a strangely light blue. "*That* one?" he asked the gypsy in amazement. "The one with the ice-blue eyes who's staring at me?"

"Yes. Indeed, indeed. That vun."

The girl below, noting Lotherwood's stare, raised her eyebrows in cold disdain and turned away. The look was a decided set-down, but Lotherwood continued to peer at her. "How can you make such a ridiculous statement?" he demanded of the gypsy. "I'm not even acquainted with that creature."

"No?" Madame Zyto shrugged her thin shoulders under her fringed, rose-embroidered shawl. "Then ye soon vill be."

Lotherwood, annoyed with himself for falling under the gypsy's spell, turned and looked at her with one eyebrow cocked disapprovingly. "I think, ma'am, that I shall tell my aunt, Lady Wetherfield, that you are a fraud."

The gypsy woman's eyes glowed as they traveled over him from head to toe. "Ye've a good leg, too, ye 'ave. Muscled as fine as a Romany stallion."

"An *incorrigible* fraud." He withdrew a gold coin from his pocket and threw it on the table. "But entertaining, I'll grant you that."

She picked up the coin, bit it, and grinned a black-toothed grin at him. "I thank ye, m'lord. Yer aunt, she know'd I be entertaining. But I varned 'er I tell the truth if I see it plain. I seen it plain just now. The girl vith the ice-blue eyes'll be yer bride."

Lotherwood glanced over the railing and down to the women on the divans. The dark-haired girl was not looking up this time.

The gypsy was suddenly standing beside him. "Aye, m'lord, she's the vun. Yer true bride. Me crystal ball don't lie."

Lotherwood stared at the gypsy woman for a moment in wonder; she seemed so utterly sincere. Then he threw back his head and guffawed. "I almost wish it didn't!" he said when the paroxysm had passed. He continued to chuckle as he walked away, shaking his head and muttering, "My true bride! Indeed, indeed!"

After the last carriage had rolled away down the street, and the lights in the Wetherfield house had darkened, a gypsy wagon rolled up to the back door. The gypsy woman, huddled in her fringed shawl, came hurrying out of the house. Just as she stepped into the street, a cloaked figure emerged from the shadows of the shrubbery. "Madame Zyto? Over here," came a lady's voice.

The gypsy woman told someone in the wagon to wait and went quickly to where the lady in the cloak was standing.

"You did well," the lady said.

With a nod of agreement, the gypsy put out her hand. The lady—a dark-haired girl with ice-blue eyes—wordlessly handed the gypsy woman a bag of coins and disappeared into the shadows.

❧ One ❧

It was almost exactly six months earlier—and hundreds of miles north of London—that Jeremy Beringer paid a call on Tess Brownlow, the girl with the ice-blue eyes. He hesitated in the doorway and glanced across the room at Tess with an expression that was half laughing and half sheepish. His hands were hidden behind his back, his hat was askew, and the tightly curled blond locks of hair that were uncovered by his hat were wet with droplets of melted snow. "May I come in?" he asked with unaccustomed diffidence.

Tess Brownlow, who was negligently lounging in an armchair near the fire with her stockinged feet toasting on the hearth, had been only a moment before staring glumly into the flames. But at the sight of Jeremy Beringer her mood brightened at once. She was always glad to see him. His round, open face exuded cheerfulness, and his eyes held a glow when he looked at her that they held for no one else. Although he had a wide circle of intimates in Todmorden, none of them were as close to him as she. It was a closeness that came from having grown up together and having shared a lifetime of youthful experiences. It was only lately (since the day two months ago when he'd first offered for her) that a tension had sprung up between them. Their friendship had been strained by his declaration of love . . . love that she could not requite. Nevertheless, she now grinned up at him with unalloyed delight. "You gudgeon, Jeremy Beringer! Did you

9

do it *again?* I don't see why you insist on stealing in without Mercliff seeing you. Why do you so dislike being properly announced?"

The young man stepped into the sitting room, closed the door quietly behind him, and grinned back at her. "One, because it's a challenge to find new ways to thwart your mother's stuffy butler. Two, because it's fun. And three, because I love to catch you unawares, as you are now, with your shoes off."

Tess immediately sat up and reached for her slippers. "You're incorrigible! Still behaving exactly as you did when you were twelve."

Jeremy ignored the mild rebuke and crossed the room. With a ceremonious bow, he removed from behind his back the beribboned nosegay he'd been hiding and tossed it into her lap. Then he unceremoniously ruffled her dark, short-cropped curls, planted a kiss on her nose, and dropped down on the hearth before her. He took her slippers from her hands and proceeded to put them on for her. "I *don't* behave exactly in the same way," he corrected. "At twelve, I stole over for a game of spillikins. At fourteen it was, if memory serves, silverloo. Now I have a quite different purpose in mind."

Tess knew very well what his purpose was. He was going to offer for her again. She'd just endured a violent argument with her mother on the subject. "He's going to ask you *just once more,*" her mother had warned, "so if you have a grain of feeling, you'll have him."

But Tess had strenuously objected. She and her mother never could see eye to eye on the subject of love and marriage. Mama considered her some sort of misfit for having reached the advanced age of twenty-three without ever having experienced what Mama liked to call the Grand Passion. "Freakish, that's what you are!" Mama always reminded her. "I've never heard of anyone who's refused to fall in love by your age!"

But Tess didn't see how she could make herself fall in love. She would certainly do so if she could. She would especially like to feel the Grand Passion for Jeremy. There was no one in the world more gentle, more congenial, more suitable for her to love. But her feelings for him were no stronger than sisterly. Shouldn't she wait, she'd asked her mother, until she found someone toward whom her feelings were stronger?

Mama had groaned with exasperation. "If you searched for *years,* you'd not find a better man for you than Jeremy. Come to your senses, my girl. You're not such a great beauty, you know, that you can expect to pick and choose. You're more than a shade too tall for most men, and your eyes are decidedly piercing. What's more, you're rapidly approaching the age of spinsterhood. So you may as well fall in love at once, or you'll be too late!"

Tess had been saucy enough to laugh. "That's an amusing speech, coming from you, Mama," she'd responded. "You're the one who always likes to prose on and on about the Grand Passion. Should I not wait for the man who can inspire the Grand Passion in me?"

"No, you should not!" her mother had retorted. "You can't wait forever for something that may not occur! Perhaps you're the sort who will *never* feel it. By the age of three-and-twenty any other girl would have fallen in love a half-dozen times! I don't understand you at all, Teresa Brownlow, not at all. How can you be so cruel? Everyone knows the boy has loved you since he was in short coats! We've prayed all these years, Lydia Beringer and I, that you would have him. It's a match made in heaven! Listen to me, Tess. Lydia tells me that Jeremy means to make you another offer this evening, but it is for the last time! Even Jeremy cannot be expected to withstand rejection forever. You've often told me that he's as dear to you as a brother. Then *take him!* If you have any heart in you, love will come later. I've heard that is often the case."

Tess had fixed her "decidedly piercing" eyes on her mother's face. "But what if it should turn out *not* to be the case?" she'd asked pointedly.

Her mother had thrown up her hands in impatience. "Then you will be no worse off than the majority of wives! Do you think *my* life was ecstatic with your father? I may have thought of him as my Grand Passion at first, but I soon learned what a mistake I'd made. Nevertheless, I made the best of it."

"I'm sorry, Mama, but I don't wish to have to say, one day, that I'd 'made the best' of my life."

It was then that Mama had said those vituperative words that still rang in Tess's ears. "Don't think yourself so high above the rest of the world, my girl!" she'd warned in a voice quavering with angry tears. "You are merely a woman, and

women must marry if they are to live any proper sort of life."
She'd pulled a handkerchief from her sleeve and sniffed into it
furiously. "I sometimes think you've no feminine feelings at
all! I hate to admit such a thing about my very own and only
child, but the truth is, Tess Brownlow, that you're *cold!* I've
always suspected it. As cold as your father!"

Jeremy's voice cut into her reverie. "Did you hear me,
Tess? I said I have a different purpose in mind tonight from
the intentions I used to have when we were children. Don't
you want to know what it is?"

"I've already been informed about your purpose," she
answered dryly.

"Oh?" He paused in his attempt to button the strap of her
right shoe. "Who informed you?"

She picked up the little bouquet he'd dropped in her lap.
"Lady Beringer told my mother, and Mama, of course, told
me."

Jeremy frowned in annoyance. "I ought to wring my
mother's neck," he muttered, returning his attention to the
shoe. "I suppose there's no point now in making my little
speech."

Tess merely shrugged and put her nose to the blooms.
"Mmmmm . . ." She sighed, breathing in their fragrance.
"These are a delight. I don't know how you always manage to
find flowers to bring to me, no matter what the season."

"Love makes me resourceful," he responded promptly,
successfully buttoning the little strap. "If you marry me, I'll
always manage to surround you with blossoms."

She stared at him for a moment, a fond warmth toward him
welling up in her throat. *Why not?* she thought suddenly. *He
really is such a dear. And Mama would be so happy. Lady
Beringer would be happy. Jeremy would be happy. In fact,
everyone in Todmorden would be happy!* With her heart
beating rather wildly at this impetuous decision, she buried her
face in the nosegay and murmured, "That will be lovely."

"Irises in April," he went on heedlessly, "armfuls of tea
roses in June, and in July the most glorious white—" He
seemed suddenly to turn to stone. Her left shoe slid from his
grasp unnoticed, while his eyes flew up to her face. "*What* did
you say?" he gasped at last.

"I said," she repeated, smiling at him tenderly, "that it will
be lovely to be always surrounded by blossoms."

Jeremy blinked. His smile faded, and as the import of her remark dawned on him, his cheeks whitened and his Adam's apple bobbed up and down. "Are you saying that . . . that you'll—?"

She nodded at him, her eyes misty.

"Oh, my *Lord!* You're not shamming it, are you?" His expression of disbelief was slowly replaced by one of utter joy. "Do you really mean to *have* me?"

"Jeremy, you looby," she teased, "can't you comprehend a *yes* when you hear it?"

With a cry of triumph, he jumped up and seized her in his arms. Lifting her high off the floor, he swung her round and round, shouting all the while, "Tess, Tess, my darling! My *love!* I can't *believe* it!"

Tess, bereft of breath, leaned a cheek on his hair. "Put me down, you idiot!" she managed to gasp.

"No, I'm *never* going to put you down! I'm going to whirl you round like this until . . . oh, until our wedding day!"

"But you must put me down, my darling, at least for a little while. There are things we must do."

"Do?" He set her on her feet and kissed her breathlessly. "What must we do?"

"We must find my other slipper, for one thing," she laughed, holding him off.

"Yes, I suppose we must." In a blissful daze he wandered back to the hearth, picked up the neglected shoe, and knelt before her to put it on. "Though I don't understand why we must put this on right now."

She looked down and gently stroked his soft, tightly curled hair. He was so sweet and lovable that something inside her seemed to open up . . . to uncurl like the petals of a blossom. *See, Mama?* a voice inside her whispered. *I'm not cold at all!*

He was looking up at her quizzically. "Well? Are you going to tell me?"

"Tell you what?"

"Tell me why are you so concerned about putting on this dashed shoe!"

"Because, my dear," she murmured, kneeling to help him button the little strap, "it would be quite shocking for me to be only half-shod when we go."

"Go?"

"Yes, go." She kissed him quickly, then drew him to the

door. "We must go and tell the news to our respective mothers."

Abruptly he paused in the doorway. "I say, Tess," he mumbled, his face clouding over, "they haven't tried to . . . I mean, you weren't *coerced* into accepting me, were you?"

She put a hand to his cheek in a gesture of reassurance. "When have you ever known me to be coerced into anything?"

"That's right," he said, smiling in relief. "Too mulish by half." He took her two hands in his. "Tess, you don't know how happy you've made me tonight."

"Yes, I do, my love. Because I'm happy, too." And, surprisingly, she did feel happy . . . quite astonishingly happy, considering that only a half hour before she'd had no intention in the world of marrying him.

They proceeded hand in hand down the corridor toward her mother's dressing room, Tess inwardly marveling at her amazing about-face. If he hadn't brought her those unseasonal flowers—

The flowers! She suddenly stopped in her tracks. "Oh, wait just a moment, Jeremy. I've forgotten my nosegay."

She ran back to the sitting room and picked up her bouquet, but instead of hurrying out again, she found herself staring at the blossoms in fascination. Could the course of a life turn on such a little thing as this? she wondered.

After a few moment's hesitation, however, she turned and went purposefully to the door. Yes, it was true that the decision she'd made was impetuous, but she was not having second thoughts. Not at all. She was sure her decision, for all its abruptness, was a good one. If what she felt for Jeremy was not a Grand Passion, it was surely the next best thing. Surely. Wasn't it?

❧ Two ❧

By midnight the passengers who'd gathered at the Bull and Mouth Inn in St. Martins-le-Grand began to grumble. They were bound for Manchester on the night mail, and they'd just been told that their departure would be delayed for another half hour. Since this was the second half-hour delay, and since the weather was decidedly nasty, it was not surprising that the news was greeted with curses and groans. However, it was apparent that standing about in the courtyard in the icy rain would bring them no solace, so six of them (five men and an elderly lady) betook themselves inside to the taproom to warm their innards with mulled ale. Only two passengers, both middle-aged men, remained outdoors. They huddled under the balcony that edged the second story, watching glumly as the postboys splashed about in the downpour loading the baggage atop the stage.

The rain seemed to turn to sleet before their eyes. Most of the windows of the coaching inn were dark by this time of night, but enough light spilled from the taproom windows to show them that the road was getting slick. Though the two travelers were unknown to each other, they exchanged worried glances. Then, as if each could read the other's mind, they both peered up at the dark sky and shook their heads. Everything that surrounded them—the entire surface of the earth—was turning glassy. The wooden gateposts of the courtyard took on a sheen as if they'd suddenly turned to polished silver,

the cobbles of the roadway began to reflect back the faint light
from the taproom windows, the branches of the spindly trees
in the corners of the yard began to glisten, and, most depressing of all to the two travelers, the twigs tinkled every time the
wind blew, the brittle sound evoking a feeling of imminent
danger.

One of the pair, a portly gentleman with a tall hat and a
woolen muffler wound tightly round his neck and over his
chin, tested the roadway with his boot and shook his head. "I
shouldn't like to be coachman on a night like this," he muttered aloud, keeping his eyes fixed on the postboys so that he
wouldn't seem to be addressing his remark to someone to
whom he hadn't been introduced.

The other man was not troubled by such niceties of manners. "Think ye they'll call it off?" he asked, facing the portly
gentleman with blunt directness.

"Call it off?" He threw his fellow traveler a doleful glance.
"Not bloody likely. Not the mail."

The other man frowned. "Are ye thinkin' that per'aps they
should?"

"The stage will depart whether I think they should or not,"
the portly gentleman responded. "The only question is
whether they should depart with us or without us. If I hadn't
sent my solemn promise to be in Manchester by Friday to examine a sick uncle, I would certainly think twice about
going."

"Oh? Ye're a doctor, are ye?"

"Yes, I am. Permit me to introduce myself. Josiah Pomfrett, at your service."

The other man took the proffered hand eagerly. "I'm
William Tothill. Honored to make yer acquaintance, sir. I
mysel' am on my way to Leeds. On business, y' know.
Lookin' at property t' establish a cotton mill. There's a land
agent expectin' me, but the appointment ain't so urgent that I
should endanger m' life—"

At that moment a covered high-perch phaeton wheeled into
the courtyard at breakneck speed and skidded to a halt beside
the mail. One of the postboys ran to grasp the horses' halters,
and another hurried round the side to let down the steps. But
before he could reach the door, it flew open. A young man
leaped to the ground, a portmanteau in one hand and an enormous bouquet of flowers wrapped in layers of tissue-thin

paper in the other. "We made it!" he shouted happily at the driver of the phaeton. "Thanks, Algy, old fellow!"

The driver, Algy, grinned down at him in triumph. "Told you so!" he shouted through the wind. Flourishing his hat at his friend, he signaled the postboys to step aside. Then, without a moment's pause, he wheeled his horses about and departed. The young man who'd alighted lifted his flowers in a grateful salute to his friend, waving them at Algy until the phaeton disappeared from view. Then he handed his portmanteau to one of the boys and, at last becoming aware of his surroundings, took belated notice of the sleet that was drizzling on his face, accumulating on his hatbrim, and dribbling down into the collar of his greatcoat. He tossed his untied muffler round his neck and looked about him. It was only then that he saw the two men who were watching him from under the balcony. Acknowledging their presence with a friendly salute, he loped over to join them. Once under the sheltering roof, he grinned at them with engaging self-mockery. "I was certain I'd missed it," he confided cheerfully.

"Me an' Dr. Pomfrett 'ere was just sayin' as 'ow per'aps the stage shouldn't depart a-tall in this weather," Mr. Tothill offered.

"What? Not depart?" The young man's cheerful expression changed at once. "Oh, no," he exclaimed in alarm, "that couldn't happen, could it?"

"No, I don't think it could," Dr. Pomfrett said. "Although I'm convinced that the mail coach *should* be detained, I know it won't be. The company has a reputation to uphold. The mail must go out in all weather."

"Thank goodness for that." The young man sighed, relieved.

Dr. Pomfrett studied the young man with shrewd, medically trained eyes. The fellow was well dressed and bore himself with the casual nonchalance of the very rich. However, his face had a pleasant openness about it; there was no sign in it of the smugness, snobbishness, or self-satisfaction that one often noticed in the countenances of members of the upper classes. The boy had too round a face to be considered handsome in the classic sense, but Dr. Pomfrett thought his bright blue eyes, full mouth, and cheerful aspect were most appealing. Excitement and happy anticipation seemed to emanate from every part of the young man's body. Ice or no ice, this young fellow was delighted to be going on this journey.

The doctor, being by nature perfectly suited to his profession (the sort who believes himself born to be a comforter and protector of humankind), felt it incumbent upon him to protect the young man from behaving rashly. No one, he was convinced, should board the stage unless there was a dire necessity for him to do so. "I shouldn't be so quick to give thanks if I were you," he said reprovingly. "The ice is accumulating so rapidly that a person of sense ought to think twice about going. There'll be another stage departing tomorrow, after all. Mr. Tothill was just saying that his appointment in the north is not so urgent as to risk danger. By the way, may I take the liberty of making the introductions? This, sir, is Mr. Tothill, and I am Dr. Pomfrett."

The young man said he was Jeremy Beringer, and they shook hands all around. But despite the cordiality of his greeting, young Mr. Beringer showed no intention of heeding the doctor's warning. "If the stage departs," he declared as soon as the introductions were made, "I shall be on it. Mr. Tothill's appointment may not be urgent, but mine is. I came to London for the express purpose of getting these flowers from a friend who has a magnificent greenhouse, and I want to get them back before they wilt. You see, I'm to be married tomorrow in Todmorden, and *that* appointment I don't intend to miss."

"Your bride-to-be might take it amiss if you appeared at the ceremony on crutches or with your arm in a sling," the doctor countered, "which is just what may happen if the stage slides into a ditch."

"Humbug!" Jeremy Beringer declared blithely, his smile taking the sting out of his blunt dismissal of the good doctor's advice. "These drivers know very well how to go on. I don't believe a little ice on the roads will matter."

Dr. Pomfrett shrugged. "I hope you're right, since I shall be on the stage with you despite my misgivings. I've given my word that I'll be in Manchester myself on the morrow."

"Then I'm goin' as well," Mr. Tothill said, chortling like a boy at the prospect of adventure. "If the two o' ye are game, why, then, I ain't the man t' turn tail. What I say is, let's go inside an' drink on our resolve. A bit o' spirits won't sit ill on such a night as this. Any road, I reckon we're in fer a long, cold journey.''

Ten minutes later the coachman announced that the stage was ready for boarding. Six of the passengers, including the doctor and his newfound companions, took places inside, while the other three climbed up on top to the seats behind the coachman's box. There, with only the minor protection provided to their backs by the pile of baggage, they would ride for sixteen hours completely exposed to wind and weather. ''I don't envy that trio,'' Mr. Tothill remarked as he watched through the window while they climbed up. ''They'll be chilled through.''

''And they'll come down with inflammation of the lungs before the week is out, no doubt,'' the doctor muttered. ''Damned fools!'' He looked at the four men and one woman who were squeezed in with him in the carriage. ''We're *all* of us damned fools!''

The other passengers ignored the doctor's grumbling and tried to settle themselves comfortably in the space meant for four. Mr. Tothill and Jeremy Beringer took the window seats on one side, with Dr. Pomfrett between them. Opposite Jeremy Beringer sat a gentleman with a neatly pressed coat and expertly tied cravat. Beside him was a bald, bespectacled, elderly man who seemed to be made of nothing but skin and bones. His wife, also somewhat frail, occupied the window seat opposite Mr. Tothill. No sooner was she seated than she removed some knitting needles and a half-finished shawl from her oversize reticule and began to knit.

While the others occupied themselves with finding comfortable positions, Mr. Tothill kept his nose pressed to the window. ''I say!'' he exclaimed after a moment. ''Wut's the to-do now?''

Out in the courtyard the coachman was engaged in an altercation with two gentlemen who'd ridden up on horseback. One was dressed in evening clothes and an opera cape, while the other, also undoubtedly a dandy, was costumed as a *coachman!* Tothill couldn't believe his eyes. There was no doubt the fellow was in coachman's livery, but it was the most elegant coachman's livery Mr. Tothill had ever seen. The man wore a greatcoat woven in a huge houndstooth pattern. The coat sported at least a dozen capes and as many large pearl buttons which gleamed in the dark. His superbly cut boots were so highly polished that they, too, gleamed. Even the prosaic Mr. Tothill could see that the shine of the boots could have been achieved only with the aid of an expert valet. "Wut's a gentleman doin' rigged out like a coachman?" he wondered aloud.

The doctor, wedged in between Tothill and Jeremy Beringer, shifted round and peered out over Tothill's shoulder. "It looks as if . . . as if he's handing the coachman a *bribe!* Look at that! *Damme* if he isn't!"

At this, Jeremy lifted himself up and peered out the window over the backs of the other two. "Oh, he must be an FHC man," he said calmly.

"FHC man?" The doctor looked over his shoulder at Jeremy, his brows raised. "What's that?"

"A member of the Four-in-Hand Club. Most exclusive club in town. Very *haute ton*. But even a dukedom won't get you in unless you can handle the reins like a master. Only the most superb horsemen can be FHC men."

"Yes, but what does your FHC man want with our coachman?" the doctor persisted. "A fellow like that, rich and titled, can't wish to ride on the stage, can he? He probably has all sorts of private carriages—each of them a hundred times more comfortable than this—and his own horses stabled in every coaching inn from here to Scotland."

"An' why's 'e rigged out like a bloomin' popinjay?" Mr. Tothill put in. "If it wasn't fer 'is boots an' those dandified buttons, I'd take 'im fer a driver."

Jeremy Beringer laughed. "Yes, many of them love to deck themselves out like coachmen. There's nothing they like better than driving a stage."

"Are you suggesting, Mr. Beringer," the doctor asked, appalled, "that this fellow is bribing our coachman to let him drive *this* vehicle?"

"It certainly seems so." Jeremy peered out through the sleet-coated window to corroborate his theory. "Yes, indeed. There goes our coachman now, making off to the taproom, I've no doubt. And here comes the FHC man, making ready to climb up on the box. Why, he looks somewhat familiar! I've seen him at Brooke's, I believe. I think his name's Lotherwood."

Dr. Pomfrett reddened in fury. "Of all the . . . ! What consummate effrontery! We must stop him at *once!*"

"But why, doctor?" his young companion asked. "Why do you want to stop him?"

The doctor looked from Jeremy's serene face to those of the other passengers. "Are you all mad? This man proposing to drive us to Manchester is an *amateur!* Are you all intending to put your lives in the hands of a man who thinks driving a stagecoach is a *game?*"

"Mercy me!" the elderly woman murmured, blinking at the doctor in mild alarm but not ceasing her knitting. "Are you saying our lives are at risk?"

"That is *exactly* what I'm saying!"

Jeremy Beringer laughed again. "I mean no disrespect, Dr. Pomfrett, but that's rubbish. We are now in the hands of one of the best drivers in the kingdom. I understood your concern for our safety before, but I assure you that you are now in the very best of hands. The man is *FHC!* Believe me, there are none better at handling horses."

Tothill, at least, was won over. "Makes good sense t' me," he said with a shrug.

The doctor looked at the others. "And the rest of you? Does it make good sense to the rest of you?"

"I've heard of the FHC. Top-notch club," said the neatly dressed gentleman sitting across from Jeremy.

"I'm satisfied," said the bald old man. He turned to his wife with courtly concern. "Are you, m' dear?" he asked her.

"Yes, dear," she answered placidly, continuing to knit in serene indifference to her surroundings. "I am if you are."

"So none of you intends to do anything about this?" the doctor demanded in disbelief.

"I don't know what *you're* going to do, my friend," Jeremy Beringer said, "but I intend to get some sleep." With that he slid back to his seat at the opposite window, laid his bouquet carefully in his lap, stretched his legs out as far as they could go, leaned back, put his hands behind his head, and shut his eyes.

At that moment the carriage began to move. The doctor leaned forward nervously and watched from Tothill's window as the stage was maneuvered smoothly over the icy cobbles of the courtyard. Despite the condition of the roadway, the substitute coachman turned the vehicle onto the thoroughfare without so much as a jolt. The skill with which this feat was accomplished impressed Tothill. "A pretty good beginnin', you'll 'ave t'admit," he said to the doctor.

Dr. Pomfrett, somewhat mollified, sat back in his seat. "I suppose so," he grunted, withdrawing a crushed copy of the London *Times* from his pocket. The manner in which he unfolded it and barricaded himself behind it indicated to any interested spectator that not another word would be heard from him.

Thus the occupants of the stage fell silent. The only sounds were the clatter of the horses' hooves on icy cobbles and the squeak of the coach as it rocked along. The journey northward had commenced.

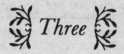
Three

It was sleeting in Todmorden with the same grim determination as in London, so Lady Catherine Brownlow and her daughter Tess sat down to dinner without any expectation of being interrupted by callers. But just as they were about to rise from the dinner table, Mercliff appeared in the dining room doorway to announce that Lady Beringer had arrived.

Lady Brownlow's eyebrows rose. "Tonight? In this dreadful weather? Is anything amiss?"

"I'm sure I couldn't say, my lady," Mercliff muttered, unable to hide a slight shrug at the strange ways of the gentry. "She is waiting in the sitting room."

But Lady Beringer pattered into the dining room just behind him. "I am *not* waiting in the sitting room," she declared eagerly. "I couldn't, shouldn't, and wouldn't wait to show you what I found!"

The unexpected visitor was obviously excited—a condition that had afflicted her the moment she'd learned that Tess was to be her daughter-in-law and that hadn't left her since. She still wore her sleet-spattered cloak and hood, and she carried a loosely wrapped package in her arms with the care and delicacy with which one would carry a baby.

"Good heavens, Lydia, what is so urgent that it takes you out on such a night?" Lady Brownlow asked, getting out of her chair.

"Don't be so pawky," the tiny but spirited Lady Beringer

berated her friend. "It takes a mere three minutes to drive over. One would think I'd come from abroad!"

"But the sleet! Give Mercliff your cloak before you catch your death."

"Never mind my cloak. I found the headdress I told you of, my dear. My grandmother's wedding headdress! Come at once to the sitting room and let us try it on the dear girl! Come, come, Tess, don't dawdle. Wait till you see it!"

Lady Brownlow and Tess dutifully followed Lady Beringer to the sitting room and watched in fascination as she unwrapped her parcel. The headdress proved to be breathtaking. It was a delicate coronet of gold wrought into a circlet of flowers with a beautiful lace veil attached to the back. The two mothers sat Tess down upon the sofa, and as Lady Beringer set the coronet on her head, Lady Brownlow arranged the veil carefully over her shoulders. Then they both stepped back and examined the girl intently.

"Oh, she looks *lovely!*" Lydia Beringer breathed.

"Yes, she does," Lady Brownlow agreed, studying her daughter critically, "although I wish she hadn't cut her hair in that boyish style."

"Oh, Kate, what a hum!" Lady Beringer said, outraged. "You told me yourself that you found the style charming."

"Yes, it *is* charming when she wears a riding habit. But it's a bit informal for a wedding costume, isn't it?"

"Informal or not," Tess informed her mother with a twinkle of amusement, "it will have to do. I can't grow much more by the day after tomorrow."

"Be still, you clunch," her mother ordered. "We are not seeking your opinions. You are only the bride."

"Come, Tess," Lydia Beringer urged. "Take a look at yourself in the mirror there. What do you think of it?"

"I don't know why I should bother to look," Tess said, nevertheless getting up and crossing to an ornate mirror that hung on the south wall between the room's two windows. "As Mama has pointed out, I'm only the bride."

The two mothers followed her across the room, and all three stared into the mirror with fascination. Kate Brownlow would not say so aloud, but she could see at once that Tess made a beautiful bride. Her dark hair and the gold coronet complemented each other, and the antique white veil seemed to emphasize the qualities that made the girl beautiful. Kate did not always find her daughter's looks to be satisfactory. The girl's eyes were sometimes too startlingly light, her chin was too strong, and her mouth too wide. But now, with her face surrounded by the mist of veiling and her hair curling over the gold circlet, she looked positively delectable.

"Perfect!" Lady Beringer murmured. "It couldn't be more perfect."

"Do you think perhaps . . ." Lady Brownlow cocked her head to the left and squinted at the vision in the mirror. ". . . a few plumes? To make it a bit more modish?"

Lydia Beringer cocked her head to the right. "Perhaps. I'm not certain," she said dubiously.

"I have some splendid ones on my blue bonnet. Wait just a moment. I'll get them." And Lady Brownlow hurried from the room.

Lady Beringer and Tess sat down near the fire to wait. Tess removed the headdress and laid it in her lap. "I've been wondering, Lady Lydia," she said without looking at her companion, "if you've ever had any misgivings about . . . about your son's choice of a wife."

"Misgivings?" Lydia Beringer looked over at Tess in surprise. "How can you ask something so silly? For me, as for your mother, this is a dream come true!"

"I know you both have dreamed of it since we were children. To cement your lifelong friendship. To join the two estates. To ensure the proper breeding of your grandchildren. I understand all that. But the truth is that I . . . I may not be the best wife for Jeremy."

"Tess!" Lady Beringer leaned forward, peering at her future daughter-in-law in sudden concern. She was a tiny woman, given to quick movements and abrupt gestures, and the feeling of alarm that Tess's words had given her made her shake her head nervously, causing the long gray-blond tresses that hung down over her ears in corkscrew curls to tremble. "What makes you say such a thing?"

Tess fingered the lace veiling absently. "For one thing, Mama thinks that I'm cold.'"

"Teresa Brownlow! That's not *so!*" Lady Beringer declared, her curls trembling even more. "She *couldn't!*"

"She could and she does. She said it to me just the other day. 'The truth is, Tess Brownlow, that you're cold. As cold as your father!' Those were her very words."

Lady Beringer, horrified, made one of her hasty gestures with her hands. "No! Oh, *no!* If she said those words, she surely didn't *mean* them. I *assure* you, Tess, my love—"

"Even if she didn't mean them, I keep wondering if they're true." Tess turned her eyes to a large portrait of her father which had hung over the mantel for as long as she could remember. "Look at him," she said with a sigh. "I *am* quite like him, am I not?"

Lord Brownlow, strikingly tall and handsome in his magisterial robes, glowered down at them from the wall. But Tess didn't mind the forbidding expression; she was quite accustomed to it. In her childhood she used to spend hours studying the face of the father who'd died when she was in her infancy. By now she was quite comfortable with that glower. In fact, she couldn't imagine her father with any other expression. She wondered if her father had ever laughed. Strange . . . her mother rarely spoke about him. But Tess had always suspected that Hubert Maximus Morden, Lord Brownlow, was a cold fish. The artist who'd painted him hadn't even tried to disguise the icy disdain with which he seemed to view the world.

Lady Beringer was also gazing up at the portrait. "No, you're not like him at all," she stated flatly, emphasizing her point with a swing of both her hands and a shake of her head. "You have some of his physical qualities, of course—long limbs, greater-than-average height, strong chin, that darker than dark hair, and lighter than light eyes. In those things you are your father's daughter. But in your nature I believe you are quite yourself."

Tess hoped her mother-in-law-to-be was right. She didn't want to be like her father. She'd always believed—at least until her mother had made that cruel accusation—that she was a woman capable of performing daring deeds for the good of mankind. She wanted very much to believe that she'd been set down on the earth to accomplish something worthwhile . . . something beyond the mere propagation of the species. There were times in her life when things happened that set her pulses racing and her spirits aflame. "I *am* capable of strong feelings, am I not?" she muttered, half to herself.

"Of *course* you are!" Lady Beringer cried with sincere vehemence. "Of course you are! Why, everyone remembers the time when your mother's bailiff attempted to oust the

Olneys from their tenancy just because Jem Olney was suspected of poaching, and you immediately and quite violently
asserted yourself on their behalf. I'll never forget how you
stamped your foot and said that they'd be turned out over
your immobile corpse! 'Shall we permit a family with six
children to be thrown out on the road just because they might
have dined on an illegal pheasant?' you declared in ringing
tones. Oh, how we all cheered you that day! You were simply
wonderful! And you should see yourself when you argue parliamentary matters with your Uncle Charles. You can be
positively passionate at such times."

Tess flicked a quick glance at Lady Beringer's face and then
looked away. Being passionate on parliamentary matters was
one thing, but being passionate in marriage was quite another.
It was with matters of love that Tess was most concerned at
the moment. Was Mama right that most normal girls had experienced the Grand Passion by their mid-twenties? Was
something wrong with her?

But this was not a question that was proper to put to Lady
Beringer. She'd said too much already. Besides, it was clear
that her mother and Jeremy's were both too elated by the
prospect of their marriage to admit the existence of any sort of
impediment. She had best drop the subject. Perhaps Mama
was right; perhaps she would learn to feel more deeply for
Jeremy after a while.

Fortunately, Lady Brownlow returned at that moment and
ended any possibility of the continuation of the conversation.
Lady Beringer turned her attention to the plumes with such
concentration that Tess almost believed she'd forgotten the exchange completely. Lydia Beringer probably didn't take
anything Tess had said at all seriously. It was the headdress
she was serious about.

The two mothers led Tess to the sofa and replaced the coronet on her head. With rapt concentration they held the
plumes against the coronet, turning them this way and that.
"Well? What do you think?" Kate Brownlow asked her
friend.

"I don't know. They may be modish, but I think fresh
flowers woven in amid the gold would be prettier."

"Fresh flowers?" Kate snorted. "Where do you propose we
find fresh flowers in the dead of winter?"

"We shall have them," Lydia Beringer said smugly.

"Jeremy's bringing an armload back with him from London.
I think he'd prefer flowers on the headdress to the plumes,
don't you, Tess, dearest?" She perched on the sofa beside
Tess and gave her hand a comforting squeeze. "Oh, I shall feel
so much better about things when Jeremy's back. And so will
you, my love," she added sotto voce. "When Jeremy returns,
you'll feel better about *everything.*"

❧ Four ❧

As the London–Manchester stagecoach rocked monotonously on through the night, the passengers, one by one, succumbed to sleep. Even Dr. Pomfrett, lulled by the rocking and the sound of the sleet drumming away on the roof, eventually dropped off. Only the old woman remained awake, her fingers busily at work on her knitting despite the darkness of the coach. When Dr. Pomfrett next opened his eyes, five hours had passed.

The good doctor peered about him nervously. Something had wakened him, but he wasn't sure what it was. Perhaps it was the dawn, which had just sent its first gray rays into the black sky. After a moment, however, he realized that something more dramatic than the dawn had jarred him awake—it was the rocking of the coach. Instead of the soothing cradlelike motion that had put him to sleep, the rocking had become violent. *Good God,* he thought, *the driver's picked up speed! Much too much speed!*

Though he could feel his stomach constrict in alarm, he didn't wish to wake the others and make a fool of himself again. Carefully he leaned over the sleeping Mr. Tothill and lowered the window. Ignoring the sting of the icy wind on his face, he stuck his head out the window. The coachman could be heard through the wind, singing a drinking song at the top of his voice. *Was the fellow drunk?* Dr. Pomfrett wondered. "I say," he shouted, "slow down!"

When there was no response, he repeated his order. But the singing continued, and the carriage proceeded on its way at what seemed to the doctor breakneck speed. "Does anyone up there hear me?" he shouted at the top of his voice. "Tell the coachman to rein in!"

The singing stopped. "Who's tha' yellin' down there?" The speaker's enunciation was slurred and his tongue thick with drink.

"I'm Dr. Pomfrett. And I insist that you slow this vehicle down!"

"Dr. Pomfrett, eh? A surgeon, are you?"

"I don't see what that has to do with—"

"You don't, eh? Then le' me explain. You're tellin' me how t' drive, are y' not? Well, doctor, how would y' like it if I came into your surg'ry an' tol' you how t' remove your patient's diseased spleen?"

"Damn it, man, the roadway's covered with *ice!* I don't have to be an expert driver to see that you're being reckless!"

One of the passengers seated above poked his head out over the little railing. His hat was tied onto his head with his muffler, and his nose and cheeks were red as beets from the cold. But his expression was surprisingly cheerful; he'd evidently become inured to sitting out in the cold. *He must be numb,* the doctor thought.

The passenger looked down at the doctor with a grin. "Don' take on so, m' good man," he advised. " 'Is lordship, 'ere . . .' e's done remarkable well so far, ain't 'e?" He waved his gloved hand over the side. Clutched in it was a bottle of spirits. " 'Ere. Catch this! A dram o' rum'll calm y' down."

The doctor made no attempt to catch the bottle, which fell to the ground with a crash. Several voices from above groaned at the sound. "Blast 'im," someone cursed weepily, " 's broken. All spilt."

"Good heavens, are you *all* drunk up there?" the doctor asked.

" 'Ow else're we t' keep warm?" someone responded.

"Lucky fer us 'is lordship supplied us wi' drink!" shouted another. "I couldn't elsewise 'ave survived the night."

"Coachman!" Dr. Pomfrett barked angrily. "I demand that you slow down at once! As a doctor, I know how drink impairs one's perceptions. You are putting us all in danger."

"Take a damper!" the unseen coachman flung back.

"Nothin's wrong wi' my perceptions. Watch how I take tha' curve ahead, and y'll see how m' percep—oh, my *God!*"

The exclamation made the doctor's blood run cold. He looked ahead to see a farm wagon coming toward them. It was so close that a collision was unavoidable. The turn in the road had kept it out of sight until the last moment. The mail was moving too quickly to stop in time. Before anyone had time to draw another breath, the horses of both vehicles reared. As if in a dream, the doctor saw the wagon's front end rise up and then fall back with a crash. The stagecoach, meanwhile, swayed dizzily from left to right and back again and then tipped over to the doctor's right. The sway threw the doctor back into the coach, causing his head to strike the window frame. It was a shatteringly painful blow, and he knew no more.

His next sensation was of a dash of icy water on his face. He opened his eyes to find Tothill bending over him. "Doctor? Can ye open y'r eyes?"

"Tothill? Wha—?"

"Thank God ye've come to, Doctor Pomfrett. If ye can stand, we've need of ye."

With Mr. Tothill's help, Dr. Pomfrett rose gingerly. His head ached painfully, but his thoughts were clear; therefore concussion was unlikely. His methodical medical mind quickly diagnosed his own condition. Cranial bruise in the dorsal area, not serious. Pelvic bone jarred but not broken. "I'm all right," he told Tothill brusquely and looked about him.

He saw that he was standing in the middle of the road before a scene of chaotic destruction. The morning light, though gray and dismal, revealed the wreckage of the mail coach in hideous detail. The vehicle was lying on its side, the underside completely caved in. It was apparent from the flotsam in the road and the condition of the carriage that it had been dragged on its side for some distance—so far, in fact, that the overturned farm wagon was almost out of sight down the road. The gentleman in the coachman's greatcoat and the man with the hat tied to his head were standing on the wreckage, tossing aside shattered pieces of wood with urgent intensity. The doctor wondered with a chill at his heart if anyone was trapped within.

At his right he could see the neatly dressed gentleman, now looking decidedly disheveled, seated on a portmanteau and holding his head in a pair of bloody hands. Behind him in the roadway lay a dead horse. The other horses were all gone. Tothill noticed the direction of the doctor's gaze. "We put the poor animal out o' its misery," he explained. "The others ran off."

Dr. Pomfrett now became aware of a soft, female wailing. In answer to his questioning look, Tothill took his arm. "It's 'er 'usband. 'E's just layin' on 'is back, unconscious. Will ye come an' take a look at 'im?"

For the next half hour Dr. Pomfrett had no time to think. Almost everyone on the coach had sustained some sort of injury, it seemed, and no one but the doctor was capable of treating the wounds. But the doctor had no idea where his medical bag was buried, and he could offer only the most rudimentary assistance. Mr. Tothill felt that the elderly man was the most seriously injured, but the doctor found that it wasn't so. The old man had fainted, but when he was brought round the doctor found nothing more serious in his condition than a sprained wrist and a large swelling on his bald head. His wife, on the other hand, who was sitting on the ground beside her husband and weeping softly, had not noticed a severe laceration on her own cheek. It had probably been made by one of her knitting needles. She still clutched the needles tightly in her hands, but she didn't seem to be aware that the shawl she'd been knitting was hanging from them in shreds. Long strands of yarn stretched from her lap to someplace under the wreckage.

The doctor, unaccountably moved by the destroyed knitting, knelt beside her and gently wrested the needles from her fingers. He bound her bloody cheek with a large handkerchief; it was all he could do for her now. Perhaps it was fortunate that the confusion of her mind muffled the shock of the accident for her. With an almost-silent sigh, he got to his feet and turned his attention to the other victims. One of the outside passengers had dislocated a shoulder; another, who had fallen from the box into the ditch on his face, had so much blood pouring from his nose that the doctor had the greatest difficulty in staunching it. And the neatly dressed gentleman, completely dazed, had suffered a torn ear and a broken arm. The doctor patched up these wounds as best he could under these straitened circumstances. It was not until he'd done all he could that he suddenly realized he'd seen nothing of Jeremy Beringer.

It was then that the nobleman-turned-coachman tapped him on the shoulder. Dr. Pomfrett turned to face a tall, dark-eyed man whose face was ashen and whose eyes were agonized with guilt. A trail of blood trickled down his face from under his high hat. "You've been injured," the doctor said flatly. "Take off that hat and let me look—"

"Never mind that. Will you come with me, please?" The thick drunkenness of his voice was no longer in evidence. The accident had completely sobered him. The doctor followed him round the wreckage to what had been the carriage roof. A small opening had been gouged out of it. Mr. Tothill and the man with the hat tied to his head were kneeling before it, staring inside with looks of horror on their faces, but when they heard footsteps they rose quickly to their feet and stepped aside.

The coachman got down on hands and knees and crept inside the hole. Dr. Pomfrett followed. There, surrounded by wreckage, Mr. Jeremy Beringer lay prone, a bouquet of blossoms, miraculously almost unblemished, sheltered in the crook of one twisted arm.

Dr. Pomfrett's heart froze for a moment in his chest. It was many seconds before he was able to expel his breath. "Shall I turn him over?" the coachman asked in a whisper, a flicker of hope mixed with the despair in his voice.

The doctor shook his head. He didn't need to turn the fellow over to learn the truth. He knew at once that the young man would never attend his wedding in Todmorden. Jeremy Beringer was dead.

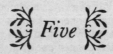

Five

The sleety rain had ended and the sky was actually showing patches of blue by late afternoon of Tess's wedding day, giving both the mother and the mother-in-law of the bride cause for optimism. Although the groom had not yet arrived from London, no one in either the Beringer or Brownlow household was particularly worried. It was to be expected that the dreadful weather of the previous twenty-four hours would have delayed the stage. Everyone agreed that Jeremy would surely return in plenty of time for the wedding.

Meanwhile, arrangements for the ceremony were swiftly proceeding. Lady Brownlow had already made several forays down to the kitchen to supervise the preparation of an elaborate dinner for thirty guests. The butler was busily at work in the library (where the vicar would be conducting the brief service), turning it into a miniature chapel by clearing out all the more massive pieces of furniture and setting the chairs into formal rows facing the fireplace before which the vicar and the betrothed couple would stand. All the housemaids were frenziedly dusting and polishing every chandelier, banister, and windowsill in the house, while Lady Beringer, who'd come over at the crack of dawn to assist in the preparations, was directing the footmen in the placement and hanging of a number of festoons and swags which she'd brought with her to decorate the doorways and stairs-rails.

Tess had been ordered by her mother to remain in her room

to rest. She'd tried to comply with her mother's wishes, but the bustle from below made her nervous, and she'd spent the past several hours pacing from the window to the dressing-room door and back again. This banishment to her bedroom, she realized, was no way to keep her mind from dwelling on her doubts.

The sound of a carriage rolling up the drive sent her flying to the window. She recognized the crest at once. It was her cousin Julia, who was to stand as her matron of honor. Julia and her husband, Sir Edward Quimby, had come all the way from London for the ceremony and had, astonishingly, arrived early! Tess flew out of her room and down the stairs to greet them. "Julia, my dearest!" she cried and flung her arms about the still-cloaked new arrival. "I've never been so glad to see anyone in all my life!"

Before Julia had a chance to respond to this effusive greeting, the entryway became thronged with people, each one with a specific and different purpose in mind. Kate and Lydia emerged from their respective activities to greet the new arrivals, the footmen from London came in from the coach to hand over the baggage to the resident footmen, Sir Edward gave instructions to his coachman regarding the stabling of the horses, and Mercliff moved about in the throng, smoothly directing the footmen to their destinations, ordering the maids to set out tea in the morning room, sending the Londoners' servants below stairs for a warm libation, and collecting from the guests all the cloaks, hats, gloves, shawls, and galoe shoes that travel in this weather required.

In the midst of all the excitement, Lydia Beringer (having overheard Julia telling her aunt that they'd covered the miles between London and Todmorden in less than fifteen hours) managed to inquire of Sir Edward how it was that they'd made the trip from London in such good time. "Why, the London stage was supposed to have left at ten last night," she told him, suddenly worried.

"We left a bit earlier than that," the calm, bespectacled Edward reassured her. "And besides, a private carriage can always make better time than the stage. I'm certain that the mail coach was forced to make stops along the way. The ice and sleet were as dreadful as I've ever seen. I wanted to stop a dozen times, but Julia wouldn't hear of it. She was determined to have a few hours of private conversation with her cousin before the other guests arrived to clutter up the premises."

"Really, Julia," Lady Brownlow said in disapproval, "if your husband wished to stop during the journey, you should have obeyed him."

Julia and her cousin exchanged a quick look of amusement. "I know the marriage service states that a wife must honor and obey her husband, Aunt Kate, but not necessarily his every little whim. Edward doesn't expect me to acquiesce in everything he says."

"Much good it would do me if I did," Edward said, laughing.

"In any case," his wife added, "he knew how much I wanted to have some time alone with Tess, so he let me have my way."

But an hour was to pass before Julia and Tess could extricate themselves from the others for a few precious moments of intimacy. Even after they'd all had tea and Edward had excused himself and gone up to his room for a nap, Kate Brownlow seemed unwilling to permit the two young women to have some time to themselves. "I don't see what you two have to whisper about that we can't hear," she said querulously.

"Come now, Kate," Lady Lydia said, rising from the tea table and making for the door, "you know how it is with young girls. We behaved in the very same way when we were young."

"We most certainly did not! We never would have hinted to our elders that we wished to dispense with their company!"

Except for a mischievous twinkle in her eye, Julia looked repentant. "I didn't mean to suggest that we didn't wish to have your company, Aunt Kate," she began.

"Of course you did," Kate Brownlow snapped, swishing to the door with a great unheaval of skirts and a nose decidedly out of joint, "but since I must return to the kitchen and see what Cook's done with the grouse filets, I take no umbrage. I shall say, however, that in my day a young woman showed greater respect for her elders. I don't know what's come over young women these days. I blame that dreadful Caro Lamb and her ilk. All those cropped curls and that wild behavior and the flouting of the authority of parents and husbands . . . ! Who *knows* where it will end!"

The young women restrained their laughter at the diatribe

until Kate had slammed the door behind her. When their laughter died down, they finally had the chance to examine each other intently. Each felt a curiosity, born of strong affection, to see what changes the past several months had wrought in the other. Having grown up in the same neighborhood, they'd been like sisters until Julia's marriage separated them. Julia was the elder by three years but now seemed even older. A comfortably plump and pleasant-faced young matron, Julia's natural warmth was now a little disguised by a slight touch of London sophistication. She sported a stylishly simple coiffure (long, dusky-blond hair pulled back from her face and tucked tightly into a bun at the top of her head) and a traveling dress of lavender ducapes trimmed with purple velvet that put Tess's country dress of gray worsted decidedly in the shade. "Julia Quimby," Tess exclaimed admiringly, "you've acquired town-bronze! I never thought it of you!"

"Oh, pooh! In town I am almost a mouse," Julia protested.

"Really? To me, my dear, you're looking complete to a shade."

"Am I indeed?" Julia's brow wrinkled. "But you're looking very pale. I thought brides were supposed to have a glow about them. Is anything wrong?"

"I'm not sure. Oh, Julia, I'm so glad you've come! I've wanted so much to have a chance to talk to you."

"Then there *is* something wrong." Julia rose from her chair at the table and perched beside Tess on the love seat. "Are they *forcing* you to wed, Tess? Is that it?"

"No, not at all. Marrying Jeremy was completely my own decision. It's just that I'm not certain that my feelings are sufficiently . . ." She paused, searching for a coherent way to describe the muddle of her feelings.

"Sufficiently what?" Julia prodded.

"Sufficiently . . . strong."

Julia frowned. "Are you saying that you don't *love* Jeremy?"

"I'm saying that I don't know if I love him *enough.*"

"I'm not sure I understand. Love is love, isn't it?"

Tess fixed her eyes on her cousin's face. "Is it, Julia? There are degrees, are there not?"

"Now I'm sure I *don't* understand. Degrees?"

"It's a bit difficult to understand, I suppose," Tess said, running her fingers through her short, troublesome curls.

"Let me see if I can explain. There is friendly love . . . that's one degree. And sisterly love, which is perhaps a higher degree. And wifely love . . . that must be an even higher degree, wouldn't you say?"

"I suppose so. Although I should not have thought of them as differences in degree but in kind."

"In kind? Now *I* don't understand."

"Friendly love and sisterly love are not lower degrees of love. They are different *kinds* of love."

"Yes, I suppose that's so. Then do you think one should marry if one doesn't feel the *wifely* kind?"

Julia, as fond of her cousin as she was of anyone in the world, was suddenly troubled. She took her cousin's hands in hers. "Tess, my love, I'm not sure I know what you mean by wifely love. But my instinct tells me to answer the question with a decided no."

"No?" Tess's eyes flew to her cousin's face. "Are you certain? Love is not the only basis for a sound marriage, is it?"

"I can't think of any other that works half so well."

The young women stared at each other for a moment with worried eyes. Julia wondered if she was saying the right thing. She'd come from London so happily, to be the matron of honor at the nuptials of her favorite cousin, who was also her best friend. She knew Jeremy, too, and was very fond of him. What right had she to give such negative advice? Even the fact that she was older than Tess and had more experience (if one could call being married all of eleven months sufficient experience) did not give her the right to speak on the subject of wedlock with the authority of a seasoned veteran.

She got up and went to the fireplace. Leaning on the mantel, she stared down into the flames and sighed. Tess had never asked her advice before. When they were young and played together, Tess had been the leader. Despite the fact that Julia was older, it had been Tess who originated their adventures and who decided what to do. It was actually rather flattering that Tess now looked to her for guidance; therefore she would not refrain from giving it. "Tess, I don't know if I'm qualified to advise you. But I've learned a little in the course of my less-than-one-year marriage, so I must warn you that it's difficult enough to establish a household with a strange man when one is in love with him. Without love, I shudder to think—"

"*Strange man?* Jeremy is no stranger to me, Julia. I've

known him all my life. And you cannot pretend that your Edward was a stranger to you."

Julia turned from her contemplation of the flames and smiled a wry smile at her cousin. "Believe me, my dear, all men are strange, no matter how well one thinks one knows them beforehand." Her smile widened as she noted the surprise in Tess's face. "Let me tell you how it is," she went on, warming to her subject. "One meets a perfectly charming man, has a perfectly delightful courtship, and goes into marriage with the highest expectations of a lifetime of contentment. And then, ha! The husband suddenly turns pompous when once you found him merely serious. He suddenly becomes jealous when before marriage he was merely protective. He suddenly becomes demanding—expecting you to wait on him hand and foot—when before marriage he was always jumping at your beck and call and fulfilling your every whim."

Tess burst out laughing. "Julia, you humbug! Do you expect me to believe all that? You cannot be speaking of Edward!"

"Of *course* I'm speaking of Edward," Julia declared firmly.

"I don't credit a word of it. You and Edward appear to be the most complacently contended couple in the world."

"Is that how we appear? Complacent?" Julia made a face of mock horror. "How dreadful! I shall take steps to change that image as soon as I return to London. I shall glare at him in public whenever I can, and I'll order him to ogle all the pretty young ladies we see. That should improve matters considerably, don't you agree?"

"As if Edward Quimby would ever ogle anyone but you!" Tess snorted. "He hasn't looked at another female since the day your friend Letty Wetherfield introduced you."

"Nevertheless, my dear," Julia assured her quite seriously, "despite our appearance of complacency, we have both learned, Edward and I, that marriage is not easy. Even if my description of the strangeness of husbands sounded like a humorous untruth, you must not interpret those slight exaggerations as real lies. Everything I said to you has more than a germ of truth. Believe me, if I didn't love Edward, I should be quite revolted with him by this time."

Tess's expression also turned serious. "Are you advising me

not to marry Jeremy? Because if you are, I'm afraid that it is too late. I couldn't withdraw now. I wish we could have talked about this a month ago. A month ago I could have taken such advice, for I'd not yet given him any encouragement. But now that I've agreed to wed him, it would be cruel to renege. He is the dearest, sweetest young man I've ever known, and he has cared for me since we were children. I couldn't bear to hurt him so."

"If you care so much for his feelings," Julia suggested, brightening, "perhaps you love him more than you think you do."

Tess fixed a pair of thoughtful eyes on the hands folded in her lap. "I've been thinking about that possibility myself," she murmured. "I know next to nothing about love, you know. Only what I've read in novels. I'm truly fond of Jeremy. I always have been, since the time we played together as children. But I've always thought these feelings weren't more than sisterly."

Julia sighed, the hopeful look fading from her eyes. "I don't think 'sisterly' is quite enough," she said frankly.

"Yes, but perhaps what I feel *is* more. Since I have no brothers, I don't know what sisterly feelings are, either. I most sincerely care for Jeremy and want to see him happy. It's just that my feelings are not . . . not . . ."

"Not what, my dear?"

Tess's dark lashes fluttered, and she lifted a pair of troubled eyes to her cousin's face. "Oh, Julia, how can I describe my muddled feelings? All I can say is that what I feel is certainly not what Mama refers to as the Grand Passion."

Julia's eyebrows rose in sudden amusement. "A grand passion?"

"Yes." Tess had to smile, too. "When Mama speaks them, those words always sound as if they're capitalized. Do you think what you feel for Edward is a Grand Passion?"

Julia laughed in relief. "Good heavens, my love, I should say not! Is *that* what you think wifely love is? Grand Passion? My dear little innocent, Grand Passions are reserved for the heroines of Italian operas, for members of royalty who are forever being forbidden to marry whom their hearts desire, and for those whose love is unrequited. We ordinary mortals who meet, love, and marry in the ordinary way do not struggle enough or suffer enough to call our affairs Grand Passions."

"But, Julia, didn't you feel a Grand Passion for Edward even at first?" Tess asked, unable to disguise a feeling of disappointment at Julia's unromantic practicality.

Julia gave the question serious consideration. "I don't think so," she answered after a moment. "Oh, I fell in love with him right away . . . and I knew without question that it was love I felt. But to call it a Grand Passion would be, I think, an overstatement. If *that's* all you think is lacking in your feeling for your Jeremy, then don't give the matter a second thought. If you ask me, a Grand Passion is probably more trouble than it's worth."

"Do you really think so?"

"I'm certain of it. All that rodomontade . . . all those declarations, accusations, misunderstandings . . . all that rending an emotion to tatters . . . all those bitter quarrels and weeping reunions . . . ! I tell you frankly, it would all be too much for me."

Tess grinned. "Yes, I see what you mean. It sounds just like the sort of thing Mama enjoys. I would hate it!" She smiled at her cousin as a cloud seemed to lift its shadow from her face. "I must admit that you've lightened a load in my heart. I was truly fearful that something essential was missing from my life."

"I'm glad that I have." The cousins embraced warmly. "And *I* must admit," Julia added, "despite the dreadful things I said before about the state of matrimony in general and my life with Edward in particular, if you and Jeremy do as well as Edward and I, you may look forward to a great deal of happiness! Now, let's make haste and go upstairs. It's almost time for the nuptials! I want to take a look at your gown before we dress."

They ran up to Tess's bedroom, but Julia's exclamations over the beauties of the lace and seed pearls which so lavishly trimmed the gown had hardly been expressed when they were interrupted by a knock at the door. "Sorry to bother you, Miss Tess," Mercliff said from the doorway, "but there's a gentleman downstairs waiting to see you."

Tess noticed an unusual pucker in Mercliff's brow. "A gentleman?" she asked, suddenly apprehensive.

"Yes, miss. Said his name's Pomfrett. Doctor Pomfrett."

"But I don't know any Doctor Pomfrett. Why didn't you call Mama?"

"He asked most particularly for you, Miss Tess. He didn't want to see anyone else. Said it was urgent. He's waiting in the morning room."

Tess threw Julia a quick glance. "Will you come with me, please?"

"He said only you, Miss Tess," the butler said.

"Never mind," Tess snapped. "He'll talk to both of us or not to anyone!"

Tess's feeling of apprehension increased as she hurried down the stairs. Julia, following closely behind, could almost see the tension in the tightness of her cousin's clenched hands and the erectness of her carriage. But the gentleman awaiting them in the morning room did not have a threatening aspect. He was, in fact, a kindly looking man with a tall hat in one hand and a bouquet of flowers in the other. The flowers surprised Julia; where on earth had the fellow managed to find so many varied blooms in the middle of winter?

Tess was also staring at the flowers. Some of them were crushed, and there was a peculiar red smudge on the tissue paper . . .

"Are you Miss Brownlow?" the gentleman was asking, obviously trying to keep his face impassive by the exertion of great effort.

Tess nodded, unable to speak. Something had frozen the blood in her veins, making her feel as stiff as a statue.

"I regret . . ." the doctor mumbled. He pressed his lips together and turned to Julia as if hoping for some assistance. "I only wish . . ." He paused, turned back to Tess, and after a deep breath, plunged ahead. "It happens, ma'am, that I was traveling on the London–Manchester stage last night—"

"With . . . Jeremy?" Tess managed, her tongue dry.

"Jeremy Beringer, yes. He mentioned your name, you see—" The doctor's eyes fell from her face. "I didn't know who else to . . ." He paused again, unable to go on. This was even more difficult than he'd imagined it would be.

The silence hung in the room like an ominous cloud. "That's blood, isn't it?" Tess asked numbly.

"Blood?"

"On the paper there?"

The doctor, startled, looked at the wrapping of the bouquet. "Oh! Yes, I . . . I hadn't noticed. I'm terribly sorry . . . !"

"Oh, my God!" Julia cried in sudden understanding. "Have you come to tell us that something has happened to Mr. Beringer?"

But Tess had already seen the answer in Dr. Pomfrett's eyes. There was not a hint in those eyes of any hope at all. The doctor, his expression of controlled detachment giving way to one of agonized sympathy, wordlessly held out the flowers. Tess took a shaking step backward. All she could see was the dreadful red smudge that seemed to her to be growing larger and darker as she stared. Her knees buckled and a low moan sounded in her throat as the darkness swelled up, over and around her until it enveloped her completely.

Six

Throughout the bleak winter months that followed, Julia sent repeated invitations to Tess to come to stay with her in London, but it was not until spring that Tess finally came. Within a few days of her arrival, however, Julia began to regret that she'd invited her friend.

Julia and her husband were a down-to-earth, practical couple who had not a touch of romantic nonsense about them. Sir Edward Quimby, a gentleman of means whose good mind was made even better by an excellent education, did not indulge in the excesses and fripperies of most of the men of wealth in London. He didn't play cards, engage in fisticuffs, or pursue lightskirts. Instead, he was an active member of the London Historical Society and spent a good part of his time in research for a book he was writing on British naval battles. His only interest in fashion was the cut of his hair. Prematurely gray, he took pride in the impressive dignity his hair color imparted to his otherwise unnoteworthy appearance. The coats he wore on his stocky frame were unremarkable, his waistcoats were dull, and his boots no more than serviceable, but his hair was always cut, brushed, and combed in the latest mode. If one saw him strolling on the street, with his out-of-fashion beaver perched squarely on his brow and his spectacles dangling from a black ribbon round his neck, one would take him for a schoolmaster rather than a well-to-do baronet.

Julia, however, found his appearance perfectly satisfactory. She was quite content with her husband and their quiet life. She spent her days rewriting her husband's notes, visiting the wonderful London museums and shops, or, occasionally, taking tea with Lady Wetherfield or one of her other London acquaintances. Although the couple would have been readily granted full membership in the *haute ton* under the aegis of Lady Wetherfield (who was a distant connection of Julia's father, and who had not only been instrumental in matching Julia with Sir Edward but who'd befriended her from the first day of her arrival in this huge, frightening city), they did not choose to take advantage of the benefits of mingling in society. They were quite content to remain quietly on the fringes. But when Julia learned Tess's purpose in coming to London, she had an uncomfortable premonition that the quiet life she and her husband so much enjoyed was in danger of coming to an end.

She said as much to Edward at breakfast on a sunny May morning a mere four days after Tess arrived. The two of them were, as usual, breakfasting early, although Julia had not yet dressed for the day. Clothed in a filmy morning robe, with her hair undressed, she sat staring gloomily at her coffee cup, leaning on the breakfast table with chin in hand. "I'm almost sorry I invited her," she muttered.

"Mmmph," Edward responded, not looking up from *The Times*. The hour after breakfast was the time he devoted to a thorough perusal of the newspaper from front page to last, and he did not readily permit anyone to distract him. Since his wife was by this time quite accustomed to this ritual, Edward assumed that she was merely talking to herself, and he didn't bother to pay attention to her.

"I think she's going to cause some sort of stir, and we shall find ourselves in the suds," Julia muttered. "Perhaps I should avoid trouble before it happens and send her back home right now."

Edward heard just enough to be startled. He knew how fond his wife was of her cousin, so her last few words were completely unexpected. His attention was caught. "Send her back home?" he asked, his spectacles dropping from his nose. "Is *that* what you said?"

"Mmm." Julia was so intent on her problem that she didn't

even acknowledge the concession Edward had made in listening to her. "You've no idea how obsessed she's become."

"Obsessed?"

"Yes, obsessed. She speaks of nothing but vengeance for the accident to Jeremy. She *thinks* of nothing else."

Edward put aside *The Times,* returned his spectacles to their place on his nose, and blinked through them at his wife across the table. "Vengeance? What on earth are you talking about? Vengeance against whom?"

"Against the driver of the coach."

Edward was completely confused. "Coach? What coach?"

His wife glared at him in disgust. "What coach do you think? The one that caused Jeremy's death! Tess has spent all these months brooding about something she overheard at his funeral. Do you remember my mentioning the gentleman who brought her the news?"

"Yes, I think so. It was a Dr. Pomeroy or some such name."

"Dr. Pomfrett. Well, it seems that he remarked to someone in Tess's hearing that the coach was driven that night by a drunken nobleman who liked to play at being a coachman."

"Ah, yes. An FHC man. Coach driving is a popular sport in those circles, you know."

"I didn't know. What an absurdity!"

"Yes, I suppose it is. But not worse than other absurdities of the Corinthian set, like boxing or cockfighting or dueling. However, I can understand why Tess feels bitterly toward the idiot who caused the accident. To endanger one's own life for sport is one thing; to cause death and injury to innocent bystanders is quite another."

Julia peered at her husband in some surprise. "Are you saying you think Tess is *right* in pursuing this . . . this madness?"

"In seeking some sort of revenge? No, of course not. I'm only saying that I can sympathize with her feelings."

"Thank you for that, at least, Edward," came a voice from the doorway, and Tess entered the breakfast room in an angry flounce of ruffles and ribbons (having been told by Julia that a morning robe was the most appropriate manner of dress for breakfast), sat down at the table and reached for the coffee-pot. "At least *someone* in this house has some sympathy for me in my 'madness.'"

"You needn't climb on your high ropes with me, my girl," Julia said, feeling not the least embarrassment at having been overheard. "If your scheme is not mad, it is something very close to it! And I would not be a friend if I didn't stop you from pursuing it."

"I don't see how you can call a scheme mad before it is even concocted," Tess retorted, pouring her coffee with a completely steady hand.

"The fact that you even *contemplate* concocting such a scheme is mad," Julia replied.

"Julia's right, of course," Edward put in calmly. "Even assuming you could identify the culprit—which in itself sounds an impossible task—there isn't much you could do to him. It was an accident, after all. There was no law broken."

"Exactly so," his wife agreed. "What would you do if you found him? Challenge him to a duel?"

"Something much worse," Tess muttered grimly. "In a duel he'd have a fighting chance. I intend to concoct a scheme in which he'll have no chance at all!"

"Do you see?" Julia demanded of her husband. "Was I not right? The girl's obsessed! Quite mad! Tess, my dear, what shall I *do* about you?"

"What you should do is to remain my friend and try to understand," Tess said. "You really don't, you know. If you did, you'd know that though I'm not quite mad yet, I shall certainly become so if I don't *do* something about the monster who caused all this."

"Feeling compelled to do something *is* an obsession," Julia pointed out reasonably. "Don't you see that?"

Tess shook her head. "I don't care what you call it. Perhaps I *am* obsessed. But there's a lump of pain inside me that I've been carrying about since the day Jeremy died, and I know it won't ease until I've done something about the perpetrator." She stood up and walked to the window. The bright sunlight made a dazzle of the small, walled garden at the rear of the Quimbys' town house, but Tess didn't even see it. Her eyes were fixed on something else . . . on a dark vision that she'd seen only in imagination but that had not left her mind for months. "A reckless, drunken gamester took a drive that night for sport—only for sport, mind you!—and by morning had ruined several lives. Several, not just one!"

Julia's firm, practical, commonsensical attitude began to wilt. "I *do* understand, dearest, truly I do. You mustn't believe I lack sympathy. But—"

"Jeremy was only twenty-four, you know. Only a boy, really. Only just beginning to live."

"Tess, *don't*—!"

Tess didn't seem to hear. "His mother is quite lost," she went on, her voice strangely empty even of sadness or self-pity. "Poor, dear Lady Lydia . . . she's only a shadow of herself. She has none of her old vitality. She hasn't left her house since that day. Mama walks over there every afternoon to make certain she takes some nourishment. I don't visit very often anymore, you know. The sight of me only makes her weep."

Julia's eyes misted. "Oh, my dear! I know the pain must be insupportable for you both."

"Yes, it is. Quite insupportable. For me it's bad enough, but I was not yet Jeremy's wife. For his mother, however . . ." She couldn't go on, although neither her stance nor her voice wavered.

Julia had to restrain herself from getting up and enfolding her cousin in a comforting embrace. But she knew that such an act would only encourage a flood of emotions, and she didn't see any good in that. "I know, love, I know," she could only murmur helplessly.

"My own pain is mostly regret for what I never did for him. Especially when I remember how happy Jeremy was about . . . about the wedding." Tess's head slowly lowered and her hands clenched tightly. "But before he . . . before I had a chance to . . . to *give* him anything—"

"Please, Tess, don't think about it. I know the timing of the accident was terribly unfortunate—"

"Unfortunate!" Tess wheeled about and glared at her cousin. "I find that word utterly inadequate."

"I only meant to say, love," Julia explained, "that you mustn't permit *yourself* to feel guilty. The accident—and the timing of it—were not your fault."

For a moment Tess stared at her cousin, arrested. Then she seemed to shake away the thought she was having. "Yes, you're right. That's why I must concentrate my thoughts on the one who *is* at fault."

Edward shifted uncomfortably in his chair. "You shouldn't

dwell on it so much, Tess. In time, you know, the pain will subside.''

Tess stiffened her shoulders and held her head erect. "I don't *want* the pain to subside. The pain will keep me to my purpose. I want to feel it just this way . . . until I can make things right.''

"But you can't make things right, my dear. You can't undo—''

"But I *can* make the murderer pay for his crime!" She turned her face back to the sunlit garden, adding more quietly, "Somehow.''

Edward and Julia exchanged helpless looks. Julia sighed inwardly. What *was* she to do about the girl? Silhouetted against the light, looking as tall and erect as a soldier on parade, Tess appeared unshakable. The sunlight streaming in the window made her pale face seem almost colorless, but it touched the curls of her dark hair with little aureoles of flame. All at once she seemed to have become older, stronger, and more imposing. Tess Brownlow had been plucky and resolute enough as a girl, but now she'd become a woman of unyielding purpose. She'd found a goal.

Julia had the sinking feeling that this glorious woman in the window would not easily be deflected from that goal. As Tess looked now, outlined in brilliance, she seemed to Julia to be gallant, intrepid, even heroic. Perhaps she was mad, but many heroic figures must have seemed mad to their contemporaries. One had only to think of Joan of Arc; even against their will, her soldiers had the urge to follow where she led. Julia felt something of that urge now. Tess's will was compelling.

Tess returned to the table. "Well?" she asked, looking from one to the other. "Do you intend to send me packing? It won't matter, you know, whether you do or not. If I can't stay here, I shall move into a hotel.''

"Of course we shan't send you packing," Edward said, rising from the table, "but whether we can support you in any wild enterprise you may concoct is quite another question.''

"As to that, Edward," his wife murmured, her resolve to bring Tess to her senses considerably dissipated, "let's wait to discuss that problem *after* she concocts the wild enterprise, shall we?''

Edward frowned at his wife in surprised disapproval.

"You've certainly had an amazing about-face in the last few minutes. Why have you changed your perfectly sensible views?"

"I wouldn't go so far as to say that I've changed them, exactly—"

Tess reached across the table for her cousin's hand. "Oh, Julia, you *are* a friend! I shan't ask you to do anything dreadful, really I shan't. Only come with me today to see Dr. Pomfrett."

"Is that what you plan to do?" Julia asked. "See Dr. Pomfrett?"

"To learn the identity of the driver, yes."

"And is that all?" Edward inquired.

"That's merely the first step."

"No doubt," Edward said dryly. "And what's the next one?"

"After we learn who the man is, then we shall see what we shall see."

Edward looked down at his wife. "Is *that* a satisfactory answer for you?"

Julia shrugged helplessly. "I suppose it must be."

Tess squeezed her hand in gratitude. "Then you'll go with me?"

Julia returned the affectionate pressure of the handclasp. "I suppose I am the greatest fool alive, or that your madness is contagious, but of course I'll go with you!"

The two women smiled at each other, happy to have recovered the closeness that had disappeared during the past few days. But Edward let out a disgusted breath. "Julia! Have you suddenly grown more hair than sense? Did you not say, less than fifteen minutes ago, that this business will land us all in the suds? Are you now intending to *support* your cousin in what you earlier called her 'madness'?"

Julia bit her lip. "No, of course not. But you see, my love, I—"

"Never mind. Don't say anything more." He strode angrily to the door and shouted to the butler with unusual asperity to bring him his hat and stick. Then he turned back, shook his head, and favored both women with a look of pained severity. "Females! I'll never understand the ways in which your minds work!" He was about to say more, but the butler appeared in the doorway. Edward took his things and waved the fellow away. "Madam Wife," he said, clapping his hat on his head, "I'm off to the Society meeting. I shall be gone all day. That gives you plenty of time to plot your mischief. But if and when the two of you decide on some sort of heinous scheme for revenge, I don't want to know *anything* about it!"

He marched out into the corridor, stopped, turned, and marched back to the doorway again. Taking a stance on the threshold and gesturing with his cane, he added in a voice of dire foreboding, "But if this business ends with the two of you dangling from a gibbet, I shall not be a bit surprised!"

☙ Seven ☙

Dr. Pomfrett proved to be a reluctant informant. "I don't see what good it will do for you to know the gentleman's identity," he said to the two young women seated on stools before him in his modest surgery on Brooke Street. "There's nothing you can do to bring him to justice. I would certainly have done something about it already, if there were something to be done."

He had brought them into his surgery to save time; in the surgery he could at least clean and rearrange his instruments while they spoke. He was not happy to see them. For one thing, they were stealing precious time from his day. Two patients were already waiting in the anteroom to see him, and there would undoubtedly be one or two more before the ladies took their leave. And for another thing, they were forcing him to remember an experience he would prefer to forget.

The surgery was small and sparsely furnished. The two stools the doctor had pulled up for the ladies were the only seats. Besides an examining table and a number of wall shelves on which were stored hundreds of bottles of chemicals and medications, the room's only piece of furniture was a large glass-doored cabinet containing a frightening array of scalpels, knives, probes, splints, and other bewildering paraphernalia. The only decoration in the room was a vulgarly colored chart of a human body without the skin, displaying a great number of muscles, veins, and organs. At the level of Tess's eyes was the body's midsection, in which the bulbous, ropy intestines were blatantly revealed. Repulsive as the picture was, Tess could not seem to keep her eyes from returning to it.

The doctor stood at his examining table, two trays of instruments before him. "Since you are no more able than I," he was saying, "to do anything about the matter, I see no point in merely satisfying your curiosity." As he spoke he kept his hands busy cleaning some small-handled knives and scissors that he took from the first tray and, when cleaned, placed in the second.

With an effort Tess tore her eyes from the ugly wall chart and fixed them on the doctor's face. His graying, streaked hair was unruly and seemed to want to stand up on end; his eyebrows, almost white, were fuzzy and thick; and his lips were tightly compressed into a forbidding frown. But something about his eyes suggested that this was a man who had seen much of human suffering and had done what he could to ease it. Tess sighed, disliking to disagree with such an obviously good man, but there was no help for it. "Perhaps there *isn't* anything I can do," she argued, "but I must know! Not in order to satisfy my curiosity, sir, no. Not for that reason, but for my peace of mind."

The doctor frowned down at the blade of the knife he was polishing. "I don't see how the information can bring you peace of mind, ma'am. I think it will only create a greater agitation in your mind than there is now."

"I don't think it *possible* to feel greater agitation, Doctor Pomfrett."

"She's right, Doctor," Julia said in support. "The thought that the man responsible for bringing so much pain to two families is walking about among us unpunished and unscarred is enough to agitate anyone!"

The doctor's hand stopped. "Yes, Lady Quimby, it is," he said, shaking his grizzled head. "If I let myself dwell on the memory of that night, I, too, become agitated. That's why I believe the best solution is not to dwell on it at all."

Tess leaned forward. "But you see, I can't *help* but dwell on it. Julia—Lady Quimby, here—says I'm obsessed."

"I'm truly sorry for it, ma'am. Truly." He put down the cloth and the scalpel he'd been cleaning and stared ahead of him at nothing. "I, too, could become obsessed if I permitted myself . . ." He walked round the table. "I admit that there

were many nights during which I lay awake reliving the . . ."
Half absently, he took Tess's hands in his. ". . . wondering if I
should have done more to prevent . . ."

"There, you see? You, too, are obsessed by it! And blaming
yourself!" She looked up into his face earnestly. "Why should
we berate ourselves, Doctor? We are not at fault! *He* is!"

The doctor shook himself from his reverie and peered at her
curiously. "Do you berate *yourself,* ma'am? Surely *you* have
no reason for guilt. You weren't even there."

Tess dropped her eyes and withdrew her hands so that he
wouldn't feel the tremor of her fingers. "Reason has very little
to do with it," she murmured.

"Surely, my dear young lady, you can't blame yourself
because Mr. Beringer chose to go to London to bring you
flowers!"

She shook her head. "That's not it. My guilt comes from a
deeper source. You see, I could have married Jeremy months
before . . . when he first asked. If I had, then perhaps he
would never have *been* on that coach!"

"Good God, ma'am," Dr. Pomfrett exclaimed, appalled,
"I've never heard such . . . such balderdash! To blame
yourself—"

"Is it greater balderdash than your lying awake blaming
yourself for not preventing what happened?" she countered.

"Dr. Pomfrett," Julia interjected, "you are *both* inflicting
punishments on yourselves that neither of you deserves. And
that's what Tess has been trying to say. If you can aim this
need for punishment in the right direction—toward the true
culprit!—then perhaps you *both* can find peace of mind."

Dr. Pomfrett leaned back on the examining table, considering her words. "But, Lady Quimby, you keep ignoring the
fact that there is no way to administer such a punishment."

"If I knew who the man was, and what his circumstances
are, I might find a way," Tess said.

The doctor shrugged sceptically. "What sort of way?"

"I don't know . . . yet."

"But there is nothing that anyone legally can do—"

"The law is not the only route for the administration
of justice. If one has a bit of imagination . . . and determination . . ."

"And Tess Brownlow is nothing if not determined," Julia
muttered dryly.

The doctor stared at Tess speculatively. Then he clasped his hands behind his back and paced about the table. When he'd made a full circle, he paused. "No," he said. "The thing is best forgotten. In the eyes of the law it was an accident, not a crime. That is how we must accept it."

"But you *know* it was a crime," Tess protested. "You said he was drunk!"

The doctor sighed. "Yes, he was. Completely cast away."

"In my view that would be unforgivable even on an ordinary day. But on a night such as that one, his drunkenness was criminal, was it not? On moral if not legal grounds?"

"I suppose it was," the doctor muttered with head lowered. "But if it was, then we must leave it to heaven to administer the punishment."

"I don't wish to wait so long," Tess retorted.

Dr. Pomfrett raised his eyes. "I'm sorry, ma'am. I'm convinced that this matter is best not pursued. I see no good in it. Now, if you will forgive me, I have patients to attend."

Tess stiffened and would have continued to argue, but Julia's hand on her arm brought her to her senses. It was clear that Dr. Pomfrett was dismissing them. He'd made up his mind, and there seemed little hope that Tess would be able to persuade him to change it; she'd already used all the arguments she could think of.

The doctor remained mulishly staring down at his instrument trays while the ladies rose to leave. "I shall try some other avenues of inquiry, Dr. Pomfrett," Tess said at the door. "You may be inclined to push this matter out of *your* consciousness, but I cannot."

Julia quickly bustled through the anteroom and out the door, Tess trailing reluctantly behind. Tess's mind was already grappling with the problem of where to turn next. She could, she supposed, interview the drivers of the mail until she found the one who'd relinquished his post to the drunken nobleman, but she had no certainty that the search would end in success. The doctor's refusal had certainly made her task more difficult and would considerably delay her plans.

The Quimbys' phaeton was waiting for them outside Dr. Pomfrett's door. Julia cast her cousin a look of sympathy and, with a sigh which was supposed to express disappointment but seemed to Tess to reveal relief, climbed up the carriage steps and took her seat. Tess, following, had climbed up the first step when Dr. Pomfrett shouted from the doorway, "One moment, Miss Brownlow, please!"

He came slowly toward her. "There's something else I ought to say," he muttered, taking Tess's arm and helping her down, "especially since you seem determined to pursue this matter . . ." He hesitated, his brow furrowed worriedly.

"Yes? Go on," Tess urged.

"Hasn't it occurred to you that the gentleman in question may have already been punished?"

"Already? How?"

The doctor's face took on an expression that she could only describe as tortured. "I have a strong recollection of his face after the accident," he said in a low voice. "The man had sobered up by that time and seemed to be quite agonized. There are some people, you know, who in such a situation cannot forgive themselves. They live in a hell worse than any we could create for them. If this is such a man—"

"Is that why you will not reveal his identity?" Tess asked, studying the doctor's troubled eyes. "Because you think he may have punished himself?"

"Don't you think it a possibility?"

"I hadn't thought before of *his* feelings," she admitted. "Yes, I suppose it is possible."

He seemed pleased by her answer. "Then you agree that the matter is best forgotten?"

"No! I don't agree at all!" Tess said vehemently. "I only agreed it was *possible* the man is consumed with guilt. But suppose the fellow has no regret at all? Suppose he has gone on with his life as though nothing untoward had happened? Should you wish, then, to forget the matter?"

Dr. Pomfrett ran his fingers nervously under his collar. "No, I shouldn't," he said frankly. "Though I think it highly unlikely that any man could go on with his life as though nothing had happened."

"Are you sure, Doctor, that you're not judging other men by your own character? You are a good man, suffering from the accident almost as much as if you'd been responsible for it. But is the perpetrator such a man as you? If he were, would he have driven that coach in the first place? And while inebriated?"

The doctor shook his head. "That's what has tormented me since that day. I don't know."

"If I discover his identity," Tess said, eagerly pursuing what she recognized as an advantage, "I shall ascertain just what sort of man he is before I act. If he is indeed living in a hell of his own making, I'll know it at once. And my undertaking will end right there."

"You're sure of it?"

"I'm not so obsessed, Doctor, that I would rub salt in an injured man's wounds. If the man shows signs of true repentance, my mission is at an end. You have my word on it."

The doctor stared at her for a long moment. Then he clasped his hands behind his back, turned away from her, and walked slowly back to his door.

Tess, fearing she'd lost the struggle again, took a step after him. "Doctor—?"

"Lotherwood," the doctor said over his shoulder. "That's the name your Mr. Beringer called him. Lotherwood. And may God forgive us all."

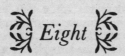

Eight

Quimby House
15 May 1812

Dear Dr. Pomfrett:

I have two reasons for writing. The first is to offer my most
sincere thanks to you for giving me The Name. You departed
from me so abruptly yesterday that I did not have the opportunity to express properly my gratitude to you for revealing
the identity of the driver of the stage that fateful night. I know
that you forced yourself to overcome some basic qualms
before you could name The Name. That you overcame those
misgivings for my sake was more than kind of you, and for
that I shall always bless you in my thoughts.

Your misgivings, however, give me my second reason for
writing. Your last words to me revealed all too clearly your inner reluctance to involve yourself in an enterprise whose
morality you find questionable. I am writing to assure you,
therefore, that you may put those qualms aside. It has turned
out that your misgivings can be put to rest. When I tell you
what I have discovered, I think it will be possible for you to
close your eyes at night with a clear conscience.

Herewith, my tale:

When I revealed The Name to my cousin Julia (the Lady
Quimby, whom you met in my company), she was very much

shocked, for she not only had heard of Lord Lotherwood but is somewhat acquainted with him. Her friend, Lady Wetherfield, is Lotherwood's aunt. The gentleman is apparently so sought-after and respected in society that Julia refused at first to believe you had remembered the name correctly. However, when I described what I knew of his physical appearance (details I had garnered from remarks I'd overheard at Jeremy's funeral), the description matched perfectly with Julia's knowledge of Lotherwood's person. And when we discovered that his lordship is indeed a Corinthian of widely touted sporting talents, a racing driver of some repute, and a member of the Four-in-Hand Club, there seemed to be no question that we'd found our man.

I immediately prevailed upon Julia to extract what information she could from her friend Lady Wetherfield. And judging from the information Julia gleaned when she took tea with her ladyship, Matthew Lotherwood, Marquis of Bradbourne, seems not at all to be a man living in a private hell! A man who is seen at all the important social functions, who is active in sports, who has a wide circle of friends, and (most significant of all) whose betrothal is this week to be officially announced in The Times, must be a man content with his life. Such a man could hardly be believed to be suffering the agonies of self-torture.

Under the circumstances, Dr. Pomfrett, I hope you will not continue to berate yourself for assisting me in the most important first step in my attempt to devise an appropriate retribution. However painful that retribution turns out to be, it seems to me that this Lord Lotherwood fully deserves it.

Yours in gratitude,
Teresa Brownlow

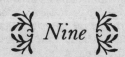

Nine

To Tess, the name Lotherwood suggested nothing more than a faceless enemy; she'd never heard it before and had no inkling of the personality of the man to whom it was attached. But to Julia, who'd heard only good things of him from her London benefactor, Lady Wetherfield, the name stood for everything that was enviable and admirable in London society. Tess's plan for revenge seemed more fraught with danger than ever.

After mulling over what she'd learned from her tête-à-tête with Letty Wetherfield, Julia could not disagree with Tess's conclusion about Lotherwood: there was nothing in the gossip concerning him that could possibly be interpreted as a sign that his lordship was suffering the slightest remorse for the accident he'd caused less than six months ago. But Julia was nevertheless unhappy that it was Lotherwood whose life Tess wished to damage. Matthew John Lotherwood, the Marquis of Bradbourne, besides being the apple of his aunt's eye, a darling of the *ton* and a gentleman of impeccable reputation, was too formidable a match for a country girl like Tess. The whole situation was certain to become an impossible muddle.

For two days after the meeting with Dr. Pomfrett, however, everything was quiet. Tess remained closeted in her room most of the time, unable to concoct even the beginnings of a scheme for her revenge, though her mind was desperately concentrating on the problem. Julia was almost lulled into believing that the whole crisis would fizzle away to nothing. But on the third day an innocuous incident occurred that set off a train of ideas in Tess's head—ideas that would lead to a plan destined to destroy Julia's euphoria, upset the peace of the Quimby household, and change the life of the unsuspecting Lord Lotherwood forever.

That day, shortly after noon, Julia invaded Tess's room in the hope of rousing her from her cogitations and enticing her to go out on a shopping expedition. She found Tess ensconced on the window seat weeping over a copy of *Childe Harold's Pilgrimage,* a work of poetry which had burst on the world only a month before and made its author, Lord Byron, an overnight sensation. "Listen to this, Julia," Tess said, wiping her eyes. "One would have thought the man wrote it for me:

"What is the worst of woes that wait on age?
    What stamps the wrinkle deeper on the brow?
    To view each loved one blotted from life's page,
    And be alone on earth, as I am now."

"Written for *you?*" Julia tossed her head scornfully. "As if you were an aged crone, alone in the world! I love the poem as much as anyone, but I will not let you wallow in self-pity over it. Besides, I didn't come up to discuss poetry. I've received an invitation card for the Wetherfield Ball! And Lady Wetherfield has included a particular invitation for my houseguest. Was that not kind of her?"

"I suppose so," Tess murmured unenthusiastically, closing her book.

"We must find you a wonderful new ballgown, my love," Julia said, pulling Tess to her feet. "Letty's balls are always quite special. I'm sure it's just what you need to shake off your doldrums."

"No, no, dearest, I've no wish to go," Tess said, resisting the tug at her arm. "Please send Lady Wetherfield my regrets. I've no interest in such nonsense."

"But you *must* take an interest, Tess," Julia persisted. "Letty is one of the very best hostesses in town. She always provides a special sort of entertainment for the evening that sets her galas apart from the others."

"Oh? What sort of entertainment?" Tess asked, more to please her cousin than to learn the answer.

"One never knows beforehand. I've been told that a few

years ago she set up a maze of mirrors through which every guest had to find his way. Last year she employed a troupe of acrobats and jugglers. The acrobats swung about on trapezes right over the dance floor, while the jugglers tossed their balls to one another over and around the guests while they danced. It was a veritable circus!''

"It all sounds very silly to me."

"Actually, it was a charming diversion. Even Edward enjoyed it.''

"Mmm. What will the woman be doing to surprise her guests this year?"

Julia grinned. "Actually, it's supposed to be a secret, but Letty confided to me when we took tea the other day that she's hired a gypsy to tell fortunes! I think it should be great fun!"

Tess made a dismissive gesture with her hand and returned to her place on the window seat, asking, "Are these the absurdities with which your London circle concerns itself, Julia?''

"It's not *my* circle, goosecap. It's Letty's. I'm only on the fringes. I assure you, Edward and I are rarely tempted to waste away our evenings at the usual squeezes. Letty's ball was one of very few we attended last season. But I should have thought *you'd* be eager to be part of Letty's circle. After all, it includes Lotherwood.''

Tess's bored expression changed abruptly, and she jumped to her feet. "Good God, I'd forgotten!" she exclaimed, a light springing to life in her eyes. "He's her nephew, isn't he?''

"Yes," Julia admitted, wishing she'd bitten her tongue off before making that last, thoughtless remark. Why had she been so idiotic as to bring up the subject of Lotherwood when she'd been hoping that Tess would forget the whole thing?

"Will he attend her ball, do you think?" Tess inquired, now all attention.

"I suppose so," Julia answered with a helpless sigh. "For one thing, he wouldn't be likely to offend his aunt by not making an appearance. And for another, his betrothal has just been announced. Letty's ball is the perfect place for the couple to receive the congratulations of the *ton*.''

"In that case, Julia," Tess said with a wicked smile, "it is very possible that I may agree to attend the ball after all." She placed her hands on her cousin's shoulders, turned her about, and gently urged her to the door. "Will you excuse me for a while, my love? I have some thinking to do."

"Thinking?" Julia echoed with a sinking heart.

"Yes. I must decide how to put this very fortuitous invitation to the best use."

Julia went downstairs to the sitting room with lowered head and faltering steps. In spite of her misgivings, Julia was quite in sympathy with her cousin's feelings. The more she heard of Tess's story, the more she understood. Tess's need for revenge was caused by something even stronger than grief. It was guilt. Julia was beginning to see that Tess was suffering from deep-seated feelings of self-blame, not only because she regretted not having married Jeremy earlier—*that* guilt even Tess herself recognized—but because she still wondered if she had loved him enough. In a hidden part of Tess's mind lay a painful awareness that her response to Jeremy's love for her had been inadequate. It seemed to Julia that Tess had convinced herself that revenge for Jeremy's death would somehow be an *atonement* . . . a sacrificial offering that she could place on the altar of Jeremy's memory that would convince not only his ghost but Tess herself that she truly loved him!

Julia sat down in her favorite chair in the small sitting room and pulled over her embroidery frame. While her fingers worked on the tiny stitches, her mind struggled with the problem of what her part in Tess's mission should be. She had to face the certainty that Tess would eventually—more probably very soon!—devise a plan that would accomplish her purpose: to make Lord Lotherwood suffer as she had suffered. And if Julia refused to assist her in her goal, Tess would undoubtedly depart from the Quimby house and proceed on her own. Julia admitted to herself that it might be better for her own and Edward's peace of mind to let Tess go on alone, but she knew she couldn't. Tess was as dear to her as a sister, and her sense of loyalty as well as her affection demanded that she remain her cousin's ally. Jabbing her needle into the fabric with a firmness that reflected her sudden decisiveness, she resolved to offer Tess all the sensible counsel and support of which she was capable. And, more important, she would make herself available to help pick up the pieces after this inevitably destructive adventure had run its course.

The afternoon shadows had begun to lengthen by the time Julia heard Tess's step on the stairs. Tess entered the sitting room with an air of decided elation. "You've thought of something, I suppose," Julia murmured, looking up from her needlework. Despite her decision to offer Tess her support, she couldn't help feeling alarmed, and the feeling revealed itself in the wrinkling of her brow.

"Yes, I have," Tess answered, very pleased with herself. "But don't look so frightened. I shall not cause you the least difficulty. At least, not very much. Will you do only two small things for me?"

Julia put aside her needlework. "What things?"

"First, when you accept the invitation from Lady Wetherfield, I wish you to tell her that my name is . . . let me see . . . what shall I call myself? It must be something a bit mysterious and inviting. Romantic, even. How about Rosamond? Or Sybil? What do you think, Julia?"

"I think you are being excessively silly. Why should you wish to take another name?"

Tess perched on the nearest chair and leaned toward her cousin eagerly. "It is the most important part of my plan. You *must* promise me never to reveal my true identity . . . and you must make Edward promise, too."

"Really, Tess, you're asking a great deal of me! You know that Edward will raise all sorts of objections—"

"Oh, pooh! You can twist him round your little finger! He does dote on you, you know. I have complete confidence in your ability to manage him. Now, let's get back to names again. What do you think of Clarissa?"

"I think it sounds like an old dowager," Julia muttered sourly, wondering if she'd made a wrong decision after all.

"Patricia, then. Or Gwendolyn. I've always thought that Gwendolyn had a rather medieval aura."

"Gwendolyn is an ugly name. And Patricia is so ordinary."

"Then what do you say to Olivia? No? Ophelia? How about Imogen?"

A reluctant giggle escaped Julia. "*Imogen?* How can you call that romantic?"

"Then *you* think of something," Tess said, getting up from her chair and beginning to pace.

Julia watched her for a moment, feeling again the dynamic strength her cousin seemed to exude. "I've always liked Sidoney," she suggested at last, shrugging and permitting herself to surrender to the game. "It always seemed to me to sound like a foreign princess."

"Then Sidoney I shall be," Tess said briskly. "Sidoney Ashdown . . . Atwood . . . Arnold . . ."

"Ashburton!" Julia smiled with satisfaction. "Sidoney Ashburton! It's a lovely name. I can't imagine one more mellifluously romantic."

Tess dropped a graceful curtsy. "Sidoney Ashburton, at your service, ma'am." She threw Julia a mischievous grin. "So will you write to Lady Wetherfield that Sir Edward and Lady Quimby will be delighted to attend her ball in the company of their houseguest, Miss Sidoney Ashburton?"

Julia sighed in reluctant agreement. "Very well. What's the second thing you wish from me?"

"Only a bit of information. Do you think you can discover from Lady Wetherfield the name and direction of the gypsy she's hired?"

"Yes, I suppose I can. But what on earth will you do with that information?"

"I will go to see her, of course. The gypsy is the centerpiece of my scheme to become acquainted with Lotherwood."

"You don't need a gypsy for that, silly. When Lotherwood appears on the scene, I can quite easily point him out to you myself. By the end of the evening you will have accomplished at least one goal: you'll have learned to recognize your enemy."

"Ah, but with the help of my gypsy, I shall have accomplished more than that," Tess chortled, striking an attitude of triumph. "My enemy will have learned to recognize *me!*"

❧ Ten ❧

When Lotherwood came down from the balcony after his visit with the gypsy, he found Dolph and Viola eagerly awaiting him at the bottom of the stairway. "Oh, *Matt,*" Viola breathed, a pretty flush still coloring her cheeks, "she kept you *such* a long time! What did she say? Was she not remarkable?"

Lotherwood had laughed all the way down the stairs, thinking of the gypsy's ludicrous prediction that a perfect stranger would be his "true bride." But now, looking down at his betrothed's eager face, his smile faded. Viola seemed to have such innocent trust in the gypsy woman's ability. How would she feel if she learned that the gypsy had predicted his marriage to someone else?

"Well?" Dolph was prodding, almost as eagerly as Viola. "What city did she predict would be your honeymoon site? Geneva? Venice? If she hit the mark, you'll have to admit she has a gift."

"Gullible flats, the pair of you," Lotherwood said, smiling but evasive. "I refuse to permit you to dwell any longer on that sham of a fortune-teller. Besides, you and she have kept me from the buffet long enough. If you don't mind, I'm for the lobster cakes before they're all gone."

"Matt! Don't be such a tease!" Viola put a hand on his arm and looked up at him with a beguiling kittenishness. "*Tell* us!"

He shook his head. "There's nothing to tell, my dear," he insisted, drawing her arm through his and starting for the buffet. "She was so far off the mark that I suspect she mistook me for someone else."

Dolph hooted in amusement, but Viola's face fell. "Oh, Matt! Really? Just what did she say that was so far off the mark?"

"Everything. Vi, my love, there's really no point in going over it. You're a silly chit for putting so much credence in the woman's performance in the first place."

"He's right, you know," Dolph said gently. "No need to take it to heart. Those gypsies are made of nothing but humbug and chicanery."

"But she was so wonderful with *me*," Viola said, crestfallen. "Are you certain, dearest, that there was nothing pertinent to you in what she said?"

Lotherwood stared down at her a moment in speculation. Perhaps he *should* tell her what the gypsy woman had said. The girl was too trusting by half. Hearing the full story might help her to become a little less gullible. "If you truly wish to know, Miss Innocence, the gypsy told me I was to be married before you."

Viola gaped at him. "*Before* me? How can that be?"

"That's just what I asked her. She replied by telling me that my betrothed would not be my true bride." He dropped her arm, took a stance in imitation of an old crone huddled over a crystal ball, and said, in an accent quite like the gypsy's, "Yer bride'll be somevun else entire."

Dolph burst into appreciative laughter, and Lotherwood was about to join in with him when a glimpse of his betrothed's face stopped him. The girl was positively aghast. She was staring up at him with eyes filling with tears. What was worse, her cheeks, which had until a moment ago been so charmingly rosy, were now white as chalk. "Vi!" he said, shocked. "You can't be taking this *seriously!*"

The poor girl merely shook her head, made a small gesture with her hands, and let her tears spill over. Dolph's laughter faded. "Vi! Don't you think it's *funny?*"

"I s-suppose I'm being g-goosish," she said, wiping a cheek with the back of her hand, "b-but what if it's *t-true?*"

"There's nothing true about it!" Lotherwood said flatly. "Goosish is a very apt word for such a question."

Viola, not finding in his tone enough of the reassurance she needed, felt a fresh flood of tears rise to the surface. "I th-think I'd like to s-sit d-down," she mumbled, reaching tremblingly for the handkerchief tucked into her bosom.

Dolph pressed his own handkerchief into her hand while Lotherwood led her to a seat behind a potted palm. "I think I'll give my aunt Letty a good dressing-down for hiring that troublemaking fortune-teller," he muttered, kneeling down beside his betrothed and taking the handkerchief from her fingers. He carefully dabbed at her cheeks while he added, "And I ought to give you one, too, for allowing yourself to be carried away by such nonsense."

The affection in his tone of voice was comforting, and after listening to his and Dolph's teasing for several minutes, Viola was able to regain her equilibrium. When her cheeks had finally dried and her usual, cheerful expression had returned to her face, she rose unsteadily. "I think we can go to the buffet now," she said. "I'm feeling much better."

"I should think so," Dolph said, helping her up. "As if anyone could steal Matt's heart from such a pretty package as you!"

"Right, Dolph," Lotherwood agreed, getting to his feet and brushing the dirt from the knees of his satin breeches. "I couldn't have said it better. Besides, you goose," he added, taking Viola's arm again, "our betrothal has been announced in *The Times*. The only way to untie the knot now is for *you* to cry off."

"I know," she said, smiling up at him tremulously. "It's just that a gypsy's prophecy has such a feeling of . . . of *foreboding* about it. I know I've been goosish. Now that I've had time to think, I don't really believe any more that the prophecy will come true."

"Well, if it *does*," Dolph chortled, taking her other arm, "you can always have me, Vi. Remember, I'm next in line."

With two gentlemen to tease and cajole her back into good spirits, Viola was able to recover the happy excitement she'd felt earlier in the evening. And when, a short while after midnight, the Prince Regent put in an appearance and came directly over to them to express his delight at their betrothal, nothing else that had happened that evening seemed to matter. Prinny had seen the announcement in *The Times,* and he not only kissed Viola's hand and twitted Lotherwood on his loss of freedom, but he promised to send them one of his favorite ormolu clocks as a betrothal gift.

By the time Lotherwood suggested it was time to take their leave, it was two in the morning. Viola was in such high spirits that it was clear she'd forgotten the entire incident concerning the gypsy's prophecy. Dolph (who'd walked the short distance from his rooms to the Wetherfield house) requested a lift home, so the three went to the doorway together. A number of other guests were departing; Lady Wetherfield's marbled, round entryway was filled with people. Every one of her huge staff of footmen was required to find hats and cloaks and to assist the guests to go promptly on their way. After only a short wait, the butler himself went to find Lotherwood's and Lord Kelsey's hats and canes, while one of the footmen brought Viola's hooded cape. Lotherwood, having taken the cape from the footman's hand, was helping her put it on when his eye fell on a tall young woman standing in the doorway. He recognized her at once. It was the girl the gypsy had designated as his "true bride."

A footman had just placed a velvet cloak over the young woman's shoulders, and she was in the act of hooking a clasp at its neck when their eyes met. Her black curls made a dark, feathery halo about her pale face, and her extraordinary eyes gleamed like a cat's. For what seemed like an eternity those eyes studied him. Despite his intention to turn his eyes from her, he found he couldn't look away. For the second time that evening, he felt a sensation like the stopping of an inner clock. If someone had told him at that moment that the girl was a witch and was turning him into stone, he would have believed it. But then, with a last look (which Lotherwood later described to himself as one of absolute loathing), the lady turned away and was gone.

As soon as he regained a sense of mobility, he looked down at Viola with an unaccountable feeling of guilt, ready to offer an apology for his long period of abstraction, but she was calmly tying the strings of her hood. Dolph, too, seemed to have noticed nothing. And the butler had not yet returned with their hats. Was it possible that only a few seconds had elapsed since he first saw the girl? *And good God,* he wondered, *who the devil was she?*

A few moments later, after Viola had climbed into his carriage, Lotherwood kept Dolph from following by putting a hand on his arm. "Who was that lady in the doorway, do you know?" he asked in a low voice.

"What lady?"

"The one standing in the doorway just now. Wearing that long cloak. You must have noticed her. She was tall and dark, with the oddest light-blue eyes."

Dolph shrugged. "I didn't notice anyone. But why do you ask?"

"Never mind," Lotherwood sighed. "Let's go home."

Lotherwood did not sleep well that night. He couldn't seem to get the girl with the ice-blue eyes out of his mind. He paced about his bedroom for a long while, trying to rid himself of the pernicious feeling the gypsy woman's prophecy had left with him, but the harder he tried, the more persistent was the feeling. And his annoyance with himself for falling under so ridiculous a spell was compounded by a feeling of disloyalty to Viola. Why, he wondered, did he feel as if he were being, somehow, unfaithful?

The thought troubled him all night long. The evening's experience even invaded his dreams. The face of the girl with the strangely light eyes made a part of every dream-image his brain conjured up, and the next morning his wide-awake mind still found itself haunted by that vision. His mouth felt dry, his tongue furry, and something was hammering away inside his skull right over his left eye. More annoyed with himself than ever, he cursed the gypsy woman under his breath. Why had he permitted himself to fall under her spell?

After another hour of pacing, he dressed himself in a long, frogged dressing gown and made his way down to the morning room. Bradbourne House, the Lotherwood London residence, was much too large for the needs of a bachelor, and his lordship kept most of the rooms closed. In that way he could keep his London staff to a minimum—just a cook, a couple of housemaids, the stable staff, two footmen, and his man Rooks, who served as butler, valet, and general overseer. But this morning, just when he was needed, Rooks was nowhere about.

Lotherwood's only hope of clearing his head was a cup of good, strong coffee, and to his good fortune, he found one of the footmen just bringing a pot to the morning room when he arrived. "Tell Rooks not to send up anything else," he said to the footman. "Coffee is all I want this morning."

But the sideboard had already been set with covered platters, undoubtedly containing shirred eggs, fish, ham, and several other foodstuffs that he had no wish to consume. With a groan, he sat down at the table with a cup of coffee, but before he'd taken his first sip, Rooks came in. "Lady Wetherfield, my lord," he announced with an air of sympathy.

"What? Here? So early?"

Before Rooks could answer, his aunt sauntered in. Her eyes were bright, her gray curls bounced under a pretty, beribboned bonnet of yellow straw, her step was light and graceful for a large-boned woman of sixty-two years, and she swung her folded parasol back and forth like an energetic young schoolboy swinging his first cane. No one would have guessed that she'd entertained one hundred and fifty of London's most select company the night before.

Lotherwood eyed her with unwonted irritation. "You are much too cheery this morning, ma'am," he muttered, "considering what a shambles your party was."

"Shambles? What on earth are you talking about?" She calmly helped herself to a bun from the pile on the sideboard and perched on a chair.

Rooks and the footman hovered over her to offer her tea or coffee, but Lotherwood dismissed them both with a wave. "Your inspired idea to hire a gypsy fortune-teller is what I'm talking about," he said, pouring his aunt's coffee himself. "Her blasted prophecies have put everyone in a foul mood."

"Have they indeed? Not that *I'm* aware of. Princess Esterhazy said the party was my greatest success. Lady Cowper insisted on taking down the gypsy's direction; she intends to go to see her for an additional reading! As for Prinny, he left the party positively beaming. Madame Zyto told him his debts would be cleared by the end of the year." Lady Wetherfield had already breakfasted, but she buttered her bun and, to ease her conscience, only nibbled at the edges. "He intends to purchase a rosewood pianoforte for the music room at Brighton entirely on the strength of her prediction."

"Then His Royal Highness is reaching his dotage sooner than expected." He eyed his aunt over his coffee cup as if she were responsible for the Regent's profligacy. "And if I know Prinny, he'd have bought the pianoforte anyway."

"You may be right about that, Matthew," she agreed, cocking her head at him curiously, "but I find it hard to believe that the gypsy could have said anything to put *you* in a pucker. You've never been the sort to let a fortune-teller flummer you."

"I wouldn't say she flummered me, exactly. But what she said to me upset Viola more than I like to admit."

"Upset Viola? How can that be? I saw her not thirty minutes ago, and she was beaming like a mooncalf. All she talked about was the ormolu clock Prinny promised to send."

"You saw her? This morning?"

"Yes, I stopped at the Lovells before I came here, to deliver a dinner invitation. I'd invite you as well, if you weren't such a Friday-faced old grouch."

"You needn't bother," he retorted ungraciously. "I want no more of your blasted invitations."

His aunt was not the least put out. She merely leaned back in her chair and raised an eyebrow. "What on earth did my gypsy say to you that's put you so far out of frame?"

"She said, my dear aunt, that I shall not wed my betrothed but someone else entirely. And she even went so far as to point out to me the very person she insists I shall wed."

Letty Wetherfield gave a trilling laugh. "You don't say! How very entertaining! Who is it she picked out for you? Don't tell me it was the Sturtevant chit."

Lotherwood made a face. "Will you forget the Sturtevant chit? You've been trying to push her at me since I was in short coats."

"Well, I still think she'd be better for you than your Viola Lovell. At least the Sturtevant girl has some spirit, which is more than you can say for Miss Lovell."

"Now, see here, Aunt Letty—" Lotherwood cut in, pushing back his chair.

But Lady Wetherfield went right on as if he hadn't said a word. "All that insipid sweetness! She'll be like a steady diet of jellies and clotted cream—they both can corrupt your blood before you're fifty."

Lotherwood rose in offended dignity. "Listen to me, ma'am," he declared in an awesome baritone, "you may have stood in place of a mother to me all these years, and you may have a claim to my greatest affection and respect, but I cannot sit by and let you malign the woman who is my affianced bride."

"Oh, sit down, Matt," she retorted, not a whit impressed. "If you want to spend your life saddled to a piece of pretty sugar-fluff, I'll say no more. I've accepted your decision, have I not? I've had her to tea, invited her entire family to my routs, taken her shopping, and done everything else a devoted aunt could do. So stop glowering at me. Sit down like the dear boy you are and finish your coffee. Yes, that's better. Now, where were we before you climbed on your high ropes?"

"Talking about your gypsy," he muttered, refilling his cup.

"Ah, yes. The gypsy. If it wasn't the Sturtevant girl, who *did* she choose for you?"

"I don't know her name. I'd never seen the creature before last night. Where do you manage to find all those eccentrics you invite to your galas?"

"I *don't* find eccentrics! But I do like to have interesting people about me. I see nothing wrong in that. What's more, if there were anyone very odd at my party, I surely would have noticed. Are you saying there was someone there last night who was truly eccentric, and that the gypsy tried to match you up with her? What was eccentric about her?"

"She was seven feet tall, had striped skin, and wore two orange circlets in her nose." His expression remained perfectly serious; only his eyes had a glint. "Is that eccentric enough for you?"

"Come now, Matt, don't tease. I want to hear about this. Did my gypsy really pick out a bride for you?"

"I've already said she did. And I've also said I don't know who the girl was."

"What did she look like? Was she actually eccentric?"

Matt shrugged. "She had very strange eyes. They were the palest blue, and when she looked at me, I had the feeling she could see right through me."

Letty's face lit up. "Oh, of course! That must be Julia Quimby's houseguest. Her name is . . . let me think . . . Ashburton. Sidoney Ashburton."

"Sidoney?" Matt's eyebrows rose in mock horror. "Are you teasing *me,* now?"

"What's wrong with Sidoney?"

"Nothing at all," he replied with a half smile. "*Sidoney*. Of course! One couldn't expect her to be called something ordinary, like Anne or Jane or Bess."

"You're quite right," his aunt said with a brisk nod. "An

exceptional name for an exceptional girl.''

Matt, who'd been so diverted by his aunt's presence that he'd forgotten his headache, now felt it returning. "Yes, I suppose she is exceptional. *I* certainly found her so.''

"Did you?" Letty looked at him interestedly. "In what way?"

"In every way, but particularly in her attitude toward me.''

"Oh?" his aunt queried. "Did she say something offensive to you?"

"No—we had no opportunity to speak at all. But considering that the girl had never met me and knew nothing about me, she nevertheless looked at me as though I were a worm.''

"That's ridiculous. Why would she do that?"

"I haven't the slightest idea.''

"Well, if I decide to invite you to my dinner party, you will meet her there and can ask her why.''

"Good God, woman," he exclaimed, "have you come this morning to invite me to a dinner party which includes that . . . that *witch?*''

Letty looked at him with an intent amusement. "Why do you call her that? Because she has speaking eyes, or because she doesn't seem to like you?"

Matt, in the act of lifting his cup to his lip, paused. "For both reasons," he said thoughtfully. Then, laughing at himself, he added, "Or neither.''

"Well, which is it?" his aunt insisted.

"How can I answer such an improbable question?" he said, shaking his head as if to clear the cobwebs from his brain. "Let's drop this subject, shall we? I hope you realize, Aunt, that this has been the most nonsensical conversation we've ever had.''

"Perhaps. But before we drop it, don't you want to know the day and time of my invitation?"

"No. Thank you, but no.''

"What? What do you *mean?*" She put what was left of her bun (now nibbled down to a mere nub) down on her plate and rose majestically to her feet. "Are you saying you are *refusing* me?"

"Yes, ma'am, that's just what I'm saying.''

"But, Matt, you *must* come! Your betrothed and her parents have already accepted, and you know perfectly well that I only asked them for your sake.''

"Sorry, my dear," Matt said firmly, getting to his feet to escort her to the door, "but I have no intention of going anywhere *near* your Miss Sidoney Whatever-her-name-is."

Letty gaped at her nephew in disbelief. "*Matt!* Has your brain gone *maggoty?* Surely you're not taking my gypsy *seriously!*"

"If you mean to ask if I believe she really has a gift of prophecy, the answer, of course, is no. But there is such a thing as a self-fulfilling prophecy. You've heard the phrase, have you not?"

"No, I don't think I have. What does it mean?"

"It means," Matt explained as they strolled toward the door, "that one can make a prophecy come true by one's own behavior that never would have come true if one had gone about one's business in the ordinary way. For example, let's say your gypsy tells you you'll find something you thought you'd lost forever. So you think: now what have I lost that I've given up hope of finding? Ah, an opal ring. Then, *expecting* to find it because the gypsy said so, you keep your eyes open and look about you more carefully than you would otherwise have done, and thus you discover it in the back of your jewel case. And you declare to the world that the gypsy is a true seer, but in reality, you *yourself* have fulfilled the prophecy."

They had reached the outer doorway, but Letty was not ready to make an exit. "Are you telling me, Matthew Lotherwood," she demanded, poking at his shoulder with the tip of her parasol, "that you're *afraid?* Afraid that you yourself might make my gypsy's prophecy to *you* come true?"

"Call me cowardly if you wish, my dear aunt, but I don't intend to go anywhere *near* that girl," he answered, removing the parasol from her grasp and opening it for her. "If that blasted prophecy comes true," he added as he watched his aunt march down the front steps in offended dignity, "it won't be through any doing of mine!"

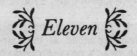

Eleven

Brooke Street
20 May 1812

My dear Miss Brownlow:

 I am in receipt of your letter of the fifteenth. I am afraid that your conclusions were not based on evidence strong enough to enable me to put aside my qualms. A man who goes about his business in the ordinary way and is seen in society with a composed demeanor may still be greatly troubled in his soul. I beg that you will consider the matter further before taking any action.

Yours, etc.,
Josiah Pomfrett

❧ Twelve ❧

Lotherwood was forced to change his mind and attend Letty Wetherfield's dinner party after all. Viola had been dreadfully upset when he told her he would not be escorting her to the affair, and when he tried to explain his motives, he realized how foolish he sounded, especially since he was avoiding all mention of the girl with the ice-blue eyes. As he explained to his aunt when he informed her of his change of intention, he'd been unable to justify himself and thus had finally agreed to go. "How could I explain myself to Viola," he asked his aunt, "without seeming to make more of the whole gypsy incident than it deserves? Besides, I *am* making more of it than it deserves."

"Yes, I suppose you are," Letty said, trying not to show the extent of the satisfaction she was feeling. "I'm delighted you're coming, of course. I think that when you meet Miss Ashburton and talk to her in the ordinary, everyday way, you'll get over this feeling of having to avoid her."

Letty Wetherfield was, in truth, hoping for an even more satisfactory outcome than that. She was quite gleeful about the whole gypsy incident. She didn't put much stock in gypsy fortune-telling herself, but this was one time she hoped there was something in it. She'd never felt that the sugary Miss Lovell would make a suitable spouse for her beloved nephew (Viola being, like sugar, the sort who would completely disintegrate in the least shower of trouble), and anything that

77

might come between that insubstantial female and Lotherwood had her approval, even gypsy witchery.

She glanced at her nephew from the corner of an eye and asked nonchalantly if Viola knew that Miss Ashburton was the "predicted" bride.

"Good God, Aunt Letty, of course not!" Lotherwood answered, appalled. "I hope you're not thinking of telling her!"

"Well, I won't if you don't wish it, but why do you think it necessary to keep her in ignorance?"

"*Why?*" Lotherwood echoed in some disgust. "I should think the reason would be obvious. Would it not be upsetting for a gentle, sensitive female like Viola to have to make polite conversation with someone who's been singled out as fated to make off with her intended spouse?"

"Surely she doesn't take all that nonsense seriously!"

Matt sighed. "I'm very much afraid she does. She was visibly shaken when I told her the gypsy said I would marry another. If she were to discover that the 'other' was a specific person—and someone with whom she was expected to sit down and dine!—well, I don't know how she might react. I think it better to leave her in ignorance about your Sidoney, don't you agree?"

Lady Wetherfield agreed. And when she was called upon to introduce the betrothed couple to Miss Sidoney Ashburton in her drawing room a few days later, she took a great deal of inner delight in the scene. Her drawing room was already crowded when Lotherwood and Viola arrived. Lady Cowper had come first, escorted by Lord and Lady Fenwick. Then Dolph Kelsey had appeared, looking as usual like an overdressed dandy in a silk waistcoat of bilious green. Mr. and Mrs. Lovell had arrived next, followed soon after by Sir Edward and Lady Quimby and their guest, Miss Ashburton. Letty Wetherfield gave the girl's face a thorough scrutiny and decided that Sidoney Ashburton was a woman of character. Earlier she'd only hoped that the gypsy prophecy would make trouble between Viola and her nephew; now she wished it would come true.

When the betrothed couple entered her drawing room, Letty hurried over to greet them and grasped Viola's arm. "Viola, my love," she purred, leading her across the room to where Tess was sitting calmly sipping sherry from a long-stemmed glass, "I want you to meet Julia Quimby's guest, Miss Sidoney Ashburton. Miss Ashburton, this is Miss Lovell, who is to wed my nephew. You've met my nephew, of course, haven't you?" she added wickedly.

"No, I don't believe I have," Tess answered, smiling up at Viola and making room for the girl beside her on the love seat.

"Then you must meet him at once." Letty turned and strode across the room. Abruptly breaking in on the conversation Matt had just begun with Edward Quimby and Dolph Kelsey, she said loudly, "Matthew, come and say hello to Julia's guest." Without giving him a moment to excuse himself, she snatched his arm and hauled him into Tess's presence. "Miss Ashburton, this is my nephew Lotherwood."

His aunt's abrupt action was disconcerting enough to Lotherwood, but his first close look at Miss Ashburton was more so. It was fortunate that his air of assurance and social facility was ingrained, for when Miss Sidoney Ashburton looked up at him and put out her hand, he experienced again that peculiar sense of shock that had struck him twice before when he'd looked at her—the feeling that all his inner mechanisms had stopped at once. If he were a callow youth, he would probably have gaped and stammered like an idiot. But years of training and experience stood him in good stead, and he was able to bring forth a perfectly normal how-de-do and bow over her hand with adequate aplomb. If he stared into those witchlike eyes a moment too long, no one noticed. Even Viola (who had no suspicion that this was a fatefully significant moment) watched with complete complacency as her betrothed performed the rituals of introduction with outward sangfroid.

When Miss Ashburton released his hand and turned away to resume her exchange of pleasantries with Viola, Lotherwood quickly escaped. Needing a drink and a moment of solitude to recover his composure, he sought out the footman with the tray of sherry glasses. *She is not so very beautiful,* he told himself with relief as he downed his glass of wine in a quick gulp. Her chin was a little too prominent for classic taste, and her skin was so pale as to seem almost colorless (and couldn't hold a candle to Viola's peaches-and-cream rosiness). There was no reason for him to react like a love-stricken schoolboy every time she looked at him. It was not the girl herself but the gypsy's prophecy that was to blame; it seemed to have affected him like some sort of malignant curse.

Lotherwood had quite recovered himself by the time the butler announced that dinner was served, so that, when his aunt clarioned, "Matt, you must give Miss Ashburton your arm, and Sir Edward will take Viola," he was able to return to Miss Ashburton's side with his usual equilibrium.

But he didn't hear the rest of his aunt's arrangements for the parade of her guests into the dining room, for Miss Ashburton had risen and was standing beside him, and her nearness was affecting him again. She was almost as tall as he, and the first thing he noticed was the fragrance of her hair. He did not dare to look directly at her, but he was aware of a shapely bosom, small waist and long thigh outlined by her shimmering blue dress. He might have convinced himself a moment before that she was not particularly beautiful, but now he had to admit that she exuded an aura of alluring womanhood.

He followed the procession and seated her at the table without quite being conscious of what he was doing. The soup had been placed before him by the time the sense of being dazed had passed. With an inward shake, he forced himself into an awareness of his surroundings. He was not a green boy, he told himself, and he would not permit the foolish ramblings of a toothless old gypsy to make porridge of his brains. He'd been seated beside attractive women hundreds of times in his life, and he'd never lost his head. Now that he was betrothed, there was all the more reason to behave sensibly.

He was seated between Lady Cowper on his left and Miss Ashburton on his right, and he immediately turned to Lady Cowper and engaged her in a lively debate about the Regent's struggle to appoint a new prime minister. The topic was on everyone's mind, because the shocking assassination of Spencer Perceval had taken place only a few days before. "I hear Grenville and his crowd have refused to be absorbed into what is essentially a Tory ministry," Lotherwood remarked.

"A good thing, too. Grenville will only make trouble if he's not in first place," Lady Cowper responded promptly.

This caught the ear of Dolph Kelsey, who was seated opposite, and Sir Edward, just two seats down from Dolph, who both joined in. Soon everyone at the table was involved, trying to guess who would be the Regent's choice. Canning, they agreed, was too young and headstrong. "He's the one who revived the name Tory and calls himself such, but he remains on the Opposition bench with the Whigs," Lotherwood said.

"It will be Liverpool," Edward offered. "Despite his early flirtation with the Whigs, Prinny is too much under the thumb of the Hertfords."

"Liverpool! Good God!" exclaimed Lord Kelsey in disgust. This started everyone talking at once, for Liverpool, though highly regarded by staunch Tories, was highly despised by everyone else. It was soon clear, however, that the staunch Tories outnumbered the others at this table: only Matt, Sir Edward, and Dolph Kelsey were opposed to the idea of Liverpool. But they were strong debaters and managed to hold their own against violent opposition from Lord Fenwick, Mr. Lovell, and Lady Cowper and minor broadsides from everyone else.

Engrossed as he was in the debate, Matt did not fail to notice that only Miss Ashburton did not participate in the discussion, nor did she exchange even a private word with Lord Fenwick on her right. When the second course was brought in, and the discussion slowed down while everyone set to work on their glazed lamb cutlets and sautéed pheasant, Matt turned to her and murmured, "You are very quiet, Miss Ashburton. Are you not accustomed to political arguments at the dinner table?"

"Oh, I quite enjoy them," she said, putting down her fork and looking over at him with disconcerting directness, "but you were expressing my thoughts so well, I didn't think it necessary to offer you my support."

"I'm happy to learn that you agree with my views, ma'am, but you should have joined the fray, not only to add to the numbers on our side but to give the others the opportunity to learn where you stand."

"I can't believe that anyone here is interested in where I stand, my lord."

"Ah, but they are, I assure you. It's always interesting to learn what a beautiful woman has on her mind."

Miss Ashburton lowered her eyes in modest acknowledgment of his compliment. "Are you speaking for the others, my lord, or for yourself?"

"For myself most of all."

She glanced at him again. "Indeed? Why is that?"

He grinned at her. "If you promise not to repeat the
nonsense, I'll tell you. I've been informed by good authority—the gypsy woman who made such a stir at my aunt's ball
last week—that you will soon become my bride. Is it not
natural, therefore, for me to be interested in your mind?"

The lady merely picked up her fork and played with the
cutlet on her plate. "I see," she murmured.

Lotherwood was startled by her lack of reaction. "You
seem not at all surprised, ma'am. Is it not shocking to you to
learn that *I* am your *fate?*"

Her lips curled. "I am not shocked, my lord. You see, I—"

But their brief tête-à-tête was interrupted at that moment by
Lord Fenwick, who was demanding Lotherwood's attention.
"I was saying, Lotherwood, that I've placed a hundred on you
for Sunday's match with Sherbrooke. You'd better not let me
down."

"He won't let you down, Fenwick," Dolph said with
authority. "When has he ever let you down in a race? Besides,
didn't Matt outdo Sherbrooke by two minutes and a half last
time?"

"Don't be too sure of me, Dolph," Matt warned. "Sherbrooke has a new pair of roans that are said to be magnificent."

"I'll still put my money on you," his friend insisted.

Julia, across the table from her cousin and near the lower
end, had been listening to this exchange carefully. She'd been
instructed by Tess to wait for just such an opportunity to bring
up the subject of Lotherwood's prowess with horses. The moment Lord Kelsey's words had been uttered, she leaned forward. "I hear that you're a most distinguished horseman, my
lord," she said to Lotherwood, and then threw a glance at
Tess.

"Julia!" Sir Edward muttered warningly, lifting his spectacles to his nose and pointedly looking through them at his
wife. "My wife knows very little about sports, my lord," he
said to Lotherwood with a touch of embarrassment. "I don't
know why she insists on speaking on the subject."

"But I am right, am I not, about your reputation?" Julia
persisted. "Have I not heard that you're one of the outstanding members of the FHC?"

"He certainly is, Lady Quimby," Kelsey put in. "There's

no one in sporting circles who doesn't recognize Matt's talent."

"Thank you, Lady Quimby. And you, too, Dolph, for your kind words. But you both make too much of me," Lotherwood said with the matter-of-fact directness that was his nature. "I admit that I've won a few races, but I think I'm getting past the age for such sport."

"Balderdash!" Dolph grunted. "You can go on for years!"

"Do you like driving stagecoaches like a coachman, as so many FHC men do?" Julia asked, leaning on her elbow and looking down the table at Lotherwood with an intent stare, quite ignoring the fact that her husband was glaring at her. "I'm told one can do that at any age."

There was a moment of silence, during which Tess noted that Lady Wetherfield and Lotherwood exchanged looks. "Matthew doesn't approve of stagecoach driving," Lady Wetherfield said sharply, a tight expression about her mouth.

"No, I don't," Lotherwood said. "I think the stage should be driven by the men who are hired to do the job. It's a foolish hobby for FHC men."

"I quite agree," Sir Edward said, still frowning at his wife.

"And now," Letty said, jumping up abruptly and forcing a smile, "I think it's time, ladies, for us to take our leave."

Lotherwood rose to help Lady Cowper and Miss Ashburton from their chairs. "I hope we can continue our conversation later," he whispered in Miss Ashburton's ear. "Your remarks were cut off at a most inopportune moment. You're leaving me in unbearable suspense."

His lordship made the remark in a joking tone, but he found the words to be truer than he thought. The conversation of the men over their brandies seemed excruciatingly dull, and the hour that passed seemed endless. Never before had he been so glad to rejoin the ladies.

He had to pay court to his affianced bride first, but as soon as Dolph joined them, he excused himself and went to Miss Ashburton's side. She and Julia Quimby had been whispering together, but at his approach Lady Quimby rose, gave him a nod in passing, and went to join the group organizing a game of silver loo. "I hope *you* don't wish to play," he said to Miss Ashburton. "I've been looking forward to continuing the conversation we began at dinner."

She looked up at him, and for a moment there was something in her eyes that reminded him of the look she'd given him from the doorway the night of the ball. A look of loathing. But the impression was only momentary, and her words were decidedly inviting. "I don't care for cards," she said, moving over to make room for him beside her on the sofa. "Do sit down, my lord."

"Thank you." He took a place beside her and turned so that he could observe her face. "Now, ma'am," he said with a friendly smile, "I wish you will tell me why you took the news that I am fated to be your husband with such complacency."

"The answer is simple, my lord," she said. "I knew it already. You see, the gypsy regaled me with the very same prediction."

"You don't mean it!" He gave a shout of laughter and shook his head in self-deprecation. "Now, why did that possibility never occur to me?"

"I had the advantage of you, my lord. When I saw you looking down at me from the balcony that evening, I realized the gypsy woman had told you the same tale."

"So you knew about it all along!" He leaned back against the sofa cushions and grinned at her, feeling the comfortable closeness that comes when two strangers discover they share a secret. "Well, then, ma'am," he teased, "what was your reaction?"

She raised her eyebrows. "My reaction?"

"Yes. Were you pleased to learn what fate has in store for you?"

She gave him a cool, appraising look. "What a coxcomb you are, my lord! Do you expect me to say that I was delighted?"

He was taken aback. It was amazing to him how easily this creature could disconcert him. He had only meant his question as an innocent joke, but he could see now that she was right; it must have sounded disgustingly self-satisfied. He ran his fingers through his hair, feeling awkward and embarrassed. "I've not been called a coxcomb before, ma'am, but you are indeed justified to find me so. I beg your pardon." His expression became rueful. "I suppose I *did* expect you to say you were delighted."

"I couldn't very well say that, my lord. I knew from the first that you were betrothed."

"Yes, of course. But I was only teasing, you know. I didn't mean to sound like a coxcomb. I was certain that, like me, you're not the sort to take a gypsy's babble seriously."

Her eyes were fixed on the hands folded in her lap. "You're quite right. I have no faith in fortune-tellers."

"Of course you haven't. Nor has anyone with a grain of sense. But I must admit to you, Miss Ashburton, that I've found the entire incident vastly entertaining. The gypsy's prophecy seems to have taken hold of my imagination. It's distracted me for days."

"Has it?" She flicked a teasing little glance at him. "Then may I ask a coxcombish question of *you*, my lord? What was *your* reaction when the gypsy pointed me out? When you looked down at me from the balcony, you didn't look the least delighted."

"I was too startled to be delighted. It's your eyes, you see. They are the most disconcerting eyes I've ever seen."

She lowered her lashes again. "Yes. My mother says they are too piercing by half."

"Piercing is too mild a word. They are bewitching."

The bewitching eyes flashed up at him. "Do you mean that as a compliment, my lord?"

He stared at her for a moment, his brows knit. "I'm not sure," he said, surprising himself by his frank and unwonted lack of gallantry. But he was remembering that, twice now, a glance of loathing from those eyes had been as painful to him as a blow.

"Not sure?" She asked the question with more amusement than offense.

"No. I'm not at all sure. Sometimes they seem to flash a look of . . ."

"Of what, my lord?"

He shook his head and turned away from her, trying to phrase an answer. But finally he shrugged and gave an ironic laugh. "It's just as well that the gypsy has no real powers of prediction," he said wryly, "for I suspect you were far from delighted to hear her words. I have the distinct impression you don't like me at all."

"Oh? Do my bewitching eyes tell you that?"

He turned back and faced her squarely. "Yes, I think they do."

"I shall not argue the point, my lord," she responded,

rising regally to her feet, "especially since your Miss Lovell has been observing us for the past few moments with an expression which bodes you no good. If you'll excuse me, I think I shall play cards after all."

He scrambled to his feet and bowed. She gave him a small nod and walked away. But it was several seconds before he was able to shake off the spell in which she seemed to have enveloped him and return to his betrothed.

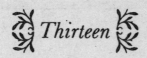

Thirteen

Quimby House
22 May 1812

Dear Dr. Pomfrett:

I am sorry that you still entertain the notion that Matthew Lotherwood, Marquis of Bradbourne, may be, in your words, "suffering in his soul." I have now met him personally, and I assure you that he is not suffering at all. In fact, I am beginning to wonder if the man has any soul in which to suffer. My cousin brought up the subject of stagecoach driving at the dinner table in order that she and I might óbserve closely how he reacted. He and his aunt exchanged glances that made it obviously clear that the question held a guilty significance for them, but aside from remarking that he did not approve of such sport, he showed not a flicker of remorse. I am not alone in that conclusion. I discussed the matter later with both my cousin and her husband, and they concur wholeheartedly. Even Sir Edward, who disapproves of this entire affair, had to agree with our interpretation of what we saw at the dinner table.

I hope this letter provides you with the assurance you need to allay your qualms, for I shall not be writing again until this affair is concluded. I intend that Tess Brownlow will disap-

pear for a while from the face of the earth. When you next hear from her, a just retribution for Lord L.'s crime will have been meted out. When that day comes, I trust you will find in the news the same satisfaction that I shall.

> Your ever grateful
>
> T.B.

✕ *Fourteen* ✕

When Tess asked Julia to accompany "Miss Sidoney Ashburton" to Islington the following Sunday in order to attend the Four-in-Hand Club race, Julia began to get an inkling of just what the mischief was that her cousin was planning. Tess had never before shown an interest in sporting activities, but now she positively glowed with excitement. She'd spread out on her bed a charmingly flounced afternoon dress of white cambric, a wide blue sash, and a wide-brimmed hat of natural straw trimmed round the crown with dried flowers and a long blue satin ribbon. The girl herself sat at the dressing table brushing her dark curls vigorously. It was plain that she was intent on impressing a man.

Julia took a stance in the doorway of her cousin's room and said in frowning disapproval, "Tess Brownlow, are you trying to make Lotherwood fall in love with you?"

"Of course not," Tess replied airily. "I'm trying to make him fall in love with Sidoney Ashburton."

"Very well, Sidoney, then. What do you intend to accomplish by that, pray?"

"I intend . . . that is, *Sidoney* intends . . . to get him to make an offer."

"An offer? Of . . . of *marriage?*"

"Exactly."

Julia began to feel a throbbing pain at her temples. "Oh,

dear. Tess, my love, do I need to remind you that the man is betrothed?''

"No, you needn't. That won't stop me. The whole idea of betrothals is that they may be broken under certain circumstances . . . as when the affianced man and woman discover they don't suit.''

"As when the *woman* discovers they don't suit," Julia corrected. "The man, once he's betrothed, cannot in honor break his word. That is the one advantage we women have in the marital stakes." Julia came into the room, sat wearily down on a corner of the bed, and leaned her throbbing head against the bedpost. "If your plan depends on the breaking of his engagement, Tess, it is hopeless. Viola Lovell will never release so good a catch as Lotherwood.''

"As to that, Julia, my love," Tess said, smiling at herself in the glass of her dressing table, "we shall see what we shall see. I've been successful so far, have I not? My gypsy trick was more effective than I dreamed it would be!''

"Yes . . . but I don't know what you intend to gain by it, even if you are successful," Julia persisted. "Is it your intention to make him mad for you and then to refuse him? Is that your plan?''

"Do you think I'd let him off as lightly as that?" Tess's face took on the look of implacable purpose that Julia had seen before. "Oh, no, my love! I intend to set a wedding date. And on the eve of that day, I intend to arrange for someone to appear at his door with the news that I . . . or, rather, that Sidoney . . . was killed in a dreadful accident.''

"Oh, Tess, *no!*" Julia gasped.

Her cousin turned and looked at her. "Oh, Julia, *yes!* Sidoney Ashburton will disappear from Lotherwood's life as suddenly and irrevocably as Jeremy Beringer disappeared from mine. Why not?''

Julia put her fingers to her now aching temples. "It is too . . . too monstrous . . . !''

"Is it monstrous?" She shook her head and stared at her reflection in the mirror, frowning at it. "It doesn't seem so to me. Mama must be right . . . I am an unfeeling, cold person, like my father.''

Julia's sympathetic nature was immediately aroused. "Tess! Your mother never meant that. You are *not* cold! Your feelings are more tender than most. But you have been much hurt—"

Tess sighed. "Yes, I have. By Lotherwood most of all. That's why I believe that my plan is the only suitable retribution. How else can I arrange for him to suffer as he made others suffer?"

Julia had no answer. She knew she couldn't persuade her obsessed cousin to change her mind. All she could do was to hope that Viola Lovell would never give Lotherwood up. With that hope to ease her mind, she rose and went to ready herself for the outing to Islington.

It was Hugh Sherbrooke who'd issued the challenge to Lotherwood: a twenty-mile race which would match just the two of them. Sherbrooke was a young hothead of twenty-two whose prowess as a horseman was becoming the talk of the sporting world. He would ride anything, drive anything, and bet on anything. Lotherwood, who was becoming tired of the endless competitiveness of sports, had initially declined the challenge, but the officers of the FHC had begged him to accept. "We can't let these callow striplings think the world is theirs," the white-haired Lord Osmond had pleaded. "Let's show 'em that they still have a thing or two to learn." Lord Osmond was a legendary driver still active at the age of seventy-four, and Lotherwood admired him too much to disappoint him. Thus the match was set.

The FHC established the rules. The two contestants would start out at Islington, each in a phaeton-and-pair. They would drive north for ten miles, immediately add another pair of horses and return to the starting line with four in hand. There would be judges and timers at the ten-mile mark and the finish line, and other FHC members would be stationed all along the route.

Members of the FHC buzzed with excitement about the match for weeks beforehand. The word soon spread beyond the membership of the FHC; by the day of the race all the members of White's, Warkworth's, and even Brooke's had become interested in the affair. Hundreds of bets had been placed, and the betting men all made plans to be present at Islington that day. Gentlemen of sporting proclivities would not permit themselves to miss such an occasion either. Even

the young dandies, who cared more about their waistcoats
than sporting events, decided it might be an entertaining
outing to enjoy with their ladies. One dismayed hostess, who'd
arranged a party for that day, had to cancel her plans, for
most of the people she'd invited were bound for Islington.

The weather on the day of the race was fine—sunny and
warm, with fresh westerly breezes. This encouraged the FHC
to expect a notable turnout, but when, that afternoon, they
discovered that the usually quiet road to Islington was
thronged with carriages, they began to realize the crowd would
be beyond their wildest expectations. By starting time the entire ten-mile stretch of road on which the race was to be run
was fringed with carriages, and the area near the starting line
looked like a fairground. Usually blasé Corinthians were
perched on the tops of their coaches, excited and eager to get a
good view; ladies in ruffles and bonnets were standing on the
seats of their open phaetons, waving and calling to one
another; sedate Londoners who, when in town, would not
have gone on foot from one street to the next, now were abandoning their carriages (which could not be maneuvered closer
than the outskirts of the throng) and making their way on foot
to the starting line.

The air was full of the carnival noise of hundreds of voices
shouting and laughing. There were even streamers and flags.
A group of young bucks had made an enormous banner
reading SHERBROOKE in large letters. Dolph Kelsey, not to be
outdone, had procured a bedsheet on which he'd painted a
huge LOTHERWOOD in red and gold. He'd attached the banner
to the tops of two long poles and attached the poles to the roof
of his carriage, one on each end. When Dolph raised that
makeshift banner in the air, the crowd roared. Despite the
loyalty of a number of young bucks who crowded together
beneath Sherbrooke's banner, there was little doubt who the
favorite was that afternoon.

Dolph's banner, hanging twenty feet in the air, was the first
thing Tess saw on her arrival. Sir Edward had refused to go,
and Julia and Tess, knowing nothing about sporting events,
had not realized that they should have left home early. The
Quimby coachman could not maneuver the carriage anywhere
near the starting line. When he found a place to stop, the
ladies couldn't see a thing. After abandoning the coach, they

opened their parasols and set out on foot through the throng.
Someone trampled on Tess's toe and didn't even look round
to apologize. Someone else stepped on Julia's dress, ripping
her hem. And when they came up to the starting point, there
was such a crush in front of them that they could not even see
the tops of the racing vehicles. "We may as well go home,"
Julia muttered irritably. "We shan't be able to make out a
thing."

Tess was about to agree when they heard someone calling,
"Julia! Miss Ashburton! Over here!"

It was Lady Wetherfield, perched on the back of a seat in
the Fenwicks' open chaise, her feet cozily resting on the arm-
cushions and her head protected by an open parasol. Lady
Fenwick was seated right beside her and Lord Fenwick opposite. "Come here!" Lady Wetherfield shouted imperiously.
"You'll see ever so much better from here."

Julia and Tess did not hesitate a moment. They climbed
aboard the carriage with dispatch, thanked Lady Fenwick for
making room for them, and perched themselves, like the
others, on the the backs of the seats. After exchanging
greetings, Julia joined the ladies in their gossip, while Tess and
Lord Fenwick studied the situation at the starting line. Two
light, open phaetons, highly polished and gleaming in the
sunlight, were poised at the starting line, one yoked to a pair
of nervous roans and the other to two perfectly matched
grays. Tess could see Lotherwood checking the breeching and
hipstraps of his grays. Sherbrooke had already climbed up on
his vehicle and was waving gaily to his cheering friends. "He
seems to be full of confidence," Tess murmured.

Lord Fenwick was thinking the same thing. "I suppose I
would be, too, if I had a pair of roans like those," he said,
brushing at his graying moustache with his fingertips. "Beautiful animals, both of 'em."

"Do you think he'll win?"

"No, but it'll be close. Those in the know're saying that
Sherbrooke's favored in the first half because of those horses.
But the betting is on Matt for the finish."

"Why is that, my lord? Do they change horses at the half?"

"No, they simply add another pair each. But even though
Sherbrooke'll still have the roans, he doesn't have the skill.
Take my word for it, Miss Ashburton, there's no one to equal

Matt with four horses in hand."

"Yes, if he isn't drunk," Tess muttered bitterly under her breath.

"What's that you said?" Fenwick asked, turning to her.

"Nothing, my lord. I only said I hope you're right."

A cheer from the crowd drew their eyes back to the starting line. Lotherwood had climbed aboard his phaeton. He waved to the crowd and then lifted his hat to a carriage on the opposite side of the road. Tess realized that it was the Lovell carriage, for Viola was jumping up and down on the seat and waving her hat wildly. Then the two contestants picked up the reins and settled themselves on their boxes as the FHC officials circled the equipages for a final check. Lotherwood, taking a last look round, spotted his aunt and waved at her. In mid-wave, he saw Tess, and his hand seemed to freeze in place for a moment. Then, just as the starter took his place and raised his gun, Lotherwood, with a pleased smile, lifted his hat to her. The gesture, coming at a time when he should have had his eyes fixed on the starter, caught everyone's attention, and every head turned to see who it was who'd distracted his lordship. Tess felt the blood rush to her cheeks, but fortunately the gun went off at that moment. There was a great uproar, and the phaetons lurched forward in a thunderous surge of motion, making off up the road in a cloud of dust and gravel. The dustcloud did not completely obscure the vehicles, however, and it was soon apparent that Sherbrooke had taken a small lead. The crowd continued to watch and shout as the carriages sped up the road and over the brow of a distant hill.

It would be forty-five minutes or more before the phaetons were expected to return, so the crowd began to mill about. Picnic baskets appeared, and wine bottles were passed from hand to hand. Betting ledgers were produced as more bets were made, the odds narrowing from five-to-one for Lotherwood to two-to-one. The roans had evidently made a great impression on the crowd.

Viola Lovell, escorted by Dolph Kelsey, came up to the Fenwick carriage to exchange greetings with Lady Wetherfield and her hosts. She seemed much more subdued than she'd been before the race, and when she made her bow to Miss Ashburton, her manner was decidedly cool. It was clear to Julia that Lotherwood's betrothed had taken due note of his greeting to Miss Ashburton and had not been pleased.

After half an hour the FHC officials began to clear the crowd from the road. The starting line had now become the finish line, with a bright red ribbon stretched across the road to mark the place. The crowd closed in on the spot, and a hush fell over them. Dolph climbed up on the roof of his carriage with a stopwatch in his hand and shouted out the time every minute. Suddenly the sound of a distant shout wafted through the air, and cries of "They're coming!" rose from the crowd at the finish line. "Good God!" Dolph bellowed. "It's been only forty-two minutes!"

A small dustcloud was noticed at the crest of the hill at that moment, setting the crowd in an uproar again. Only one carriage appeared. "Which one is it?" Fenwick shouted, but the answer could not be determined for a moment. By the time it was clear that Lotherwood was ahead, the second carriage had made its appearance. The vehicles thundered down the hill, the noise of their wheels and the pounding hooves of eight horses rising over the roar of the onlookers' screams. Sherbrooke's phaeton was a full length behind Lotherwood's, but he was slowly closing the gap. As the racers came into closer view, Sherbrooke's first pair raced up to the right of Lotherwood's carriage, passed it, and came up alongside his rear pair.

Everyone in the crowd was screaming. Both drivers were on their feet and urging their horses to their utmost. Lotherwood began to draw ahead again, and with the finish line so close, it became apparent that Sherbrooke had no chance. Whether from desperation or simply poor horsemanship, no one knew, but Sherbrooke suddenly swerved to the right, making it necessary for Lotherwood to do the same if he was to avoid a collision between his phaeton and Sherbrooke's horses. Just as they thundered past the Fenwick carriage, Lotherwood veered. His phaeton swayed dangerously on only its two right wheels. The crowd gasped as if from one throat. But Lotherwood, manipulating the reins with cool concentration, managed somehow to right it. All four of his horses galloped over the finish line before Sherbrooke's.

Everyone in the crowd, cheering wildly, surged forward to get a glimpse of the winner as he climbed down from the phaeton. The Fenwicks and Lady Wetherfield jumped down from the carriage as soon as their hero crossed the finish line, in hopes of being among the first to embrace him. Julia, carried away by the excitement, was about to follow when she noticed that Tess had slumped down on the seat, her face ashen. "Tess, my love, what *is* it?" Julia cried in alarm, kneeling down beside her stricken cousin.

"I don't know," Tess answered, breathing heavily. "It was . . . dreadful. I thought the carriage would overturn. It made me . . . *sick* . . ."

"Oh, my poor dear, you thought of Jeremy! It brought everything back!"

Tess shivered. "Yes . . . Jeremy . . ."

"You're white as a sheet!" Julia took Tess's hands in hers and rubbed them briskly. "We shouldn't have come."

"No, I suppose we shouldn't have. I didn't dream I would find it so . . . so horrifying."

"Then, Tess, my dear, let's go home."

Tess shook her head, trying to pull herself together. "We can't, Julia. Lady Wetherfield would think it strange if we disappeared without a word of thanks or farewell."

"Oh, fiddle! Who cares for that? I can explain to her another day that you were feeling ill—"

"No, I don't wish to draw such attention to myself. I don't want to give anyone the least hint that a carriage accident can affect me so. There must be no connection whatever between Sidoney Ashburton and a coaching accident."

"But you surely don't want to stay! Letty will take one look at you and know that something's wrong."

"Then, Julia, you stay. I'll go back to our carriage and wait for you. Just say that all the excitement made me feel a bit faint, so I went back to our carriage to avoid the noisy crowd."

Julia didn't want to leave her cousin alone, but Tess, as usual, managed to persuade her. Tess walked back to the Quimby carriage on legs that shook, but her mind was more troubled than her body. Why, she wondered, had she become so upset by something that was so trivial? There had been no accident. To everyone else the incident had been nothing but a momentary fright. Was it that she'd been too dramatically reminded of Jeremy lying dead under a pile of rubble? Or was it something else . . . something that she was ashamed to admit to herself?

She found the carriage deserted. The coachman had evidently gone with the rest of the crowd to cheer the winner.

Grateful to be alone, she climbed inside and sank back against the squabs with a sigh of relief. She closed her eyes and tried to remember what had made her feel ill. She recalled the excitement of the last seconds of the race, the thrill of tension when Sherbrooke's horses seemed to be catching up to Lotherwood's, the chill of her blood when Lotherwood's phaeton swerved. She'd been certain that it would fall over. At that speed the accident would have been disastrous. In her mind's eye she'd seen the disaster quite plainly . . . the rearing horses, the horrible noise, the phaeton reduced to rubble, the bloody body buried beneath it. And she'd seen the victim's face, and the sight had made her ill.

Julia had easily explained it. The incident had brought Jeremy's accident to mind. But she had to admit one fact to herself that she'd not admitted to Julia . . . the fact that the face she'd seen in her mind was not Jeremy's. It was Lotherwood's.

❧ *Fifteen* ❧

Even without rousing herself from the depth of the carriage seat into which she'd sunk to look out the window, Tess knew that the crowd at the finish line was beginning to disperse. She could hear footsteps and voices approaching, and from all about her came the sounds of carriages starting to move along the road south to London. And soon Farrow, the Quimbys' coachman, tapped on the carriage door, indicating that he'd returned to his post.

"Lady Quimby is making her farewells," Tess told him, pulling herself up to a more dignified position and adjusting the angle of her hat. "She will be along shortly."

Farrow nodded and climbed up to his place on the box. But when the carriage door opened a few minutes later, it was not Julia who looked in. "May I come in, ma'am?" Lotherwood asked.

"But . . . my *lord*, what . . . ? Where's Julia? Is anything amiss?"

"No, nothing at all, Miss Ashburton. Lady Quimby is going home with my Aunt Letty in the Fenwicks' carriage. I insisted on seeing you home myself." And without waiting for her permission, he climbed up and sat down beside her. He was still in his riding clothes, though they looked considerably the worse for wear. His shirt was wrinkled, his hat was missing, and his neckcloth was undone and hanging loosely round his throat.

"Seeing me home yourself?" Tess echoed, feeling shaken and confused.

"Yes. I wished very much to speak to you. I hope you'll pardon my coming to you in all my dirt." He made an attempt to brush his trousers. "I must be a disheveled sight. I have no idea what's become of my hat."

Tess waved a hand in dismissal of the subject of his appearance. "I don't understand," she said, concentrating on questions of more importance than his lordship's disarray. "Julia—Lady Quimby—wouldn't desert me, especially knowing that I was not . . . er . . . not . . ."

"Not feeling quite the thing?" he supplied.

"Yes."

"So she told us. She hasn't deserted you, Miss Ashburton, I assure you. My aunt Letty and I had to use all our powers of persuasion to convince her to let me take her place." He tapped on the roof of the carriage with the handle of the riding crop he still carried, signaling the coachman to start off. Then, as the coach set promptly into motion, he sat back against the seat and looked at her.

Tess was disconcerted. It was bad enough that she still felt queasy inside, but to have to face Lotherwood in this unforeseen way was not to her liking. She needed to have her wits about her in her encounters with him; she could not afford to make a slip. If her scheme was to succeed, it was obviously necessary to see him frequently, but she wanted to meet him only according to her prearranged plans, not according to haphazard chance. "I still don't understand," she said, passing the back of her hand over her forehead. "Why should you wish to take Julia's place? You are the hero of the hour. Why are you not having a joyful celebration with your friends . . . and your betrothed?"

"I shall have my fill of joyful celebrations this evening. Lord Osmond is hosting some sort of gala, I believe. That will be quite enough." He smiled in the self-deprecating way she'd seen before, that she couldn't help liking. "This is not the first race I've ever won, you know," he said with a disarming lack of pride or affectation. "The celebrations do not seem as thrilling as they once did."

"But that doesn't explain, my lord, why you deserted your admirers to escort *me* home."

He hesitated for a moment before speaking. "You became

ill during the race, is that not so?" he asked.

"Not exactly. To say that I became ill is putting too serious a face on it. I was merely a bit discomposed."

"No, you were more than discomposed. I saw you, you know."

She was startled. "*Saw* me?"

"It was just at the moment when my phaeton lurched. I saw your face. It was just for a fraction of a second, for, as you can imagine, my attention was fully occupied with the horses. But I did see you, as one might see a face in a lightning flash. Your expression impressed itself upon my brain."

"Oh?" She noticed that her fingers had begun, unaccountably, to tremble. "Why was that?"

"It was a look of pure horror, ma'am. I don't think I've ever seen such a look. And later, when I noticed you walking back to your carriage—"

"You *noticed* me?" She shook her head in disbelief. "But you were completely surrounded by your well-wishers when I—"

"Nevertheless, I noticed. You were so shaken that you were using your parasol as a cane. I realized that my little swerve had upset you badly, and that's why I've come. I wish to apologize for frightening you, and to make amends, if I can."

Tess did not know how to handle this unexpected kindness. Lotherwood had not turned out to be the sort of man she'd expected. *One's enemy should not be kind,* she thought ruefully. *It tended to muddy the purity of one's motive for revenge.* But of course, he had not been kind to Jeremy; *that* was what she had to remember. Even if in his sober moments he was generous and large-hearted, he had permitted himself to get drunk and had caused her sweetheart's death. And that was as far from kind as could be.

She turned her back on him and stared out the window at the long shadows cast by the passing trees in the late afternoon light. "You give yourself too much credit, my lord," she said coldly. "That little 'swerve,' as you call it, was not your fault. And my horror-stricken look—if it was indeed such a look— had nothing to do with you. So you see, you have nothing to apologize to me for. You've deserted your admirers to no purpose."

Lotherwood was completely taken aback by this icy response. "You have an infinite capacity to astound me, ma'am. If the look of horror that I saw on your face—and it was *indeed* such a look—had nothing to do with me, then what was the cause?"

"I don't like carriage racing, that is all. I should not have come today."

"But it's only a sport, like any other. What harm is there in it?"

"How can you ask so foolish a question?" she demanded, turning about abruptly and glaring at him. "Especially today, when you almost *overturned!*"

His brow cleared. "Are you implying, my dear, that the sport is too dangerous? Is that what troubles you? Please take my word that it is not. That swerve, today, was due to Sherbrooke's carelessness—or, perhaps, to his viciousness—but either way it wasn't dangerous. Part of the skill of driving four-in-hand is learning how to handle swerves. I used to spend hours in my youth practicing taking turns on two wheels. I learned how to handle just such emergencies. There was no real danger today."

His complacency seemed to her nothing but arrogance. This was just the sort of reasoning she expected from the driver of that ill-fated stagecoach. "You are overconfident, I think," she said, trying not to let her revulsion show in her voice. "What if you'd misjudged the situation today? What if, just this once, your much-admired skill had deserted you, and you'd turned over?"

"Then I would have been hurt, I suppose. But you said, ma'am, that your look of horror had nothing to do with me."

A feeling of fury flared up in her. "How arrogant you are, my lord," she hissed between clenched teeth, "to think that under those circumstances my concern would be for you! If I had a horror-striken look on my face, it was not at the prospect of injury to *you* but to your *victims!*"

He was utterly nonplussed by her venomous tone. "Victims, ma'am? What victims?"

"Might there not have been victims? Is it not possible that some innocent bystander might have been crushed if you'd overturned?"

"I think it extremely unlikely. Besides, I've never overturned a carriage in my life."

"*Never,* my lord?" She stared at him, narrow-eyed and scornful. "Yet one does hear of carriage accidents with fatal consequences, does one not?"

She had the satisfaction of seeing a startled look cross his face and his eyes fall from hers. "There are always coaching accidents, Miss Ashburton," he said quietly, after a moment, "but there are fewer accidents in sporting events than you would dream. We who indulge in this sport take the greatest care to avoid them."

Tess did not utter the contemptuous words that sprang to her lips. It would not serve her purpose, she realized, to call him a liar. In fact, she was uncomfortably aware that she might already have gone too far. He had withdrawn from her as far down the seat as he could go and was now staring out the window. She was sorry she'd revealed so much of her true feelings toward him and his "sport." If he was ever to offer for her, she had to make him believe she cared for him. The conversation of the last few minutes was bound to have been a setback.

She glanced over at him, but his face was turned to the window. She could see only that his jaw was clenched. Was it tight with anger? What could she now say to bridge the gap she'd so thoughtlessly erected between them? She tried various openings in her mind, but everything she thought of sounded too insincere to utter aloud.

They rode without speaking for a long while. They were almost home when she finally, somewhat desperately, broke the silence. "My lord, I . . . I should not have spoken as I did," she murmured lamely.

He turned from the window and faced her. The late afternoon sun was setting behind the roofs of the city, making the light in the carriage too dim for her to see him clearly, but she could make out the tight expression of his mouth. She braced herself for a barrage of angry words.

Instead, he gently picked up her hand and looked down at it. "On the contrary, ma'am," he said, surprising her by the lack of rancor in his voice, "you had every right to speak so. I forced my presence on you this afternoon. I realize now that it was arrogant. I seem always to play the coxcomb in your presence. But I did so only in the hope that I might ease your mind and allay the terror that I saw in your face. However, I seem to have upset you more than before. I'm very sorry, ma'am."

Her heart seemed to leap up in her chest. She hadn't expected so generous a response to what must have seemed to him a bitter, sharp-tongued set-down. She lowered her head contritely. "It is I who should be sorry. I have taken the joy from your triumph."

"Yes, you have. But only because I sense that you've taken a strong dislike to me, and I don't know why. Have I done something to offend you, Miss Ashburton, that I've stupidly overlooked?"

Under the sheltering safety of her wide hat brim, she smiled to herself. How lucky she was! The man was offering her the opportunity to regain the ground she'd thought she lost. "I don't dislike you, Lord Lotherwood," she said, looking up at him coquettishly from beneath the brim. "Whatever made you think something as foolish as that?"

But his lordship did not smile back at her. "I'd be foolish to think anything else," he said, regarding her suspiciously. "You're playing some sort of game with me, Miss Ashburton. I only wish I knew what game it was."

Sixteen

Viola Lovell's parents (having proudly watched their daughter embrace the victorious Lotherwood after the race) naturally assumed that the girl would return to London with her betrothed, and so they left Islington without her. But Viola, after surrendering her place beside Lotherwood to the dozens of other well-wishers who were surrounding him, discovered to her chagrin that he'd suddenly disappeared. One moment he was surrounded by a cheering mob and the next he was nowhere to be seen.

Deserted and bereft, she wandered about in confusion for a while, too embarrassed to ask mere acquaintances if they'd seen him. But when she spotted Lord Kelsey, engaged with a circle of friends who were still crowing over their man's victory, she did not hesitate to draw him aside. "Do you know where Matt has gone?" she asked, not able to disguise the quiver in her voice.

"He must be somewhere about," Dolph answered cheerfully. "Can't have gone away already. He's probably hiding himself. Hates to have everyone clapping him on the shoulder, you know."

"But I don't see him anywhere! Can he have gone back to town without me?"

"Not likely, if he was expecting to take you up."

"Well, he *should* have been expecting to, should he not?"

She bit her underlip worriedly. "Mama and Papa have already left."

"Don't look so frightened, Miss Jinglebrain," Dolph teased. "You don't think you'll be left stranded here, do you? Look there! There's Lady Wetherfield with the Fenwicks. Wager my day's winnings she'll know where your fellow's hiding himself. Fenwick! I say, *Fenwick,* hold on there!"

Lord Fenwick, who had just ordered his coachman to depart, signaled the man to stop. When Lady Wetherfield realized it was she to whom they wanted to speak, she leaned over the side. In answer to Viola's breathless question about Lotherwood's whereabouts, the troublemaking aunt explained (with a barely visible smile of satisfaction) that Matt had excused himself to escort an ailing Miss Ashburton back to town.

"Miss *Ashburton?*" Viola gasped, her face paling.

Letty Wetherfield pretended not to notice her dismay. "Did you want a ride back with him? We can make room for you right here, can we not, Fenwick?"

But Dolph Kelsey, much moved by Viola's stricken expression, immediately offered her a seat in his curricle. "Much more room with me," he declared, giving Lady Wetherfield a reproving look.

"Thank you, D-Dolph," the girl said, her chin quivering. "That's very g-good of you."

The Fenwick carriage drove off, and Dolph and Viola went back toward his carriage. As they walked, Dolph threw several surreptitious looks in the girl's direction. Viola's face was clenched tightly to hold back tears, and her lips were pressed together in a tense line. Her hat had slipped off and was hanging by its ribbons on her back. She was obviously in distress, but Dolph thought he'd never seen a creature so endearing; a ride back in her company (during which he was certain to cheer her up) would make a charming end to a very pleasant afternoon.

After whispering to his friend Lord Merivan (who'd driven up to Islington with him) to find travel accommodations elsewhere, he helped Viola into his rig and climbed up beside her. As soon as they were on the road, the poor girl surrendered to sobs. "I'm s-sorry, Dolph," she stammered, sniffing into her handkerchief. "I c-can't seem to h-help myself."

"Oh, I don't mind," he said comfortingly. "Go ahead and blubber to your heart's content. Though I must say I don't see why. What is there in Matt's being gallant to someone who's taken ill to make you turn on the waterworks?"

"B-But it's . . . it's with M-Miss *Ashburton!*"

Dolph turned his eyes from the road to throw the girl a puzzled glance. "What's special about Miss Ashburton?"

"I d-don't know. It's just a f-feeling I have. Did you s-see him l-lift his hat to her today?"

"Lift his hat to her?"

"Yes. Just when the race b-began. His attention should have b-been on his horses, but there he w-was, smiling and d-doffing his hat to her as if there were n-nothing else on h-his m-mind. It s-seemed to m-me that everyone remarked on it."

Dolph's brow wrinkled. "Mmmm. Now you mention it, I *do* recall it. Thought at the time that Matt was going to lose a second or two on his start because of it."

"Oh, Dolph!" She burst into a fresh flood of tears. "You n-noticed it *too!*"

"Yes, but I don't see any particular significance in it. Certainly nothing to cause such a downpour as that."

She tried to stem the flood from her eyes with her already soggy handkerchief. "I s-suppose I'm making much of n-nothing, but I'm so m-miserable! Ever since Matt t-told us about the gypsy's prophecy, I've—"

"Prophecy? What prophecy? Do you mean that silliness about his marrying someone else?"

She peeped up at him with a glimmer of hope. "Do you really think it's silly?"

"It's utter rubbish! How can you even *think*—?"

"I don't know, D-Dolph. It occurred to m-me today that she . . . she . . ."

"She who? The gypsy?"

"No, you g-gudgeon, Miss *Ashburton*." She dropped her head in her hands. "What if she's the one the gypsy meant?"

Dolph gave a snort of disgust. "Vi, this is the outside of enough! If you insist on taking seriously the babbling of a gyspy woman, I wash my hands of you!"

Viola lifted her head and expelled a tremulous breath. "I s-suppose you're right. But even if we f-forget the gypsy, there is still t-today. He tipped his hat to her . . . and t-took her home. And the other night at L-Lady Wetherfield's, he sat p-prosing with her for hours and hardly sp-spoke to me at all!'' She brushed the wetness from her cheeks and turned to her escort with earnest intensity. "Tell me the t-truth, Dolph. Do you th-think he's *t-taken* with her?''

"Taken with her? Do you mean in an *amorous* way?'' He gaped at the girl beside him in complete surprise. "You must be touched in your upper works!''

"Why?'' Viola turned a pair of still-watery eyes up to his. "Don't you think she's beautiful?''

"Beautiful? Miss *Ashburton*? She's as tall as I am! Besides, she peers at everyone like a distrustful schoolmarm. Puts me in mind of a governess I had when I was a tyke. Frightened me out of my wits, that woman did.''

Viola glanced up at him gratefully. "You're n-not just saying that to c-comfort me, are you, Dolph? You truly don't believe that Matt is attracted to her?''

"When he has *you?* He'd have to be six ways a fool! See here, Vi, you're the prettiest creature in all of England, and everyone knows it. So you can put aside these addle-brained notions once and for all.''

"Truly, Dolph?''

"My word as a gentleman.''

She took a deep, trembling breath of relief and leaned her head on his shoulder. "Thank you, Dolph,'' she murmured. "You are my d-dearest friend in all the world! You've made me f-feel ever so much better.''

He looked down at the golden head resting on his shoulder, feeling very pleased with himself. Viola had been on the verge of a serious quarrel with her betrothed, but he'd calmed the ruffled waters. He had a golden tongue, he told himself. He'd managed to soothe the pretty creature beside him and to help his friend at the same time. "If you're feeling so much better,'' he said with benevolent self-satisfaction, "you can dry off those tears. I won't have you dampening my favorite coat!''

Dolph's golden tongue might very well have prevented a quarrel between Viola and her betrothed if Letty Wetherfield had not arranged an outing which brought Miss Ashburton again to Viola's attention. Nevertheless, for a fortnight following the race, Viola was able to dismiss Miss Ashburton from her mind. She and Matt did not encounter Miss Ashburton at any of the social gatherings which they attended, nor did her name cross anyone's lips in Viola's hearing. Matt certainly never mentioned her, and he gave no sign that he remembered her at all. So completely did Miss Ashburton seem to disappear from their lives that Viola allowed herself to hope that the girl had gone back to wherever it was she'd come from. It did not occur to her that Dolph had reported every word of their conversation to his friend, and that Matt had taken steps to keep Miss Ashburton out of their way.

But Lady Wetherfield did not intend to let Miss Ashburton disappear from their lives. Although Matt had twice refused to attend gatherings at her home, she did not give up. She racked her brain to find a way to bring her nephew and Miss Ashburton together again, but it was not until Julia remarked to her that her friend had not yet seen the Elgin marbles that Letty Wetherfield was able to concoct a successful scheme.

Lord Elgin had brought the magnificent Greek antiquities to England nine years before, in 1803, but since the sculptures were housed in a temporary building attached to his home in Park Lane, they were not commonly seen. Lady Wetherfield, being somewhat acquainted with Lord Elgin, had viewed them a number of times and had always found them breathtaking. When she learned from Julia that Miss Ashburton had never seen them, the idea of the outing took shape in her mind.

"Has Viola ever seen the Elgin marbles?" she asked her nephew when she paid one of her unexpected calls on him and caught him at breakfast.

"No, I don't think she has. Why?"

"I'm arranging with Lord Elgin to visit the exhibit again, with a small group of friends. Perhaps you'd like to join us."

Lotherwood eyed her suspiciously over his coffee cup. "Join whom?" he asked.

"I've only asked the Fenwicks and Lady Cowper so far. I'll include the Lovells, if you like."

"Very well, we'll gladly join you. I know Viola would wish to see the marbles. But I hope, Aunt Letty," he added, reaching for a slice of toast and buttering it with concentration, "that you won't ask anyone else. I dislike viewing works of art in a crowd."

His aunt said nothing else. She fully intended that the Quimbys and Miss Ashburton should be part of the group, but she saw no reason to mention it. Three more people would not make a crowd, she told herself. She felt no touch of guilt. If anyone had accused her of acting dishonestly, she would have laughed and said that an evasive silence was not quite a lie.

Viola was not as enthusiastic about seeing the marbles as Matt had expected. She and her mother had arranged to visit the exclusive modiste who was making her wedding gown on the day of the outing, and she explained to Matt that Madame Durand was very temperamental and did not do her best work for clients who missed appointments. But she promised to join the group at Lord Elgin's exhibit as soon as her fitting was over.

Lotherwood, having no lady to escort, arrived at the exhibit before any of the others. Pleased at having the opportunity to view the sculptures in privacy, he went immediately to the alcove which housed his favorite of all the pieces, the fragment from the east pediment of the Parthenon representing the head of one of the moon goddess's chariot horses. Something about this sculpture particularly moved him. The chariot that the horse was supposed to be drawing had ostensibly sunk below the horizon with the setting moon, and all that could still be seen was the horse's head, looking tired and spent. Its great eyes were wide with weariness, and its lower jaw hung limply open almost as if the animal were gasping for breath. But despite the weariness, the horse had a power and strength that were unmistakable; there was a grandeur in the massive profile that Lotherwood loved. He liked to imagine that, if the goddess had needed him, the tired animal would have summoned the strength to gallop like the wind.

"I might have suspected that you'd be with the horses," said a low-pitched voice behind him. "You look as if you'd like to stroke his nose."

He turned to find Miss Ashburton smiling at him, and before he had a chance to reign in his emotions, he felt a surge of gladness at the sight of her. She wore a dress of deep amber, with a dark, wine-colored shawl thrown over it. One gloved hand was untying the ribbon of her straw bonnet, while the other was held out to him. Standing poised in the doorway of the alcove, with the rays of sun from the high windows lighting her face, she seemed magnificent, like the subject of a Renaissance portrait or the heroine of an opera. His eyes drank her in, as if they'd been starved for color by having gazed too long at the pallid stones.

But he recovered quickly. "Good afternoon, Miss Ashburton," he said, removing his hat and bowing over her hand. "Yes, I have a strong affection for horses, even those of marble." He turned back to the sculpture, wondering why he didn't feel at all like murdering his aunt for lying to him. "This one is especially beautiful, don't you agree?"

She came up beside him and studied the sculpture. "Marvelous. But a little sad, too, I think . . . as if he'd been driven too long and too far."

"Yes, I feel that, too."

They stared at the horse's head for a long moment, Lotherwood finding himself unduly pleased at her reaction. "But you mustn't believe that I find horses the only work of art worth noticing. There are many pieces here I could recommend to your attention. Have you seen the Herakles in the next room?"

"Good heavens, my lord, you astound me. Are you an expert in classical sculpture? I thought you knew only horses."

"Now, that is a set-down if ever I heard one!" He laughed, taking her arm and strolling out toward the main room. "But you were quite right in your first assumption. I know very little about classical sculpture or anything else, other than horses. Of the four levels of gentlemanly types, I stand on the very lowest."

"Four levels?" she asked, looking up at him curiously. "What levels are those?"

"Haven't you heard of the four types of gentlemen? Then allow me, ma'am, to enlighten you. This method of classification may stand you in good stead when you decide to choose a husband. On the highest rung you will find the Religious Gentleman, who, even if he doesn't take holy orders, spends his days in doing good works for the benefit of humanity. One step below is the Scholarly Gentleman, who studies the classics, reads the great thinkers, and writes philosophical treatises in his mature years. On the third rung is the Military Gentleman, to whom the development of his mind and soul may not be of primary importance, but who is willing to give his life for the protection of his country and is therefore also admirable. But on the bottom rung, alas, we find the Athletic Gentleman, who has nothing at all to recommend him but his sense of sportsmanship and his well-developed muscles."

She laughed, a full-throated, gurgling laugh that delighted

him. "You are too modest, my lord. I know you have more to recommend you than that."

"Do you, ma'am? But didn't you just remark that you thought I knew about nothing but horses?"

"Yes, but I am already amending that opinion."

He stopped in his tracks in mock astonishment. "You don't say! Then tell me, please, what is it you've discovered?"

But before she could respond, they came upon the others in the group and had to separate. While Lotherwood made his greetings to his aunt and her guests, Lady Cowper took Tess's arm and led her to view some of the sculptures in the far corner of the room.

By the time they returned, an unexpected sight greeted Tess's eye. Lotherwood had evidently been describing to Lord Fenwick his theory of how the various marbles had appeared on the ancient Parthenon, and the others in the group had, one by one, come up behind to listen. Lotherwood did not know that his aunt, Lady Fenwick, Julia, and Edward were quietly grouped behind him and eavesdropping on his words. Lotherwood was suggesting that the sculptures of the Parthenon's West Pediment (which were so much damaged that it was difficult to make sense of them) represented the contest between Poseidon and Athena for possession of ancient Attica. He pointed out that the weathered torso of a huge, powerful figure could be the sea god, that the reclining figure (which had undoubtedly filled the left corner of the pediment) might be a minor god watching the contest, and that a third torso might represent the divine messenger Hermes, who, according to legend, had accompanied Athena to the contest. Tess could not help being impressed by his lordship's knowledge of mythology, his eye for sculptural detail, and the modest yet persuasive manner in which he spoke. And when Edward came forward (startling Lotherwood by declaring enthusiastically, "By heavens, old man, I'm dashed if you haven't got the right of it!"), she broke into applause with all the others.

Lotherwood flushed in embarrassment. "We're not likely ever to learn whether I've got the right of it or not," he muttered, looking about him for a way to escape, "so I'm quite safe in spouting my theories. Come, Miss Ashburton, I want you to see some other horses that I like."

As he ushered her boldly out of the room and into another

small alcove, Lady Fenwick threw Letty a quizzical glance. Lady Fenwick had been privy to much of the behind-the-scenes activity on the day of the race, and it suddenly occurred to her to wonder if the betrothed Lotherwood was showering too much attention on the attractive Miss Ashburton. She wondered if she should drop a word of warning into Letty's ear.

Meanwhile Lotherwood had stopped before a fragment showing the head of a horse rising up from the base of the pediment. In the midst of his explanation that this was probably the horse of the rising sun god, contrasting with the horse they'd seen earlier which drew the chariot of the setting moon goddess, he suddenly stopped speaking. Tess looked at him curiously. "Is something the matter, my lord?"

Abstracted, he shook his head. "Must you be forever calling me 'my lord'?" he asked in irritation. "My name is Matthew, although that's too biblical for me. I prefer to be called Matt."

"I don't think it would be suitable for me to do so, my lord, any more than it would be for you to call me Sidoney."

He gave a sudden laugh. "Sidoney. I should have great difficulty calling you that, even if it *were* suitable. Never have I heard a more ridiculous name."

"Then it's just as well you can't use it," she answered tartly.

"Very well, don't eat me. I meant no offense." He looked down at the hat in his hand and fingered the brim absently. "I suppose it was unsuitable for me to take you away from the others like this, too," he muttered.

"Quite unsuitable. I only hope there will not be talk to reach Miss Lovell's ears. We must be going back."

"Dash it all," he said, taking her arm as if to keep her from running off, "why is it I never find the opportunity to have a proper conversation with you?"

"I beg to differ, my lord," she teased. "Nothing we've ever said to each other has been *im*proper, has it?"

"I'm serious, ma'am." He dropped her arm and took hold of her chin instead, tilting her head up ever so slightly. "I have a keen desire to sit beside you somewhere in private, with no one about to disturb us and at least two hours of time ahead of us, where I can ask you questions and learn what goes on behind those eerie eyes of yours."

"That, sir," she said, removing his hand from her chin, "would be more unsuitable than anything else you've suggested."

He sighed. "I suppose it would. Do you ride?"

"What?"

"Do you ride? Perhaps we could meet one morning and ride in the park for an hour or so."

She shook her head and started toward the door. "That is quite impossible, and you know it. Come, my lord. Our absence will be noted."

When they returned to the group, they found that Viola and her mother had arrived. Viola was engaged in an animated conversation with Lady Cowper, but when she looked round and saw Miss Ashburton she turned quite pale. Lotherwood went over at once to greet her. "You are looking lovely, my dear," he said in her ear. "I'm glad you're finally here."

"I don't think you've m-missed me," she answered in a small voice.

"Yes, I have. I've been waiting to show you my favorite piece in this collection. It's in an alcove over there. It's an absolutely wonderful horse's head. Come and let me show it to you."

Viola kept her head lowered, but the position did not hide the pout of her lovely underlip. "I don't wish to see any old horses," she said in a shaking voice. "I want to go home."

"Are you sure, Vi? There are so many marvelous things here to see." He took her arm in his and leaned down so that he could see her face. "After spending an hour among these masterpieces, you'll feel so inspired that—"

She pulled her arm away petulantly. "I want to go home! If you don't wish to escort me, then I can go with Mama."

They were standing a little apart from, but in full view of, all the others. Lotherwood could see that everyone was aware of their quarrel and its cause. He reddened in embarrassment. "I'll be glad to escort you, if that is what you wish," he said quietly. "We need only to say our good-byes."

He put on a public face and moved among his friends with perfectly appropriate smiles and bows. He said and did everything he ought, but inside he felt ill. He found himself wondering if he'd made a terrible mistake in offering for Viola. The little incident had made her seem to him like a spoiled child; he felt as if he'd seen her throw a tantrum. He hated having been party to that public scene. The fact that he himself was very much to blame did not lessen his revulsion. One's own conduct is never quite as repugnant in one's eyes as someone else's.

He was, however, quite aware of his guilt. This afternoon's encounters had forced him to admit to himself that his attraction to Miss Ashburton was an actuality, stronger and more real than any gypsy could conjure up in a crystal ball. He felt more excitedly alive in her presence than he'd felt in any race, and in her absence his memory of her consumed him. In contrast to her, his betrothed seemed childish and dull.

But perhaps he was being unfair. He was infatuated, and Viola sensed it. She was jealous, and jealousy was known to distort one's character. It often made people behave in humiliating ways. He must be careful not to blame Viola for his own faults. And in any case, he was betrothed—shackled for a lifetime—and he knew he had no choice but to make the best of it.

He came up to Miss Ashburton to say good-bye, determined to make it their last encounter. If he kept himself out of her way, he was certain he could overcome his infatuation and face his betrothed with a clear conscience. "Good-bye, Miss Ashburton," he said, taking her gloved hands and looking intently into those bewitching eyes. "Thank you for making this afternoon so memorable for me."

She smiled and nodded with a gracious, mannerly detachment, moving her lips as if she were saying a perfectly polite good-day. But what he heard was, "I always ride on Wednesdays."

He was sure he hadn't heard properly, but his inner clock stopped again. "What?" he asked stupidly, wondering if everyone in the room could hear the strange thump of excitement in his chest.

Her smile widened by the merest millimeter. "At eight," she murmured, dismissing him with a wave of her hand. "Good day, my lord." Her voice was loud and clear as she walked away. "Thank you for an instructive afternoon."

❧ Seventeen ❧

Tess departed from Lord Elgin's exhibit very pleased with herself, but as soon as she and the Quimbys returned home, Edward turned on her. They had barely set foot in the door when Edward rounded on the two women and loudly declared, "I've had just about enough of this business!"

Julia paused in the act of removing her gloves. "What business, my love?"

"What business? Can you ask? This business of Tess's. All this secret plotting, all this false-name nonsense, and now this latest mischief!"

"Mischief?" his wife asked with exaggerated innocence.

"Don't pretend you didn't see that scene between Lotherwood and Miss Lovell!" He lifted his cane and waved it beneath Tess's nose. "It's a *damnable* pass to upset so sweet a creature as Miss Lovell," he growled. "And as for Lotherwood, he's as fine a fellow as I've come across, whatever he's done in the past!"

"*Whatever* he's done?" Tess echoed indignantly, thrusting the menacing cane away. "Whatever he's done is not something to push aside so cavalierly!"

"Yes, really, Edward, I quite agree with Tess," Julia said, trying to placate him without taking his side. "You can't ignore what he's done as if it were a mere peccadillo, however fine you find him now."

"Quite right," Tess said, starting up the staircase, swinging her bonnet saucily by its ribbons. "You know, Edward, I would like him, too, if I didn't know his secret shame. He has many surprising facets, I admit. If I didn't hate him so, I might really enjoy this flirtation."

"Flirtation? *Flirtation?*" Edward stalked to the stairway, perched his pince-nez on his nose, and glared up at her. "Is that what you're doing? Flirting with a man who's *betrothed?* And what do you intend to accomplish by this shocking behavior?"

"What I intend to accomplish, my dearest cousin-in-law, is to marry the man." She leaned over the banister and grinned into Edward's angry face. "Almost."

"*Almost?* What does that *mean?* What does she mean, Julia?"

Julia dropped her eyes and fiddled nervously with the gloves she'd just removed. "She means that she intends to entice him to offer for her and then to die on the eve of their wedding."

Edward's spectacles fell off his nose. "*Die?*"

Julia shrugged. "Well . . . *pretend* to die."

"*Miss Sidoney Ashburton* will die," Tess amended.

Edward gaped at her. "Die? I don't understand."

"It's quite simple, really. That's why I created her. To die."

Julia patted her bewildered husband on the arm. "I shall explain it all to you, my love, as soon as you make yourself comfortable. But Tess, I don't see why you are so complacent. If his lordship should *not* offer for you—and frankly, I don't see how he can, being betrothed as he is—you will have engaged in this elaborate masquerade for nothing."

"He will offer for me," Tess said with a serene smile. "In a fortnight or less." And with that arrogant prediction, she waved her bonnet at them in a gesture of adieu and sauntered up the stairs.

Julia, realizing that the time had come for Edward to know all, coaxed him into his favorite easy chair in the downstairs sitting room and ordered the butler to light a fire and bring in a cup of Edward's favorite Indian tea. This done, she perched on a footstool at his feet. "Promise me that you won't lose your temper," she urged, patting him fondly on his knee. "If Tess is correct in her prediction that Lotherwood will offer for her within a fortnight, the whole matter will be over in a month's time. She will, by then, have gone back to Todmorden, and we shall be at peace again."

He sighed deeply. "Very well, I shall *try* to stay calm. Just tell me what this 'dying' nonsense is all about."

"It's a rather clever plan, really. And the retribution is almost biblical in its fitness to the crime. An eye for an eye, you see."

"No, I don't see. Go on."

"Well, all depends on Lotherwood's offering for her, of course, but even *you* could see today that he's taken with her."

"Yes, even I could see that," Edward muttered dryly.

"Right. So when he does offer, she will set a prompt wedding date, telling him that since she has no family—"

"But she *has* a family. What about her mother?"

Julia frowned at him impatiently. "*Tess Brownlow* has a family. *Sidoney Ashburton* does not. And so she will ask Lotherwood to arrange a very private ceremony, which he no doubt will very happily do. Then, on the eve of the wedding . . ." Here Julia hesitated and looked up at her husband with trepidation. "Now, you will not fly into alt over this, Edward, will you?"

He groaned. "Go on. On the eve of the wedding—?"

"On the eve of the wedding we will go to Lotherwood's—"

"We? You and *I*? Listen to me, Lady Wife, I promised to stay calm, but I did *not* agree to play any part in this affair!"

Julia sighed. "Please hear me out, my love. How can we discuss this when you don't know all?"

"Very well. Proceed with this preposterous plot. On the eve of the wedding you and I are to go to Lotherwood's. For what purpose?"

"To inform him, with heartfelt sympathy, that there's been a carriage accident in which Miss Sidoney Ashburton has, most tragically, been killed."

Edward gaped at her in disbelief. "You've lost your wits. *Both* of you!"

"That's what I said, too. But when one thinks about it—"

"There's nothing to think about," Edward declared firmly, putting his teacup down on the nearest table with a finality that almost shattered the delicate china. "It's too ridiculous to consider."

"No, it's not. It can be accomplished quite easily. Just before we make the announcement to Lotherwood, Tess will steal home to Todmorden and never be seen in London again.

She says she doesn't care much for life in town anyway. Before she goes, she will arrange to bribe an actor to perform the role of a clergyman who will conduct a brief funeral service a few days after she leaves. It's rather neat, really. Sidoney Ashburton will be dead, Lotherwood will have been dealt a just retribution, and everyone will get on with their lives."

Edward stared at his wife in horror. "It's . . . *ghoulish!* Positively ghoulish! I can make some allowances for Tess, considering the devastation of her loss, but *you*, Julia! I never would have believed that *you*—"

"I know, dearest. I reacted just as you are doing when Tess first explained it to me. But when I thought about it, I realized that it's a better plan than some others she might have concocted. No one is really *harmed*, you see."

"No one harmed? Are you *mad?* What about poor, adorable little Miss Lovell, for one?"

His wife threw him a look of disgust. " 'Poor, adorable little Miss Lovell' will have gained more than she lost. What happiness would she have had married to a man who doesn't love her enough to resist the first temptress to come his way?"

Edward was forced to concede the point. "There is something in that, I suppose," he muttered. "But there are several others who will be harmed. Tess, herself, will be forever banished from town. *We* will forever be deprived of her company. And all this is nothing compared to the harm to Lotherwood."

"Tess is willing to pay the price of banishment for the satisfaction of knowing that Jeremy's death is avenged. As to our loss, we will visit Tess in Todmorden, just as we've always done. But as to Lotherwood—"

"Yes, Lotherwood. How are you going to convince me that there's no harm *there?*"

Julia got up and went to poke the fire. "I can't pretend that Lotherwood won't be hurt. That is the intention, after all. Tess says it is simple justice: he will be made to suffer as she has suffered." She looked round at her husband with pleading eyes. "It *is* just, is it not, Edward?"

Edward tried to convince himself that there was some justification in all this, but he remained troubled. "I don't know, Julia. I am not a jurist. I only know that Tess has no right, either legally or morally, to play the avenger."

"I know, love," Julia said sadly, "but she will go ahead

whether we support her or not. If we refuse to help her, she may concoct some alternative that would be worse." She returned to the stool and sat down, resting her head on his knee. "It won't be too dreadful, will it? After all, Lotherwood *is* guilty of a terrible act. We mustn't forget that. And after a while he'll get over it. He may even marry someone else in a year or two."

Edward snorted mirthlessly. "Is that what you mean when you say there'll be no real harm? That he may someday marry?"

"Yes. At least, there'll be no *permanent* harm."

He was silent for a moment. When he spoke, it was in the regretful, weary tone of one who has surrendered. "We shall be tampering with people's lives," he said, stroking his wife's hair gently, "and I don't think anyone can know what permanent harm may come from that."

Tess was much relieved to learn from Julia that Edward had "come round," although Julia admitted frankly that her husband had quite serious reservations. Nevertheless, Tess wanted to celebrate. There was to be a performance of *Cosi Fan Tutte* at the King's Theater, and, knowing how much Edward loved Mozart, she insisted on taking them as her guests. It was difficult to procure seats, for all of the boxes of the theater's five tiers were sold by subscription for the season, but Julia's butler showed himself to be unexpectedly knowledgeable in these matters and managed (with a well-placed bribe) to obtain a box for them for Monday evening. Tess promised that it would be an evening of relaxed pleasure; there was to be no connection at all with, in Edward's words, "the business with Lotherwood."

It was a relief for all three of them to put the Lotherwood business out of their minds for an evening. Tess could be herself, and Edward and Julia would not have to worry about remembering to call her Miss Ashburton. They dressed up in the splendor required for an evening at the opera, they laughed and joked over dinner as if none of their heads had ever contained a serious thought, and they climbed into the carriage in the most festive of moods. The box to which they were shown was well situated—in the second tier just a little left of center—and they took their places with a sense of real exhilaration. Edward had just leaned over to Tess to point out the newly appointed Prime Minister, Lord Liverpool, and his wife sitting just two boxes away, when Julia drew in a gasping breath. "Good God, Tess, they're *here!*" she whispered, hiding her face behind her program.

"Yes," Edward said, "I've just pointed out Lord Liverpool—"

"Not Liverpool," Julia hissed. "*Lotherwood*. With Miss Lovell and other friends. There, just below us to our right."

"Oh, my *word!*" Edward turned to Tess in irritation. "You promised that this would be a quiet evening! Especially for my pleasure, you said! Tess Brownlow, if this is another of your idiotic schemes—"

"No, really it isn't! I swear to you, Edward, I had no idea he would be here," Tess said with sincere chagrin.

Edward glared at her suspiciously. "Is that really the truth?"

"Of course. I'm as dismayed as you. I hate having to meet him by chance. Unless I've planned an encounter and am fully prepared with what to say, I'm quite uncomfortable in his presence. I'm always afraid I shall forget myself and say something to give myself away."

Edward sighed. "Then I suppose we had better leave."

"Oh, Edward, no," Tess demurred, very reluctant to rob him of his promised treat.

"I don't think that will be necessary, my love," Julia pointed out hopefully. "They *are* below us, after all, and the overture is about to begin. Perhaps they won't take notice of us."

Edward shook his head dubiously. "They need only glance over their shoulders and look up. Even if their fascination with the opera keeps their eyes fixed on the stage, they're bound to notice us during the interval."

"During the interval, Edward," Tess declared firmly, "I shall hide myself in the ladies' retiring room. Thank goodness *Cosi* has only one. In the meantime, let us sit back and enjoy the music. I, for one, refuse to have my evening spoiled."

The gaiety and charm of the music soon relaxed Edward's tension, and the first act passed without incident. Before the curtain fell at the intermission, Tess excused herself and hurried down to the retiring room. There she took a chair in a corner almost completely obscured by a screen and watched surreptitiously as hundreds of chattering ladies came and went. She did not emerge until she heard the music start up again. When she did, she found to her relief that the wide staircase was deserted. As she made her way up the stairs, she anticipated the second act with pleasure; now that the interval was over, there was no likelihood that she and the Quimbys would have to endure an encounter with Lotherwood and his party. The only way they could meet now would be in passing when they left the theater, and, in that unlikely event, the only exchange necessary would be a brief greeting and a bow.

As she approached the landing at the first tier, a handsome young man appeared above her at the top of the stairs, making his way down. As he took his first step, he lurched and lost his balance. "Ouppff!" he grunted as he tripped and stumbled down the two steps that separated him from Tess.

It was obvious that he was about to pitch forward and fall headlong down the stairs. Acting completely by instinct, Tess braced herself with one hand on the banister and, with her free arm and shoulder, managed to catch hold of him. The fellow, also acting on instinct, flung one arm round her neck and clutched her about the waist with his other, clinging to her for dear life. But the force of his weight threw her off balance, and the two of them teetered dangerously on the edge of the stair. Only Tess's grip on the banister kept them from toppling over. Finding strength from the fear that she could be dragged down the stairs in this stranger's grip, Tess pushed heavily against his chest, causing him to teeter back in the opposite direction. This eased the force propelling them forward, and she was able to regain her balance.

The whole incident took only a moment, but the moment was long enough to indicate to Tess that the fellow was utterly foxed. His breath reeked. The smell of spirits seemed to exude even from his pores. As soon as they were both firmly on their feet, she tried to push away from him. But the fellow did not let go. Instead, keeping both arms tightly about her so that her arms were pinned against her sides, he leered into her face. "Saved m'life, ma'am," he grinned. "Mus' say I'm might'ly obliged t' you."

"Yes, but I would be obliged to *you*, sir, if you would release me and let me pass," she said, struggling to move her head from its proximity to his.

"In a minute, m' lovely, in a minute. Saved m' life. Wish t' express m' gratitude."

"It's not necessary. Please, sir, let me go! You are making me miss my favorite aria."

He clutched her even tighter. "Pish-tush an' rubbish, ma'am, no one cares 'bout opera. Dull's ditchwater, if y'ask me."

"I am not asking your opinion on opera, you lout!" she muttered, trying with all her strength to push away from him. "I am asking you to *let go of me!*"

"Not yet, m'lovely, not yet." The fellow leered lasciviously at her, causing her chest to constrict in alarm. "Not till I give you a li'l kiss. A reward, y' might say, f' what y' did f' me."

Tess struggled in such desperation to keep her face away from his that she feared they would tumble down the stairs after all. "If you don't release me at once," she said in icy warning, "I shall scream."

But at that moment they heard a step above them, and the drunkard turned his head to look. Before Tess could see what was happening, the fellow's arms dropped from her sides as he seemed to levitate into the air. It took her a moment to realize that someone had lifted him off the ground by grasping him under his arms. "I say!" the boozy fellow squealed, kicking helplessly in the air. "Le' me *down!*"

"I *ought* to let you down!" barked a familiar voice. "Right down the stairs!"

"Lord Lotherwood!" Tess gasped, leaning back against the banister and trying to catch her breath.

His lordship stood the bounder on his feet but kept a tight arm about the fellow's neck. "Are you all right?" he asked Tess.

"Yes, I'm fine. Quite unharmed." But she reddened, suddenly feeling hideously shamed at being discovered—and by him, of all people!—in such humiliating circumstances, and she immediately did what any woman would do in such straits: she glanced down at herself to ascertain the extent of the damage the inebriated idiot had inflicted on her gown. "Only a bit rumpled," she added with an embarrassed little laugh.

He had been studying her carefully for signs of injury, and he'd been struck once again by the effect the sight of her had on his insides. To him she seemed unspeakably lovely at this moment, the dark red velvet of her gown and the embarrassed flush of her cheeks coloring her face with a vivid glow. "You look quite marvelous to me," he couldn't help saying.

"T' me, too," the drunkard agreed.

"Hold your tongue!" Lotherwood snapped, glaring down at the fellow imprisoned in the crook of his arm. "What possessed you, eh? Can't a lady climb the stairs of the King's Theater alone without being attacked?"

"Didn't attack 'er. She saved m' life."

Lotherwood raised his brows. "*Did* she, indeed?"

"That is rather an exaggeration," Tess explained, "although I did prevent him from falling headlong down the stairs."

The fellow nodded. " 'S what I said. Saved m' life."

"And that's how you repay her?" Lotherwood asked. "By trying to maul her?"

"Wasn't tryin' t' maul 'er. Only tryin' t' kiss 'er."

"Oh, is *that* all?" His lordship threw a teasing glance at Tess but spoke to his captive. "I can understand the desire," he said, an amused glint in his eyes, "since I've wanted to kiss her myself. But even I, who am acquainted with the lady, would never have dared to try it in so public a place. And you, I'll wager, haven't even been introduced."

"No, but she saved m' life."

"So you said. Does that mean she has to let you *kiss* her, too?"

The fellow hung his head. "I s'pose . . . I'm a bit lushy."

"Lushy? You're completely cast away! Now, tell the lady how sorry you are, and I'll let you go. And if you have the sense you were born with, you'll take yourself home and put your head under the pump!"

The fellow gave Tess a stumbling apology and made his escape down the stairs. Lotherwood took Tess's arm and escorted her up. At the first tier's turning they had to make their way through a small group of onlookers who had gathered on the landing to watch the to-do. Among them was Lord Kelsey, who'd come out of the box to see what had happened to delay his friend. But Lotherwood was too engrossed in his companion to notice his friend, and Tess, still embarrassed by the humiliating encounter, did not raise her eyes. Tess and her escort continued on their way up to the second tier, and Lord Kelsey quietly returned to the box. But he was troubled for the rest of the evening; he had assured Viola that

Matt was not "taken" with Miss Ashburton, but this glimpse of them together had shaken his confidence. If anyone looked "taken," it was his friend.

Lotherwood escorted Miss Ashburton to the door of her box feeling strangely elated. The two days since he'd last seen her had been difficult; there had been an unpleasant scene with his betrothed. Viola had been badly shaken by seeing him with Miss Ashburton at Lord Elgin's exhibit. "You don't love me," she'd sobbed, "and it will all turn out just as the gypsy predicted!" The girl had wept bitterly and had made him feel like a vile adulterer. He'd had to reassure her that his love for her was as strong as ever, but he knew as he spoke that it was no longer true. Though his words seemed to have appeased her, his conscience pained him, and he'd made a vow to himself that he would put Miss Ashburton out of his life. But this meeting today had not been of his making; therefore, he intended to enjoy it without berating himself with guilt.

When they arrived at her box, Miss Ashburton offered him her hand. "I don't know how to thank you, my lord. You saved me from a most embarrassing contretemps."

Instead of bowing over it, he took her hand and held it. "You should thank Miss Lovell. If she hadn't sent me for a glass of negus, I never should have known you were a few steps below me, struggling with a drunken assailant."

"I would ask you to thank her for me, but I'd prefer that you not mention the incident at all. I found it all rather embarrassing. It's not something I would wish to be the subject of gossip."

"I shall respect your wishes, of course," he assured her, "but I don't see why you should be embarrassed. *You* were not the one inebriated."

"While we are on that subject, my lord, I must compliment you on your handling of the foolish young man. You were appropriately severe, but kind, too."

Lotherwood shrugged. "Oh, well. I've been foxed myself in my time."

At those words Tess felt a chill in her chest. She had, for a while, forgotten that this was the Lotherwood who, wildly drunk, had cracked up a stagecoach and snuffed out a life. "I must get back to my seat," she said, her face stiffening and her hand wriggling from his grasp.

He was again startled by the change in her mood. "Yes, of

course," he said politely, but he was puzzled and irritated. Was this the best reward he could expect for his service to her—a cold dismissal? *The devil take her!* he thought. *I'm weary of trying to understand her mind.* "Good evening, ma'am," he said, making an abrupt bow and striding off.

She stood with her hand on the doorknob, watching him go. *I've angered him again,* she thought with a pang. *If I'm not careful, I'll lose the whole game.*

But after he'd taken a half-dozen steps, he stopped in his tracks, hesitated, and then turned round. "Miss Ashburton?"

Her heart leaped up into her throat. For the second time she'd cut him, and for the second time he was offering her a reprieve. "My lord?" she asked, letting him hear a slight note of eagerness in her voice.

He heard it, and he would have liked very much to wring her neck. Her backing-and-filling was driving him to distraction. He'd promised himself two days ago to cut her from his life. If he had any sense, he would stalk off and never turn back. But with an inner sigh of defeat, he surrendered to the impulse that had made him stop. He had a question to ask, and he was incapable of keeping himself from asking it. "You did say, did you not, that you ride on Wednesdays?"

The corners of her lips curved up in the smallest of smiles. "Yes, I did say that. Wednesdays. Good evening, my lord."

❧ *Eighteen* ❧

It rained on Wednesday. It poured down buckets, torrents, oceans. Sheets of water fell from a leaden sky and splashed down on roofs, overflowed the drainpipes, and rushed down the streets in streams. It was a day unfit for bird or beast, and only an occasional human, because of some dire necessity, ventured out of doors under the protection of, if not a carriage, at least an umbrella. Lotherwood wondered if he were the only one in all of London who was out in the downpour unprotected.

He sat astride a large chestnut stallion at a turning of the bridle path in Hyde Park where he could see anyone who was approaching from the stables. He'd dismissed his groom, insisting that the fellow take the umbrella back with him to the stable. He knew he was being idiotic to sit out there with the rain drenching his coat and pouring from his hat brim down his back. Miss Sidoney Ashburton wouldn't be coming out on a day like this. Nobody with sense . . . But in case she did, he would be there.

In more ways than one he was a fool to be here. Ever since he'd seen her at the opera, he'd berated himself for being a fool. It was not only because he was betrothed, although that was reason enough; it was not in his character to take that commitment lightly. But it was also clear that something about him was disturbing to Miss Ashburton, and only a fool would permit himself to become involved with a woman who found him abhorrent. There was no question that this entanglement with Miss Ashburton had to end. Throughout the long hours of the two nights since he'd last seen her, he reiterated the vow he'd made to himself to put her out of his life forever. He swore it. Forever. After Wednesday.

He'd looked forward to Wednesday like a schoolboy to a birthday. His desire to look once more into her enchanting eyes was like an ache within him. It would be a last fling, a final taste of youthful irresponsibility before putting on the yoke of middle-aged respectability. He could hardly wait for Wednesday morning to dawn. But when the dawn came, so did the rain. It was almost like a warning that he was transgressing. The blasted rain seemed to him a sort of heavenly rebuke.

After several minutes of waiting—and feeling more foolish than he'd ever felt in his life—he was ready to acknowledge the futility of remaining. She wouldn't be coming. He hadn't really expected it; even if the weather were fine, she would probably not have come. She was playing some sort of deep game with him, a game in which he would be the victim. He was as certain of it as he was sure the gypsy was a fraud. With a shrug that said it was just as well, he turned his horse back in the direction of the stables. It was then he saw her horse approaching.

She, at least, had had the sense to carry an umbrella. She held it over him as they exchanged greetings. "I never dreamed you'd come on such a day," she said with a shy laugh.

He'd never known her to be shy. It warmed him. "Nor I you," he said. "We are a pair of fools." They sat there for a moment, smiling idiotically at each other, neither one quite able to believe that the other had really come.

After a while he lifted a hand to brush a dripping tendril from her forehead. "Why did you ask me to meet you, ma'am? You pointed out to me quite firmly at the exhibit the other day how unsuitable such a meeting would be."

She lowered her eyes. "I know. I don't know why I did it. Perhaps it's because fate is directing me."

"Are you referring to the gypsy's prophecy? No, I can't let you off so easily as that. That excuse won't wash. You once said you had no faith in it. A woman of your intellect must believe that we ourselves, not gypsies, determine our own fates."

"I do believe it. But chance or fate or whatever you wish to call it plays some part, does it not?"

Her mare made a little sidestep, and he leaned forward and steadied the animal. "No, I don't think so. *'The fault, dear Brutus, is not in our stars.'* "

"Shakespeare has the answer to everything, it seems. But, my lord, what about the rain today?" she asked thoughtfully. "Either one of us, or both, could quite sensibly have decided not to come. Might it not be fate that brings us here now?"

"Not in my case. Believe me, my dear, it was a quite conscious decision on my part. In fact," he admitted with a boyish grin, "I could hardly wait for this day to come."

His frankness startled her into a blush. "Truly, my lord?"

"Very truly. Too, too truly."

"Oh." Her voice was very small, not much more than a breath, but her pulse unaccountably began to race. She dropped her eyes from his face. "But if one believed in fate," she said, clinging to the impersonal subject in sudden fear of the intimacy which she could feel impending, "one might take this rain to be a warning that we should *not* have met."

"Yes," he agreed, watching her face closely, "perhaps we shall be punished for ignoring the warning. But must we go on discussing the problem of fate versus self-determination? I think you're trying to deflect the conversation away from my original intention, my dear, which was to find out why you suggested this meeting."

She kept her eyes lowered, but her lips curled in a mischievous smile. "My suggestion that we meet today was . . . well, in truth, it was a wicked impulse. I never should have succumbed to it." The eyes flickered up again. "Shall I be sorry?"

"Not on my account," he said in a voice that was firm and reassuring in spite of the fact that his instinct was again warning him that she was playing with him. "You know how much I've wished for the chance to talk to you."

"Yes, so you said. But why, my lord?"

"I wish I knew. Who can explain what attracts a man to a woman? Perhaps it's that you're like a mystery I'm driven to unravel."

"And when you unravel it, what then?"

Now it was his eyes that fell. For them there was no future in which he could unravel the mystery of her, much less a what-then. But before he was put to the necessity of framing an answer, his horse shied, shedding a spray of water upon them. "Miss Ashburton . . . Sidoney, my dear, this is insane. We can't hold a conversation like this in such a downpour. I have a carriage waiting just beyond the stables. Shall we make for it and get out of the wet?"

They left the horses in the care of the stable grooms and ran for his carriage, a closed phaeton with his crest on the door. He'd driven it over himself, causing both his coachman and his tiger to eye him with reproach when he'd departed, but now he was glad he'd been firm. It would have been awkward to have to dismiss them now.

He opened the door and helped her up. Once settled inside, she took off her wilted riding cap while he dispensed with her umbrella, shook off his hat, and took out his handkerchief to wipe off her face. But when he looked at her with the wetness glistening on her pale skin and the dripping tendrils framing her face, his heart clenched. "I once thought you weren't beautiful," he murmured in amazement.

Her eyes widened, and some wetness that had no relation to the rain trickled down her cheeks. "Oh, *Matt*," she said with a sad sigh.

He'd had no intention of kissing her, but there was simply nothing else he could do. Neither fate nor self-determination had anything to do with it. It was just her nearness, her face tilted up just a little (for she was almost as tall as he), and her eyes looking mistily into his and revealing for the first time the depth of her feeling. He took her in his arms without conscious intent and suddenly found himself kissing her hungrily. He felt her give a little shiver at first . . . a sort of instinctive resistance . . . but almost at once she sagged against him. He tightened his hold on her as if the pressure of his arms would keep her close to him forever, and she, too, seemed to cling to him with the same frenzied desperation. Locks of his hair dripped water, all unnoticed, down her cheeks, while her hands, as if of their own volition, fondled his hair and the sides of his face. He could taste the rain on her mouth, feel the throbbing of her heart against his chest. How could a woman so tall and strong become so soft and pliant in his arms?

No woman he'd ever held had stirred him like this, to his very core. He wanted never to let her go.

Never before had he felt so shaken by an embrace. When he finally released her, they were both trembling. It took him a moment to regain his equilibrium, a moment in which a host of feelings burst on him all at once—guilt, joy, desire, shame, all of them. But he heard a little sob that came from deep within her throat, and when he looked at her, everything else fled from his mind.

She was staring at him with eyes wide with horror. "Oh, my *God*!" she gasped breathlessly.

He recognized that look. He had seen it in a flashing moment during the race. "Good Lord, what *is* it?" he asked in alarm. "What have I done?"

The look remained in her eyes for just a moment more. Then she blinked and, trying to catch her breath, made a dismissive movement of her hand. "No, it's . . . it's nothing . . ." she managed.

"It's not nothing!" he insisted, grasping her by the shoulders as if he would shake an answer from her. "What's amiss?"

She shut her eyes as if in pain. "Nothing, truly. I just didn't expect . . ."

"I know. I didn't expect it, either." He put an arm about her and let her head rest on his shoulder. There was so much he wanted to say to her, but at this moment their feelings seemed beyond words. It was as if they'd known from the first that they would come to this unutterable closeness, and no explanations were necessary. "I've never felt so . . . shattered . . ." he murmured into her wet curls.

"Yes," she said, taking a deep breath. "Yes."

"I am not accustomed to feeling things so deeply. We Corinthians train ourselves to avoid deep feelings."

"I don't think I've felt things deeply, either," she said, a note of surprise in her voice. "Though I was not trained to avoid it."

He stroked the side of her face in thoughtful silence. "But that's not what I saw on your face just now," he said after a while. "What is it, my dear? I wish you'd tell me. Is there something about me that frightens you?"

She shook her head. "I'm ashamed, that's all. Ashamed!

Of both of us. We shouldn't have permitted ourselves to behave so wickedly."

"That is *not* all," he said, deeply chagrined. "But you don't intend to tell me, do you?"

"No," she said, pulling herself away from him. She turned her back to him and stared out at the rain. "If I did," she added in a voice heavy with mockery, "there would be no mystery for you to unravel."

"Ah! Then you admit there is a mystery?"

"I'm very much afraid you'll never know."

He knew from her tone that her answer was final. "What a vixen you are, Sidoney Ashburton," he said, taking hold of her shoulders and forcing her to face him. "A veritable witch. I knew it the moment I clapped eyes on you."

She lowered her head and sighed. "I suppose you rue the day."

"No, but I should."

He tried to lift her chin, but she shook her head. "I think it would be wise if we ended this . . . interview, my lord."

He wanted to object, but he had no right to keep her. He had no right to be here at all. "I'll take you home," he said in gloomy acquiescence.

With a stiffening of his whole body, as if he were preparing himself for a difficult physical endurance contest, he let her go. He let down the front window-panel, picked up the reins, and started the horses. The rain still poured down, the streets were rivers of rushing water, and the sky showed no promise of brightening. The atmosphere could not have been more perfectly suited to his mood. As the horses splashed slowly down the street, he turned back to her, his face taut. "You realize, of course," he said huskily, "that I can't indulge . . . that we won't be meeting again."

"Yes, I know." Her voice was cold and distant.

He winced in pain. He wanted to say something, do something, to recapture one last bit of closeness and warmth. "It will be difficult for me," he said with a quiet but unmistakable regret, "knowing that you're somewhere close by and that I'm not able to—"

"You will survive. Besides, I shan't be close by for very long. I can't remain with Julia indefinitely, you know. I'm merely her guest for the month."

"I see." He was shaken by the realization that the girl was a stranger to him. Despite their moments of intimacy, he still hadn't learned very much about her. "Then will you be going home to your parents?"

She looked down at the hands she'd folded in her lap. "I have no parents. I shall be going to a country home where I've found employment as a governess."

"Good God! I had no idea." He turned to her in deep concern. "Is that the only choice you have for your future?"

"You needn't look so stricken, my lord," she said. "I am quite content. This has been my plan for a long while. And my weeks in London have provided many memories to mull over when my post becomes a bore."

"Where is this country place to which you're going?"

"I'd rather not say."

"See here, my girl, there's entirely too much you'd 'rather not say' to me!"

"Don't flare up at me, my lord! What right have you—?"

His jaw tightened, and he turned away and stared out ahead of him at the horses' heads. "No right. I beg your pardon."

They rode on without speaking until he drew up at the Quimby house. She picked up her soggy riding cap and umbrella and reached for the door handle. "Good-bye, my lord," she said, brittle as glass. "I wish you happy."

But he could not let her go. "Dash it all," he muttered, pulling her roughly to him again, "tell me what it is about me that makes you swing so wildly from warmth to ice! What *is* it?"

Her expression was unreadable. "I have nothing to say, my lord."

"Is there something you want of me? If there is, you have only to ask. There's no need to play games. Just *ask* it."

Her eyes grew scornful. "There is nothing I want of you that you are free to give."

He groaned and pulled her closer, cradling her head in the curve of his shoulder. "Oh, God," he said miserably, "if only that blasted gypsy had pointed you out to me a few weeks earlier."

"Yes, isn't it sad?" She withdrew from his arms and moved to the door. "But there's nothing to be done now, is there?"

There was something in the angle of her head, the strange edge in her voice, the opaque look in her eye that he was beginning to recognize. It was her "game" technique, a certain unnatural, calculating manner that told him she was playing with him. "I wish I understood the mystery of you, ma'am. It is driving me to the brink of distraction."

"Is it? That is something else you will survive, I think." She studied him coolly for a moment, but then her expression softened. "I'm sorry, Matt," she said, her voice low and melancholy. "I shouldn't poison our last meeting with dissension. Since it will be for the last time, perhaps . . ."

"Perhaps. . . ?"

"Perhaps you'd like to kiss me again, in farewell."

Though still convinced he was being used as her pawn in some mysterious game, he could not refuse this last gift. He put his hand gently on her cheek and lifted her face. Slowly, with a tenderness even he did not know he possessed, he kissed her mouth. It was a light kiss, barely touching, but it managed to shake him up again. "I love you, Miss Sidoney Ashburton," he murmured with his lips still on hers. "For what little it's worth, I love you. Mystery or no mystery."

She withdrew from his arms and smiled at him, a smile that was somehow both teasing and sad. "And I love you."

He shook his head. "No," he said flatly, "I don't think you do. You needn't offer me Spanish coin, ma'am. When I first kissed you, I did believe for a moment that I'd touched something real in you. But now, no."

A shadow seemed to cross her face. She turned away abruptly and threw open the carriage door. He made a move to jump down and assist her, but she shook her head. "Don't come round, my lord. I shall manage," she said, and climbed down.

He picked up the reins, but before starting up the horses he turned to take one last look at her. She was standing facing the open carriage door, the rain dripping down her face like tears. "For what little it's worth," she said, meeting his eyes with a look of self-mockery in her own, "I *do* love you. It's so funny! I've been waiting all my life for the Grand Passion. And now, when it finally comes to me, I discover that I feel it for the very *last* man in the world I should have chosen!" With a laugh that was also a sob, she turned and ran through the rain to the house.

❧ *Nineteen* ❧

Viola Lovell was known to be a young lady of rare good nature and sweet disposition, but she was not often described as clever. Sweetness and cleverness are not characteristics that are supposed to go hand in hand. And since cleverness in a woman was not a requisite virtue—and not a virtue *at all* in the minds of many wife-seeking gentlemen—Viola did not bother to prove the evaluation to be mistaken. She knew that she was considered both lovely and amiable, and that was enough.

But despite the innocence of her wide-eyed gaze and the vulnerability in her trusting smile, Viola Lovell was no fool. She knew very well how to add two and two, and in the case of her betrothal, she had added up all the advantages before she'd given her hand. She'd known exactly what she was doing. Her value on the marriage mart was high—she had (1) a respected if not titled family name, (2) her reputed amiable disposition, (3) a pretty face, (4) a softly feminine form, and (5) a complexion that was the envy of every girl she knew. These advantages added up to an impressive total. She'd made the best possible trade for those advantages: Matthew John Lotherwood, the Marquis of Bradbourne. He, on his part, had (1) breeding, (2) titles, (3) a sizable income and a magnificent estate in Essex, (4) virile good looks, and (5) a charm of manner that made him sought after by every female he met. The match had a beautiful mathematical symmetry. It seemed to add up to the most glowing prospects for her future comfort and happiness. Until just a short while ago, she had considered herself to be the luckiest girl alive.

But now her prospects for the future appeared to be seriously flawed. She'd avoided facing the problem squarely for almost a fortnight, unwilling to believe that anything could spoil the neatness of her arithmetic. But signs were accumulating that his lordship was beginning to believe he'd not made the best of bargains in committing himself to her. It was not merely the gypsy's prophecy that had shaken her confidence, although that had certainly been a blow. (She was willing to concede that Matt and Dolph were right in denying that gypsies had magical powers, but even if gypsies weren't supernaturally gifted, they did have, she was convinced, an uncanny ability to read people's characters in their eyes. Lady Wetherfield's gypsy might not be a true seer, but time had proved she undoubtedly knew *something*.)

However, with Dolph's encouragement, she'd put aside her doubts. But a strange event during the night at the opera had added another clue to a rapidly accumulating body of evidence pointing to the fact that Matt no longer wanted her. It was time, she realized, to give the matter some serious attention.

It was not ignorance or innocence that had kept her from facing her problem before this. Viola was not the bubblehead that everyone thought her. She'd taken note of Matt's apparent attraction to the peculiar young woman staying with Julia Quimby almost immediately, and she'd made some scenes and shed some tears. But in her deepest heart, she hadn't been unduly alarmed, because Miss Ashburton did not strike her as a formidable rival. Other than her strikingly odd eyes, Miss Ashburton had little to recommend her. She was (1) much too tall, (2) too strong in chin and nose (and colorless in complexion!) to be considered beautiful, (3) cool and distant in manner, and (4) so far out of the common way that Viola found her almost eccentric. Nor was Viola alone in her assessment; Dolph Kelsey was in complete agreement with that judgment. Thus Viola had easily convinced herself that whatever it was that Matt had seen in Miss Ashburton could not possibly be serious. It didn't add up.

But the night at the opera gave Viola what she believed was the definitive clue to prove that she'd been too complacent. During the intermission a number of well-wishers had invaded their box, and when the members of Matt's party had finally settled into their seats for the second act, she'd asked Matt to bring her a glass of negus. He'd teased her about her taste for that tepid concoction ("Adding hot water and spices to wine," he'd quipped, "is like pinning a flower on Dolph's orchid-hued waistcoat—too many sensations from one source."), but he'd gone off in perfectly good spirits to do her bidding. When he didn't return for what seemed an unduly long time, Dolph went off to look for him. Dolph returned a moment later saying that he couldn't find Matt anywhere, but Viola thought that he seemed disturbed. When Matt returned shortly after-ward—and without her drink—she thought the incident quite strange, but she decided not to question him. It didn't seem important, and it would have been too awkward to discuss anything while the opera was in progress anyway.

After the opera, however, when they stood waiting under the portico of the King's Theater for Matt's coachman to bring round the carriage, she caught a glimpse of Miss Ash-burton and the Quimbys coming down the stairs. She was about to draw the attention of her party to their presence when she noticed that Dolph, too, had seen them. Dolph's ears grew red, and he glanced up at Matt with a look of concern. It was then that Viola realized that Matt's absence from the box and his failure to bring back her drink had had some sort of con-nection with Miss Ashburton. It was clear to her at last that something was amiss. It was something perhaps not havey-cavey but serious nonetheless.

She thought about it all that night and the next day. She remembered all the little warning signs: Matt's interest in Miss Ashburton at Lady Wetherfield's dinner party, his attentions to Miss Ashburton on the day of the race, his look of admira-tion for Miss Ashburton at Lord Elgin's exhibit, and his air of abstraction when he returned to the box that night at the opera. In addition, she realized that he'd been, of late, very different in his manner toward her, his own intended bride. Instead of becoming closer since their betrothal, his manner had become more formal and distant. She'd tried her usual wiles to ease the strain between them, but they had little effect. She now admitted to herself that she'd been finding herself more and more uncomfortable in his company. All this surely added up to serious trouble.

By Tuesday evening she still had not decided what to do. She supposed she should confide in her mother or father, but she knew what they would say: "You must do nothing, child. Nothing at all." She could hear her mother's jittery whine: "I *knew* something like this would happen! I *knew* it! It was too good to be true, your snaring Lotherwood! This is all that uppish Lady Wetherfield's doing. She didn't want you for her precious nephew from the first!"

And her father would be no better. "Nothing to worry about, if you hold fast," he'd say, puffing on his pipe. "You're safely betrothed. Banns posted, announcement in *The Times*. As good as wed. Nothing he can do about it now. So hold on fast. Many a woman has to bite her tongue while her husband cavorts about. There's only one woman who wins in the end, and that's the legal wife. So hold on."

That sort of advice from her parents was not what she wanted to hear, so there was no point in seeking it. There was only one person whose presence might be soothing and whose advice might be useful to her, and on Wednesday morning she sent a footman through the rain with a note for him.

The note only contained a simple request that he call at his earliest convenience, but Dolph knew at once what she wanted to talk about. Late that afternoon, as soon as the rain lessened, he presented himself at her door. Viola told her mother, who was at that moment wandering through the hallway looking for a mislaid piece of needlework, that she wished for some private words with Lord Kelsey. Without heeding the look of astonishment that crossed her mother's face, she took Dolph's arm, pulled him into the sitting room and shut the door.

"If you're going to ask me something about Matt's doings at the opera the other night, Vi, you're wasting your breath," Dolph said flatly, putting down his rain-spattered hat. "I don't like tattling."

"There's no need for you to tattle," she said, sinking down on the sofa and folding her hands into a tight, tense knot. "I know he must have met Miss Ashburton. I don't need any details."

"Good. Because I wouldn't blab any even if I knew them, which I don't." He pulled up a straight-backed chair in front of her and perched nervously on the edge of it. "What *do* you want of me, then?"

"Only some advice." Her eyelids lowered pathetically, and her underlip began to quiver. "Oh, Dolph, I'm so confused!"

Dolph shifted on his seat uncomfortably. "Thought you might be. Dashed unpleasant situation."

She clasped and unclasped her hands. "Then you admit that there is a situation. Just what is it, Dolph? Can you tell me that much?"

"I don't really know anything to tell you. It's only a feeling I have."

"Yes, just as I have. It's Miss Ashburton, isn't it? You once said that he couldn't care for her. But now you're not so sure, are you?"

Dolph shook his head unhappily. "Wouldn't have thought it of Matt. True sportsman, Matt is. It isn't like him to play foul."

"Play *foul?*" Her eyes flew up to his face in dismay. "Do you think matters have gone as far as that? That he's actually been . . . *unfaithful?*"

"*No!* Good God, no! I didn't mean . . . !" He reached out and grasped her hands in his. "I *do* beg your pardon! It's only my way of speaking. Confound it, Vi, he's not a *cad!* I only meant that it's foul of him to treat you so. So sweet and good and lovely as you are, you don't deserve . . . ! It's foul of him even to *look* at anyone else."

The feeling in those words undid her. "Oh, *Dolph!*" she cried, the tears spilling over. "It's *you* who's sweet and good. I only w-wish . . ."

"Wish what?" Dolph asked, awkwardly dropping his hold on her hands in order that he might pull out his handkerchief and dab at her eyes.

She let him mop her cheeks for a moment and then shook her head. "I can't tell you!" she cried, pulling the handkerchief from his fingers and weeping into it. "I just c-can't!"

She jumped up and crossed the room to the window. The rain still dribbled down the panes, making the world outside seem utterly dismal. It seemed to her at that moment that the sun would never shine again. With her back to Dolph, she let the tears run freely down her cheeks, but he knew she was still weeping. With a sigh, he stood up and followed her. "You can tell me, Vi. I'd do anything for you, you know. I'll talk to Matt for you. This business with Miss Ashburton can't be serious. I'm sure he wouldn't stay for a moment in her company if he knew it made you unhappy. That's what you wish, isn't it—that I go to see Matt in your behalf?"

"No!" she exclaimed, wheeling about. "That's the last thing in the world I wish!"

"Then what—?"

Bursting into sobs, she threw herself into his arms. "Oh, D-Dolph! What I w-wish is that *you* were my b-betrothed instead of him!"

"*Vi!*" His jaw dropped down in astonishment. "You can't mean that!"

"Why not?" she demanded with a sudden burst of spirit. "*Why* can't I mean that?"

"Because it's *Matt* we're speaking of. Matt! He's the best! In every way the fellow's better'n me. In riding, in boxing, in—"

"Who cares for that?" she cut in furiously. "You're better than he for *me! You* never speak to me as if I were a spoiled child! *You* never make me feel uncomfortable when I'm with you. *You* never make me feel ashamed to say what I really feel about things. I'd rather have a conversation with you than with him . . . or anyone else, if you want the truth!"

"Good God!" Dolph exclaimed in stupefaction. "You must be addled in your upper works!"

But Viola's upper works were far from addled. She'd done her arithmetic carefully this time. As a prospective husband, Dolph had almost as many advantages as Matt. True, he was not a marquis, but viscount was not a title to be sneezed at; and true, he was not so famous a Corinthian or so outstanding in sports as Matt, but she cared nothing for that. For the rest, Dolph was really a superior choice for her: (1) his income was rumored to be enormous, (2) his taste in attire was not so somber as Matt's, and (3) he was by far easier to control. Perhaps her parents and the rest of the world would think she'd taken a step down, but she'd decided last night that she would rather be married to a viscount who truly desired her than to a marquis who felt trapped.

She turned her sweet, tear-streaked face up to his. "It's not too late for us, is it, Dolph?" she asked softly.

There was hardly a man in the world who could resist such an invitation. To Dolph's credit, he did hesitate for a moment. He was beset with a flood of confused doubts. Was he in love? he wondered. Was he a rotter? Was he being disloyal to a long-admired friend? What was he doing here at all? An hour ago he'd had no intention of getting himself leg-shackled, but at this moment it suddenly seemed a very real possibility. How had he gotten himself in this position?

But that lovely, creamy-skinned, soft-lipped face was tilted up, the eyes moist with yearning, and the urge to kiss her proved to be irresistible. With a sigh of surrender, he took her in his arms. Later, he told himself, they would talk things out. Later they would face Matt and tell him all. Later they would make things straight. But this embrace, these sighs, this pressing together of hands, of lips, of hearts . . . these were for now.

❧ Twenty ❧

It continued to rain all night, not heavily but steadily. Tess knew all about it, because she'd lain awake and listened. The dripping sounds on the eaves and windowpanes seemed a fitting accompaniment to her thoughts. Not that starlight or moonshine would have made any difference; there was no celestial atmosphere that nature could provide that would be bright enough to affect the brooding darkness inside her. The inescapable fact was that Tess was miserable.

She should have been happy, she told herself, for she was on the verge of success in her plot against Lotherwood. After this morning she knew she'd caught him. The dreadful irony of the situation was that she'd caught herself, too.

What she'd said to him was true: she *did* love him. What a shock she'd felt when she realized it! She had no idea how it had happened. She'd concentrated so intently on her plot for revenge—on every step in the carefully mapped route toward his seduction—that she hadn't noticed that she herself was being seduced. It was only when she lay trembling in his arms after he'd kissed her that the awareness burst on her like a sharp blow to the face: she loved him.

Until that moment it had seemed so certain that the game was hers. At every crucial crossroad, when he could have chosen a path away from her, she'd won. Even when she'd played the game badly, like the day at the race or the other night at the opera, he'd succumbed. It had seemed so easy.

Too easy. Why hadn't she seen it before? Lotherwood was too clever (and probably too experienced a lover) to be taken in by a woman playing a game. He was not fooled by pretense. It was her *real* feeling that had taken him in!

But she herself had not recognized the fact that she *had* real feelings. Not until he'd kissed her. Her reactions during that embrace had been utterly beyond her expectations. They had had nothing to do with playing a role. They were too spontaneous, too intense to have anything to do with pretending. They had come from her very depths.

Even now, so many hours later, she was still shaken by the recollection of that experience. She had completely lost her head this morning. Never before had she so wildly abandoned all inner restraint. She'd pressed her body and her lips to his . . . she'd clung and clasped and clutched in a burst of such unbridled passion that she hadn't known where she was or why she was there. But she did remember thinking, during one moment when her mind was still functioning, that this must be what her mother had tried to explain—the intoxicating blending of body and spirit that makes a passion Grand.

How the gods must be laughing at her, she thought. What an ironic twist her so-well-calculated road had taken! Was this the price the gods intended to extract for her hubris in taking it upon herself to inflict revenge? Was she to be punished for giving Lotherwood his punishment?

Tess was so shaken by this discovery that for a short while she actually considered the possibility of abandoning her plan and running home before matters developed any further. If she left things as they were right now, no one would be much affected. Julia and Edward would be relieved, Lotherwood would marry his Viola, and Tess would not have to suffer the torture of torturing the man she loved.

But then she remembered Jeremy. Poor Jeremy, to whom she'd never said a word of love. At last she understood the full extent of what she'd withheld from him. She'd never even *kissed* him properly! He'd died without having experienced even a bit of the Grand Passion. She owed something to his memory. Lotherwood had snuffed out Jeremy's life and had gone on with his own without caring. *We train ourselves not to care deeply*, he'd said. It was only simple justice that Lotherwood be made to pay! And if she was now to share the cost, in the pain of giving him pain, perhaps that, too, was simple justice.

Morning came, bringing with it a decisive frame of mind. *She would proceed as planned*. And, as if the gods were giving her a sign that they agreed, the rain stopped at that moment.

She remained in bed, staring up at the ceiling of her small bedchamber. She heard the sounds of the waking household. She heard Julia and Edward go downstairs. She heard the sound of the door as Edward left the house. She heard the clock strike nine and then ten. And then she fell into a doze.

The clock was striking eleven when Julia tapped on the door. "Tess?" she whispered urgently. "Tess? Are you up?"

"Yes, love, come in," Tess answered in a voice thick with sleep. "I'm sorry I'm such a slugabed. I don't know what made me—"

"Never mind that," Julia hissed, coming in and closing the door carefully and quietly behind her. "You've got to come at once. He's *here!*"

Tess froze in the act of stretching her arms. "*Who's* here?"

"Lotherwood! He seems a bit unstrung. I left him pacing about like a caged lion." She looked about her nervously, as if she suspected the presence of an eavesdropper, before she went on. "Honestly, Tess, I think he's going to make an *offer!* If ever a man had the appearance of a hopeful suitor, it's he!"

Aghast, Tess stared at her cousin for a moment and then leaped out of bed. "He can't be here for that!" she muttered, searching about madly for her robe. "It's too soon. What about Viola? Why, only yesterday, he—!" Her eye fell on her reflection in her dressing-table mirror. "Oh, good God, just look at me! I'm a veritable *fright!*" She dropped down on the bed and put a shaking hand to her forehead. "Tell him to go away. I can't see him looking like this. Tell him to go away and come back later. Tonight. Tomorrow. But not now."

"I can't tell him that," Julia said, pulling her up. "He insisted that I drag you down just as you are. It is urgent, he said. We've already kept him waiting too long." She put Tess's arms into the sleeves of her rose-colored robe and pulled it up on her shoulders. "There, that's presentable enough. Now tie the sash and run a brush over your hair!"

That done, Julia pushed Tess to the top of the stairs.

"That's as far as I go," she whispered. "From this point on, you must make your own way." And before her cousin could object, she flew down the hall and into her bedroom.

Tess stood at the top of the stairs, her heart pounding. She knew very well that she was not properly prepared for this interview, whatever the subject of discussion was to be. She looked dreadful. She had dark circles under her eyes, her hair was unkempt despite the hurried brushing she'd given it, and her robe was a silly, flouncy bit of fluff that was quite out of character for her. Worse, she had not decided just what mood and tone she should adopt for this meeting. She would be at a decided disadvantage this time. It was quite possible that she could lose the game today.

However, the game had to be played. She took a deep breath, stiffened her back, and descended. As she came to the half-landing, she saw him standing below waiting for her. He was dressed in riding breeches and a tweed coat, looking every inch the dashing, worldly Corinthian he was reputed to be. But his hair was boyishly tousled, and his eyes held an unmistakable glint of youthful anticipation. Her pulse began to race at the sight of him. She had an almost irresistible urge to repeat to him the lovely words he'd said to her the day before: *I once thought you weren't beautiful.* But all she did was stare down at him and utter a breathy, "Oh!"

"Good morning," he said, a grin lighting his face. "I see I've roused you from your bed."

Her hand unwittingly flew to her hair, but she immediately brought it down, telling herself angrily that she refused to let him see her embarrassment. "So you have," she said, lifting her chin in an attitude of proud reproof. "It was very rude of you. A true gentleman does not call on a lady before noon." *There*, she thought, *that should give him a set down. The best defense is a strong attack.*

But he showed not a sign of mortification. "You're right, of course," he agreed, "but since I knew that you are on the bridle path on Wednesdays by eight—and in all weather, too —I naturally assumed that you're an early riser."

"On *Wednesdays* I am on the bridle path at eight. On *Thursdays* I sleep until noon," she informed him coldly, raising her chin higher. "One would think, my lord, that by your advanced age you would have learned that ladies are notoriously inconsistent."

His grin widened. "I'm rather glad I haven't learned it, for if I had, I *would* have waited until noon and missed this glimpse of you in your charming disarray. You do look charming, you know. Even at my advanced age I've never encountered a more delectable vision."

It was hard to maintain her pose of chilly *hauteur* when struggling against an urge to laugh. She leaned over the banister and made a face at him. "*Now* who's offering Spanish coin?" she teased.

"I never offer Spanish coin, ma'am. Blunt to a fault I am." He moved closer to the stairway so that he was right below her and lifted up a hand to her. "I hope you don't intend to linger there on the landing for very long. Please take my hand and come down, my dear. At my advanced age, it's hard on my neck to keep looking up this way indefinitely."

Laughing, she slipped her hand into his. He led her down the stairs, the banister making an ever-decreasing barrier between them. "What brings you here, my lord?" she asked as she descended. "Wasn't it only yesterday that we exchanged final farewells?"

"We should have known better," he said, coming round to the foot of the stairs. He dropped her hand, picked her up by the waist and lifted her up over the few remaining steps. "Final farewells can't possibly be exchanged between us."

He held her to him for a moment before he set her on her feet. The brief bodily contact left her breathless. She backed away from him and hurriedly turned round so that he wouldn't see how his touch affected her. "Seriously, my lord, why have you come?" she asked, leading the way to the library.

He followed her in and closed the door behind him. "I came, ma'am, to suggest a fifth category of gentlemanly types for you to consider."

His words made no sense. "What?" she asked, feeling thick-headed and bemused.

Smiling a roguishly secret smile, he led her to the sofa. "You remember, don't you, that I once described four categories of gentlemen for you: the religious, the scholarly, the military, and the athletic? I think we both agreed that the athletic was beneath your consideration for wedlock. And since I certainly cannot claim membership in any of the other three, I've thought of a fifth: the Country Gentleman. He is sturdy, hardworking, reliable, and is responsible for the advantageous use of the land for the prosperity of the nation. Do you think you might consider such a one?''

Sinking down on the sofa, she put a hand to her forehead. "Whatever are you talking about, Matt?"

"I'm speaking of myself, ma'am," he answered, taking a seat beside her with an air of such amused self-satisfaction that she had an urge to box his ears. "I admit that I haven't made a mark in that category thus far, but I'm not without experience. While concentrating all these years on my foolish sporting activities, I've nevertheless managed my Essex estate with enough skill to keep it unencumbered. And now, with you beside me, I'm certain I shall soon make a quite respectable Country Gentleman."

She gaped at him for a moment, wide-eyed. "With *me* beside you?" she gasped.

"Yes, my love, exactly." The teasing look faded from his eyes. "I'm asking you to marry me," he said earnestly, taking both her hands in his. "You see, all of a sudden I find that I'm quite at liberty to do so."

"At . . . *liberty?*"

He nodded. "Since last night. Miss Lovell paid a call on me, in company with my friend, Lord Kelsey. She informed me that she feels she and I do not suit. It seems I've been a most unsatisfactory betrothed. I've been inattentive, insensitive, abstracted, uncaring, and neglectful. While Dolph, on the other hand, has been devoted, sympathetic, affectionate, and kind. So I was given my walking ticket."

"Oh, *Matt!*"

"Don't look so dismayed, my dear. It's a perfect solution to everyone's dilemma. Viola seemed quite smitten with Dolph, and Dolph, bless him, was very content to take my place with her. As for me, I felt as if I'd had a reprieve from a prison sentence! Now there's only you to hear from." He lifted her hands to his lips and kissed them each in turn. "I wanted to rush right over last night to tell you," he added softly, "but it seemed too opportunistic to do so. I decided to wait till this morning. It was the longest night I've ever endured."

"I see," she murmured, gently withdrawing her hands from his clasp.

"You *see?*" His brows lifted in restrained surprise. "Is *that* the best response you can make to my recital of these momen-

tous events?'' He moved a small distance away from her so
that he could scrutinize her face. "Good God!" he exclaimed,
the lightly mocking tone of his voice at variance with the sudden tightening of his jaw. "I believe I've been a coxcomb
again. You're going to *refuse* me!"

She threw him a quick glance. "What makes you think
that?"

"Well, my dear, your reaction has been somewhat lacking
in maidenly delight."

Her eyes fell. "I'm trying to restrain my maidenly delight."

"Why, ma'am? Why should you restrain it?" He leaned
back against the cushions but kept his eyes fixed on her face.
"Don't tell me that you feel this is too sudden! Surely Miss
Sidoney Ashburton is not the sort to think in such clichés."

"But it *is* too sudden," she murmured, keeping her head
resolutely lowered. If only he knew how very sudden his offer
was. She was struck with terror at the necessity of giving him
an answer. She would have liked to have a little more time.
She'd made up her mind last night about what her course of
action would be, but this was her very last chance to change it.
We are heading toward a precipice, my love, she cried inside,
and you are urging us headlong to the edge. She could still
withdraw, still run back home and save them both from the
grief her plot would bring. But once she accepted him, there
could be no turning back.

"Too sudden? Everything that's happened between us has
been too sudden." He leaned forward and pulled her abruptly
into his arms. "Look at me, girl. You said yesterday that you
loved me, did you not? Was it the truth, or was it part of this
game you're playing with me?"

She looked up at him obediently, her eyes brimming with
tears. "It was true. It *is* true. I *do* love you, Matt."

"Then, damnation, what is the impediment?" He waited a
moment for an answer that didn't come. Then, expelling a
long breath as if he were releasing the tension of his frustration, he cradled her head in the curve of his shoulder and
stroked her hair. "Sidoney, my love, why won't you speak to
me? What is it about me that frightens you so?"

She shook her head and hid her face in his coat, unable to
speak. She was poised, terrified, at her life's most significant
crossroad, but each path led to a dismal end. Whichever she
chose, there was no hope of happiness for her. But if she

refused him, she could at least keep *him* from the full brunt of the suffering she'd devised for him. If only he would show one slight sign that he regretted his thoughtless past and the error which had caused Jeremy's death.

She turned her face up to him. "You *can* be frightening sometimes, Matt, don't you know that? You have the reputation of having been very wild."

"I have?" He stared down at her in sincere bewilderment. "Who on earth could have told you that? Lady Quimby? Sir Edward? Whoever it was, he was mistaken."

His earnestness was almost convincing. "Have you never done *anything* you consider wild?" she asked, hoping he would feel impelled to confess his crime. If he showed even the slightest repentence, she would forgive him. She wanted with all her heart to be able to forgive him and to go away.

His brow knit in an intense effort to understand what it was that troubled her. "Is it the race you're thinking of, my dear? I know there was something about it that shook you. If you consider *that* to have been an act of wildness, then I suppose I'm wild. I've raced horses all my life. But I've never hurt anyone."

Never hurt anyone? The words seemed to reverberate in her head. How could he lie to her like that? He claimed to *love* her. Didn't love mean sharing, even one's darkest secrets? She would give him one last chance to confess. She would make her voice warm, enticing him with the offer of complete and sympathetic understanding. *Dear God,* she prayed, *let him tell me the truth.* "Never hurt *anyone?*" she asked gently.

But the softness of her voice and the pleading look in her eye did not mask the intent of the question. "Good God, girl," he demanded furiously, "what do you take me for? I may not have done much good with my life, but there's not a man, woman, or child in this world whose life was made *worse* because of me!"

His words made her heart sink in her chest like a stone. She felt herself stiffen in his arms. She'd failed. *He'd* failed. There was no doubt left in her mind of what her course of action would be. She lowered her head to keep him from reading the feelings that were undoubtedly revealed in her face.

But he didn't miss the look that flared for the briefest moment in her devastating eyes. "Sidoney, *don't!* Why do you look at me so? Dash it all, why won't you ever tell me what you're thinking? What is this game you feel impelled to play with me?"

She had to say something, she realized. She had to go on with her scheme. She had no choice, now that she knew him for the miscreant he was. He appeared to be so open and honest on the outside, with his sportsman's bluntness and his unaffected charm, but they were only coverings that masked a craven, indifferent soul. He was a man who could ruin lives and then forget he'd done it. She didn't know how she'd come to fall in love with such a man, but she couldn't help that now. But she could, and would, punish him for what he'd done to Jeremy, no matter what the cost to herself.

He'd taken her chin in his hand and forced her to look up at him. "Can't you tell me, you ice-eyed witch, just what is going on in that brain of yours?"

"I'm thinking, Matt, that you've been captured by this so-called game. It's the *mystery* of me that's attracted you. You said so yourself, did you not? But I'm not a witch. I'm a quite ordinary girl. If you knew what I was thinking, you might not love me at all."

"Not love you?" He laughed shortly. "I think it more likely that the sun won't go down!" With both hands he tilted up her face to his and kissed her, gently at first but soon with a fervent desperation. His hands moved from her face to her neck and down her arms. She shivered and flung her arms about him, pressing herself against him with a low, almost gutteral moan. The sound stirred something deep within him, and he lifted his head to stare at her. He didn't understand her, but she inspired feelings in him he didn't dream he was capable of. They were the kinds of feelings that a true Corinthian would scorn, but only because he'd never felt them. "If that was a game," he murmured, trying to catch his breath, "I'm willing to play it all my life."

"No, that was . . . not a game," she said, furious at herself for letting him shake her again.

With an effort he pushed her from him but held her arms in a tight grip. "Then, confound it, say you'll marry me!" The words were harsh, but his expression was touchingly tender. "I shall be the gentlest and most loving of husbands," he pleaded, his voice choked. "I'll never frighten you, I promise.

No one will ever call me wild. Once we're wed, I'll prove to you that there's nothing in me to be afraid of."

She gave a little sob and flung herself against him. "I'll marry you, Matt," she said, burying her face in his shoulder.

She tried not to enjoy his reactions to her words—his breath of relief, the tightening of his arms about her, the touch of his lips on her forehead. She despised him, really. He was a coward, a liar, and a killer, and she was glad she'd just pushed him over the precipice to his destruction! In less than a fortnight he would come crashing down to a terrible emptiness, a terrible loneliness and the terrible pain of living forever with what might have been. Of course, she was hurtling down with him, locked in his arms as she was. She would come crashing to the same disastrous end.

But she did enjoy his reactions . . . she couldn't seem to help herself. *Oh, well,* she thought, *for the moment there's no real harm in it.* For the moment she might just as well enjoy these inexplicable sensations that overwhelmed her when she lay in his arms like this. Soon enough there would be nothing to feel . . . nothing, that is, but regret and pain.

❧ Twenty-one ❧

Matt put forth several good reasons for setting an early date for their wedding, the most logical being a necessity for them to leave London as soon as possible. He explained that it did not behoove a decent gentleman to be seen going about everywhere in the company of a new love when just having broken with an old. It would not be kind to Viola if his behavior encouraged speculation among the gossips of the *ton* that she'd broken with him because he'd found someone else. It was all very well for Viola to be seen with Dolph, of course, but Matt would be a cad to behave in that way. Everything possible had to be done to maintain the fiction that it was the *female* of the pair who broke the troth; the male had to pretend to be the party to be pitied. He had either to appear in society in a lonely state and with a long face, or he had to disappear. And since Matt could not bear to appear anywhere without being in the company of his new beloved, the only answer was to leave London. If they were married, he explained, they could go abroad for a month or two and be constantly together without constraint. By the time they returned, their marriage would have ceased to be a subject for gossip.

Tess was happy to acquiesce. The sooner this business was over, she knew, the better it would be for everyone. She found his companionship too wonderful to bear, and she realized that the longer she enjoyed it, the more difficult the end would be. Therefore it was agreed between them that they would keep their "understanding" secret, that Matt would arrange for a special license, and that a small ceremony would be held in Lady Wetherfield's library with only Lady Wetherfield, the Quimbys, and the bride and groom in attendance. With arrangements thus simplified, the wedding could take place in a week.

It was a week that Tess would never forget. She and Matt rode together every morning at first light, before the bridle path was generally used, either ambling along side by side engrossed in whispered conversation or racing madly down a stretch of path feeling the wind whip at their faces. In the afternoons they strolled down unfashionable streets, poking into out-of-the-way shops and buying each other ridiculous presents like a briarwood pipe for Matt, who never smoked, and an enormous and completely impractical Russian sable muff for her. They took tea and dinner at either Letty Wetherfield's or Julia's, and both their hostesses were kind enough to allow them several hours alone.

Those could have been the best times of all, if Tess had been able to be herself. They sat together, sometimes deliciously entwined, sometimes with Matt stretched out on the rug in front of her chair with his head resting on her knee, while he told her about the estate in Essex—the manor house with its turrets, its hidden passages and its enormous public rooms; and the grounds, with their beautiful gardens, shaded walks, and unspoiled woodlands. Sometimes he spoke seriously about his plans for the modernization of the farms; sometimes jokingly about the sort of pompous Country Gentleman he would someday become. He liked to tease her, too, about her forthcoming role as countess, as hostess of the estate, as housewife, and mother. Because she so often seemed abstracted, he had the impression that she was terribly absent-minded, and he drew amusing word-sketches of the new Marchioness of Bradbourne getting utterly lost in the manor house's miles of corridors and not finding her way back for days.

Tess, on the other hand, could not speak freely. Since she was locked into her role as Sidoney Ashburton, she had to guard her tongue at every moment. Once she forgot herself and almost made a serious faux pas. He had given her an entertaining account of the first time he'd jumped a fence on horseback and had fallen into a shallow brook. He'd broken his ankle and had lain helpless in three inches of bubbling water until he was rescued by the pretty barmaid of the local inn who'd come wandering into his vicinity to keep an assignation with her swain. This reminded Tess of *her* first spill from a horse, and she was halfway into the tale when she remembered that *her* rescuer had been none other than Jeremy! That was a name that Lotherwood was certain to find familiar, and her brain raced about like a crazed rat in a cage to fabricate a fictitious name that would sound convincing. She managed to complete her narration with a minimum of awkwardness, but she resolved never again to indulge in reminiscences.

Another topic that had to be avoided was the wedding trip. Matt had made out an itinerary that would make any girl's heart dance in anticipation: Naples to see the blue grotto, a fortnight each in Rome and Florence, and then an indefinite period to, in Matt's words, "rest in dissolute luxury" amid the breathtaking beauties of Venice. Planning this dreamed-of journey (that she knew they'd never take) caused her too much pain. To silence him on the subject, she told him that she wanted the details of their wedding trip to be a surprise.

It was only when they engaged in the sort of lovers' badinage that all betrothed couples exchange that Tess could permit herself to be natural. It was delightful to participate in such conversation: to identify with absolute precision the very first moment they each knew they were in love; to describe with gurgling laughter each one's very first impression of the other; to recall each early encounter in exact detail and reveal the quips, comments, and retorts each had been tempted to deliver but resisted. For that sort of conversation there was no need for her to inhibit herself, and she enjoyed it to the full.

After each delightful evening Tess found it necessary to remind herself of the reasons she was living this terrible lie. As she lay tossing in her bed, she told herself over and over that he was a coward, a liar, and a murderer. Never once, in all their intimate exchanges, did he indicate by so much as a word or a look that he harbored a horrible, guilty secret. As far as she could tell, he'd put the coaching accident completely out of his mind. It was as if he had no conscience at all. *There's not a man, woman, or child in this world whose life was made worse because of me*; not only had he said those words, but he seemed actually to believe them! It was difficult to remember, when she was with him, that this warm, charming, straightforward-seeming fellow was in reality a blackguard. Only by constantly repeating those words to herself was she able to strengthen her will to proceed with her plans.

They were to be married on Thursday, one week to the day following their betrothal. On Wednesday, after their morning ride, she permitted him to drive her back to the Quimby house in his carriage, but she informed him on the way that it was to be their last encounter until the wedding. "You must stay away for the rest of the day," she told him. It took all her self control to keep her voice steady, for she knew it was the last time she would ever see him. At this moment all her bags were packed and ready for her return to Todmorden, and a carriage had already been hired to come for her as soon as darkness fell. Julia and Edward were rehearsed in their roles for the evening. By this time tomorrow, Matt would be in mourning, and she would be back home, her London "idyll" over. But there must be nothing dramatic or significant in her farewell to him today. To become overly emotional would be to give the game away.

He was handling the ribbons, as he had done the day of the rainstorm, preferring his own driving—and the privacy it afforded—to the presence of his coachman. "Stay away?" he asked, his eyes on the road. "Whatever for?"

She gave a flippant wave of her hand. "You are not permitted to see the bride till the wedding day," she declared, keeping her voice light.

"But why, my love?" He took his eyes from the horses for a moment to throw her a look of amusement. "You've consistently denied it, but I think that in the secret depths of your mind you're superstitious. Do you honestly think my dropping in for tea will bring bad luck?"

"No, but I shall not tempt fate. Besides, I have too much to do. Julia's dressmaker wants to put the finishing touches to my gown, and I must complete my packing for our trip. And one thing more . . ." She smiled at him with what she hoped was bridelike fondness. "I must pick up a special wedding gift I had made for you."

"Wedding gift? From the bride to the groom? That's a custom I've not heard of before. Is it a family tradition of some sort?"

"Not that I'm aware of. It's my own idea. You'll be giving me a ring tomorrow that I shall wear forever. It seems only fair that I give you something, too."

"Splendid idea. I accept." He pulled back on the reins lightly to slow the horses' pace. "What is it?"

"I think it should be a surprise, don't you?"

"No, I don't. You know you'll receive a ring from me. Why can't I be similarly informed?"

She hesitated. She hadn't intended to tell him about it, but, on consideration, she supposed there would be no harm to her plot if she did. "It's a fob for your watch chain." She gave a gurgling little laugh. "I've thought of the most appropriate design for it."

"Oh?" Catching the teasing note in her voice, he turned from the horses with eyebrows raised suspiciously. "Appropriate, is it? Let me guess. If it's a fob, it must be a gold piece of some kind. I know. A gold disk with a diamond set in, to represent your diamond of a husband-to-be."

She tossed her head scornfully. "Conceited jackanapes, aren't you? Diamond indeed! As if I could afford such a thing. I'm not a marchioness yet, you know."

Unperturbed, he went on. "A gold heart, then. With our initials all intertwined in florid script, surrounded by dozens of curlicues and flourishes."

"Oh, pooh! I am neither so sentimental nor so commonplace. It's a gold *cock's comb*, if you must know. And well you deserve it!"

He laughed. "Your point, my dear! I never would have guessed, but I can't think of a more appropriate symbol. I shall wear it for all eternity, as a constant reminder to stay humble."

They drew up at the Quimbys' door. While he concentrated on stopping the horses, she stared intently at his profile. She wanted to remember every detail of his face . . . the strong line of jaw, the narrow, vertical crease that dented his cheek, the dark eyes, the heavy brow, the thick hair that, despite its short-cropped Corinthian style, never looked properly combed. But his attention to the horses was momentary, and as soon as he turned to her, she dropped her eyes.

He climbed down from the carriage and came round to her door. "This is good-bye, then," he said cheerfully, assisting her to alight. "Until tomorrow at ten."

"Yes," she said, unable to match his tone. "Until . . . tomorrow."

He lifted her hand to his lips. "After tomorrow, thank heaven," he said with a rakish glint, "I shall be able to kiss you properly when we say good-bye."

She lowered her head and gulped down the tears that had suddenly gathered in her throat. "No one seems to be about," she suggested, attempting a mischievous smile. "Why don't you kiss me properly right now?"

He was delighted to acquiesce. He pulled her close and lifted her chin. "*Damnation*," he muttered before he could proceed further, "here's comes Julia's blasted butler."

There was nothing to be done. He let her go, bowed over her hand, and returned to his seat in the carriage. She watched numbly as he waved farewell and, without remaining to see the carriage disappear down the street, turned and followed the butler into the house. She handed him her riding crop and walked slowly up the stairs. There was no hurry; her hired coach would not be arriving for hours. She had all day to weep.

With his impending nuptials a secret, Matt could not celebrate his last evening of bachelorhood with the traditional carouse, but he went to White's anyway, hoping to forget his impatience for the morrow by indulging in cards and drink with his cronies. After the usual exchange of pleasantries, however, and two hours of piquet, he'd had enough. He arrived home before eleven, three hours earlier than was his wont, but he was nevertheless surprised to find his man waiting for him. The fellow had standing orders not to stay up for him on the nighs he attended his club. "Why aren't you in bed, Rooks?" he asked, handing him his hat and stick.

"Visitors, my lord." Rooks couldn't hide a look of concern. "Sir Edward and Lady Quimby. I've put them in the drawing room."

A premonition of disaster struck Matt like a body blow. Frowning, he strode across the hall to the drawing room and threw open the doors. "Julia? Edward? What—?"

They had been sitting silently side by side on the sofa, but they both rose at the sight of him. "Ah, here you are, Matt," Edward mumbled, and cast an enigmatic look at his wife. Then he cleared his throat. "We've come on . . . er . . . a most unfortunate . . . that is, I am sorry to . . ." He paused and looked at his wife again in obvious discomfort.

"Good God," Matt exclaimed impatiently, "speak up, man! Something is obviously wrong. Is it Sidoney?"

Edward dropped his eyes. It was Julia who answered. "Yes, Matt," she said in a voice that shook. "I . . . we . . . don't know how to tell you—"

"Has she taken ill? Is that it?"

"There's been an accident," Edward said, keeping his head lowered.

"A terrible accident," Julia amended, taking a step toward him.

Matt felt himself suddenly transplanted into a nightmare —the kind in which one tries to move quickly but everything is slowed down as if the air were made of water. "Please," he muttered hoarsely, "just tell me. How badly is she hurt?"

"She is . . . gone," Julia said.

"Gone?" Matt stared at her in utter disbelief. "You don't mean *dead!*"

"Yes," Edward said flatly. "She's been killed."

No one spoke or moved for a long moment. It was Matt who broke the silence. "This can't be! It's a game, isn't it! This is Miss Sidoney Ashburton's idea of a game!" He took two strides to Julia and grasped her by the arms. "If this is some sort of joke, you can tell her for me it is *not* amusing. In fact I've a good mind to go over there right now, pull her out of bed, and *wring her neck!*"

"It's no game, my dear," Julia said, a tear slipping down her cheek. "I think you'd better hear the whole. It . . . happened about three, I think. She'd walked to Bond Street to pick up a parcel. The jeweler would have sent it round, but she insisted on getting it herself. She wanted to assure herself that the work had been done properly, you see, and . . . and she said she needed some air." Julia slipped out of Matt's slackened hold and sank down on the sofa, burying her face in her handkerchief. "It seems she picked up the parcel and then decided to hire a hack to take her home. There was a collision, and . . . and . . ."

Matt stared numbly down at her. Then he turned to Edward. "Is this *true?*"

Edward turned away. "I'm so sorry, Matt," he said with a sigh.

Matt felt the blood drain from his face. He swayed on his feet. Edward came up and steadied him. "Shall we ring for your man?" he asked gently.

Matt shook his head. "No, it's not necessary. I must . . . I can't seem to *think*. If you'll both excuse me, I'll . . ." With an abstracted, dismissive motion of his hand, he turned to the doorway.

Julia rose and followed him. "They found this parcel in her hand, Matt," she said, holding it out to him. "The one she'd gone to fetch. It was her wedding gift to you. We thought . . . Edward and I . . . that you might like to have it."

Matt stared down at it in horror. The little parcel was wrapped in tissue-thin white paper and tied with a silver ribbon. Tess had, in reality, done it up herself. And as if the dramatic scene she'd so carefully composed were not grim enough, she'd added a final, artistic touch: she'd daubed the white paper with a little smear of blood.

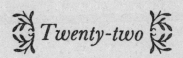

Twenty-two

Todmorden

22 June, 1812

My dear Dr. Pomfrett:

As you can see by the above, I have returned home, but
before I settle back into the old routines of my life before London, I am taking this opportunity to write to you. I promised
to let you know when the goal I set for myself in regard to
the Lotherwood matter had been accomplished; you will be
pleased, I think, to learn that it has. Lotherwood has been
given his just deserts in a manner and degree completely appropriate to his crime. I was not present when the sentence was
meted out, but my accomplices inform me that his suffering
was not "hidden in his soul" but quite apparent to the onlookers. I am certain that he will never again deal carelessly
with human lives.

I admit, dear doctor, that this experience was extraordinar-
ily difficult and painful for me, but despite all, I am convinced
that I was in the right to seek and achieve this retribution. It
was only simple justice that Jeremy Beringer and all of you
who suffered in that stagecoach accident be avenged. I must
believe in that justice, or the thought of what I've done would
be unbearable to me.

This letter to you is my last task in this affair. Now I intend to put the whole matter behind me and try to find, if not contentment, at least some peace of mind. I hope that now you, too, will be able to do the same.

Yours,

Teresa Brownlow

❧ Twenty-three ❧

Throughout the summer Lady Brownlow watched her daughter with increasing alarm. Something dreadful had evidently occurred to Tess in London, for the girl who'd come home was not the same as the one who'd gone away. She was quiet, introspective, pale, sad of eye, and devoid of the youthful energy that had been so much a part of her before. The girl rose reluctantly from her bed in the morning, pushed herself without enthusiasm through the routine of the days, and took herself up to bed at night with a sigh of hopeless weariness.

Lady Brownlow tried, by both direct and indirect questioning, to find out what had happened, but Tess would not speak of her two-month absence from home. She would only say that her visit to London had gone very well, thank you, Mama; that Julia and Edward had been the very best of hosts; that she had seen London Bridge, the Tower, St. Paul's, and the Elgin marbles; and that she intended never to visit the city again as long as she lived.

One day in late July, when the weather outdoors was too sultry to bear, Lady Brownlow sat with her needlepoint at an open window in the drawing room, wondering where her worrisome daughter was hiding herself. The girl's bedroom faced south, so it was hardly the coolest room in which to spend so humid an afternoon. Determined to find her and drag her down to the relative comfort of this northern exposure, she put aside her needlework and crossed the hallway to the stairs.

Before she mounted them, however, she glanced inside the open door of the downstairs sitting room and saw Tess slumped in an easy chair, her eyes fixed on the portrait of her father that hung over the fireplace. "Goodness, my love, whatever are you thinking of, sitting there like that?" Lady Brownlow asked from the doorway.

Tess barely stirred. "I was wondering about Papa. Tell me, Mama, was he a good magistrate?"

"A good *magistrate?*" She crossed the threshold and stared at her daughter in bewilderment. "I don't know what you mean."

"I mean was he considered to be a good judge of men? When criminals were brought before him, was he kind? Fair? Forgiving?"

"Good heavens, child, how should I know? I was never present at the trials."

"No, I didn't think you were. But you must have some impression. He told you about some of the cases he judged, did he not? And you must have heard others speak of him. Judges have reputations, don't they, of being easy or hard, honest or corrupt, prejudiced or fair?"

Lady Brownlow shook her head, wondering if her daughter was turning queer. But she nevertheless knit her brow and tried to answer the question. "Well, your father was not corrupt—that much I can say with certainty. He never lied; it was not in his nature. And from that I assume that he was also fair. But as to his being *kind*, well, I rather think not. He was quite unbending in his standards for himself, so I presume he did not bend them for others."

"Hard and unforgiving, then," Tess murmured.

Her mother shrugged. "I suppose so. But what difference does it make to you now?"

"No difference, really," Tess said, pulling herself up from her chair. "Except to determine if I am like him. I rather think I am."

"Hard and unforgiving? I would not describe you so, my love," Lady Brownlow said, taking her daughter's arm and strolling to the doorway. "In any case, since you are not a judge of criminals, what does it matter whether you are like him or not?"

Tess paused and looked once more over her shoulder at the haunting portrait. "Not a judge of criminals," she muttered to herself. Then, with a shake of her head like a puppy shaking off raindrops, she turned to her mother with a reassuring smile. "You're right, Mama. It doesn't matter at all. Come, let's go to the drawing room where it's cooler."

After two months of watching this behavior, her fears becoming more worrisome each day that her daughter was descending into an irreversible decline, Lady Brownlow consulted with her friend Lydia Beringer about the problem. Lady Beringer's health had seriously declined since the death of her son—a condition that required frequent bed rest and a style of living much more sedentary than it had been a year ago—but her mind was as sharp as ever. "Take her abroad," she advised the troubled Lady Brownlow. "When I was young, a trip abroad was considered the best cure for girls with broken hearts, broken troths, or broken spirits. I should think travel would be as effective now as then. Close up the house for a couple of months—I shall miss you dreadfully, of course, but it will be worth it if Tess is cured!—and go off to Florence or Lisbon or Geneva. Too bad that the dreadful Bonaparte keeps Paris out of our reach, but there's a whole world of exciting places the British nobility can visit with impunity. Take her abroad, my dear. It will do wonders for her, see if it doesn't."

To Lady Brownlow's surprise, she had no trouble persuading her daughter to agree to the plan. Tess was unenthusastic but perfectly willing. She had no objection to taking a journey; as much as her mother did, she wanted to shake off the depression that had engulfed her. She had no real confidence in the curative powers of a voyage to a foreign city, but she was willing to try. Any distraction from her misery, even a temporary one, would be welcome.

The only subject of contention was where they might go. For some strange reason, Tess was adamantly opposed to visiting any city in Italy. She would not explain herself but merely declared that Italy was out of the question. "You may choose any other place on the globe," she told her mother, "but not Italy."

It was Lydia Beringer who actually made the final decision: Lisbon. Having done a great deal of travel in the early years of her marriage, when Lord Beringer had been in diplomatic service, she had many helpful hints to pass on to her friends who'd never been abroad before. "When visiting a foreign city," Lydia Beringer told Lady Brownlow, "it is always comforting to have in one's possession the address of a few friends (or friends of friends) on whom one can call. Such acquaintance helps one to become less strange; one learns one's way about, one makes other acquaintance, and before one knows it, one develops a circle in which to . . . well, in which to circulate! And I have a friend in Lisbon who will admirably answer those needs.''

She gave Lady Brownlow the address of a certain Senhora Carlotta da Greja, a London heiress born Charlotte Finch, who'd married a Portuguese merchant and now made her home in a charming villa in the heights of Ajuda, just outside the city. ''Be sure to call on her at once. She will know just where all the visiting English congregate and will help you to find gentlemen companions for Tess.''

But Tess found herself a companion even before she and her mother called on the Senhora. In the entryway of their hotel near the Terreiro do Paco (which the British visitors called Black Horse Square because of the huge equestrian statue at the center) Tess literally bumped into a round-cheeked young student evidently making his Grand Tour. Mr. Barnabas Thomkins, his head buried in a book, blundered into her and knocked her down when she was leaving the hotel on her very first outing. Red-faced and agonized, he helped her to her feet while uttering a profusion of apologies. In the midst of a sentence he gazed into her eyes and fell helplessly in love. From that moment on he took every opportunity to be at her side. He was quick to inform her that he'd taken leave from Cambridge, where he was a student of Romance languages, in order to take his tour. He'd been in Lisbon for almost a month, he said, and his expertise on the ways and byways of the city would be of enormous help to her. He insisted that he would be ''excessively delighted'' to put himself at her disposal as escort and guide. Since he gladly included her mother in his offer, Tess accepted his escort. For the first few days of their stay, the fellow proved indispensible and was almost always in their company.

After a week had passed, Lady Brownlow paid a call on Senhora da Greja, who received her most graciously. The result of the visit was an invitation to accompany the Senhora, in two days' time, on a trip to Cintra. ''It is the most picturesque mountain spot in the world, my dear,'' the senhora told her. ''There is a Portuguese proverb that says 'To see the

whole world and leave out Cintra is to travel blindfolded.' "
But the invitation was not merely for sightseeing; it included a
stop at the Beckford Palace, an estate that an eccentric and
wealthy Englishman named William Beckford had built two
decades before. "It is an astonishing sight," the senhora explained. "Pure white stone wrought in the Moorish style, with
a surrounding park of plants, giant ferns, and flora from all
over the world! There will be a fete, and every well-connected
Briton in Lisbon will be there."

Lady Brownlow returned to the hotel in a state of high excitement. When she told Tess and Barnabas Thomkins about
it over dinner in the hotel's dining salon, the young man
agreed that a visit to Cintra and the English palace would indeed be desirable. "I was going to arrange an invitation for
you myself," he said.

"Oh? Are *you* going?" Lady Brownlow asked with a touch
of dismay.

"Yes, I've been invited," the boy said. "The Beckfords are
acquaintances of the Marquis of Anglesey, who is somehow
related to my father."

If this explanation was incomprehensible to Tess, it was not
to her mother, for Kate Brownlow was well aware of the efficacy of good connections. But Barnabas Thomkins's good
connections notwithstanding, Lady Brownlow was not happy
at the prospect of having him as escort. After dinner, when
Tess excused herself and went up to bed, Lady Brownlow requested that the boy remain for a few moments at the table
with her. "Now, Barnaby," she said with blunt fondness (for
intimacy comes quickly to compatriots who make friends on
foreign soil), "I don't want you to take this amiss, but I don't
wish you to hang about Tess too closely at the Beckford
Palace. It is essential that she become acquainted with some
other, more eligible young gentlemen, and they won't approach her if you are always in the way."

"I *say*, Lady B.," the boy objected, "you can't be serious.
I'm as eligible as anyone else, ain't I?"

"You're an absolute dear, and Tess and I both adore you.
But she doesn't consider you a proper suitor, and you know it.
You're *years* too young for her."

"*Years?* I'm twenty-two!"

"Bosh! You're not half over twenty, if I have eyes in my
head. And though Tess is only twenty-four, she is years older

in experience. To her you are the little brother she never had."

Barnaby, pouting, propped his chin on his hands. "Yes, she seems to treat me so. But I've been hoping that in time—"

"In time, my boy, you will forget this infatuation as if it had never been."

"Infatuation!" He lifted his head, his round cheeks quivering in offense. "How can you call it infatuation? You can't know what I feel."

"But I do, Barnaby, I do," she said, reaching across the table and patting his hand soothingly. "I know that you will feel love for many and many a girl before you settle down. You have many such adventures before you. But Tess . . ." She paused, sighed, and began to fiddle with a teaspoon.

"What about Tess?" Barnaby prompted, leaning forward interestedly.

"She's suffered a great deal, you see," Lady Brownlow admitted. "She was to be wed, but on the eve of the wedding her betrothed was killed." She fixed a pair of pleading eyes on the young man's face. "She has not yet recovered from the blow, though it's been almost a year. If you truly cared for her, Barnaby, you would help me to help her."

Barnaby looked down glumly at the teacup still before him on the table. "So that's it. I wondered why she so often seems to be somewhere else in her mind. Very well, Lady B., I won't stand in her way. I'll even introduce her to one or two chaps with whom I'm acquainted." He rose and came round the table to help Lady Brownlow from her chair. "But if it ever should come to pass that Tess takes a fancy to *me*," he added, his usual optimism reasserting itself, "I hope that *you* won't stand in *my* way!"

They rode to Cintra in Senhora da Greja's open carriage. It was a fascinating ride through rugged, mountainous roads. Tess had brought along her copy of *Childe Harold's Pilgrimage* in order to read aloud the stanzas describing Cintra, but the lively senhora was already familiar with them and enchanted everyone by declaiming them aloud. When the high peaks ("the horrid crags, by toppling convent crowned," Byron had written) came into view, Tess found herself speechless at the awesome sight. The Beckford Palace was bound to be an anticlimax, she thought.

But of course it was not. It was like a magical oasis in the midst of Cintra's rugged mountain mass. The white stone of the building gleamed orange in the late afternoon sun, and the lawns, spread like carpet on the surrounding mountainside, were as lushly green and perfect as any in England. The reception was well under way when they arrived, the guests all gathered on the south slope, wandering about with their glasses of Amontillado on the graveled walks and among the wonderful trees and shrubbery that edged the lawns. Senhora Charlotte, as Barnaby called her, immediately bore Lady Brownlow away to meet their hostess. "Don't forget your promise," Lady Brownlow muttered to Barnaby before she was swept away.

"What promise, Barnaby?" Tess asked him curiously.

Barnaby frowned disgustedly. "I promised I would stay out of your way so that some other fellows might have a chance with you."

"Oh?" Tess laughed and patted his arm comfortingly. "Well, there's no need to take a pet. No 'other fellows' seem to be crowding about me to elbow you out."

"Yes, but they will, as soon as I introduce you to a few of them. Not that I see very many acquaintances here today whom your mother would consider eligible. There's Trevithick, mooning over there by himself near that grove of palms. He's all right, if you like moody Cornishmen. And there's Rob Westall, the fellow in the Hussar boots, talking to Lord and Lady Horleigh. He's going to be an earl, but he ain't much older than I. Oh, *there's* someone who might interest you. He drinks, but there's no telling what the influence of a good woman might do for him." He walked a few steps down the path and waved to someone in a group of ten or twelve people some distance away. "Lotherwood! I say, *Lotherwood!*" he shouted. "Over here!"

❧ Twenty-four ❧

Tess's heart stopped beating. She felt her knees turn to water and the blood drain from her face. "Barnaby, *don't*—!" Terror-stricken, she looked about her for a place to hide, but the world was spinning about in a dizzying pace, and she couldn't see where to go. If only she could sink into the ground, evaporate in a fog, or just die.

"What?" Barnaby had turned back and was looking at her strangely.

"Please! You mustn't *let* him . . . he mustn't *see* me!"

"But why not?" He glanced over his shoulder. "It's too late, anyway. He's heard me. Can't you see him coming this way?"

She looked round again, more desperately, for a place to hide, but she seemed unable to move. The only thing capable of motion was her mind. *He mustn't find me here!* her mind screamed. She had to find a hiding place . . . but where? And what if he'd already *seen* her! In absolute dread she covered her face with her hands, and, peeping through her fingers, lifted her eyes to Barnaby's face and followed the direction of his gaze.

There was a man making his way through the milling guests toward them, but it was nobody she'd ever seen before. She took her hands from her face as her pulse began to pump again. "That's . . . that's not Lotherwood," she breathed as the world slowly steadied itself.

"Ah, but it is," the strange gentleman said, coming up to them. He took a swig from the glass he carried before studying her with interest. "I'm a little squiffy, but I'm not drunk enough to forget my own name."

Tess's obvious agitation had unnerved Barnaby. He had to perform the introductions, but he did it with distinct unease. "Miss Brownlow, may I . . . er . . . present Lord Guy Lotherwood?"

"*Guy?* Guy *Lotherwood?*" She stared up into his face. This Lotherwood had thick black hair and broad shoulders, but there was no other resemblance that she could see. He was younger than Matt, one or two inches shorter, and more than a stone heavier. His features were handsome, but they were already somewhat coarsened by drink, the nose in particular. It was swollen and covered with the small red lines that come from heavy indulgence in alcohol.

"You are surprised, ma'am," he was saying. "I take it you are acquainted with my brother."

Tess stared at him in wonder. "If your brother is Matthew Lotherwood, the Marquis of Bradbourne, I *am* somewhat acquainted with him."

"Ah, yes," Guy Lotherwood said bitterly, taking another swallow of his drink, "but you find no family resemblance. Is that what so surprises you?"

"What surprises me, my lord, is that you exist at all. No one in his circle every mentioned to me that he had a brother!"

"It doesn't surprise me, however. You see, my dear, I am the proverbial black sheep. Quite unmentionable in family circles."

Tess was dizzy with these revelations. "I'm afraid," she said, putting a hand to her forehead, "that I must sit down. Is there somewhere we might go, Lord Guy, where we can talk?"

"I say, Tess," Barnaby cut in, "let *me* take you to a quiet spot. Guy, here, ain't in the best condition to keep a lady company. Said himself he was squiffy."

"Squiffy, old man, but not drenched. I'll take her to the grove of palms over there. You can trust her with me, I assure you," Guy Lotherwood said, waving the boy off and taking Tess's arm—

"Tess—!" Barnaby objected.

"It's all right, Barnaby," Tess said, abstracted but trying to smile at him reassuringly. "There's something I wish to ask his lordship that is of most urgent interest to me. There's no need to worry about me. If I don't return to your side in half an hour, you may come and fetch me."

She leaned heavily on Guy Lotherwood's arm as he led her down the path, her mind whirling with the possibilities this man's identity suggested . . . possibilities that terrified her to think about. There were things this man could tell her that might affect her very life.

He brought her to the palm grove, but in the cool circle of trees there was only one seat—a carved marble bench on which the gloomy Cornishman whom Barnaby had pointed out before was brooding. The Cornishman looked up at the sound of their footsteps, glared at them for intruding, and rose. Before either of them could apologize and back away, the fellow marched past them through the trees and out of earshot. "That was obliging of the fellow, I must say," Lotherwood said, laughing as he led her to the bench. "Do sit down, ma'am. May I go to find a drink for you? You look as though you could do with one."

"No, thank you, my lord. It shocked me to learn your name, but I shall soon recover. Please sit down. There is a great deal I wish to ask about you."

Guy Lotherwood raised one eyebrow curiously. "I can't imagine what about me should interest you, ma'am. I'm nothing more than what you see . . . the proverbial second son, the proverbial black sheep, the proverbial *persona non grata*." He took a seat beside her and sipped at his drink. "But I am quite at your disposal. What is it that you so urgently wish to know?"

Tess drew in a trembling breath. "A number of things, I'm afraid. I hope you won't think me idly curious. I have good reasons for taking this interest in you."

"I can tell from the excessive pallor of your cheeks, my dear, that your curiosity is more than idle. Fire away, then."

"You are Lotherwood's younger brother, I take it. Isn't it unusual that he never mentioned you in the two months I knew him?"

"I *told* you, Miss . . . Miss Brownlow, is it? . . . that I'm the black sheep. No family likes to refer to its black sheep."

"But what makes you the black sheep, my lord? Did you . . ." she paused and bit her lip nervously ". . . did you do something . . . d-dreadful?"

"I did several dreadful things," he said, draining his glass. Then he looked directly at her and smiled bitterly. "They were so dreadful he banished me."

"*Banished* you? *Matt* did?"

" 'Matt,' is it?" He raised his brows in a manner that reminded her of his brother. "You must have known my brother well."

She stared at him for a moment and then, with a little shiver, dropped her eyes. "Perhaps not well enough," she murmured, half to herself. It was another moment before she looked up again. "What do you mean, banished?"

"You know the word. *Banished. Exiled.* I am given a generous livelihood in return for having pledged my word never to set foot on English soil."

"I see. Would it disturb you very much to tell me what dreadful things you did to cause this banishment?"

He shrugged. "Again, I don't know why this should interest you, ma'am, but I suppose there's no harm in telling you. I cracked up three vehicles with devil-may-care driving. Destroyed two horses. Made any number of drunken scenes. Wounded a scoundrel in a duel. I should say for my brother that through all of this he stood by me, picked me up, dusted me off, set me on my feet, and saved me from punishment and disgrace. But then I did one thing more."

Tess felt her fingers begin to shake. "One thing m-more?"

He stared at the empty glass in his hand. "One thing that pushed him past his endurance. The last straw." He gave a mirthless laugh and threw his empty glass crashing against the nearest tree.

The sound of shattering glass coincided with a little cry that came from deep in Tess's throat. The look on Guy Lotherwood's face when he'd thrown the glass had cut her like a knife. It was the look Dr. Pomfrett had once described as "suffering in one's soul."

He turned back to face her, but his eyes did not see her. They were looking at some vision from his past he could not erase. "Do you want to know what that last straw was?" he asked. "I—"

Tess put out a hand as if to ward off what was coming. Two silent tears rolled down her face. "You wrecked a stage-coach," she said quietly, "and a man was killed."

He blinked as his eyes returned to the present and focused

slowly, bewilderedly, on hers. "Confound it, who *are* you? How did you—?"

There was no anger in the voice that cut him off. Only an unutterable sadness. "Jeremy Beringer was my betrothed."

"Oh, God!" Guy Lotherwood muttered, shutting his eyes in anguish. "Oh, God."

They sat there unmoving for a long while. Then he got to his feet and paced back and forth among the trees. When next he looked at her, he was startled by her appearance. Her face was as white as chalk, her hands were clenched in her lap, and her strange eyes were staring straight ahead of her with an expression of utter shock. It was as if the death of her betrothed had just occurred instead of having happened almost a year before. The look in her eyes undid him. That he could have been responsible for it was more than he could bear. In an agony of guilt he ran up to her, fell to his knees on the ground before her, and grasped her hand. "Forgive me," he whispered in despair. "Forgive me! I never meant . . . ! I would give my life if I could only . . ."

She looked down at him and laid a hand on his cheek. "No, no. There's no need," she said in a low, hoarse voice. "I haven't asked you all these questions to berate you. You have my forgiveness, for what it's worth."

"For what it's *worth?* If only I could *tell* you what it's worth!" He lowered his head until his forehead rested on her hand. "For all these months I've wished . . . ! Perhaps now it will be possible, someday, to forgive myself."

"I hope someday you will, my lord. If you do, you will be more fortunate than I."

There was a crack in her voice as she spoke that brought his head up. "What do you mean? What have *you* to forgive yourself for?"

She shook her head, withdrew her hand from his, and rose. "I think," she said, starting to walk away, "it is something worse."

"Something worse?" He got to his feet and stumbled after her.

"Oh, my God, it's *true!*" she said, looking back at him with an expression he would not ever forget. It was as if the truth she'd just discovered was the darkest truth one could learn. "It's something much worse than you've ever done!"

❧ Twenty-five ❧

Matt's summer passed in a fog of grief that was unrelieved by the solace society usually provides for those who suffer loss. Because there had not been any familial or legal connection between him and the deceased Miss Ashburton, society did not offer the usual mourning rituals: no wreath was hung on his door, no clergyman called with words of comfort, no stream of visitors came to express condolences, no friends gathered to share his grief. Because he'd had to keep his wedding intentions secret, very few of his circle even knew that Miss Ashburton existed. Sometimes he himself didn't believe she existed; his only tangible proofs of her presence in his life were the special wedding license, which had never been signed, and a little gold watch fob shaped like a cock's comb.

His aunt Letty knew she existed, of course, as did Julia and Edward Quimby. Letty tried to offer what comfort she could, but Julia and Edward seemed ill-at-ease in his company after the night they broke the news to him, and after a while he avoided them. Most of the others in his circle of friends had never even met Sidoney. Dolph and Viola, the two who had, were involved in preparations for their nuptials, and though they took brief notice of Miss Ashburton's sudden absence from the scene, they simply assumed that Matt had lost interest in her and that she'd gone back to wherever it was she'd come from. (It occurred to Viola, in a sleepless hour late one night, that she'd perhaps been hasty in severing her betrothal to Matt, but she put the thought aside. As her old nurse used to say: better to be a lesser man's first choice than a greater one's second.)

Matt did not regret that most of his friends knew nothing of his tragedy; he simply didn't believe that their sympathy, if they *had* known, would have been any real comfort to him. The blow of her death had left him reeling as nothing that had happened in his life had done before, and he soon realized that, if he was to regain his equilibrium, he'd have to do it for himself.

Letty did not neglect him, but sometimes he wished that she would. She visited him with devoted regularity, but her attitude toward his grief was not particularly soothing. "It was such a brief acquaintance," she'd point out repeatedly. "Too short to leave a lasting wound. You'll get over it. By fall, we shall find a new prospect for you. I've been thinking that perhaps it's time you began to think seriously about Miss—"

"I know . . . I know." He'd cut her off each time with a wry smile. "Miss Sturtevant. Cut line, Letty. I've no interest in new prospects."

For a while he continued to follow his usual daily routine. He dressed, he rode in the park, he met with friends, he boxed at Cribb's Parlor, he spent evenings at one or the other of his clubs. He even attended a ball or two and stood up with Dolph at the Lovell-Kelsey wedding. But the activities which had in former years seemed exciting and fulfilling were now empty and meaningless, and one by one he dropped them. His friends remarked from time to time that Lotherwood was turning mopish, but since sporting types were not inclined to be analytical, they did not pursue the matter.

More and more he preferred his own company. He spent hours each day walking through the London streets, letting his feet take what direction they would. His eyes did not notice much of what passed before him. His thoughts roamed where they willed, while the fingers of his right hand played with the little fob he'd hung on his watch chain. He spent much time thinking about that fob, for he'd discovered that Sidoney had had a few words engraved in tiny letters on the back: *I love you anyway*. The words now seemed to him an enigmatic message from the grave—a message that was, somehow, rather important to decipher. What exactly had she meant?

The *I love you* was clear enough, but what did she mean by *anyway?*

As the summer passed and the winds brought in the cool smell of fall, he continued to tramp the city streets. The sharp pain of shock had eased, leaving him with a dull ache in his chest that was even more depressing than the earlier, more stinging grief, for it bore with it the heaviness of permanence. But he'd begun to think about his future, which was a sign of the curative—though limited—powers of time. He decided that London held nothing more for him and that the only hope of a new life lay in Essex. On his estate in the south he would make himself heal. He would become the Country Gentleman he'd always planned to be. The prospect was the only brightness in what had become a grim, gray world. He did a great deal of planning during those long rambles, but even then his mind still occasionally gnawed, like a dog at a bone, on the question of the words on the watch-fob: *I love you anyway.* What had she meant by them?

The most obvious explanation was that she meant she loved him in spite of his being a coxcomb. It was a perfectly logical interpretation for a sentence of four very simple words, but somehow it didn't satisfy him. There was just enough ambiguity in that fourth word to keep him puzzling; it's indefiniteness had the same aura of mystery that was part of his memory of the girl herself. Sidoney had always been troubled by something in him, some serious flaw he himself did not recognize. He'd hoped that their marriage would sooner or later bring the secret to light, but now, of course, it was too late. Was this little message another indication that she had serious reservations about his character? Did she mean she loved him in spite of *that?*

He couldn't answer, nor could he guess that an answer would soon be found. And it was about to be found right there on the city streets.

It happened on a crisp day in late October. He had wandered east from Oxford Street, along High Holborn, across Gray's Lane and into Grevil Street. The streets were noisy and crowded with pedestrians and vehicles of all descriptions, for the Clerkenwell section of London was a far cry from the prosperous elegance of the West End. Today, however, there seemed to be greater confusion than usual, and he was forced out of his abstraction by an unusual burst of noise emanating from round the corner on Leather Lane. He walked round and discovered that a farm wagon, heavily laden with potatoes, had lost a wheel and tilted over. Some of the sacks of produce had slipped over the wagon's side and were now fair game for looting. While the farmer struggled with three of the looters, others came running over from all directions, tearing open the sacks or even lifting whole sacks on their shoulders and making off with them. Matt, feeling quite ripe for a good fight, waded into the throng in support of the farmer, throwing his highly praised right hook at any target that looked promising.

The force of his fist, combined with the din of the farmer's outraged shouts, were just beginning to take effect when a particularly enthusiastic pillager conceived the idea of using the loose potatoes as a weapon. He picked up a few of the hardest he could find and began to heave them about wildly. One of them struck Matt's forehead, right above his left eye. It felled him at once.

He toppled back and lay stretched out on the cobbles unmoving. A woman screamed. The noise and looting stopped at once, and the miscreants immediately ran round the corner to the busier Grevil Street and melted into the passing crowd. Only the farmer and the man who'd thrown the missile remained, staring down at the fallen pugilist with worried frowns. "I'm bum-squabbled," the potato-tosser muttered. " 'E looks t' be a *nob*."

"Aye. That's trouble for 'ee. An' serves ye right, I say."

"Is 'e dead, do y' think?"

"Nay, I sh'dna think so." He knelt down and listened at Matt's chest. "E's breathin'."

"Praise be. I din't mean 'im no 'arm, y'know. There's a doctor roun' on Brooke. Will ye gi' me a hand to take 'im there?"

"Be 'ee daft? There wouldn't be a sack remainin' t' take t' market when I came back!" the farmer declared.

"There wouldn' be a sack remainin' *now*, if 'e hadn' took yer part." He rubbed his stubbled chin speculatively. "Seems t' me a nob like this un 'd be 'appy t' pay ye fer yer trouble. More'n ye'd get fer *double* that load."

It was a convincing argument. The farmer lifted Matt under the arms, the looter took his legs, and they awkwardly dragged him back down Grevil to Brooke Street, to a neat, two-story edifice with a brass plaque near the door reading JOSIAH POMFRETT, PHYSICIAN AND SURGEON.

Matt's first conscious thought was to wonder where the dreadful, stinging odor was coming from. He opened his eyes to find a stranger with wild gray hair and thick white eyebrows bending over him and holding a vial of spirits of ammonia under his nose. "Uch! Take it away," Matt muttered.

"Ah, that's better," the stranger said cheerfully and helped him to sit up. "Now, just sit still for a bit. I want to look you over."

Matt found himself in a bare, neat surgery, sitting on an examining table. His forehead throbbed badly, but he seemed otherwise in good condition. "How did I get here?" he asked the stranger, who'd turned aside to replace the spirits. "Are you a doctor?"

"I'm Dr. Pomfrett," the man said, returning to the table. "You were brought here from the Grevil Street corner by two loobies, one of whom admitted to throwing a potato at your noggin." As he spoke he lifted Matt's upper eyelids, one at a time, and peered into his eyes. "The scoundrel was full of apologies, of course. Said he didn't mean you harm. The other one seemed to want you to buy his load of potatoes." He ran his fingers skillfully over Matt's skull, feeling for signs of injury. "Since I gather that you'd sustained this injury by going to his assistance—and quite heroically, too, from the sound of it—I read them both the riot act and sent them on their way. There, now, let's get you on your feet and see how steady you are."

"Thank you, Doctor, for dealing with those louts," Matt said, rising carefully and putting a hand to his aching head. "I'll think twice, next time, before I let myself be drawn into a street-corner mill."

Dr. Pomfrett made him walk back and forth and then sat him down on the table again. "I don't think you've sustained a concussion," he said, turning to his shelves and taking down a bottle, "but you will have to be watched for a day or so. I'll give you some laudanum for the pain, which I'm afraid will be considerable tonight, but you should send for your own physician right away and let him examine you."

"I have no physician, Dr. Pomfrett. And you seem to me to

be quite competent. I'd be grateful if you yourself would provide whatever future examinations or treatment might be necessary."

The doctor paused in the act of pouring the drug from a large bottle to a small one and looked up at Matt quizzically. "I? Are you sure? I'm not the sort of doctor to attract your set, you know. I haven't a single member of the nobility on my list of patients."

"Well, you have one now," Matt said, smiling. He slid down from the table and offered his hand. "I am Mathew Lotherwood, Marquis of Bradbourne."

Dr. Pomfrett, in the act of putting out his hand, froze. "Lotherwood?" He blinked up into the taller man's face in confusion. "You can't be!"

Matt studied him curiously. "Oh? Why can't I?"

"Because I . . . I've met Lord Lotherwood. I remember him well. He was . . . stockier than you, a bit younger, features somewhat . . . coarser—"

Matt's expression hardened. "I think, sir, that you must be speaking of my brother."

"*Brother?*" The doctor's whole face seemed to go slack. His hands went about the business of closing the bottles of laudanum, but his eyes did not leave Lotherwood's. "I have never heard mention of a brother!" he said, placing the bottles down on the table like an automaton.

"Probably not, since he resides abroad." Matt's response was cool and aloof. "I'm afraid I don't see why the subject is of concern to you."

"Abroad? He resides *abroad?*" He came round to Matt's side of the table, rubbing his forehead nervously. "Has he been abroad for very long?"

Matt stiffened, bracing himself for who-knew-what sort of tale of his brother's involvement in yet another scrape, although it did not seem possible after the remorse he'd showed the last time. "I don't think I care to answer these questions, Doctor, unless you give me sufficient reason why I should do so."

"You *must* tell me!" the doctor insisted, a note of desperation in his voice. "Has he been away for more than a year?"

"No, something less than a year, I believe."

Dr. Pomfrett sank down on a stool. "It was *he*, then, and

not you!'' He buried his head in his hands. ''Oh, my God, what have I done?''

Matt wondered if the potato blow had affected his ability to think. ''I don't understand, Doctor. *What* have you done?''

The doctor couldn't bring himself to meet his eyes. ''I think I've done you a great disservice,'' he said miserably.

''How can that be? We've never met until today. You haven't done me a disservice by *treating* me this afternoon, have you?''

Dr. Pomfrett shook his head. ''How can I explain? I never thought . . . ! You see, he called him Lotherwood that night. Simply Lotherwood. He did not give a Christian name.'' He looked up at Matt with an expression of anguish. ''How could I have guessed he was a younger brother without hearing the Christian name?''

''What night was that, Doctor?'' Matt asked, a glimmer of light dawning at the back of his brain. ''The night of the stagecoach accident?''

''Yes, yes! No one *ever* spoke of a younger brother. How could I have guessed?''

Matt tried to cut through what seemed to him mere babbling. ''*You* were on the coach that night?''

''Yes, I was. And the boy . . . the one who died . . . he recognized your brother when he climbed up on the box. *Lotherwood* is all he said. And I assumed . . . *assumed* . . . !'' He dropped his head in his hands. ''How could I? I am a man of science. I am trained *never* to assume!''

''But I see no reason for this agitation,'' Matt pointed out calmly, although his mind was racing about trying to understand the doctor's ramblings. ''You assumed it was I who drove the coach, and now you learn it was my brother. Does it make so great a difference to you which Lotherwood it was?''

''Not to me,'' the doctor answered, looking up. ''To *you!*''

''To me? I don't understand.''

The doctor's eyes fell. ''I think you have lately endured something which brought you considerable suffering, is that not so?''

''What *is* this?'' Matt demanded, a pulse beginning to throb in his temple. ''What are you trying to tell me?''

''Simply that when she came to ask . . .'' He wrung his hands in abject shame. ''. . . *I told her it was you!*''

Matt's heart lurched in his chest. "She?"

"Miss Brownlow."

"Miss Brownlow?" Matt's whole body tensed itself as if waiting for a blow. But the blow had actually struck him already, in the explosion of understanding that had suddenly broken upon his brain. It was not coherent; he would have to sit down and think over what had actually happened, step by painful step. But in the essentials, he *knew*. Nevertheless, he had to ask one last question. He had to *know* he knew. The words came out slowly, each with its own breath. "I . . . don't . . . know . . . any . . . Miss . . . Brownlow."

The doctor looked at him sadly. "Are you sure? I can describe her to you. She is tall, quite tall, with dark hair cut in a short, curly fashion, and—"

Matt had backed away as the doctor spoke until he was stopped by the wall. With a sound that was not a sob or a groan but something between the two, he turned and let his bruised forehead fall against it. "You don't have to tell me," he said, clenching his fists. "She had . . . *has* . . . ice-blue eyes."

❧ *Twenty-six* ❧

Soon after her meeting with Guy Lotherwood, Tess insisted on returning home. She was too miserable to endure traveling. She could not put on a bright morning face and accompany her mother through castles and cloisters, for every beautiful church, every frescoed tower, every magnificent mosaic and painting seemed especially designed to break her heart. Lady Brownlow, recognizing the increased unhappiness in her daughter's face, agreed that she would be better off at home. Lydia Beringer may have been right about travel being curative for some, but in Tess's case, it seemed to have made her worse.

They came home in late October to a chill, damp English autumn. Tess immediately retired to the hermitlike existence she'd indulged in before they left, seeing no one outside the household except for occasional visits to Lady Beringer, speaking only when absolutely necessary, moving about the house with a morose listlessness, and, when the long days were finally over, crying herself to sleep. Her mother, who sometimes listened outside Tess's door to the forlorn sobs, often wept herself, wondering what had brought such misery to her daughter and how it would all end.

One afternoon of a crisp fall day, Tess returned from a long walk to find her mother waiting for her right inside the front door. "Thank goodness you're back," Lady Brownlow said in a worried whisper. "You have a caller."

"A caller? Who—?"

"Sssh! Do you want him to hear you? He's right back there in the drawing room. He seemed too grand for the sitting room, so I put him in the drawing room and closed the doors."

"But, Mama, why did you find it necessary to close the doors, for goodness sake? Whoever it is will think you very inhospitable."

"I wanted to *warn* you. If I'd have left the doors open, he'd have seen you as soon as you came in."

"Warn me? Of what?"

Lady Brownlow wrinkled her brow. "I don't know, exactly. It's just a feeling. The way he asked for you . . . it made me jittery."

"Jittery? Why? Did he ask for me in some special sort of way?"

"I can't explain. It's just that he sounded so . . . so forbidding! 'Is this the residence of Miss Brownlow? Miss *Tess* Brownlow?' From his tone he might have been an exciseman looking for a smuggler, except that there's no exciseman in all of England with so exquisite a coat."

"What is this exquisite-coated fellow's name, Mama?"

"He wouldn't give it . . . not to Mercliff or to me. And there's something else that's strange. Mercliff told me that when he informed the gentleman that you were not at home, he ordered Mercliff to have his carriage taken round to the stable. Mercliff thinks he didn't want you to see it at the door. There was a crest on the side, you see, and Mercliff suspects that your caller feared you would recognize it and not see him."

"A crest? That *is* strange. What crest is there in the surrounding fifty miles that Mercliff wouldn't recognize?"

"Oh, my dear, this gentleman isn't from these parts. Didn't I tell you at once? He's from London."

"*London?*" Tess gasped, turning pale. "Good God, it can't be—! *He* couldn't have learned—!"

"Tess? What *is* it? Who—?"

But one of the double doors of the drawing room opened at that moment, and the London gentleman in the exquisite coat stood framed in the doorway. "Good afternoon," he said, his eyes on Tess. "Miss Brownlow, I presume?"

"*Matt!*" Her hand fluttered to her breast and clenched. "Oh, God!"

"Tess!" Lady Brownlow exclaimed. "Do you *know* this gentleman?"

"Yes, Miss Brownlow," the gentleman said. "Answer your mother. Do you know this gentleman?"

Tess's breath came in short, painful gasps. "Please, Matt . . ."

He turned to Lady Brownlow. "It seems she knows me," he said dryly. "In that case, may I have your permission, ma'am, to have a brief interview with your daughter in private?"

Lady Brownlow looked from his rigid face to her daughter's agonized one. "No, you may not," she declared firmly. "In view of my daughter's obvious distress, I think it better for you to say what you have to say before me."

"No, Mama, it's all right," Tess said, her voice shaking. "I will see Lord Lotherwood alone."

"You will do no such thing," her mother insisted. "See here, Tess, I don't know what this is all about or who this Lord Lotherwood is, but you are a young lady of proper up-bringing, and I will not permit you to closet yourself in a room with this stranger unprotected."

"Lord Lotherwood is not a stranger to me." Tess stiffened her shoulders, walked to the drawing room and opened the second door. "Come in, my lord."

"Tess!" her mother cried as Matt gave her a brief bow, walked past Tess, and went inside. Lady Brownlow stormed across the hall. "Step aside, Tess Brownlow, and let me in."

"Go upstairs, Mama," Tess said with a quiet authority that brought her mother up short.

Lady Brownlow's show of matronly consequence wilted. There was something in Tess's expression that told her this meeting was something momentous in her daughter's life. "Tess," she pleaded, "why won't you let me—?"

"I will come up to you later, Mama." With that, she closed the doors.

Tess stood for a moment with her back to the room, trying to dredge up the courage to turn round. But he did not wait for her courage to come. "So you do have a family after all," he remarked. "It seems that everything you ever said to me was a lie."

"Almost everything," she admitted, facing him. It was her first close look at him in months. "Oh, my *dear*," she exclaimed, her arms going out toward him in an involuntary gesture, "how gaunt you are!"

"I haven't come to discuss my appearance, ma'am," he said curtly. "I just came to ascertain with my own eyes that the woman I idiotically took to be the deceased Sidoney Ashburton was really the living Tess Brownlow."

She took a step toward him, twisting her fingers behind her back. "How did you—?"

"I came upon a Dr. Pomfrett, quite by accident. When he heard my name, he was quite overcome. He realized at once that he'd sent you to the wrong man."

"Oh. I see," she said in a small voice.

He raised his brows. "You don't seem surprised to learn that you wreaked your monstrous vengeance on the wrong man."

"Well, you see, I'd learned it already. I met your brother, quite by accident. In Lisbon."

"Did you indeed?" He gave a sneering, contemptuous laugh. "I shudder to think of what must have occurred. What did you do to *him*, Miss Brownlow, when you learned the truth? Push him off one of Portugal's high crags?"

"Please, Matt, *don't!*" she begged, dropping down on one of the sofas and burying her face in her hands. "I know I did a t-terrible thing to you. I am s-so very sorry—"

"*Sorry?* How good of you!" He strode across the room to her and pulled her to her feet. "So you're sorry, are you?" The words whipped out at her, little knives cutting into the marrow of her bones. "Do you have any idea of what you put me through? Can you imagine what it was like for me these past months, trying to keep myself from visualizing you crushed and bleeding under the wreckage of a carriage? Reeling from the suddenness of it? Trying to make myself accept the finality of your absence from the world? Do you think your *sorrys* are an adequate atonement?"

His grip on her arms was bruising, but she didn't feel it. Anguished tears fell from her eyes. "Oh, Matt!" she moaned.

"Oh, the tears are splendid," he jeered acidly. "You always were convincing with tears. But I'm afraid your uncannily successful scheme worked so well that it hardened me." He threw her back upon the sofa and turned away. "I'm quite impervious to them now."

"What can I do, Matt?" she pleaded softly. "I would do anything—"

"Do you really think there's something you can *do?*" He went to the window and stared out at the leaves blowing about in the wind. "Can you erase the last six months and bring us back to the day before I laid eyes on you? Witch though you are, that is beyond your powers."

She tried to stem the flow of tears with shaking fingers. "I made a d-dreadful mistake, I know that. B-But I believed you to be guilty of a heinous crime—"

"That's just it, ma'am," he said, wheeling round. "That's just the point that I think you *still* fail to understand. Even if I *had* been guilty, any civilized purveyor of justice would have given me the right to *face my accuser.* Good Lord, woman, why did you never *ask* me?"

"I d-don't know! I wanted . . I waited for you to c-confess."

"No, ma'am. That's not good enough! Knowing me as you did, did it never occur to you that *just possibly* I might have had nothing to confess?"

"No, it n-never did," she said miserably. "The evidence seemed—"

"But the evidence was misleading, wasn't it? In the end it proved to be utterly wrong. The fact that evidence can sometimes be misleading is the reason why, in any enlightened court of law, the accused is given the right to speak before he is sentenced. *Before,* ma'am! Only a tyrant, a barbarian, or a supreme egotist would believe he knew all the answers before he asked the questions!" He turned back to the window and waited until the fury that had churned up into his throat receded. "You must have had yourself a grand time playing all the roles—Tess Brownlow as judge, jury, even *hangman!*"

"I kn-know you're right," she said, trying to swallow her sobs. "I *was* b-barbaric."

"The fact that you agree with me, my dear, doesn't change a thing." The words were said with an air of finality, and after he said them he strode to a table beside the sofa on which he'd placed his hat, gloves, and stick. "Knowing that anything we might say would be pointless, I hadn't intended to discuss the matter like this. I didn't drive all the way from London for recriminations, explanations, or apologies; they are all equally repellant to me. I only came to see Tess Brownlow with my own eyes." He placed his hat firmly on his head. "Well, I've seen her. That makes an end of it."

She watched as he pulled on his gloves with calm deliberation. She tried urgently to find something to say to melt the rigid coldness of his expression. There had to be something! He'd loved her once. He had been angry with her before, and she'd managed to win him back. Was it possible, even now, for her to do it again? But there was nothing she could think of to say that would in any way lessen the enormity of what she'd done. "I suppose you hate me now," she mumbled in helpless, childish desperation.

"You surely don't expect an answer to so ridiculous a question, do you?" he said, starting for the doors. "Good day, Miss Brownlow."

"Matt?" She jumped up and blocked his path. "Please! Is there no way for us to . . . to even *speak* to each other any more?"

Coldly, he placed his cane under one arm, put both hands on her waist, and lifted her out of his way. "No way in the world, my dear," he said, proceeding to the door. "I could never trust anything you'd say to me now. Now that I realize you lied about your name, your family, your past, your future, your feelings, your hopes, your intentions—about everything, in fact—it is not possible for me to believe you again."

"I didn't lie about *everything*, Matt. I *do* love you, you know."

"I don't know anything of the sort, though you've said it convincingly enough in the past. Even engraved it on the watch fob, didn't you? A masterly touch, that." With an abrupt twist of his wrist, he snapped the little cock's comb from his watch chain. With three quick steps he returned to her side, lifted her hand, and wrapped her fingers about the fob. "Here. It's yours. If what it says on this fob *is* true," he added with an unexpected softness, "it's a strange sort of love. I couldn't have done to someone I loved what you did to me."

The truth of those words was the greatest blow. Wincing with the pain of it, she had to lean against the back of the sofa to keep from reeling. When she regained her balance, she held the gold piece out to him. "I would rather that *you* kept it," she said. "Please!"

He wouldn't even glance at it but turned and strode to the door. With his hand on the doorknob, he paused. "I suppose, in a way, you should be complimented. Everything turned out exactly as you planned. I was completely duped." He shook his head as if everything was still incomprehensible to him. "I've never encountered anyone so adept at concocting falsehoods. If it weren't my aunt Letty who'd hired that blasted gypsy, I'd even be inclined to believe you bribed— Good God!" He turned and regarded her with an almost admiring revulsion. "Not that too! You *didn't—!*

Somehow, though her cheeks were wet, her lips were trembling, and her heart ached in her chest, she lifted her chin and said proudly, "Yes, I did! But I am not a liar. Not usually. I thought . . . I believed . . . that the end justified the means. I was very wrong. But you needn't insult me by assuming that I would lie to you now."

"Well, it hardly matters at this point, does it?" He threw open the doors and stepped into the hall. "I'll say good-bye again, Miss Tess Brownlow," he said, taking one last look at her. Then he smiled a wry, ironic smile. "So your name is Tess. *Tess,* of all names! So unpretentiously English. It suits you. How could I have been so stupid as to swallow a name as patently false as Sidoney? Of all the ways you made a fool of me, ma'am, it now strikes me that making me call you Sidoney was probably the most mortifying."

❧ *Twenty-seven* ❧

When the sound of Matt's carriage could no longer be heard, Tess retreated from the window, sank down upon the sofa, and waited for misery to overwhelm her. But it did not come. At first she didn't understand herself. He had left her forever, and with words as final and unforgiving as any could be. Why was she not awash in tears?

It took a several minutes of rueful contemplation before she discovered the single-worded answer: truth. What she was feeling was the blessed *relief* of knowing the truth and knowing that Matt knew it, too. The truth was indeed wonderful; only in its light could she see how dismal and grim living a lie had been. Some words that John Milton had once written sang in her spirit like a hymn: *Daylight and Truth meet us with a clear dawn.*

Relief flooded over her with the restorative powers of a fresh breeze. A short while ago she'd thought that her life would be forever devoid of hope. When she'd seen him standing in the library doorway, she'd been overwhelmed by shame. Revealed as a liar, a schemer, and a fraud, guilty of the cruelest misjudgment, she felt that her life had sunk to its nadir. But that low point had passed. In this new light of truth, both she *and* Matt could now begin to find a way out of the morass she'd created.

It was amazing how good it felt to know that he'd learned her true identity. Even if he hated her, at least he knew her now as she really was. No longer would she have to hide in shame. No longer would she have to carry in her heart the painful guilt that had weighed her down since her interview with his brother Guy; for Matt, freed by truth as she had been, would no longer be mourning the death of the imaginary Miss Ashburton. He was hurt and very angry, yes, but he was no longer crushed.

Tess's spirit, like a healthy bird kept too long in a dark, covered cage, flew up into the bright air of hope on wildly flapping wings. Someday, she told herself, she would see Matt again and make him love her. If he had once loved Sidoney, he was bound to love Tess, for in normal circumstances Tess was really an open, honest, loving girl. Sidoney had been calculating, dishonest, and manipulative, but time would prove to him that Tess was not. Someday she would find a way to make up to him for all the pain she'd caused. There had to be a way! She was determined to find it.

It was a letter from Julia that set her inventive mind working again. *We had a visit from Lotherwood,* Julia wrote, *in which he took us severely to task for our part in the deception. I must say, Tess, that he brought me several times to tears. I tried to defend Edward, but my dear husband would not let me. He told Matt that he was without defense; women were emotional creatures, he said, and one expected them to jump to idiotic conclusions, but he, a male, should have known better. I was hard-pressed to know how to defend him on the one hand and berate him for his insults to womankind on the other! In the end, however, Edward's abject regret for what we'd done impressed itself on Matt, and he forgave us. And oh, my dear, what a relief it is to feel like a truthful person again! If ever the occasion arises in which you find it necessary to concoct another scheme, you may be sure that neither Edward nor I (much as we love you) will aid or abet you in any way.*

Later that week we dined with Lady Wetherfield, the Kelseys, and the Fenwicks at Matt's table. (None of them are privy to the truth about you, by the way. I suppose Matt does not feel it necessary for them to know.) Matt took the occasion to announce that he is closing his townhouse and taking up permanent residence at Bradbourne Park, his estate in Essex. He seemed quite enthusiastic about the prospect of facing his duties as landowner and turning himself into what he

*calls a Country Gentleman. Dolph Kelsey spoke for all of us
when he raised his glass and said that the extent of our sorrow
at his departure is equal in degree to the fervency with which
we wish him happy.*

The letter was interesting to Tess in all its particulars, but
the item that stimulated her instinct for invention was the news
that Matt was leaving London. His Essex estate was huge, she
knew, and on its vast acreage all sorts of opportunities might
be found that her imagination could shape to her advantage.
Her very first thought was that, in a newly opened household,
someone (even someone inexperienced in the ways of the
working classes) might find employment. And employment at
Bradbourne Park might be the very means she was looking
for! She held the letter aloft and danced about her bedroom in
girlish excitement. Perhaps she had a future after all! At least,
at this moment, there seemed to be the prospect of a clear
dawn.

The manor house at Bradbourne Park, impressive though it
was from the outside (its wide "panoramic" lines achieved by
three long rows of windows and two flights of balustraded
steps which led to a portico whose pillars and triangular pediment were acknowledged in architectural circles to be among
the finest in England), showed the neglect of absentee owner-
ship within. Of the one hundred rooms under its roof, half of
them had not been used for a generation. But beyond ordering
that all the rooms be closed but for a mere handful he needed
for daily use, Matt took little interest in the interior of the
house. His concerns were exterior: to learn the best ways to
breed cattle, to help his farmers make use of new ideas and
new machinery, to bring about some much-needed im-
provements to the homes of his tenants and to the out-
buildings on his own lands. To assist him he hired an able
Scot, Alistair MacCollum, as his bailiff, and it was with Mac-
Collum that he spent his time. The management of the inside
of the manor house he left to Rooks, whom he had brought
with him from London, and to Mrs. Tice, the housekeeper
who had run the household since the day his mother had come
there as a bride.

Despite the fact that his lordship was using only fifteen
rooms, his presence in the manor necessitated a sizable in-
crease in the household staff: a cook and two kitchen maids, a

baker, an additional scullery girl, a new upstairs maid, a general housemaid, and two footmen. Beyond giving his permission to Rooks and Mrs. Tice to hire whomever they needed, Lord Lotherwood did not take notice of the staff who attended his comfort. He had been bred to expect all household details to be taken care of without any effort on his part. He paid generous salaries and said "please" and "thank you" at all the right times. In return he expected tasty meals to be served, hot, whenever it pleased him to eat; to have his bed made daily and warmed before he retired, to have his clothes washed and pressed and waiting for him in their proper drawers or cupboards; to have fires burning in the grates of every room he deigned to enter; and to have everything he touched, leaned on, or sat upon clean and free from dust. *How* all this was done interested him not at all.

What interested him at this time of his life was the estate. He had much to do and much to learn. The enterprise which most demanded his attention was the expansion of the stables, which required the services of what seemed to him a small army of architects, stone cutters, masons, carpenters, and assorted other craftsmen and workers. This project, added to the duties he'd already taken upon himself of improving the farms and the tenants' homes, kept him busy all day and half the night. The problems of the household staff had no place on his mind.

It was surprising, therefore, when the name of one staff member seemed to come to his attention more than any other. Annie, the upstairs maid. The first time it came to his notice was a chilly night in November, when Rooks was pulling off his boots at bedtime. He noticed a bowl of bright red flowers on the table near his bed. "Where did those come from?" he asked curiously.

"From the greenhouse, my lord," Rooks explained. "If nobody picks the blooms, they only die on the vine, so we thought we might just as well use them to brighten your lordship's bedroom."

"That was most kind of you, Rooks," Matt said pleasantly. "Thank you."

"No need to thank me, my lord. It was the new maid thought of it. Annie's her name."

"Then thank this Annie for me, will you?" his lordship said, and thought no more about it.

The next time it was MacCollum who mentioned the name. Matt received a note from a Mrs. Whittle thanking him—in words of misspelled but sincere gratitude—for having fixed her dangerously crumbling doorstep. "What's this?" he asked his bailiff. "I don't know anything about fixing a doorstep."

"Dan Whittle's one o' the cottagers, m'lord. Seems yer upstairs maid . . . Annie's her name . . . paid 'em a call on her half-day, and she brought the matter t' my attention. I asked ye if I might send o'er one 'o the masons t' mend it, if ye recall, an' ye agreed."

"Well, I don't recall, but I'm glad it was done. Give this Annie my thanks, MacCollum."

Then there was the night Rooks served him a portion of some sort of poultry in a greenish sauce that he found most delicious. "What is this I'm eating, Rooks?" he asked.

"Couldn't say, my lord. I'll ask Mrs. Tice."

Mrs. Tice bustled in, beaming. "Do you really like it, my lord? Cook will be in transports. It's hazel hen in a puree of celery. Our Annie gave her the recipe."

His lordship raised his eyebrows. "Annie? The upstairs maid I've been hearing about?"

"Yes, my lord. A treasure, she is. Worth her weight, that one."

"Well, give the cook my compliments, Mrs. Tice. And Annie, too."

The very next morning Mrs. Tice sang the girl's praises to him again. On the way down to breakfast he passed the housekeeper hurrying along the corridor with an armload of linens. The woman was humming to herself happily until she caught sight of him. " 'Morning, your lordship," she said, dropping a curtsy.

"Good morning, Mrs. Tice. You're wearing a very cheerful face today."

"And so would you be if you'd seen your linen cupboards made over. Y'see, my lord, over the years everything got so confused like, I didn't know how I would ever make 'em straight. But now they're as neat and orderly as they could be. I tell you, your lordship, it's a joy the way she's set the arrangement to rights."

"She? Your Annie, I suppose."

"Oh, yes, my lord. She's a—"

"I know," he said wryly, making his escape. "A treasure."

It occurred to him as he ate his breakfast that he didn't know the name of anyone else on the household staff except Rooks and the housekeeper. The first footman, who was always on attendance at the door, might possibly have the name of Charles, but he wasn't even sure of that. But he could not avoid knowing Annie's name. This Annie was certainly making her presence felt in this house.

But the most impressive encomium the new maid received was from MacCollum a few days later. The two men were at the desk in Matt's study, a dim room on the second floor that faced north and was chilly even with a roaring fire. They were bending over the plans for the extension of the stables, discussing the direction the expansion should take. A wing on the east end of the present stable building, going northward, would make the most desirable design, but it involved destroying a lovely summerhouse that Matt's grandfather had built for his bride eighty years before. The summerhouse was made of stone, with graceful, fluted columns and a round base, and Matt had often played in it as a boy. "It's a shame to have to knock it down," he said with a sigh, "but it's the best thing for the stables."

"Y'know, m' lord," the Scotsman mused, "I was speakin' o' this verra problem in the kitchen today . . . takin' a wee bite o' luncheon, y'see . . . and yer maid Annie asked why we couldna just *move* the thing."

"Move it?"

"Aye. Lock, stock, an' barrel. 'Twould be a bit o' labor, mind, takin' the stones apart, but it could be done."

"It's a deucedly good idea," Matt said, studying the plans. "I don't suppose this Annie suggested a place where we might put it, did she?"

"Aye, she did that!" MacCollum laughed. "She said she spied a pretty promontory on the far side o' the lake. With a goodly bit o' shrubbery about the base, she said, it would make a fair scene, 'specially from a distance where one could see it reflected in the water."

Matt shook his head in admiration as he rolled up the plans. "This Annie appears to be quite the treasure Mrs. Tice says she is. We'll take a look at her promontory tomorrow, shall we, MacCollum?"

"Aye, we'll do that. 'Twouldna surprise me t' find she's picked the perfect spot."

They stowed the plans away on the bookshelves behind the desk and strolled to the door. "One of these days, I must take a look at this Annie, too," his lordship remarked with a grin. "If this house has a treasure, I ought to see it for myself."

❧ *Twenty-eight* ❧

They did not go to see the promontory after all, for a deep snow fell in the night and kept everyone imprisoned indoors the next day. With nothing better to do, Matt decided to tackle the account books, a task he'd been long avoiding. To his surprise he became completely engrossed, and even after hours had gone by he didn't look up from his labors. Day turned into evening. The wind picked up in the north and howled at the windows. And although the footman or Rooks came tiptoeing in every hour to replenish the fire, Matt had to blow on his fingers or hold them over his lamp to keep them warm. At dinnertime, Mrs. Tice stalked in and delivered a scold. "No need to do a year's work in one day, is there, my lord? It feels like the North Pole in here, it does. Why not come away and have a good, hot dinner. Cook's made some wonderful filets of veal and a pearled barley soup that'll warm you right through—"

"I don't want to stop right now, Mrs. Tice," his lordship said, not even looking up from his work. "Just bring me a bowl of that barley soup to drink right here, if you don't mind. And tell Rooks I could use a warm blanket to put over my shoulders. I'll be fine."

He went to bed very late, his fingers and toes almost numb. But his bedroom was cozy, his sheets had been warmed with hot bricks, and he went promptly to sleep. The next morning he was wakened by a streak of snow-bright sunlight which had crept in through an opening in the draperies and spilled across his face. When Rooks came in to help him dress, the butler looked as cheerful as the day. "We've a surprise for you this morning, my lord," he said with very unbutlerish glee. "I can't wait to show it to you."

As soon as his lordship was dressed, Rooks led him down to the second floor. "This way, my lord, just past the yellow saloon. Look!" And he threw open the door of a room that had been closed for years.

Matt gaped. The room had been newly painted an eggshell white and sported shiny new draperies of flowered chintz. There was a mulberry-and-cream-colored Persian rug on the floor that Matt remembered vaguely as having come from one of the long-unused bedrooms, and a velvet-covered wing chair near the window. His desk had been moved from his study and stood, gleaming with new polish, near a large fireplace over which a George Stubbs painting of two nuzzling horses (a work that had long been a particular favorite of his) was hung. His bookshelves, too, had been moved in, cleaned, polished and their contents replaced. "What *is* this, Rooks?" he asked, bemused.

"It's your new study, my lord," Rooks said with satisfaction. "We've moved you."

"But, good heavens, man, *why?*"

"Why, my lord? Because we all agreed that, if you were going to spend half the night at your accounts, you shouldn't do it in the coldest room in the house."

"But I don't mind the cold. I don't understand this, Rooks. Most of these things were in the other room just a few hours ago. How could you have moved everything in so short a time?"

"We did it after you retired, my lord. Mrs. Tice, Charles, Annie, Ben from the stables, and myself. We wanted to do it all at once so that you wouldn't guess what we were planning. To surprise you, you see."

"Well, you certainly succeeded. I'm dumbfounded." He walked about the room examining the details. "It was very thoughtful of you."

"But you don't seem very pleased, your lordship," the butler said, crestfallen. "Don't you like the room?"

"Oh, yes. It's a pleasant room. But I'm accustomed to my old study, I'm afraid."

The butler nodded knowingly. "Annie *said* you might not be pleased. 'Gentlemen can be very set in their ways when it comes to their workplaces,' she said."

Matt frowned. "Was this *Annie's* idea?" he asked.

A note of disapproval in his voice made Rooks shift his weight uncomfortably from one foot to another. "I suppose it was, my lord. Mrs. Tice and I were remarking, in the servant's hall, about you spending so much time in that drafty room, you see, and Annie wondered why you didn't change it, what with so many empty rooms to choose from. So one idea led to another, and we made the plans. There's still the wallpaper to be hung in the panels and another chair—" He glanced up at his lordship askance. "We'll put things back as they were, my lord, if you're displeased."

"No, it's a sensible change. I'm quite grateful, really. But I would like to have been consulted first. I know you all meant well, Rooks, but it seems to me that this Annie of yours has been taking a great deal on herself. Send her to me at once, will you? I'd like a few words with her."

Rooks bowed in acquiescence but bit his lip. At the door he paused. "Your lordship," he ventured, "you won't be too harsh with her, will you? She didn't mean any—"

Matt was already rearranging some of the books on the shelves. "You don't think I'll put her in chains, do you?" he said, turning and waving the butler off. "Just fetch her, and don't trouble yourself—" He stopped speaking, having noticed something gleaming on the rug. "Wait a minute, Rooks!" he said in a completely different voice. "What's *that?*"

"What, my lord?"

His lordship had turned white to the lips. "This!" he demanded, picking up a little gold piece and holding it out to the butler.

"Oh, that's nothing, my lord. Just a trinket. I think it's meant to be a cock's comb. It belongs to Annie. I've seen her wearing it on a chain round her neck. She must have dropped it. I'll take it to her."

"No, thank you," his lordship said between clenched teeth. "I'll take it to her myself." His eyes were blazing, and an angry muscle twitched in his cheek. He strode past the astonished butler and out the door. Then he swung about. "Where can I find her, Rooks?"

Rooks was both startled and disturbed by his lordship's sudden change of mood. He was not unfamiliar with his lordship's character, having been his butler and valet for more than fifteen years, and he recognized restrained fury when he saw it. For some reason quite beyond Rooks's understanding, Lord Lotherwood was about to vent the full force of his spleen on poor Annie. "Right *now*, my lord?" he asked, temporizing.

"Yes, right now!" his lordship barked.

"Doing up your bedroom, I surmise, my lord. This time of day is customarily—"

But his lordship had already taken off down the corridor. Rooks ran after him. "Do you wish me to accompany you, my lord?"

"I wish, dash it," his lordship muttered, wheeling round, "that you'd go about your business. I don't want to see you again this morning! Do I make myself clear?"

"Yes, my lord." Rooks watched as his lordship disappeared up the stairs. *Poor Annie*, he said to himself with a sigh and, shaking his head in bafflement at the peculiar ways of the nobility, went down to the servants' hall.

Matt threw open the door of his room with a crash. The draperies had been opened, and the room was flooded with white sunlight. Almost silhouetted by the brightness was an aproned, mobcapped female whom no tricks of light could disguise. Caught in the act of shaking out his comforter, she jumped and uttered a frightened little scream.

He surveyed her icily for a moment while his eyes adjusted to the glare. Even in her neat black housemaid's dress with its starched white collar and apron, and that silly cap covering her dark curls, there was something imposing about her. He wondered how that special quality had been overlooked by his household staff. He supposed it was her talent for dissembling that made them accept her so easily as one of their own. "So you're Annie this time, eh?" he said with devastating contempt. "Can't you *ever* use your own name?"

Tess, clutching the comforter to her chest, dropped a curtsy. "G-Good morning, your l-lordship," she stammered.

He leaned on the doorjamb and folded his arms. "What sort of game are you playing this time?"

"Nothing harmful, I promise you," she said, giving him a tremulous little smile.

"You aren't so foolish as to believe I would take your word, are you? What are you doing here, ma'am?"

She took a step toward him, the comforter dragging on the floor. "Please believe me, Matt," she begged softly. "I only wanted to do something to . . . to make amends."

"Good God, woman, do you think that hiring out as a housemaid and making my bed is making *amends?*"

She shrugged helplessly. "It was all I could think of. Besides," she added proudly, "I do more than your bed, my lord. Have you seen your new study?"

"Yes, I've seen it. Did you really think it could make a difference? I don't want your services, ma'am," he flared. "I don't want your good works." He strode across the room to her, pulled the comforter from her grasp, and threw it on the bed. "I don't want you in my bedroom, I don't want you in my house, I don't want you anywhere in my vicinity!"

The bitter anger in his voice seemed to have no effect on her. She kept her eyes fixed on his face. "But you needn't know I'm in your vicinity. I've been here a month, yet you didn't know until today that I was anywhere about."

"Only because I'm an idiot. With all the talk I'd been hearing about Annie, I should have *guessed.*"

She smiled. "You would not have guessed. You are only here now because you found the fob."

That startled him. "Are you saying you left it there on *purpose?*"

Her eyes searched his face questioningly. "It was an impulse. I was so proud of having done up your new study. Oh, dear. I've made a mistake, I think. It was too soon . . ."

"Everything you *do* is a mistake! Don't you see it even yet? You make everything into some sort of . . . charade! A watch fob becomes a symbolic talisman, a racer becomes a murderer, a spoiled girl becomes a housemaid. You change identities as easily as I change my coat! What on earth is *real* to you? Tell me, ma'am, do you think all of *life* is a game?"

She had anticipated having some difficulty with him, but she hadn't expected his bitterness to be so lasting. If this *was* a game, she was playing it badly. Alarmed, she put a hand lightly on his arm. "I know that coming here as a housemaid is, in a sense, playing a game. But I didn't know how else to do something tangible to make up for what I'd done. I shouldn't have revealed myself today. It was indulgent of me. Can you pretend that today didn't happen? Let me stay, Matt. I'll never bring myself to your notice again. Let me try, by working here, to do something useful for you."

He brushed her hand away. "Don't be a fool," he said, turning away. "I want nothing to do with your pretendings." He went to the window and squinted into the sunlight. "Go to your room and pack your things. I'll have my carriage made ready to take you back to Todmorden. The snow is melting. You'll be able to leave as soon as the roads are passable."

She didn't move. "It isn't a game to *me*, you know. Coming here and serving in your household made my life bearable again. It made me feel a little less . . . blameworthy. If you send me away, it will be like a prison sentence to me."

"And what do you think it would be to me if you stay?" He whirled on her furiously. "Do you seriously think I could bear living here knowing you were somewhere in the house?"

For the first time her eyes wavered. "Oh, Lord!" she muttered, dismayed. "Do you hate me as much as that?"

He shut his eyes for a moment, as if he wanted to blot out the sight of her. "My feelings for you are quite beside the point," he said, trying to behave sensibly in what seemed to him an utterly implausible situation. "The point is, ma'am, that you are playing a role again . . . a role you obviously can't continue to play indefinitely. Go home, and for once in your life, try to live it as yourself."

"How can I, without you?" she murmured sadly. "Loving you as I do."

For some reason that innocent remark infuriated him. It seemed to him to be too facile, too lacking in sincerity. It sounded like Sidoney, toying with him again. "Stop it!" he said between clenched teeth. "I don't want to hear those words from you again!"

"*Matt*," she cried in chagrin, "why won't you *believe* me?"

"I believed you once and paid for it dearly." He held the gold watch fob out to her. "Here, ma'am, take your bauble and go. It will be better for us both to make an end of this."

Her eyes searched his face for any sign of vacillation, but there was none. She took the fob from him and walked slowly to the door, defeated. The grim days, like all those she'd suf-

fered through before, were about to envelop her again. She
had no choice but to follow his orders and leave. *But, dash it
all*, she thought suddenly, *I am not a housemaid! I don't have
to depart like a meek little mouse!* Taking a deep breath, she
drew herself to her full height and wheeled about. "Very well,
Matthew Lotherwood, I shall go. We'll make an end of it. I
shall play no more roles. But before I go, you will listen to me
speak my true mind for once! I know I've lied, I've dissem-
bled, I've treated you with the cruelest injustice. But I've
never, *never* lied about the words on this 'bauble.' It says I
loved you even when I thought you a liar and a murderer. It
says that, whatever you were, I loved you *anyway*." She was
making an earnest effort to speak calmly, but her voice began
to shake and a tear slipped down her cheek. She dashed it
away angrily with the back of a hand. "You are my Grand
Passion, whether you choose to b-believe it or not! If you
think I would come here as a *servant*, to rise in the morning
before five—which I assure you I'd never done in my *life*
before!—to wash in a tiny bowl of ice-cold water, to wear this
ugly black bombazine monstrosity, to scrub floors and empty
chamberpots and do all manner of lowly things if it were not
for love of you, then you haven't the brains you were born
with!"

He stared at her, overcome. Standing there in the doorway,
tall and proud, she looked as magnificent as she'd looked the
day at the Elgin marbles, in spite of the incongruity of her
apron and mobcap. He didn't know what to make of her or
his own feelings. He was essentially an uncomplicated man, he
believed. He'd spent his life in sporting pursuits where every
contest was very clear. The goals were marked, the opponents
recognizable, the results conclusive. But these matters of love
were much more confusing. In his mind he and this girl had
had a match in which he'd been the loser. She had not played
fair, of course, but he'd taken his loss like a gentleman. Was
she here for a rematch? Could love be played like a boxing
match, in which the opponents return for another go? But
even if it were, he didn't dare step into the ring with her after
the beating he'd taken. Oh, no, not he!

She turned on her heel and marched out the door with her
chin in the air. In that second, like a momentary flash, he
knew that he *had* to enter the ring again. There was no hope
for any happiness in his life if he didn't. The truth was that no

matter what name she called herself or what she did to him, he would love her *anyway!*

He took a stumbling step toward the door. "*Tess,*" he muttered hoarsely, "Tess!"

She heard him. He'd never called her by her own name in that way before. Hesitantly, not trusting the shiver of joy that had bubbled up in her veins at the sound of his voice, she glanced over her shoulder at him. That one look was all she needed. "Oh, Matt!" she sobbed in relief as she flew across the room to him and flung herself into his arms.

They kissed until his knees grew weak, and then he sank on the bed, drew her on his lap, and kissed her again. It was a long while before they could speak. It was she who finally broke the silence. "I told Mama this might happen," she said with a sigh, "but I didn't really believe it."

"Your mother must be a queer sort of parent, to permit you to leave home to become a housemaid," he remarked.

"She *didn't* permit it. Even when I told her I would wed you or no one. I had to steal out of the house in the dark of night. You know, of course," she added plaintively while nevertheless snuggling contentedly in his arms, "that we can never be wed."

"Oh?" He took off her mobcap and, nestling her head on his shoulder, placed his lips on her hair. "Why not?"

"How can we? How could we explain it to the world? How could you present me to Lady Wetherfield or the Fenwicks or your friend Dolph? What could you say: 'I'd like you to meet my wife, the deceased Miss Ashburton'? Or, 'This is my wife, the Sidoney Ashburton that was'? It's quite impossible."

"Is it?" he murmured, blissfully entranced by the charm of a tendril that had curled around her ear.

"Unless we can concoct a plausible explanation. Sidoney could have had a *twin*, perhaps, or—"

"Not on your life!" he declared, lifting his head sharply. "We shall be wed quite properly with our true names, and when the time comes for me to present you to the world, you will tell the *truth!*"

"The truth?" she exclaimed, appalled. "Matt, no! I promise I shall always tell the truth to *you*—always!—but, my love, it would be quite awkward to have to—"

"Awkward or not, you will face everyone squarely and admit *everything*. There has to be *some* punishment for your heinous crimes. If you ask me, you are getting off much too lightly." But he softened these stern pronouncements by kissing her again.

"Lord Lotherwood!" came a shriek from the doorway. The lovers lifted their heads to find a scandalized Mrs. Tice gaping at them. "I can't believe my *eyes!*" she gasped in horror. "That *my* Lord Lotherwood would ever be found fondling a housemaid is something I never thought to live to see! *Fondling* a *housemaid!* It's the most shocking sight these old eyes of mine have ever *seen!* Have you no *shame?*"

Matt looked down at the girl in his arms with a barely disguised gleam. "Well, ma'am, are you just going to sit here gloating while my reputation as a gentleman is torn to shreds? You're the one with the remarkable talent for scheming and concocting tales, are you not? Well, then, let's see you concoct something to get me out of *this!*"